SLAYERS

FRIENDS AND TRAITORS

SLAYERS

FRIENDS AND TRAITORS

C. J. HILL

FEIWEL AND FRIENDS

A FEIWEL AND FRIENDS BOOK
An Imprint of Macmillan

Feiwel and Friends books may be purchased for business or promotional use. For
information on bulk purchases, please contact the Macmillan Corporate and Premium Sales
Department at (800) 221-7945 x5442 or by e-mail at specialmarkets@macmillan.com.

Library of Congress Cataloging-in-Publication Data Available

ISBN 978-1-250-02461-9 (hardcover) / ISBN 978-1-4668-4845-0 (e-book)

Book design by Véronique Lefèvre Sweet

Feiwel and Friends logo designed by Filomena Tuosto

First Edition: 2013

1 3 5 7 9 10 8 6 4 2

macteenbooks.com

*To Guy, who helps me
slay my dragons.*

SLAYERS

FRIENDS AND TRAITORS

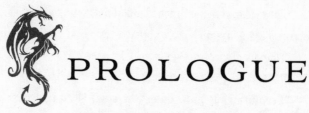

PROLOGUE

It would be ironic, Brant Overdrake thought as he paced around the cabin of his jet, for a man who could fly to be killed in a plane crash. Life was full of ugly little ironies, though.

Bianca, his wife, sat nearby, clutching a water bottle tightly in her hand. They had come from their plantation on St. Helena, one of the most remote islands in the world, a place hidden away in the south Atlantic. The flight to Virginia took sixteen hours, hours that had taken their toll on Bianca. Her long blonde hair was disheveled. Only hints of makeup remained on her face. Pillows were strewn around her seat—an effort to get comfortable in seats that weren't meant to accommodate women who were eight months' pregnant.

She took a drink of water. "Pacing won't make the storm go away."

He ignored her. The usual hum of the plane engine was swallowed up by the sound of rain clawing at the wings. Out the windows, the sky was an angry gray. Every few minutes distant slices of lightning illuminated the clouds.

Bianca lowered her voice. "The pilot already asked you twice to sit down and put on your seat belt."

Overdrake walked to his chair, leaned over it, and peered out the window. "Yes, but I pay him, which means I give the orders, not the other way around." The seat rattled underneath his fingers as though it were trying to shake off his hand. Storm turbulence. The plane kept bumping and shuddering along.

Bianca let out a high-pitched moan that sounded like a kitten trapped somewhere. Through panting breaths, she said, "Another contraction."

"How far apart are they now?" he asked.

She held up five fingers.

"Keep drinking your water," he said. She'd had false labor at six months. The doctor said she'd probably just been dehydrated. Once they had gotten enough fluids into her, the contractions stopped.

Overdrake knew none of his current problems were Bianca's fault. She hadn't chosen to have contractions a month early on the day they were moving to the United States. After she lost their first baby, she'd done everything she could to ensure this pregnancy went well. More than everything, actually. She turned into a health Nazi, ordering their chef to cook with organic ingredients, insisting that none of the staff smoke anywhere on their plantation—as if somehow the whiffs of secondhand cigarette smoke would make it through the air filters she erected in their house.

Still, even knowing how badly Bianca wanted this baby, Overdrake felt an illogical annoyance with her. Producing a son was the one task he needed from her, the one thing he couldn't do on his own. She wasn't supposed to go into labor early while they were in the sky, waiting out a storm. Why couldn't she control her body? How hard could it be to carry a child and give birth to it at the right time? Women across the world had managed this task for thousands of years. He didn't need the extra stress right now.

Overdrake left the window and strode to the cockpit to talk to the pilot. Peter Divers was an older man with a face like a bulldog's and a temperament that wasn't much better. He'd fought in the Gulf War and after that did some business for drug lords and arms dealers. Overdrake hired him as his personal pilot for three reasons. The man was cool under pressure, didn't ask questions, and could keep a secret.

Overdrake looked at the monitors on the instrument panel. He'd flown enough that he could tell the plane was running low on fuel. Waiting out the storm had cost them. "What's the latest on the weather?"

"Not good," Divers said. "Just more of the same for the next hour. You'll have to decide where to land soon."

"I have decided. We're landing on my airstrip in Winchester."

Divers kept his gaze forward. "Well, until the weather decides that's an option—"

"For the amount of money I pay you," Overdrake snapped, "you should be able to put this plane down on the White House lawn if I ask you to do it."

Divers checked the flap settings and the stabilizers. "No matter how much you pay me, I can't change the weather or the laws of physics."

"Brant!" Bianca called from the cabin. "The last one was three minutes!"

Great. The contractions were getting closer together instead of further apart.

"Did I mention," Brant said coldly, "that my wife is in labor?" It was a rhetorical question. Divers had already called for an ambulance to meet the plane on Overdrake's property in Winchester.

"That's another factor I can't change," Divers said. "But I can call BWI and ask them to have medical staff standing by." He glanced over his shoulder, looking for Overdrake's reaction, some sign that he was relenting.

Overdrake didn't speak.

"Even if we land at BWI," Divers said, "it doesn't mean the feds will come aboard and search your plane. As far as they know, this isn't an international flight. And even if they did search us—what are they going to find? Some boulders. It's odd, but so what? No law against that."

The cargo carefully nestled inside seven meters of Styrofoam weren't boulders. They just looked like boulders and were nearly as heavy. That was how dragons camouflaged their eggs. When the mother first laid them, the eggs were a translucent white with colored, glowing veins fingering across their milky surface. They looked like giant opals—nature's artwork at its best. Within minutes, the shells took on the color and texture of the rocks around them. The shape of the eggs shifted, too, settling into a form that wasn't so perfectly oval. The shells became stonelike and would remain that way for the next fifteen to twenty years. After that, the shells thinned and dragon hatchlings the size of lions would claw their way out.

Divers didn't know the exact nature of what the plane carried, and Overdrake wasn't about to tell him. "I won't go to a public airport," Overdrake insisted. "If you can't land on my property, then find a private airstrip in an isolated place."

Divers gestured to the flight plan at his side. "What do you mean by isolated? If you wanted isolated you should have told me to fly to Nebraska, not D.C."

"The government must have some airstrips away from the populated areas. Make up a story. We'll land there, wait out the storm, and then fly to Winchester." Overdrake was grasping at straws. He knew that.

Divers actually turned in his seat to give Overdrake an incredulous stare. "Make up a story? My story is that I don't go near the feds. You knew that when you hired me."

Overdrake didn't push it. He didn't want anyone from the government checking his papers or his story, either. He just wanted Divers to come up with another solution. One that didn't involve a place where crowds of people would be exposed to the unborn dragons' signals.

That was another irony. In the last couple of weeks he'd flown two adult dragons from St. Helena to his compound in Winchester. Those were the trips he'd worried about. It would have been impossible to get around custom agents in England with a forty-ton dragon, so he took a three-day boat ride to Namibia, paid off officials there, then loaded the dragon onto a cargo plane and flew twenty-five hours from there to the States. He only stopped once to refuel.

He'd made that trip twice. Once for each dragon. Trying to contain an adult dragon in a confined space was tricky at best. Trying to do it for days verged on suicidal. Overdrake couldn't tranquilize them. Dragons were naturally resilient to poisons and drugs, and his vets couldn't say exactly how much tranquilizer would be needed or what prolonged exposure would do to their systems. So Overdrake had to stay linked to each dragon's mind the entire trip, putting it in a trancelike state to keep it calm, quiet, and immobile.

Those flights went off without a hitch. But even if one of them had needed to be rerouted to a public airport, it might not have mattered. Overdrake had fittings that covered the diamond-shaped patches on the dragons' foreheads, blocking the signals that originated there. As long as no one searched the plane, everything would have been fine. No signals would have leaked out into the public.

Overdrake couldn't cover the foreheads of unhatched dragons. To block the eggs' signals during their transportation, he would have had to put them behind tons of concrete and steel. It hadn't seemed practical or necessary to fly that way. The containers would have been so heavy they would have required another cargo plane, and since his personal airstrip in St. Helena wasn't big enough to accommodate one of those, he would have had to make the long boat trip to Namibia again with its hassles and hush money.

Overdrake wanted the rest of the move to be quick, and Bianca wanted to be settled in the U.S. before she gave birth so their son would have automatic citizenship. Overdrake had packed the eggs in Styrofoam, put them on his jet, and they flew from St. Helena. It was supposed to be a simple trip.

And now this. A storm, dwindling fuel, and Bianca having contractions three minutes apart. Overdrake turned away from the cockpit and went back to check on her. He cursed himself as he did. He should have been more careful. He should have taken the means to protect against every possibility of the eggs' signals coming in contact with any Slayer knight descendants.

In the Middle Ages, when dragons roamed the sky unchallenged, the Slayer knights took an elixir that changed their DNA to give them powers to fight dragons. The knights passed on those genes to their descendants, but the dragon-fighting genes became active only when a baby in the womb came in contact with the signal a dragon emitted from its forehead.

If the Slayer genes weren't activated during that nine-month slot, they remained forever dormant and useless—like they should.

When Overdrake got to Bianca, she was gripping her armrest, eyes closed. A sheen of sweat covered her face. The water bottle had dropped to the floor and lay jiggling against the side of the plane.

He wouldn't let himself panic about this. She would be fine. Contractions, even when they were real ones, could last several hours. When Bianca lost the last baby at five and a half months, it had still taken six hours to deliver it.

He didn't like to think about that son, a tiny gray curled figure that didn't look quite human. This son would be healthy. He had to be. Overdrake needed another dragon lord to help him, and only boys inherited that trait. If this baby died, who knew how long it would take for Bianca to produce another son for him. The wives of dragon lords always had a hard time getting pregnant. It was the one drawback of having ancestors who had mixed their DNA with dragons.

Bianca stopped gripping the armrests, took a deep breath, and let herself go limp in the chair.

"How far apart was that one?" he asked.

She glanced at her watch. "Two minutes."

"Two minutes?" he repeated.

She put her hand over her stomach and her shoulders shook with a silent sob. "You have to land the plane. I'm in labor."

Rivulets of water coated the windows. The clouds looked as if they had rolled in charcoal. Thunder was rumbling hungrily, looking for something to consume. "We can't land until the storm stops."

Bianca's voice rose. "The storm isn't going to stop, and neither are these contractions. I need a doctor." Tears spilled from her eyes, and she put her arms around her stomach, cradling it as though she could cradle the baby that way. "This is too early. Something is wrong."

Overdrake didn't tell her it would be all right. He didn't know if it would be. The memory of the last labor still clung to the edges of his mind. With a sigh, he sat beside her and took her hand in his. "If we land at BWI, the eggs' signals will reach all the people at the airport, all the people sitting in planes. Some of them are bound to be descendants of the Slayer knights." Back when those knights had ruled the Middle Ages, they'd spread their genes far and wide. Conquerors always did.

"Yes, but how many of those descendants will be pregnant?" she asked. "There can't be that many."

"How many Slayers does it take to kill a dragon?" Overdrake meant to counter her argument, but instead found the sentence comforting. Even if the eggs' signals did activate genes in a few unborn babies, giving them powers later on—it didn't mean those children would be able to grow up and kill the dragons.

Over the generations the Slayer knights' powers splintered apart. Descendants no longer inherited all of the abilities their ancestors had, just a few. And what could a handful of half-equipped Slayers do against his dragons?

Bianca shifted in her seat, gripping the armrests again. Another contraction was coming. "We've got to land. We don't have another choice and waiting will only put our son's life in danger." Her eyes seared with pain. "Who are you more concerned about—Slayer babies that might not even exist or your own baby who needs your help right now?"

She was right. Overdrake put his hand over hers, giving her what comfort he could. "I'll tell the pilot to land at BWI."

Three hours later, Overdrake sat beside his wife on her hospital bed. The doctor and nurses had finally left, giving the couple some privacy. Smiling and satisfied, Bianca handed Overdrake their son to hold. Even though the baby was four weeks premature, he was still seven and a half pounds. Perfectly healthy and waiting to be admired. He had strong, smooth skin, wisps of fair hair, and knowing eyes. Ones that showed intelligence. It was as if he already understood that he was a dragon lord.

"You can swim through the sky," Overdrake whispered to him. "You can control the kings of the air."

Bianca laughed. "You'll let him learn to walk before you train him to do all that, won't you?"

Overdrake grinned at her. "Maybe." He could enjoy these moments without worry, because Divers had already left BWI and landed in Winchester. Overdrake's staff were now carefully transporting each egg into the dragon enclosure.

Bianca reached over and stroked the baby's cheek. "How many . . ." She didn't finish the sentence.

Overdrake knew what she was thinking. "How many Slayers did our detour here create? I guess we'll know when the dragons attack and a bunch of teenagers show up to fight them."

"Teenagers," Bianca repeated, letting the word drift off. "They'll still be children when the dragons are full grown . . ."

Bianca was beautiful and Overdrake loved her, but she was much too soft when it came to thoughts of war. "Those teenagers won't just be the dragons' enemies," he reminded her. "They'll be our enemies, and our son's enemies, too."

Overdrake bent down and kissed his son's forehead. This was the person who would help him start a new dynasty. Overdrake ran a finger over his son's small hand and felt a surge of protectiveness and regret. He should have been more careful when he'd transported the eggs here. He'd taken risks and inadvertently created enemies for his son—children who would be born with a destiny already genetically stamped into them.

Overdrake would take care of his mistake, though. He would think of a way to find the Slayers and do whatever he needed in order to eliminate them.

CHAPTER 1

At six foot four and two hundred pounds, very few things frightened Ryker Davis. Dragons were one of those things, but they hardly counted since dragons weren't real.

Or at least, they weren't supposed to be real. They weren't real yesterday. Today might rearrange that fact. Ryker had just finished building the machine that would prove one way or the other whether he inherited superpowers to fight dragons. Were dragons just myths from the Middle Ages—the work of wild fears turned into legends—or was reality about to make a 90-degree bend?

The dragon heartbeat simulator was a metal box the size of a cedar chest and about as boring looking. According to the specifications, when it was turned on, it sent out energy waves that would fool his body into thinking a dragon was around. His dormant Slayer abilities would be triggered and he'd have extra strength, the ability to see in the dark, and one of the other dragon-fighting skills. Something along the lines of flight, throwing shields up, dousing fire, sending out freezing shocks, sending out fireballs, healing burns, or seeing what the dragon saw.

So far, all the machine did was make a humming-thumping sound, like something was loose inside.

He stared at it, not sure whether to feel discouraged or relieved that nothing amazing was happening to him. It was hard to feel anything but foolish while his cousin, Willow, stood by, making little quips to show that she thought the whole idea of dragon slayers was hilariously funny. "So if you're a superhero, are you going to start wearing brightly colored tights under your clothes?"

"No, I've always thought that jeans were good superhero fashion."

Ryker hadn't known that anyone considered dragon Slayer a career option until two years ago when he did an Internet search of his name and found the website RykerDavis.com.

The site proclaimed, "All You Ever Wanted to Know about Ryker Davis." It had a password to get past the first page. The clue was, What does Ryker dream about?

How could he not try to guess the password? For all he knew, one of the jerk-wad senior guys from the football team had put up the site to harass him. It bugged a few of them that the coach made Ryker starting varsity when he was a freshman. They'd never forgiven him for it. And they'd especially never forgiven him when he quit football a year later and went out for cross-country instead. Guys who could play varsity football weren't supposed to like cross-country better.

Ryker had typed in a few things he thought the jerk-wads would say he dreamed about, but when none of them worked, he typed in the real answer. Dragons. Although strictly speaking, those weren't dreams. They were nightmares.

Ryker didn't find any jokes or stupid pictures of himself. He found something completely different. And in many ways much worse.

> *Ryker, although you're unaware of it, you belong to an elite group of teenagers called the Slayers. Dragon eggs are here in the country, lying dormant, and will hatch*

within a few years. The resulting dragons won't be humankind's friends. You've inherited powers necessary to fight them. Your subconscious already knows this—which is why you've always had an obsession with dragons.

Granted, for as long as Ryker could remember, and he was seventeen, he'd liked weapons. As a child, he constantly stole the vacuum cleaner's hose attachment to use as a sword. Ditto for his dad's golf clubs. In kindergarten he turned a coat hanger into a bow and pencils into arrows. He started fencing lessons in third grade and now had a collection of swords that barely fit in his bedroom. And, okay, maybe he had a habit of buying plastic dragon toys, throwing them up in the air, and then seeing how many times he could slice through them before they hit the ground.

But that didn't mean he had a dragon *obsession.*

If he was obsessed with anything, it was hang gliding.

I need to train you, the site read, *but it must remain a secret. Tell no one.*

As if Ryker would tell anyone about the website. He was constantly worried someone he knew would find it and think he'd created it. Ryker didn't want to go through high school known as the weird guy who believed in dragons.

The site gave a phone number, an e-mail address, and a name. Or at least part of one: Dr. B. Ryker hadn't contacted him. The guy was probably some wack job, and besides, Ryker's parents were ultra-paranoid about identity theft, strangers, and all things that went bump in the night. If it weren't for the fact that there were two other Ryker Davises who had information all over the Internet, his parents would already be freaked out that a website existed with his name.

Ryker had kept tabs on the website over the last two years. He even started believing it. Or at least believed it enough that he had to know whether it was true.

A couple weeks ago, Dr. B posted schematics on how to construct a dragon heartbeat simulator, and Ryker built it. He stared at the machine now. He didn't feel extra strong. Nothing changed in his vision. The light in the basement was as dim as it always was.

Ryker picked up a screwdriver, walked over to the simulator, and twisted a screw tighter. It didn't need tightening. He had picked up the screwdriver to test his strength without being obvious about it. As he stepped away from the simulator, he took the screwdriver in one hand and tried to bend it. It remained straight.

Willow swished her long blonde hair off her shoulders dramatically. She was tall, thin, and graceful—willowy—which was a good thing since it would be hard to live down a name like Willow if you were short and dumpy. "Can I be your sidekick?"

It had been a mistake to let his cousin see the simulator. She had promptly e-mailed Dr. B and asked if a Batmobile came with the Slayer job description.

Immediately after she sent her e-mail, Dr. B contacted her, giving his phone number and asking that Ryker call him.

Yeah. Ryker wasn't going to do that. He fingered the screwdriver again. It still didn't bend. He tossed it onto the floor near his dad's toolbox and decided it served Willow right that she'd e-mailed Dr. B. The guy would probably send her daily spam trying to sell her tinfoil hats and elf repellent.

Willow looked upward, thinking. "For my sidekick costume, I want a cute headband like the one Wonder Woman wears but not the star-spangled bathing suit. I mean, fighting crime shouldn't require a girl to shave her legs. That's asking too much."

"I don't think you have to worry. I'm not experiencing any superpowers—at least not ones I didn't already have. I think my innate genius probably qualifies." Ryker kept his voice light, but there was a sort of numb disappointment filling him. He was normal. Like everybody else. Which meant he had an entire mundane, unimportant life to look forward to.

"Maybe you're not trying hard enough," Willow said. "See if you can shoot spiderwebs from your palm."

"Sorry," he said. "As much as I'd like to encase you in a web and leave you dangling somewhere, I can't." On the other hand, Ryker didn't have to worry about dragons attacking cities, or about his genetic responsibility to fight them. When he looked at it that way, a mundane, unimportant life wasn't such a bad thing.

Dragons. Sheesh. When had he become so gullible?

Willow let out a dramatic sigh. "I guess we'd better inform Dr. Alphabet Letters that you're not as cool as he thought." She picked up her Kindle. Dr. B's e-mail to them still sat on the screen.

"Don't," Ryker said. With one swift motion he grabbed the Kindle out of Willow's hands. "Don't encourage whoever . . ." He stopped talking when Willow let out a gasp. She stared, openmouthed at his hand.

Ryker looked down. The Kindle had cracked. The screen was nothing but a starburst of lines and colors.

Willow took a step toward him, her hands lifted in frustration. "What did you do that for?"

Ryker peered at the broken Kindle, dumbfounded. "I didn't grab it that hard. It just shattered."

Willow yanked what was left of the Kindle from his hand. Pieces of plastic fell onto the floor. "These don't *just shatter*. You must have . . ." Her voice trailed off, her anger fading away.

They looked at each other. Then they looked at the simulator. It was still making the same soft thudding sound. They looked back at each other. Neither said anything for a moment.

"Do you feel extra strong?" Willow asked tentatively.

"No," he said. "I still feel the same."

Willow scanned the room, saw the screwdriver, and picked it up. "See if you can bend this." She handed it to him, then took a step back from him as though the screwdriver might not only shatter, but explode, too.

Ryker laughed at the change in her expression. He already knew he couldn't. "I bet anyone can break an e-reader if they grab it wrong." He put one hand on the tip of the screwdriver and slowly applied pressure to show Willow it was pointless. "I'll buy you a new—"

He didn't finish. His mind couldn't form words. The metal spike of the screwdriver was bending into a horseshoe shape. He did have extra strength. It had just taken a few minutes to kick in.

Willow let out a high-pitched squeal. "You did it!" She bounced on the balls of her feet, a bundle of excitement. "This is so awesome!"

Ryker turned the ruined screwdriver over in his hand. "No, it isn't." His heart beat against his chest in a fast rhythm, a drumbeat pounding out a new and insistent call. He wasn't normal. He wasn't like everybody else. "This is really bad. Do you know what this means?"

The excitement drained from Willow as quickly as it had come. Her mouth opened into an O of understanding. "It means," she said in a voice that had gone still, "that the other stuff is true, too. Dragons are real. They're going to attack."

Ryker paced around his living room waiting for his parents to come home. He and Willow had just had a long talk about secrecy and caution, about what they should say and who they should tell. Slayer or not, signing up to fight dragons was going to take some thought. Especially since Dr. B had written about Overdrake, the dragon lord, who was lurking around somewhere, waiting to pick Slayers off.

Dr. B also reported on his site that he had met with Ryker's parents when his mom was pregnant with him. Dr. B didn't give many details about what led to the meeting. He just said that, instead of agreeing to let him train their son, Ryker's parents had moved without a trace. It was the reason Dr. B now kept Slayers from revealing any information about their training to their parents. It was the reason why Ryker wasn't supposed to tell his parents anything now.

But then, maybe his parents had good reasons for keeping him away from Dr. B. Maybe the man was dangerous. Or crazy. Or had an agenda of his own.

Ryker looked out the living room window to the street in front of their house. No cars were heading in his direction. It wasn't a surprise. They lived on a cul-de-sac. Ryker turned and paced back the other way.

No matter what Ryker's parents thought of Dr. B, they still should have told Ryker he was a Slayer. That part really ticked him off.

Willow and he had spent the last couple of hours trying to find other powers. He jumped off his trampoline about fifty times. He could leap huge distances, but he hadn't flown anywhere. He dragged every candle his parents owned onto the back patio and tried to extinguish their flames. That hadn't worked either. He wasn't sure what throwing a shield up entailed, so he waved his hands around, attempting to create some sort of force field over the basketball hoop while Willow shot baskets. That experiment was probably doomed from the start. Willow kept trying to make wild, impossible shots. He might have had a working shield up there half of the time and wouldn't have known it.

Next, Ryker went into the guest bathroom to test his night vision. The bathroom didn't have any windows, so it was the best place for that sort of test. Even in the dark, he could make out the gray shapes of Willow's shampoo bottle and conditioner in the shower. He could see the tangled silhouette of her blow dryer and iPod dock sitting on the counter, and see her makeup junk that was scattered everywhere. Seriously, why did girls need all of that stuff?

After that experiment—while Willow informed him that, yes, she really did need all that makeup junk, and guys should appreciate what girls did to look nice—they took cups of water out on the patio. Ryker dipped his fingers into his, then tried to send out freezing shocks to the hydrangeas. No frost formed, and if the hydrangeas felt chilly, they didn't let on. Before long, that experiment deteriorated into Willow and him throwing water at each other.

Besides the strength and night vision that all the Slayers had, he and Willow didn't discover any extra powers. But then the website didn't say how to access them. Maybe there was a trick to it that Dr. B hadn't mentioned. It could be his way of making Ryker contact him.

Or maybe it just took more practice.

Ryker heard the garage door open. His parents were home from work. They both worked at the same doctors' office: his dad as the office manager, his mother as a nurse. They were later than usual because they had to pick up Ryker's twelve-year-old sister, Jillian, from basketball camp.

Willow probably heard the garage door open, too. She was down in the basement hiding the simulator behind boxes of Christmas decorations. The website said his powers would last for half an hour after the simulator was turned off. He'd started a countdown in his mind, already dreading the time his extra powers would leave him. He'd just found them. He didn't want to give them up yet.

Ryker sat on the couch and picked up his laptop from the coffee table. It was already open to RykerDavis.com. A few moments later his sister Jillian and his parents strolled inside. His father was still fit for a man in his forties. His receding black hair and the wrinkles that creased the corners of his eyes were the only things that gave away his age. He prided himself on being able to occasionally beat Ryker at a game of one-on-one. Ryker had never told him, but beating his father at any sport had stopped being a challenge around seventh grade. Ryker lost on purpose sometimes because it didn't seem right to make his father lose all the time.

Ryker's mother was blonde, thin, and efficient in everything she did. She was the type of woman who could talk on the phone, stir three different things on the stove, and use hand motions to instruct her children to clean up their stuff, all without breaking stride.

As she came through the door, she was sorting through mail, already making a stack of things to shred. "The dog needs to be fed," she told Ryker, without looking up. "His bowl is empty again."

Griffin's bowl was frequently empty because the dog was a glutton. "Mom," Ryker said calmly, "I need to talk to you and Dad alone."

His tone of voice made her look up from the mail. "What's wrong?"

Ryker's gaze slid to his sister. Jillian let out an offended huff. "Nobody ever lets me hear anything."

His mother fluttered her hand toward Jillian's bedroom. "Go find something to do for a few minutes."

Jillian clomped down the hallway, still huffing, and shut her door with a loud bang.

"What's up?" his father asked, coming to stand in front of the couch.

Ryker flipped the laptop around so that RykerDavis.com was showing. "Have you ever heard of Slayers?"

Ryker's father squinted at the screen, then took the laptop from Ryker's hands. His mother stood rooted to the spot, an envelope still clutched in her hand. "What are you talking about?"

"According to the website," Ryker said, "I've inherited powers to fight dragons. A guy named Dr. B wants to train me."

His parents stiffened. His mother strode over to read what was on the laptop. Two spots of angry color formed in her cheeks. "I don't know what sort of scam this man is running, but you're not going to have anything to do with him. Just forget you ever saw it." She was speaking too fast, worry overshadowing her anger. "This Dr. B person is obviously making things up. Con men will tell you anything to get your trust."

Ryker pulled the screwdriver from his pocket. It shouldn't have fit in there, and wouldn't have if he hadn't twisted the metal around the handle. He stood up and handed it to his mother. "This used to be a screwdriver. It turns out I can bend steel."

Ryker's mother stared at the screwdriver and let out a gasp.

His father handed the laptop to his mother and took the screwdriver from Ryker's hand. He tugged at the metal. It didn't move. "How did you do this?"

Ryker wasn't about to tell them about the simulator he built in the basement. "Slayers have extra strength," Ryker said. "I can also toss my weights around like they were Frisbees." He leaned forward. "Did you guys really skip town after Dr. B told you he needed to train me?"

His parents exchanged a glance, one of fear and frustration. "How did Dr. B know Ryker's name?" his mother asked his father. "We never told him."

Ryker knew the answer to that question. "You stenciled my name on the nursery wall. After you moved, Dr. B came by to talk to you again. He looked through the window and saw it."

"He peered in our windows?" His mother let out another gasp, as if this were the worst part of the story—not running away after you found out your son was needed to protect the country.

Ryker's father glared at the computer screen. "Don't tell anyone about this. Not about dragons, not about Slayers. It isn't safe."

It isn't safe? They were talking about dragons attacking the country. They were talking about a dragon lord who was trying to hunt down Slayers. How was any of it going to be safe? Ryker stood up sharply. "I thought you guys had a good reason for running off, but you didn't, did you? All along, you knew what I was. Why didn't you ever tell me?"

"Because we want you to live." His mother's eyes were wide, and her voice spiraled upward, nearing hysteria. "You have no idea about dragons. I dreamed of them while I was pregnant with you—it's genetic memory. I saw one pick up cars and toss them around like they were toys. They're huge, they're fast, and you'll be killed if one finds you."

Ryker wasn't sure which surprised him more, that his mother had dreamed of dragons, or that she thought he hadn't. He'd dreamed of them before he even knew what they were. They hovered around the edges of his crib, snapping their jaws and flicking their tails. "Mom," Ryker said, trying to calm her so they could talk about it reasonably, "I'll be safer if I know how to use my powers. Dr. B has a camp—"

"No." She didn't let him say anymore. "You don't have our permission to go to camp or anywhere near that man." She was pale, trembling. Even her lips had lost their color.

Ryker stared at her, not sure what to say. He expected there to be some grand and noble reason they'd kept his identity hidden from him—or at least one that made sense. He expected his parents to feel guilty for running away. They didn't, though. They were mad he'd found out the truth.

Ryker's father gripped the laptop hard, still reading. "Did you contact Dr. B? Did you tell him where we lived?"

"No." Which was true. Ryker hadn't e-mailed Dr. B—Willow had. Dr. B couldn't trace the e-mail, though. Ryker's father had installed software that rerouted their IP addresses. One more paranoid thing his parents did, which suddenly made sense. They weren't hiding from identity theft or Internet predators. They were hiding from Dr. B.

Ryker's dad shook his head at the laptop screen. He was nearly growling. "What sort of man tells you not to tell your parents that he wants to train you for life-threatening missions?"

"The sort of man," Ryker pointed out, "that knows you ran away the first time he told you about dragons. The other Slayers at that camp know about me. They've saved me a spot every year, waiting for me to come." This, surprisingly, had been one of the harder facts for Ryker to realize was true. The other Slayers were at camp right now, wondering if he would ever show up. They must think he was a coward.

Mr. Davis spun on Ryker, his finger pointed in accusation. "We're trying to save your life. That man will throw it away."

Ryker raised his voice to match his father's. "You should have told me who I was. When I was little and was worried that dragons were going to pop out of my closet—you knew why I was afraid of them. You never said one thing about it." Until Ryker started elementary school, he'd made his father check his closet every night. It was a ritual—his father pushing shirts and toys aside to show that nothing lurked in deep shadows.

"What should I have told you?" his father asked. "That they were real and you were supposed to fight them? *That* would have given you good dreams."

"What about now?" Ryker asked, incredulous. "You knew it was in my DNA to fight dragons, but you never did anything to prepare me for it."

A flush of anger reddened his father's throat. "I don't care who your ancestors were. You're a *child*. It's not your responsibility to fight dragons. If you ever hear about an attack, you stay away from it. Do you understand?"

"It's my life," Ryker threw back at them. "You can't make my decisions."

His mother's eyes narrowed and her lips tightened into a line. "We can until you're eighteen. I swear I'll put a restraining order on Dr. B if he comes near you." She turned to Ryker's father, shaking even more now. "We need to read the entire website. We need to know what it says."

Ryker's father put his arm on her shoulder and guided her across the room. He shot Ryker a look over his shoulder that said this was far from over, and then his parents disappeared down the hallway to their bedroom.

Ryker stared after them, gritting his teeth. This was turning out really well. They didn't listen to anything he said, didn't ask him what he wanted to do. They were determined to treat him like that same five-year-old who had cringed from shadows in his closet.

He stormed downstairs to talk to Willow. It wouldn't take his parents long to read all the pages on the website. Maybe an hour or two. Once they found the blueprints for the dragon heartbeat simulator, they would realize that's where Ryker had gotten his strength from. They would come for it. Ryker wasn't about to give it up.

When he reached the bottom of the stairs, he found Willow leaning against the doorway that led into the rec room. She'd listened to the whole thing. Which was good since it saved him the trouble of having to repeat any of it.

Griffin, Ryker's dog, sat at Willow's feet, looking up at her as though he knew she was upset, and was just waiting for her to bend down so he could lick her hands to make her feel better. Stupid dog. Griffin hadn't even cast a glance at Ryker and he was the one who fed him every day.

Willow sighed. "I just realized why superheroes wear masks. It's so their parents don't ground them."

"We were right not to tell them everything. If they knew—"

"Don't say it," Willow looked up the stairs. "They might hear you."

Ryker strode into the rec room so his voice wouldn't carry. "What are we going to do?"

Willow followed him, Griffin trotting along at her heels. "What can we do? They won't let you anywhere near Dr. B. And if you ran away, they'd have the police scouring that camp to find you."

Ryker turned this over in his mind. Willow was right. Dr. B wouldn't want police questioning him or looking into his camp. Ryker had been wrong to ever confront his parents about what he'd learned, to think it would make any difference to them that he could pretzelize screwdrivers or leap ten feet into the air. They didn't care about protecting the country. They were afraid and apparently couldn't even imagine Ryker might win in a fight against a dragon.

"I'm going to train whether they like it or not," Ryker said. "They can't stop me from doing that. I'll call Dr. B and ask how to access my other power." He turned and walked toward the boxes where they'd hidden the simulator. Restless energy filled him. He pulled the boxes away from the machine, lifting each as though it were empty. "We need to find a place to hide the simulator."

"D.C. isn't that far away," Willow said, thinking. "We can find a way to see Dr. B without your parents knowing."

"I'll have to build a fake simulator—something my parents can get rid of so they think they're solving the problem." Ryker had messed up enough times while building the simulator that he had extra parts. He could put something together quickly. It didn't have to do anything except switch off and on.

He reached the real one. It was silent now and no longer vibrating; still, the thing was big enough that there weren't many places in the house he could hide it. "I'll take this to Kyle's, tell him it's a science project on measuring hang-gliding trajectories or something." His friend wouldn't ask too many questions about why Ryker couldn't keep it at his house. "I'll pick it up every time I go hang gliding, which I'll be doing frequently since you just decided you wanted to learn how to hang glide. We'll train up on the ridge."

Willow's lips twitched. She'd never wanted to hang glide and was probably worried she'd have to show some proficiency at it if they went with that story.

Ryker pulled the simulator into the middle of the room. It had wheels, but with his extra strength, he could carry it. He hefted it onto his shoulder. "I'll put this in my truck, then I'll go talk to my parents again—distract them while you drive this to Kyle's."

Ryker hadn't heard Jillian walk downstairs and didn't know she'd come into the room until she gasped out, "No!"

Then he realized what he should have known all along. When his parents sent Jillian to her room, she hadn't gone there. She went into the guest bedroom—Willow's bedroom—right next to the family room. She heard everything he and his parents had said.

Jillian clutched her iPad. He didn't have to ask what site it was open to. She walked toward Ryker and her hands shook, jiggling the image of a dragon that was on one of the website pages.

"Is this stuff about dragons true?" she asked. "It says their scales are bulletproof. It says they eat people. And what is EMP? What does that mean?"

Ryker put the simulator back on the floor and sighed. Dr. B's website had lots of gory dragon details on it. They ate voraciously for their first year—people or animals, whichever was easiest to catch—adding to their size until their bodies alone were the size of a large commercial bus. With their wings, tails, and necks added to the picture, they looked more like dinosaurs than animals from this day and age. Dragons could outmaneuver planes and helicopters, and their skin absorbed radar, making it impossible for people to shoot missiles at them from a safe distance.

Those details, however, weren't what made dragons so dangerous. When dragons screeched, they sent out an EMP: an electromagnetic pulse that destroyed anything with electronics. Vehicles, lights, cell phones, TVs, computers—so many of the things people depended on—none of them worked if a dragon screeched in the area. A few flybys from a dragon, and entire cities would be crippled.

Ryker stared at Jillian, unsure what to say. He didn't want to scare her more than she already was, but he didn't want to lie to her, either.

Willow walked over and took the iPad from Jillian's hand before she dropped it. "It's going to be all right," Willow said.

Jillian scowled and grabbed her iPad back. "You want Ryker to fight dragons. I heard what you said about training and sneaking off to D.C." Without waiting for Willow's response, Jillian stomped over to the simulator, looking like she would kick it. "If you call Dr. B, I'll tell Mom and Dad what you're doing."

Ryker strode over and grabbed her arm. "Don't you dare say a word about it to anyone."

"I will," Jillian said. Her face scrunched up until her eyes squinted with emotion.

"You won't," Ryker told her firmly. He didn't know he was squeezing her arm too tightly until she grabbed at his fingers, crying out. Then he realized her emotion had been pain, not stubbornness. He immediately dropped her arm. Red lines circled her skin. His fingerprints.

A wave of sickness washed over him. He hadn't meant to hurt her. "I'm sorry," he stammered. It seemed a limp apology next to the welts he'd left on her arm.

Tears dribbled down Jillian's cheeks. She held her arm and whimpered. In the quiet of the room, the noise sounded even louder. "I don't care what you do to me," she whispered. "I'll tell if you go see Dr. B."

Her words slapped Ryker. Jillian thought he'd meant to hurt her. The red lines were swelling now. If he had applied a little more pressure—if he'd been a little angrier—he would have broken her arm without meaning to. "I'm sorry," he said again, and his voice caught. "I didn't mean to. I forgot about my extra strength. Here, let me see it."

He reached for her arm as if he could undo the damage, as if he could keep the bruises from forming. Instead of showing him the injury, Jillian wrapped her arms around his neck and hugged him. She was still crying. "I don't want you to die. Promise me you won't join the Slayers."

He hugged her gingerly, carefully, so he wouldn't hurt her again. She seemed so small and thin, so breakable. "I won't," Ryker said. "At least not until I turn eighteen. That means you can't tell Mom and Dad anything about what I'm doing. Promise?"

Jillian clung to his neck and muffled her words into his shoulder. "I don't want you to train at all."

Willow walked around Ryker's side so she could look into Jillian's face. "He has to learn how to use his strength," she reasoned. "Otherwise he might accidentally hurt someone again—or do something worse. Besides, Ryker will be safer if he learns how to use his powers."

Ryker felt Jillian sigh against him, relent a little. "All right. But you can't go see Dr. B."

Ryker patted Jillian's back so softly he was barely touching her. His gaze went to Willow's. He could read her expression. *The more our family knows, the harder all of this will be.* He nodded at her. She was right. Which was why they couldn't tell anyone the other secret they'd discovered today.

CHAPTER 2

THE BEGINNING OF AUGUST, DRAGON CAMP

Tori Hampton faced the mechanical dragon. Its golden eyes glowed with electric malevolence and steam leaked from its gaping jaws. Tori's flame-retardant suit was hot, uncomfortable, and every time she took off her helmet to wipe sweat from her face, she ended up getting soot in her eyes.

When you came right down to it, having superpowers was a lot less glamorous than Hollywood made it seem. Spider-Man didn't have to work out hours a day to stay in shape. He just swung between buildings as if he were on an amusement park ride. Superman didn't have to take flying lessons. He'd never turned too fast midair and slammed into a tree so hard he broke off branches. Tori, on the other hand, left the trees around her cabin looking maimed and offended. Batman—well, Batman didn't count. He didn't have superpowers. He just had awesome fashion accessories.

Every day after practicing at the rifle range and the archery range—after horseback riding, motorcycle riding, sword fighting, and martial arts—the Slayers assembled in the dragon hall to fight two van-size, flame-shooting mechanical dragons that swooped around the three-story pavilion.

If the twirling beams that represented the dragons' claws touched you, you were dead. If the hundred-pound swinging tail hit you, you were dead. If one of your teammates accidentally shot you with their pellet rifle, you were dead. If the flames that shot twenty feet out of the dragons' mouths reached you, you were burned. For real. It was real fire.

The machinery on the ceiling clanged, wires tightened, and the dragon lifted from the floor, its state-of-the-art hydraulic system hissing. The claw-shaped beams at the end of the dragon's legs began their slow twirl.

Tori had already fought the dragon three times this afternoon. It killed her twice, which ought to be enough for one day. Still, she checked her pellet rifle for ammunition, slipped the gun into the sling on her back, and gripped her wooden sword. She was ready. She waited for Dirk, A-team's captain, to start the round.

"Get in position," Dirk called. He wore the standard black helmet, fire-repellent pants, and jacket. His jacket was undone around the collar, and even Dr. B's lectures on safety couldn't make Dirk zip it up. No one hassled him about it. Dirk was fast and his instincts were flawless. In all the years he had come to camp, he had never been burned.

Lilly edged toward one side of the dragon. Her bleached-blonde hair was pulled back into a ponytail that swayed underneath her helmet like a white flag. Her hair was the only thing that would ever wave a white flag. She—for some indiscernible reason—actually enjoyed these practices, enjoyed fighting.

Kody moved around closer to the other side of the dragon. His jacket was partially open in the front, too. Not because he meant it to be. Kody was just the most muscular of any of the Slayers. Sort of a combination between a cowboy and the Incredible Hulk. His shoulders were so broad the jacket didn't fit him right. Halfway through every practice round, the front always came undone. Dr. B had ordered him a new one, but it was the last day of camp, and it still hadn't come.

Kody and Lilly were fire control. They tried to stay on opposite sides of the dragon. Alyssa, A-team's healer, stayed behind Dirk. She didn't take a dangerous position unless everyone else died first.

Healer would have been an awesome job—hang back out of the fighting and heal people's burns. Tori wished she had it. Instead, she was A-team's flyer.

Flying had seemed like a cool talent until Tori realized that the fly-ers had to do most of the work to kill a dragon. All the other Slayers' powers were simply support. They kept the dragon from charring people while the flyers battled the monsters in the sky. The flyers had to strip away the dragon's protections so that someone was able to shoot the dragon's vulnerable underbelly and pierce its heart.

The mechanical dragon in front of Tori wasn't attacking, not yet. Tori hovered off the ground, waiting for Dirk to call a play. She stole a quick glance at the other side of the dragon hall. Team Magnus had already started their round. Four black-clad Slayers darted over the practice arena while their dragon swooped and spun around that part of pavilion.

The sound of cables moving drew Tori's attention back to her side. The dragon lunged forward, claws twirling, toward Tori.

"Eight of clubs!" Dirk called. He and Lilly sprinted around to one side of the dragon. Kody and Alyssa ran toward the other. Tori flew up over the dragon's head, then looped back down so that she was over the dragon's back. She had to do two things before anyone was able to go for the dragon's heart. First, she had to run her sword along the sensors on both sides of the dragon's back to simulate that she'd cut the two Kevlar straps that held bulletproof plating over the dragon's underbelly. Second, she had to hit two different pairs of sensors with a blast from her pellet rifle to simulate that she'd blown through the chains underneath the Kevlar straps that also kept the bulletproof plating in place.

That was one of the new items of information the Slayers learned earlier in the summer when Overdrake set a real dragon on them. The bulletproof plating had two layers to cut through.

Tori wasn't able to get close enough to the mechanical dragon's back before it turned and flew upward, coming after her. She darted out of the way, made a hand signal for an under-the-belly dive, and plunged downward, heading underneath the machine. One of the hardest things about maneuvering around the dragon was remembering to make the corresponding hand signals so the rest of the team knew what she was doing.

The dragon somersaulted after her, metal joints screeching. Theo, the techno geek who worked this dragon's controls, wasn't supposed to know what the Slayers' hand signals were. Tori was pretty sure he did, though. The dragon always followed her movements without hesitation. She heard the hiss of gathering fuel in the dragon's mouth and knew what would come next.

Fire blazed out of the dragon's mouth at her. Heat licked against the back of her legs until Lilly managed to flick her wrist in Tori's direction and extinguish the flames.

You would think that since the job only took as much physical effort as waving good-bye, Lilly would be faster about snuffing out flames. But no. She seemed to enjoy making Tori even hotter.

Tori flew toward Kody, giving him the signal to distract the dragon. He wound his arm back, like a pitcher throwing a fastball, and sent out a freezing shock. Moments later it hit the dragon squarely in the face. The metal on its neck shuddered. The dragon turned its glowing yellow eyes on him and hurled toward him.

Kody leapt out of the way of the dragon's claws, and then leapt again to get away from its swinging tail. All the Slayers could leap at least eight feet in any direction. Kody could leap ten.

Tori hated putting him in danger, but it was a part of the practice. While the dragon was busy with him, she swept her sword across the top of the dragon's back. One light on the dragon's back lit up indicating the first Kevlar strap had been cut. Her fastest time yet. Maybe she would not only kill the dragon this round, maybe she'd do it before Jesse, Team Magnus' flyer.

The thought made her smile. Not because she didn't like Jesse— she did. He had spent all summer teaching her how to fly and fight in the air. It would mean something to him if she finally slew her dragon faster than he did. Half of the time during practice, Tori was the first one killed on either side, and then her team had to do their best to stay alive until Jesse beat his dragon and could come over and take care of A-team's as well.

Tori didn't have time to cut through the second strap. The dragon pulled upward and swung its tail at her. She barely managed to dodge away.

"Roll!" Dirk called to her, which meant she was supposed to attack on the left-hand side. She circled around the dragon and made the hand signal to request a distraction.

Any of the Slayers on the ground could have shot the dragon with their rifles. That was usually enough to provoke the dragon into an attack. Dirk signaled for Kody to send another freezing shock. Maybe because the two of them had a running bet with Team Magnus as to who could knock off their dragon's head first.

Kody pushed his hand forward. The air shimmered in a line until the freezing shock hit the dragon's mouth with the force of a baseball bat. Metal clanged. The dragon's head jerked backward. A circle of frost appeared on the side of its head and then just as quickly melted. The dragon turned and plunged toward Kody.

Tori dived at its left side, keeping one eye on the dragon's tail. The tail was how she usually met her untimely deaths. The dragon swooped and wheeled, chasing Kody across the middle of the practice arena. Tori zoomed along beside it, slashing downward across the sensors. A second light came on. Both Kevlar straps were gone. Now she only had to blast away the chains. That was easier. She didn't have to get as close to the dragon to do it.

Tori swung her sling forward, putting her rifle into firing position.

Lilly sprinted toward Kody, trying to cover him. She wasn't fast enough. Fire erupted from the dragon's mouth, a blaze that ballooned outward like a reaching orange hand. Kody leapt sideways, spinning around to send out a cold blast to intercept the flames. His blasts could push fire away, but this time it wasn't soon enough and it wasn't strong enough.

Half of the fire stream reached him, hissing and spitting as it intersected with the freezing gust of air. Flames pummeled Kody's chest for several seconds before Lilly managed to extinguish the fire.

Tori's shots at the dragon had missed the sensor. It was a small target and had to be a direct hit. Dirk shot the dragon's neck, drawing its attention to him. While the dragon jerked its head toward Dirk, Kody rushed toward Alyssa. He held up two fingers, indicating he needed burn help. Smoke mingled with the acrid scent of charred skin.

Tori flew over the dragon, glancing at Kody's wounds as she did. Red, oozing spots covered his neck and the exposed part of his chest.

Guilt twisted her stomach. Kody had distracted the dragon for her and he'd ended up burned and in pain because of it.

The dragon twisted toward Dirk, making gusts of wind with its wings, then decided to ignore him and go after Kody again. The weak and the injured—those were a dragon's favorite prey.

Tori needed to hurry and blast through the chains. Once that was done, someone on the ground could kill the dragon and the round would be over. Keeping her distance so the dragon couldn't suddenly turn and lunge at her, Tori took aim and shot. Her hand shook. She missed the sensors.

Dirk rushed toward the dragon, firing at its head. The pellets made pointless plinking sounds. Even armor-piercing bullets wouldn't do anything to a dragon except annoy it. The dragon turned from Kody, roared, and hurtled toward Dirk.

Tori shot at the sensors again, quicker this time. The dragon dived after Dirk, jolting the target away from her. Her bullet fire swept down onto the ground and a light on the front of Lilly's jacket lit up, indicating she'd been hit. Not good.

Lilly threw her arms up in aggravation. "Really?" she yelled at Tori. "You didn't notice me standing here? You're so beyond worthless!"

Lilly at her charming best.

It didn't do any good to argue with Dr. B that in a real fight the Slayers would wear bulletproof outfits and Tori wasn't using armor-piercing ammunition for that reason. Rules were rules. Lilly was dead and one hundred points would be taken from A-team's score because Tori had accidentally killed her.

Tori flew after the dragon, trying to keep up and aim accurately while the dragon chased after Dirk. The last thing she wanted was to kill him, too. The dragon was flying low, leaning one way and then the other so the target was never still. The dragon swiped a black spinning claw at Dirk. He leapt over it and was nearly bludgeoned by the dragon's tail. Theo knew that move and had anticipated it.

Dirk flipped through the air, landed on the dragon's tail, then leapt up again and took a midair shot at the dragon's back. The sensor lit up. He'd blasted through the chain. One more chain to go, and any of them would be able to fire at the dragon's underbelly, killing it.

Tori smiled. Dirk was good. Her strategy should be to fly low to the ground so the dragon chased her, and let Dirk take care of the straps and chains.

Tori zoomed in toward the dragon's back again, making sure none of the Slayers were close before she aimed her gun. The extra two seconds of precaution cost her. Before she shot, the dragon flipped upward, coming after her.

Down below, Dirk shot at the dragon. It ignored him this time and kept after Tori. She zipped upward, then arced across the roof. The dragon kept pace with her. She heard the fuel building up in its mouth. In another second she would be engulfed in flames and she'd already killed her team's only fire extinguisher.

Tori sped up, zigzagging sideways. The fire-repellent suits helped but still melted after about fifteen seconds. Protection and mobility were always at odds with each other when it came to a battle.

Tori had run out of room. She wished she could fly over into Team Magnus air space. Bess, one of Team Magnus' Slayers, could throw a force field up that shielded a fifteen-foot area from the dragon's flames. Tori would lose points for that, though—bringing another dragon over to Team Magnus area before they'd killed theirs.

Tori dived downward, completely forgetting to use her hand signals. She flipped around in midair, expecting a blast of fire to come at her. Hopefully, she could fly through it before it scorched her. She was good at making it through curtains of flames, could dive through them like they were water. She'd never gotten burned during practice—unless you counted her first day at camp, when a rogue fireball singed off a chunk of her hair. That was a burn she was still smoldering about—so to speak—because it had happened after practice ended. And, okay, Dr. B was always telling them that they couldn't let their guard down, but still, it was her first day. Someone should have warned her that regular rules didn't apply in this place.

The fire came, a billowing molten stream reaching for her. Tori sliced through it, diving even closer to the dragon. Her first clue that something had changed, that the dragon was different, was the sound— the whirring of its claws stopped. Broken, she thought. That was bound to happen after two months of shooting, freezing, and whacking the thing.

She should have learned by now never to make assumptions about dragons.

A chain shot out of the dragon's left front claw and hit her below her ribs—hooked into her with a pinch of pain. Immediately, it reeled her toward the claw.

"Hey!" she yelled, pulling at the hook. "Since when do dragons have fishing poles?" She knew Theo and Dr. B could hear her. They had audio in the control room.

Tori's short attempt to free herself ended when she slammed into the bottom of the dragon's claw. The impact knocked her helmet loose and dug the hook into her stomach. Her helmet tumbled to the ground and landed with a crack.

Before Tori could draw a breath, two metal straps shot out from each end of the dragon's claw. They curved around Tori, attached together in the back, then tightened. The hook in her stomach dug even deeper into her skin. She let out a yelp of pain.

The dragon zoomed upward, flying out of range of her teammates. She turned her head and saw them staring up at her, openmouthed. The dragons had never captured Slayers before, only killed them.

Tori felt a wave of panic. She was going to be burned if she didn't escape and her helmet had fallen off. Theo wouldn't care about how much a blast to the face hurt or whether there would be scarring. Alyssa could cure burns and this was part of practice.

Tori thrashed, trying to loosen the bands that clamped her arms to her sides. They didn't budge. Dr. B always made sure his equipment counteracted the Slayers' extra strength. Tori was up so high, that only another flyer would be able to rescue her. Across the pavilion, Jesse darted around the side of his dragon, getting in place to shoot its chain sensors.

"Jesse!" she screamed. "Help me!"

Jesse turned to see what was wrong. It was a mistake. The second his attention left the dragon, it twisted and lashed its tail in his direction. The swinging metal smashed into Jesse's stomach with a sickening *thwack* that flung him through the air.

Being knocked out of the practice area meant Jesse was technically dead. Tori didn't care. She thrashed against her bands, still calling for him. Slayers had stronger skin than normal people, but at this close range, her nose and ears would probably burn right off. She didn't know how Alyssa was at healing the charred remains of noses and didn't want to find out.

The sound of fuel hissing inside the dragon's mouth meant in a few seconds it would spit out fire. "Jesse," Tori yelled again. "Get this thing off of me!" She couldn't see where he was, didn't know if he could break the bands anyway.

The dragon flew a bit lower, taunting the other Slayers. It was still too high up for any of them to reach. Dirk ran along beside it. "Bess!" he hollered to Team Magnus' area. "Put a force field underneath me!"

Without waiting for her reply, he leapt into the air. Dirk could jump the highest of any of the Slayers. Fifteen feet. When he'd reached that height, instead of falling back to the ground, he only sank a few inches and then stopped. He'd hit Bess' force field. He leapt up again, this time grabbing the dragon's left leg, right above the claw that held Tori.

The blast of fire came, hitting Dirk's back instead of Tori's face. She felt the heat fingering around his body, brushing against her exposed skin. Smoke rolled through the air. Finally the flames vanished. Kody had managed to send out a cold shock to push away the fire before it could completely melt Dirk's jacket.

Tori gulped in relieved breaths. "Thanks."

Dirk smiled, took off his helmet, and placed it on Tori's head. "You need this more than I do." Then he climbed hand over hand up the dragon's leg.

Tori caught sight of Jesse. He was hovering in the air near her side of the arena, watching but not interfering. Dead Slayers were supposed to stay out of the practice area. He was staying close by, keeping an eye on the new direction the round had taken.

Tori struggled against the bands, pushing them with all her might. They creaked, unyielding. Wasn't it bad enough that she'd already been killed twice today? Did she have to be the only Slayer that died a slow ignominious death, stuck on the dragon's claw like something it had stepped on and hadn't managed to scrape off its talons yet?

Dirk sent a distract signal to Kody, and Kody happily shot a round into the dragon's head. With flames already spurting from its mouth, the dragon plunged after Kody, swerving on its side as it turned. The turn allowed Dirk to swing up onto the dragon's back. He pulled his gun forward to blast through the last chain.

The dragon didn't give him time. It immediately flipped over on its back, shaking Dirk loose. The move swung Tori around to the top of the pavilion so she faced downward. She caught a glimpse of Dirk falling. He aimed his gun upward and fired at the dragon's back. Tori couldn't see the shot or the sensor, but she heard the click of the fourth light as it came on. Dirk's shot had been good.

Dirk, Kody, and Alyssa let out yells of triumph. Good. This would be over soon. A reprieve from her ignominious death. The dragon turned upright again, and Tori had to crane her head to see the others. Dirk landed on his feet, the impact of the fall making him stumble forward before he caught himself.

Kody raised his rifle and fired at the dragon's underbelly. He managed to hit the heart target on his first try and didn't kill Tori in the process. Always an added plus. The dragon went limp on the wires.

The bands around Tori loosened, letting her fly away. The chain was still attached to her jacket, part of it embedded into her skin. She ripped out the hook, undoubtedly leaving a hole in her skin as well as the one in her jacket. No time to worry about that now. She soared across the pavilion to Team Magnus' dragon.

With Jesse gone and the dragon's bulletproof plating still attached, Team Magnus hadn't made any more progress in slaying their dragon. Mostly it was diving toward Slayers, and Bess was throwing shields up in front of it to slow down its progress. Tori zoomed along overhead. This time, she would make sure she stayed well away from its claws.

Tori swung her rifle into position. She only had one chain to shoot through; one good shot and the Slayers on the ground would be able to take care of the rest. She aimed, angry with herself for being caught by A-team's dragon and angry with Dr. B for throwing something new at them on the last day of practice. The anger gave her a sort of determined focus.

She shot and hit the target. The last sensor light turned on, all of them glowing green to show that the dragon's bulletproof plating had been cut away. Green was a beautiful color.

The dragon turned and wheeled toward her, eyes flashing, wings pressed tight to its body. The flight was short lived. Shang, Team Magnus' fire extinguisher, punched a round of ammunition at the dragon's heart.

The second dragon went limp on the wires.

Only then did Tori unzip her jacket and feel along her stomach to see what damage the hook had caused. Her fingers came away bloody. Wonderful. That would be one more injury she would have to explain to her parents when she got home. Slayer healers cured burns, but couldn't do anything for cuts or bruises, which was what Tori always collected during practice.

On the ground beneath Tori, Jesse walked toward the weapons

lockers. He took off his helmet with tense, deliberate motions. She flew over and paused in the air beside him. "Sorry I got you killed."

"Not your fault," he said. "Sorry I couldn't save you."

She flew toward Dirk then. She owed him. Big-time. Tori didn't even want to think about what that fire blast would have done to her face if Dirk hadn't shielded her. And he had given her his helmet—put himself in harm's way to protect her.

Dirk was sauntering over to the weapons lockers, joining the rest of A-team. He was tall and muscular like all the Slayer guys. He had surfer-boy blond hair and the sort of face that could have been used to sell cologne—to sell anything probably. The strut in his walk said he knew exactly how impressive he was. Kody high-fived him. "Awesome shooting, man. I can't believe you shot the target while you were falling."

Alyssa's gaze went over Dirk as though checking him for a limp. "I can't believe you didn't break a leg."

Tori landed next to Dirk and gave him a quick hug. "Thanks again. You saved my life."

"Or at least her hair," Alyssa put in.

Lilly snickered. The two of them liked to bring up Tori's first-day hair-singed-off debacle. Rather than cutting her hair to even it out, Tori had skipped out on camp, gone to a salon in the nearest town, and gotten extensions in the damaged part. Her long, honey-brown hair was restored to the point that with any luck, people wouldn't notice the change.

Tori ignored Lilly and Alyssa and kept walking alongside Dirk. "I can't believe the dragon harpooned me." She fingered the blood-rimmed hole in her shirt. That was another piece of clothing camp had ruined, bringing the total to—well—just about everything she'd brought. "I don't think Theo should be allowed to work the controls anymore. He clearly doesn't grasp the difference between a challenging practice and inflicting hideous deaths on all of us."

"Clearly," Dirk repeated. "Except I'm pretty sure Dr. B was controlling our dragon this round."

Tori let out a disbelieving gasp. "Are you kidding me?"

Before Dirk could answer, the door to the control room opened, and Dr. B and Theo started down the stairs that led to the practice arenas.

Theo was a twenty-something guy who would have looked normal enough in another place. Next to the Slayer guys, he always seemed pale, gawky, and so stringy that a strong wind could blow him away.

Dr. B looked like an ordinary middle-aged man—tall, slightly overweight, with unruly gray hair and wire-rim glasses. He often had an expression on his face that indicated he was pondering some aspect of the cosmos, which he probably was. He was a medieval history professor during the school year and acted like a concerned teacher most of the time—caring, kind, encouraging. Always, always so deceptively mild. He constantly praised them with plaque-worthy sayings. *You have the power to overcome anything. You are what victory is made of. I love each and every one of you.*

And then immediately afterward he would lead a staff ambush against the Slayers while they ate dinner. Throughout camp he peppered anyone he could with paintballs and then cheerfully deducted team points for their careless deaths.

Tori couldn't decide whether he was a brilliant leader or a sociopath. Today, she was thinking sociopath. Definitely sociopath.

Dr. B blew his whistle. It was his way of getting the Slayers attention to let them know he had comments about their performance.

Dr. B frequently had comments.

As he finished walking down the stairs, he called out, "What have you learned from this round of practice?"

You've got an uncharacteristic sadistic streak, Tori thought. Although technically that wasn't something new she learned. It had crossed her mind several times during the summer. Tori didn't say these words. She'd been raised to be polite, and besides, Dr. B was Bess' father. She couldn't insult her friend's father.

"The dragons now have fishing lines and hooks," Tori called back to him. "Apparently they've evolved since yesterday."

Dr. B waved away her point. "The hook was to simulate the dragon's ability to reach out and grab you. It can do that."

Bess pulled off her helmet. Her brown curls were matted against her head in sweaty tendrils. She didn't look much like her father, but she had inherited his curls. "We've learned that we need both teams to work together." She said the phrase like it was the obvious answer. "I had to help Dirk free Tori. She had to help us kill our dragon."

Dr. B didn't ever yell. The closest he got was a sharp tone of exasperation. He used that tone as he walked across the floor to them. "You already know you have to work together. That's not what happened here." His gaze went to Jesse. "Why were you killed?"

Jesse stiffened. He hated making mistakes. "I wasn't paying attention."

"You *were* paying attention," Dr. B corrected. "You were just paying attention to Tori instead of your dragon."

Dr. B's gaze swung to Dirk. "You not only abandoned the rest of your team to rescue Tori, you used one of Team Magnus' members to do it—thereby endangering both teams—and why? Tori was already dead."

Dirk didn't flinch, didn't show any signs of regret. "Tori sounded pretty alive while she was screaming."

Dr. B held up a hand. "The rules state that if any Slayer is hit by dragon claws they're considered dead. We can assume the same is true for Slayers gripped in dragon claws. In a real battle, even if Tori had been alive for a few moments, she wouldn't have been alive by the time you got to her. The dragon would have sliced her in half."

Tori winced. It was always cheery to hear people talk about her gruesome demise.

Dr. B put his hands behind his back and divided his time between staring at Jesse and staring at Dirk. "So essentially what happened is that both teams lost their flyers. You had no way to kill the dragons and your only functioning team captain stopped functioning and turned into a one-man rescue mission."

Dr. B let out a huff of frustration. "I want you to protect one another. That's a good thing. But you can't do it at the expense of the mission. Killing the dragon has to be your top priority. You need to learn to react with logic and not emotion. If you react emotionally, you'll try to save your friends, even though logically it may be the worst mistake you can make. I know this is hard . . ." Dr. B's voice dropped and his gaze swept over the group, meeting each Slayer's eyes. "Don't sacrifice the lives of two people—let alone your whole team—to try to save one person." His gaze landed on Jesse again. "You're our most experienced flyer. You can't let anything or anyone distract you."

Jesse nodded, somber.

Dirk was immune to guilt trips, though. He only smiled at Dr. B. "But you have to admit—shooting the target while falling was a sweet move."

"All right—yes." A smile tugged at the corner of Dr. B's mouth. "That was quite well done."

Dr. B turned to Tori and his voice softened. "You've come a long way from the start of camp. However, your frequent deaths lead me to believe you're still not ready to become A-team's captain."

Ever since Dr. B discovered Tori could fly, he insisted that one day she would be A-team's leader. Tori never wanted the job. It was bad enough that she occasionally got her team members killed in practice. She didn't want to be the one responsible for their lives when it came to a real battle. She nodded. "That's probably for the best."

While Dr. B addressed Team Magnus and gave them specific feedback on their fight, Tori turned to Dirk. She gave him a look that said, *See, you have nothing to worry about. You're A-team's captain and always will be.*

Dirk's extra Slayer power was the ability to see what the dragon saw. No one was quite sure how the links worked, but Dirk had a connection with one of Overdrake's dragon eggs. A part of Dirk's mind always saw what the unborn dragon saw—which was darkness at night and a reddish light during the day.

That particular talent didn't do much good in a fight, and yet Dirk was such a good Slayer, Dr. B had made him A-team's captain four years ago.

"I think you should already be captain," Dirk said in mock seriousness. "A-team might need their captain to die a martyr's death in order to rally them into action."

Tori smacked him.

Dirk laughed and put his gun on a peg in his locker. "You always fly too close to the dragon and stay there too long. Are you purposely getting yourself killed so you don't have to be captain or do you have a risk-taking side I don't know about?"

Tori placed her wooden sword on the floor of her locker and shut the door. "I figure it's better to see how well I can maneuver in here than in a real attack. This is the place to push my limits, to make mistakes."

Dirk shook his head. "When it comes to dragons, there isn't a place to make mistakes."

He was right about that—at least while Theo and Dr. B ran the controls. "You're so wise," she purred at him. "Which is why you'll always be A-team's captain. Well, that and the fact that I don't want to deal with Lilly any more than I have to."

"Coward," Dirk whispered.

Neither of them said more after that because Dr. B had finished with his assessment of Team Magnus and turned to give A-team its critique. Most of his comments were directed at Tori. She needed to utilize the other Slayers' abilities to optimize her strategy. She needed to make sure she was always covered. And she needed to rely less on her sight and more on her instincts. Her Slayer senses picked up things her conscious mind didn't.

Dr. B must have seen her discouragement because he ended his assessment with, "Overall, you're doing very well. Better than I expected. It just takes time."

That was the problem, though. None of them knew how much time they had before Overdrake began attacking cities with his dragons and his mercenary fighters. Overdrake wanted to take over the government and would lay waste to as many cities as he needed until the nation agreed to his terms. Dr. B thought the only reason Overdrake hadn't launched an assault already was that he was waiting for his dragon eggs to hatch. Once they did, they would mature within a year and be ready for Overdrake to use.

Dr. B walked back in front of the room and raised his voice, addressing the group again. "Before camp ends, I wanted to say a few words about safety."

Safety. An ironic topic after he'd trapped Tori with a flame-throwing dragon and nearly roasted her.

"I know you've all been concerned about an informant or some sort of leak at camp." Concerned was an understatement. At the beginning of the summer, the Slayers figured out where Overdrake kept the dragon eggs and launched a surprise attack to destroy them. Not only had Overdrake been waiting for them, he knew their names. The Slayers barely managed to escape from the dragon enclosure.

They had never figured out who tipped off Overdrake or how he knew their names. After the attack, Dr. B moved the Slayers to a hidden backup camp an hour away from their original one. Theo checked all their belongings for bugs and took their phones to search for anything suspicious. The Slayers all had special satellite phones with EMP and tracking protection—or at least they did until Theo confiscated them. The regular kind didn't work well in the forest and wouldn't work at all after a dragon strike. Dr. B needed to make sure he always had a way to contact the group.

In the name of security, Dr. B had added more cameras and sensors along the camp's boundaries and had given the Slayers a few new rules.

Camp already had dozens of rules. The Slayers couldn't give one another any personal information about their outside lives. Not where they lived, what they did, especially not their last names. They couldn't take pictures of camp or each other. They had a complicated system for going home after the summer to make sure no one followed them. At home, they couldn't talk about camp to their family or friends. They couldn't use any of their Slayer powers in a way that would draw attention to themselves. They couldn't contact one another, except in an emergency.

"The bad news," Dr. B went on, "is that I can't tell you where Overdrake got his information. The analysis of your old phones and your old cabins didn't turn up anything. You'll still have to be more careful, more diligent than you've ever been."

A fair amount of murmuring went through the group at this news. If it wasn't some sort of bug, what was it? How did they know Overdrake didn't still have a way to spy on them?

"The good news," Dr. B said a little louder, "is that Theo has designed a new, more secure communication device."

Theo held up a large black plastic watch for everyone to see. It didn't just scream tacky, it shrieked it while flashing out the time. "This is the prototype of our new emergency phones," Dr. B said. "You'll get yours tomorrow as you leave camp. Always keep it with you."

Tori hadn't realized she'd groaned until Dirk leaned toward her and whispered, "What's wrong? Will it clash with your Dior outfits?"

"It'll clash with any outfit." Tori allowed herself another groan. "Maybe I could wear it around my ankle so no one will see it."

"Hmm," Dirk said, while Dr. B demonstrated how to send and receive calls. "It sounds to me like you're not taking your safety seriously."

She did take it seriously. During their failed raid, Overdrake had captured Tori and pulled off her helmet. He'd seen her face. If he came after any of them, it was going to be her. "Of course, wearing that watch around my ankle won't work with shorts or skirts. Do you suppose the band would stretch around my thigh?"

"I'd like to see you answer a call if it did." Dirk let out a low chuckle. "I'll have to phone you frequently and see how that goes."

"You're only allowed to call in emergencies," she reminded him.

"And I consider making your thigh ring at inappropriate times an emergency."

"I'm relatively certain," Dr. B went on, sending Tori and Dirk a reproving look for talking while he was, "that Overdrake doesn't know the locations of your homes. I don't keep that information written down anywhere, you have nothing with ID in your belongings, and none of you would have spoken your addresses out loud anywhere at camp. Still, be careful." He emphasized each word. "Your Slayer senses will only keep you safe if you listen to them. Don't become so distracted by your iPod, your friends, your studies—that you ignore your instincts. And if anything suspicious happens, call me at once."

Tori nodded. Dr. B was really speaking to her. Overdrake hadn't only seen her, he'd recognized her. She was the daughter of Senator Hampton, one of the front-runners for the next presidential election.

Tori pushed away the worry. No point in dwelling on it. Having a father who was a powerful senator had benefits. Her home, her neighborhood, her school—they had gates, security staff, and safe-guards that protected her not just from stalkers and disgruntled con-stituants, but would also work to keep megalomaniacal dragon lords away.

At least she hoped they would.

CHAPTER 3

Tori flew out of the Dragon Hall, literally, and waited at the top of a nearby tree for Jesse to catch up with her. He spent the last part of most afternoons giving her flying lessons.

She had already improved enough over the summer that they could have discontinued the sessions a week or two ago, but neither suggested it. The lessons always seemed to end with the two of them hidden in some sunlit section of the forest, their arms draped around each other, while Jesse dropped kisses onto her lips.

It was all wrapped together in Tori's mind: the magic of skimming through the trees, the enchantment of the wild growing forest around them, and the euphoria of being with him. She didn't want it to end. And here it was already—the last day of camp. As she waited for Jesse, she felt a desperate ache twining around her insides. The two of them would have to find a way to see each other over the school year. Even if they weren't supposed to.

One of Dr. B's many rules was that Slayers couldn't have contact with each other outside of camp. Tori understood the reasoning. If

Overdrake caught one of them, he wouldn't be able to extract information about the other Slayers.

She didn't need Jesse's last name, though. She just needed to persuade him to meet her someplace. Regularly.

Jesse soared up to her tree branch, six foot two of muscles and good looks. Even when his dark hair was mussed from working out and he was covered with singe marks, he looked kissable. He looked perfect.

Jesse hovered in the air in front of her and gave her a smile. He didn't smile enough during the day. He was always too focused on training, on strategy—on keeping alert for possible attack. It made his smiles to her all the more meaningful. She felt as if she'd won a prize when he looked at her like this. "You officially made it through the last dragon-slaying practice," he said.

"Just barely." She stepped from her branch and joined him in the air. "I'm covered with bruises, I've ruined my last shirt, and it's a miracle I still have eyebrows left."

Jesse laughed—another prize—and glided slowly through the trees away from the main camp.

Tori followed after him, so seamless in her flight that she didn't have to concentrate on how to move her body when they sped up or turned. She shadowed him, enjoying the lifting sensation of soaring through an ocean of sunshine and leaves. Everything around her was fresh, green, laden with the scent of life. This feeling, this freedom flowing through her fingertips, made the risk of being a flyer worthwhile.

For her lesson, Jesse went through all of the advanced moves, spinning, diving, flying straight at the ground and then pulling up inches before impact. Tori practiced, savoring the feeling of flight and wishing she had a way to keep it. Tomorrow afternoon she would be back home in McLean, back living her normal life. Or pretending to. Things would never quite be normal again.

When Tori was done going through the advanced moves, she

and Jesse practiced speed flying. This was Tori's biggest weakness. She couldn't fly as fast as Jesse and wasn't nearly as accurate with her turns when she tried.

She didn't mind rocketing along at seventy miles an hour when she had a helmet or goggles on, but Jesse liked to remind her she might be caught in an attack without either of those things, so she had to practice without them. At high speeds, the wind tore at her face and made her eyes water. It was hard to see or hear anything.

Luckily the two of them couldn't fly fast for long. The simulator had a range of about five miles, which meant it only took a few minutes to get out of its range. After that, they had half an hour to get back in range or their powers would disappear and they would fall from the sky—or in the very least have a long walk back to camp.

Jesse had some sort of internal clock that let him know how much time had gone by. He said all Slayers did, but if that was true, the feature had never kicked in for Tori. She was supposed to signal Jesse when they'd flown for ten minutes, so they could turn around and fly back with plenty of time to spare. She was usually off by a few minutes in either direction.

Today she signaled early on purpose. She wanted to spend time lazily floating through the treetops with Jesse. She wanted to ask him to break another rule.

When they got back in range, Tori took hold of Jesse's hand, and they glided around a few trees until they found one with enough space for both of them to stand in. The tree had an empty spot where a few of the upper branches had been knocked off; probably victims of Tori's maneuvering attempts earlier in the summer.

Jesse leaned against the trunk, still holding Tori's hand. It was also against camp policy for the Slayers to get romantically involved with each other. Dr. B didn't want those sorts of distractions while the Slayers trained. So while she and Jesse were with the others, they pretended none of this was happening. Jesse was better at that than she was. During practices, Jesse always concentrated on being Team Magnus' captain so intently, Tori doubted he thought about her at all. She, on the other hand, needed frequent doses of stolen glances. She was an addict.

Now Jesse surveyed her with his warm brown eyes, eyes that had depths she could fall into. Tori leaned into Jesse and kissed him lightly. She didn't feel bad about breaking the camp's dating rule. If she had to risk her life fighting dragons, she was entitled to one perk. Jesse.

Jesse didn't kiss her back. Instead he wound his arms around her waist and held her in a loose embrace. She could feel the tension of the muscles in his chest, a rigidness that ran through him. He was thinking about tomorrow, too, about all of this ending.

She rested her head against his chest, listening to his heartbeat and wishing she could sever the connection she had to the dragon eggs so she didn't have to hear that noise, too.

Part of her Slayer powers was the ability to hear what a dragon heard. Like Dirk's eyesight link, she seemed to connect to whichever dragon was closest. Since her Slayer powers had kicked in at camp, she'd had a constant pipeline to a dragon egg.

At first, Tori thought this new Slayer ability was pointless and would most likely send her into bouts of insanity. Curled up in its shell, the loudest thing the unborn dragon heard was its own heart-beat. And worse still, the noise didn't fade away every night after Dr. B turned off the simulator. Her strength, night vision, and power of flight all disappeared at bedtime, but the sound of the dragon's heartbeat remained: a creepy thump-thumping in a corner of her mind, a relentless reminder that dragons were out there, somewhere, waiting to hatch.

Then Tori had overheard some of Overdrake's men talking nearby the eggs. They inadvertently gave away their location. That's what led to the failed raid earlier in the summer. Now to keep Tori from overhearing anything else that might be useful to the Slayers, Overdrake played a constant stream of music next to the eggs. And he wasn't nice about it, either. The first week, he'd played nothing but the Bee Gees greatest hits. Apparently one week was as long as his vets could listen to nonstop Bee Gees because after that the music changed. Now it was a mixture of music from the eighties and nineties. Tori could turn it way down, but not completely off.

At moments like this, her head resting against Jesse's chest, the music bothered her the most. She didn't want to hear anything except the sound of Jesse's heart underneath her ear. Instead she heard the faint sounds of M. C. Hammer's "U Can't Touch This."

Overdrake knew how to ruin a moment.

Jesse stroked Tori's hair, letting the breeze pick up pieces and flutter them around his fingers. "Next summer seems so far away."

Tori lifted her face to see Jesse's expression. "We don't have to wait until next summer to see each other. We can find a way to meet during the school year."

Jesse's hand moved from her hair to her back, caressing a soft path down her spine. Even then she could tell it was an apology. "It's too dangerous to contact each other outside of camp."

"I'm not asking for your address. We'll meet someplace. On the second Saturday of the month, I'll just happen to be at the Natural History Museum, admiring the stuffed elephant in the main lobby. Let's say noon, so we can go somewhere for lunch." She said all of this as though it had just occurred to her, a butterfly of an idea that had just fluttered in. Butterflies were harmless.

He didn't answer. His hand was still making apologies on her back.

"Or," she added, "we could meet *every* Saturday, if you'd rather."

Jesse let out a sigh. "I'm a team captain. I'm supposed to enforce the rules, not find ways to break them." His hand made its way back to the tangle of her hair again. "I know. Call me a hypocrite. I've been kissing you all summer."

"I'm not going to criticize you for that." She smiled and threaded her fingers together against the small of his back. "Go ahead and break another rule."

She felt like Eve right then, luring Adam to take a bite of the forbidden fruit—wicked, but too desperate to care. The rule was stupid. Anything that kept them apart was wrong. He had to see that.

Jesse didn't move, didn't even bend down to kiss her. He would have done that yesterday—joked about her corrupting him and then pressed his lips to hers. Tori searched his eyes, trying to read her future in them. She only saw flickers of gold, patches of reflected sunlight.

It was doubly frustrating. She and Jesse could both fly; that made them counterparts. Or at least it was supposed to. Slayer counterparts could sense things about each other—moods, feelings. If they were close enough, one could tell where the other was without looking. It helped them while fighting.

Sometimes Tori was sure she sensed what Jesse was thinking and feeling. Most of the time, though, the ability completely abandoned her. She had no idea what was going on in his mind right now.

She would have thought that her romantic feelings messed up her connection, but her other counterpart abilities with Jesse were sketchy, too. She couldn't tell where Jesse was without looking. Not like she was supposed to. Sometimes Tori could feel Jesse watching her, and when all the Slayers were in a group, a part of her automatically kept track of where he was. It wasn't quite the same as counterpart-knowing, though.

Tori knew how it was supposed to work, because she was also counterparts with Dirk. In Slayer genetics, apparently seeing what the dragons saw was close enough to hearing what the dragons heard to give she and Dirk counterpart abilities.

When Dirk came within a radius of a dozen yards, she knew where he was, could feel his presence without seeing him. When they were together, she felt his moods in the same way she felt the sun warming her shoulders or a cloud moving to blot out the light. It was just there, obvious.

She hadn't told Dirk that Jesse kissed her, but after the first time it happened, Dirk had looked at her and known. He hadn't said anything. He hadn't needed to. She had felt his sharp disapproval easily enough.

Counterparts were supposed to have one other ability. If Slayers were away from the simulator for more than half an hour and lost their powers, they could recharge their powers by touching a counterpart who still had them.

It didn't work on Tori, not with Jesse or Dirk. Once she lost her powers, she didn't get them back until she was within five miles of the simulator again.

Tori stared at Jesse, watched him standing against the rich green backdrop, and tried to sense what he was thinking. She couldn't. Or maybe she could and didn't want to accept it. "We both live in the D.C. area," she pointed out. "We could easily run into each other. It would be like coincidence . . . but with a helping hand."

Jesse dropped his arms from around her. She felt the distance in that movement before he even stepped away. "Tori, there's a reason for the rules. We shouldn't . . . We can't . . ." He let out another sigh. "My feelings for you are already getting in the way of the mission. We've got to be careful."

She blinked at him. "What are you talking about?"

"Today at practice," he said, as though it proved his point. "You called out for help and I completely lost focus. I can't afford to make those sorts of mistakes. I can't let my feelings get in the way of my judgment."

A stone of dread formed in Tori's stomach: a hard piece of reality that she didn't want. She shifted away from Jesse. "Okay. If a dragon captures me, I'll try not to distract you with my screams for help."

"Tori," he whispered. It was as though he hated saying the words even at a low volume. "Unless we stop the dragons, people will die. Cities will fall, maybe the entire nation will. With the dragons helping him, Overdrake might have enough men and weapons to pull it off." Jesse paused, still trying to make her understand. "If today's practice was the real thing, how many people would have died because I didn't want to lose you? We need to be better—at least, I do."

"Okay," she said slowly. The stone of dread was still there in her stomach, heavy, cold, and growing larger. "So I guess the second Saturday doesn't work for you."

The wind fluttered a strand of Tori's hair into her face. Jesse pushed it back into place. "We're only making this harder on ourselves. It's better if we make a clean break of it for the school year."

"'A clean break' . . . ," she repeated. It sounded like something you did in surgery—cut through bone or muscle with a quick scalpel stroke.

"Only for the school year," he said. "It wouldn't be fair if I asked you to give up dances and all that stuff, just because I can't be there for it. I don't want you to put your life on hold, waiting for next summer."

"Oh." It was the only word she could say. Jesse didn't want to meet her and he wanted her to date other guys. She felt as if gravity had taken effect again, as if it were pushing her downward. This wasn't a good-bye, it was a breakup. Her heart began racing, although she couldn't tell if it was anger or pain that made it beat so frantically.

She felt his gaze on her, knew he was looking at her with sympathy. His voice was soft. "I don't want it to be this way."

Tori doubted that. He wouldn't have broken up with her if he didn't want it to be this way. He probably had a girlfriend back at his school. After all, Jesse was not only tall, dark, and handsome; he was smart, responsible, brave . . . and he was breaking up with her.

Don't cry, she told herself. He wasn't emotional about this, why should she be?

Tori stared at the leaves stretching out around her. They were still so bright and green. They hadn't realized yet that summer was ending.

"We'll be together again next June," Jesse said.

And next June he would be willing to break the rules for her? He could do that at camp—kiss her in the treetops—but not outside of camp?

"Say something," he said.

There was no point in saying anything. You couldn't debate someone into loving you. "We should get back to camp," she said. Without waiting for his reply, she dived from the branch into the waiting air.

# CHAPTER 4

Tori went directly to her cabin and began packing her things. She had put it off before. Packing up things meant that camp was really over. Now she put her clothes in her suitcases with a numb sort of speed. *Just get through this*, she told herself, *then everything will be fine*. She would pack up her feelings for Jesse and never open them again.

Tori had more luggage than any of the other Slayers. She had brought actual outfits, a half a dozen different shoes, jewelry, books—the sorts of things she'd used at other camps. Tori hadn't realized she would spend two months training to be a Slayer. She hadn't even realized she would be here that long. She'd only signed up for the first session and then had to persuade her parents to let her stay an extra five weeks.

Lilly and Alyssa had already finished packing most of their stuff. Their duffle bags and backpacks sat waiting by the end of their bunk bed. Alyssa was braiding Lilly's blonde hair into a French braid, identical to the one she wore. Lilly and Alyssa usually looked like they were trying to be copies of each other.

"Don't forget to bring your iron next year," Lilly called to Tori. "It made the perfect doorstop." Lilly and Alyssa had not only mocked Tori for bringing an iron to camp, they constantly took it off her dresser and used it to prop open the cabin door whenever they wanted a breeze.

"And bring the designer sheets again," Alyssa added. "Those were just divine." Alyssa and Lilly both snickered.

Tori wasn't going to miss them at all.

Rosa, Team Magnus' healer, had finished packing and now sat on her bed reading a romance novel. All the Slayers were athletic, although Rosa hardly looked it. She was petite with long black hair, flawless dark skin, and large brown eyes that made her look more like a doll than someone who could pick up a grown man and throw him across the room. Every once in a while she gave the cabin an update from her novel. "Fleur's carriage is going down a lonely country road. *Pues*, that can't be good."

"Of course it's good," Bess said, tossing a couple of shirts into an open duffle bag at her feet. "Fleur is either going to run into a handsome highwayman or she's going to be saved from vile highwaymen by some passing hot single duke." Bess added some shorts to her pile. "That's why, after we're done being Slayers, I'm going to do nothing but roam lonely country roads. Apparently that's where all the action is."

Bess was tall, with chin-length curly brown hair that was frequently in states of disarray. Her bright blue eyes and pointed chin made her look elflike, as though she really belonged here in the forest. "How much do you want to bet that within five pages Fleur's lips will be quivering in unspoken passion?"

Normally Tori would have added a comment about Fleur, lonely country roads, or Bess' definition of action, but she wordlessly kept putting things in her suitcases. She'd hardly said anything since she'd come inside.

Rosa put down her book and studied Tori. "Are you all right?"

"Yes," Tori said. She didn't bother faking a smile. "It's just, you know, camp is ending." Even though Bess and Rosa were Tori's friends, she couldn't tell them that Jesse had dumped her. Not when she'd never told them that Jesse and she were a couple to begin with.

Bess wouldn't have told her father that Tori and Jesse were breaking the rules—Bess was the biggest practical joker in camp, so her respect for the rules was questionable at best—but Rosa would have felt the weight of keeping that secret. Rosa was the type that looked for things to worry about. And it had never felt right to tell one friend and not the other.

Rosa watched Tori for another moment. Rosa was also the type that noticed pain lurking in the corners of people's eyes. She didn't press Tori, though.

A few minutes later, everyone got up and left for dinner. Tori didn't go with them. "I'll come in a little bit," she said. She was lying. Her appetite was gone and she wasn't about to sit at the same table as Jesse and pretend everything was fine.

Outside, she heard the guys leaving for dinner, too. Kody called out, "Bess, don't think I'm going to forget about this next year. You're toast—or at least a few of your belongings will be."

"I don't know what you're talking about," Bess said airily.

Shang let out a disbelieving grunt. "You blocked our cabin door with your shield."

"Hmm," Bess said. "Maybe your doorknob is just stuck."

"Right," Kody said, drawing out the word with his Southern accent. "That's why we all had to haul ourselves out the window."

"Aren't there bars on your window?" Alyssa asked. Both of the cabins had bars to keep intruders from breaking in.

"Used to be," Kody said. "I yanked them clean off. I'll let you explain that one to your dad."

"You know," Bess said, unconcerned, "you're all going to miss me tomorrow."

Murmuring to the contrary went through the group.

"You will," Bess insisted as the group walked away. "Especially once you realize I've stolen all your car keys."

Tori kept packing. A clean break. She didn't want to hear Jesse's words repeating in her mind. It was already a loud enough place. Still the phrase was there, its volume irrepressible. Jesse wanted a clean break? It was a stupid thing to say. You couldn't break a heart into anything but jagged pieces.

Tori lifted a stack of books off her dresser. A pink wildflower she'd pressed between the pages fluttered down onto her bed. Jesse had given it to her. Once while teaching her to fly low, he'd skimmed along the forest floor, plucked the bloom, and put it in Tori's hair.

Tori held the flower by its threadlike stem. She had pressed it between the pages so she could keep it forever, so it wouldn't wilt or fade. Ironic. It hadn't, but Jesse's feelings had. She stared at the flower, wanting to crumple it up and wanting to keep it, and then felt furious at herself when she couldn't do either. She could only stare at it and blink away tears.

She wasn't going to cry about this. She had never cried over a guy before and she refused to start now. She would go fly somewhere, find a place to be alone, and not come back until she could pull herself together. She dropped the flower on her bed and walked out the door.

Dirk was leaning against the stair railing that led to her cabin's patio. It surprised her to see him. She'd been so caught up in her emotions, she hadn't sensed him there at all.

He looked like he was waiting for someone or something.

"What are you doing?" she asked.

He gazed at her casually. "Deciding whether to come in and talk to you."

Tori stopped, one hand not quite reaching the railing. "Did Jesse tell you to talk to me?"

Jesse and Dirk had been close friends ever since they came to camp. Jesse might have sent Dirk because he figured she needed her other counterpart's consolation.

Dirk let out a scoff. "No." The way he said the word made it clear that guys didn't do that sort of thing. He gestured to her door. "I noticed waves of emotion rolling out of your cabin and figured you might want to talk about it."

Tori walked down the stairs. "I'll be fine."

Dirk watched her silently, looking right through her. "Come on," he said, taking hold of her hand. "Let's go talk."

"I don't want to talk," she insisted, but she went with him, letting him lead her toward the trail that went to the lake. Her feet thudded against the packed dirt in noisy, graceless steps. She dropped his hand. It didn't seem right to keep holding it.

"You don't have to talk," Dirk said. "We could make out instead. That's the perfect way to get back at guys you're mad at." He was teasing, trying to joke her out of her bad mood. "At least it would be perfect for me." He gave her a wicked grin, an encouraging one. "At any rate, you should give it a try."

She rolled her eyes and didn't answer. Even before Tori had realized she was Dirk's counterpart, she had suspected he was a player—the type of guy who flirted for sport and collected girls' hearts like they were trading cards. Romance was always a game for those sorts of guys. And not one she wanted to play.

They kept walking through the forest. Curtains of trees on both sides of the trail held out their branches and shimmered their leaves like peddlers displaying their wares.

"Tell me what happened," Dirk prodded.

What had happened—that was the question, wasn't it? Yesterday Jesse loved her and today, well, not so much. It was all for the good of the country, of course—because that breakup excuse sounded way more noble than "It's me, not you." It was much better than "I just want to be friends."

She had probably always been just a summer distraction, a way to kill time until he got back to his real life. She didn't want to talk about any of it. If she tried, the shards rattling around inside of her would come loose and cut her to ribbons. Dirk would get the information out of Jesse, if she didn't say something—and that seemed worse, Dirk going up to Jesse and asking him why she was so upset.

"Jesse said I should date other people over the school year."

"Score," Dirk said. "You can start right now. I'll be your first date."

Tori ignored his suggestion. "That's the thing that makes me the maddest about this. Jesse is pretending he's doing this for me, when in reality he just dumped me."

She told Dirk everything then. How Jesse said their separation would only be for the school year, and then in the next breath told her they needed to keep the rules so he wasn't influenced by his feelings for her.

When Tori finished, they were at the lake. The canoes had already been packed up somewhere. The worn wooden dock sat forlorn and empty in the water. Dirk didn't go to the water's edge. Instead he sat down on a large boulder not far from the trail. "That's the difference between Jesse and me. I don't feel guilty for rescuing you today."

Tori sat down beside him, focusing on the slate-blue lake water in front of her. "But what if it had been a real battle and we all died, and the country fell because of it?"

Dirk shrugged. "I guess I'd be too dead to feel guilty over it."

She tilted her chin down. "You're not taking the question seriously." Dirk took very few things seriously. It was part of his rakish personality.

"What's your point?" he asked.

She picked up a rock and tossed it at the lake. Normally her rock wouldn't have made it to the water's edge. With her Slayer powers going, the rock sailed over the dock and disappeared with a tiny splash far in the lake. "The point is, it's bad enough that I have to rearrange my life to train for combat, and I have to risk my life to fight dragons—I can't even have a regular boyfriend. A normal guy won't understand the Slayer stuff, and a Slayer won't be my boyfriend because caring about me might taint his judgment while he's fighting. All of this sucks." And then despite her best intentions, she cried. Not a little bit. Not delicate tears that trickled unnoticed down her cheeks. She gulped like she couldn't breathe and her shoulders shook.

Dirk put his arm around her and she nestled into his side. She rested her head against his chest, shut her eyes, and cried until the emotion drained out of her. Dirk didn't say anything, just kept his arm around her and waited.

Finally, he said, "It won't always be this way."

"Yeah," she agreed. "Eventually we'll all be too dead to care about the rules."

She felt Dirk smile. "We might not *all* be too dead."

"You're an optimist."

Tori had always liked the reflection of the trees across the lake's surface. Now the image just seemed smudged, upside down. She picked up another rock and hurled it into the water.

"There are two types of people in the world," Dirk said. "Those who are loyal to principles, and those who are loyal to people. The problem with dating Jesse is that he's in the first group and you're in the second. You were bound to get hurt."

Tori considered this while she picked up another rock. "I'm loyal to principles. I'm fighting dragons to protect my country."

Dirk shook his head. "You're fighting dragons to protect the people you love."

She opened her mouth to protest, then realized he was right. When she first found out she was a Slayer, she hadn't wanted to stay at camp, had almost gone home. She had told Dr. B she decided to stay because of her father. He would give his life for his country; she couldn't do less. What had weighed more heavily on her mind, though, was Jesse—the only flyer. She couldn't stand the thought of him fighting the dragon without all the help he could get.

"When Overdrake's dragon attacked us," Dirk said, "you joined in the fight even though you only had a few days of training. You weren't thinking about your country. You were thinking about saving our lives." Dirk looked upward. "I bet you money Jesse was thinking of saving the country. If he had to sacrifice one or all of us to do it, he would."

Tori picked up another rock. "Who's right?" She had the nagging feeling that people who were loyal to principles were right, and she didn't like it. She didn't want to be sacrificed, even if it was for the greater good.

Dirk gave her a wry smile. "You shouldn't ask me. I've already admitted that I didn't feel guilty for rescuing you. I'm loyal to people." He took the rock from her hand and threw it far over the lake. "Especially you."

Especially her. The words were sweet and soothing, because she could tell they were true. Dirk was her friend. She still had that.

"Thanks." She rested her head against his shoulder.

He put his arm around her again. "You'll get through this. You'll be okay."

She didn't answer. Ever since she'd learned about the dragons and Overdrake, being "okay" seemed a fleeting goal at best.

CHAPTER 5

Brant Overdrake laid out pictures of the Slayers on his desk, covert snapshots taken by his son the first day of camp. Each photo had a fact sheet underneath it. Overdrake was hoping that having them all in one place would help him think better, that he would see something he'd missed while flipping through computer files.

Jesse's parents were both teachers. He had two younger brothers. He was a fourth-degree black belt in tae kwon do and a top-level fencer. Overdrake's men had looked for him in the D.C. area dojang records, but never turned up anything. The same held true for fencing tournaments. For all Overdrake knew, Jesse wasn't even his real name.

Shang spoke and wrote fluent Chinese. He either lived in a multi-generational home or his grandparents lived close by, because Shang talked about them as much as he did his own parents. He had several Chinese friends, which might indicate he lived in a Chinese district. D.C.'s Chinatown consisted mostly of restaurants. So Shang might live outside of the D.C. area, or perhaps he was just involved in a lot of Chinese groups.

Lilly still hadn't gotten her license because her mom couldn't afford the car insurance. She would live in a poor area somewhere. Unfortunately, there were too many poor areas around. His men couldn't search them all. They were already scouring through every high school yearbook in Virginia, Maryland, and D.C.

Overdrake had the same sort of information on the other Slayers. Hints, but not enough details to find out where they lived. What he needed was access to the computer program Dr. B had for tracking the Slayers. Overdrake had been so close to having it. He'd spent years training his son to steal that sort of thing, and now the Slayers had disappeared and disabled their phones. He hadn't heard from his son since the attack at the beginning of the summer. Nothing at all. It wasn't a good sign.

Overdrake swiped his hand across the desk, sending several of the photos fluttering to the ground. He picked up the picture of Jesse, crumpled it, and threw it into the fireplace. The paper curled and blackened in the flames until the fire devoured it. There was something satisfying about seeing Jesse's image destroyed that way. Something fitting.

Overdrake picked up the paper for Ryker next. It had no picture and the only information on his sheet was his parents' names. Overdrake crushed the paper in his hand. He had been greedy. That was his problem. He put off striking the Slayers at their camp because he had been waiting for any stragglers, waiting for Ryker to show up. Overdrake had been every bit as optimistic about Ryker's arrival as Dr. B had been. Well, that would teach him to put any stock in Dr. B's beliefs. Ryker would never show up. Overdrake should have realized that and attacked camp long ago. It wouldn't have been hard to wipe out the Slayers that way.

Granted, the Slayers had ultra-tuned senses that alerted them to danger. It was hard to sneak up on Slayers even when their superpowers weren't turned on. However, the Slayers also had their own version of kryptonite, and it wasn't hard to come by: drugs. Any drug strong enough to render a Slayer unconscious also destroyed the pathway in his brain that let him access his powers. If you put the Slayers out, they woke up without superpowers. And best of all, their memories of being Slayers were affected, too. They didn't remember having powers, so their brains made up new memories to compensate for all of the old ones that no longer made sense.

Overdrake could neutralize the Slayers and they wouldn't even remember that he'd done it. It should have been so easy, would have been if Dr. B hadn't moved the Slayers to another camp. Now Overdrake had no idea where they were.

He threw Ryker's sheet into the fire, then picked up Tori's profile. She was the only other Slayer whose last name he knew. She would be out on the campaign trail with her father. So easily accessible. Like shooting fish in a barrel.

He would enjoy seeing Tori go down. It was her fault the Slayers had gotten away from him. At least mostly Tori's fault. Dirk was the one who freed the other Slayers from the dragon enclosure. Still, Overdrake took his anger out on Tori's picture. He ripped it into little pieces, then dropped them one by one into the fire. They trembled as they fell into flames, wavered until they were nothing but ash. Dirk cared about Tori, so it was only fitting that she suffer.

Overdrake would find a way to locate and take out all of the Slayers, but Tori would be first.

# CHAPTER 6

Dirk said his good-byes to everyone as normally as he ever had. Normal was a coat he could take on and off without thinking about it. He joked around, he hugged everyone, he said he'd see them next year. When he hugged Tori, he held on to her for a couple of seconds longer than he did everyone else. She was warm, soft, and smelled like gardenias. It was some perfume she'd brought from home and insisted on wearing even though by the end of the day they all smelled of horses, smoke, and sweat.

"Thanks," she told him. She didn't have to say for what. He knew she meant about last night.

"No problem."

Letting go of her felt like ripping something off his skin. But then, saying good-bye to his friends each summer always felt that way. He was used to it.

Dr. B had elaborate systems for making sure no one trailed or put any tracking devices on the Slayers' cars. Before camp, he texted the Slayers the code name of a meeting place in D.C. The Slayers either had their parents drop them off there or they drove their cars to a long-term parking lot and took a bus, train, or cab to the meeting place. A camp van picked up the group. At the end of camp, the reverse happened.

When new Slayers showed up, Dr. B called their parents before camp ended and offered the camp van service for the trip home. Parents always agreed. It saved them hours of driving time.

This time, Dr. B had driven the Slayers to a street near the National Mall.

Tori turned away from Dirk, pulling her luggage toward a waiting blue BMW. It was probably a good thing she was still so wrapped up in her thoughts about Jesse that she wasn't paying attention to him. Otherwise, she might have sensed something was wrong. She would have worried, tried to pry into it.

Jesse watched Tori go. He looked like he wanted to go after her, but he turned his attention to Dirk instead. "Hey, take care."

"Always do."

Jesse gave him a quick hug, a sort of half pat on the back. "Don't do anything I wouldn't do."

"Now you're asking too much."

"Well then, at least don't get caught doing it."

Good advice. Dirk didn't plan on getting caught.

Jesse picked up his duffle bag and moved off to say more good-byes. Dirk said a few more himself. It was a blur. Everyone else was going home. He was running away. Well, maybe it wasn't technically running away. Dirk's father probably didn't want him to come home. Not after the way Dirk had betrayed him in June.

Before Dirk headed down the street, he looked back at Dr. B and hesitated. What would Dr. B do if Dirk told him that he had nowhere to go?

"Dirk?" Dr. B asked, catching his stare. "Is something wrong?"

Dirk smiled and shook his head. "No." He knew what Dr. B would do if he confessed his situation. Dr. B would be concerned, sympathetic—as caring as if Dirk were his own son. Dr. B loved the person he thought Dirk was, and somehow Dirk couldn't destroy that image. He couldn't answer the questions Dr. B would ask. It was better to do this on his own. He could find someplace to live. He could take care of himself.

Dirk turned and walked away, duffle bag thudding against his back. It was late afternoon and he had things to do.

He took a cab to his bank. Had to. He needed more money than an ATM would deliver. Luckily he had enough in his bank account to cover rent and food for a few months. Dirk went through the motions of emptying his account with calm proficiency. Funny how he could do that when he felt a wild desperation growing inside of him.

Last night while Tori cried on his shoulder, she said there was no such thing as a clean break. She was probably right. How would Dirk make a break with his family and not have it leave a gaping hole inside of him? His sister, Bridget, was only seven years old. Would she even remember him when she was old enough to leave home herself? What would their father tell her about him? Had he already ripped Dirk out of all the family pictures?

Dirk didn't let himself think about it. He'd already made his decision at camp. Now he just had to carry through.

From the bank, he went to a store and bought a few things he'd need for a road trip. Then he dropped off a letter to Tori at a post office. He didn't know her address, but her father's senate office address was easy enough to find. She'd get the letter. Picking up his car was trickier. Dirk was half afraid his BMW either wouldn't be where he'd left it or that his father would be sitting in the front seat, waiting for him. Dirk hadn't told his father where he parked, but there were only so many long-term parking places in the D.C. area. It wouldn't have been hard for his father to check them.

It might have been better for Dirk to walk away from the car. He didn't want to do that, though. Driving was the easiest way to get to California unnoticed, and he could sell the Beemer once he got there. The money would see him through until next summer.

Dr. B had taught all the Slayers how to do surveillance work. Dirk never thought he would use it to stake out his own car. His first task was to look around the perimeter of the building at possible places other people might be doing surveillance: the roofs of nearby buildings or suspicious maintenance vans on the street. Homeless people who sat near the building's entrance were also suspect. When Dirk didn't find anything suspicious, he walked a few streets over, found a homeless guy who looked moderately sober, and paid him twenty dollars to walk inside the parking garage and see if any of the cars near his had people waiting in them.

When that checked out clear, too, Dirk finally went in. His BMW was just where he left it. Still locked, nothing moved. He was almost disappointed. Maybe his father didn't want to find him. Maybe his father didn't care that Dirk wasn't coming back.

No, that wasn't it. His father was so positive that Dirk would return home, apologetic and contrite, that he hadn't bothered to track down his BMW.

Dirk was tempted to turn on his phone and check his messages, but he didn't. He knew he would have to listen to message after message of his father screaming at him, and besides, cell phones could be tracked. Better to leave it turned off until he decided what to do with it.

With one last measure of precaution, Dirk took out a flashlight and checked the underside of the car for a tracking device. He didn't see any. He got in the car and drove away.

By the time Dirk made it onto the beltway, it was six o'clock. The highway was jammed with commuters going home. He'd heard the only place where the traffic was worse than D.C. was L.A. He made a note to avoid that part of California. He would go to a university town somewhere. He'd fit in there. No one would notice one more teenage boy around. No one would question why he was there. No one would care.

An image of Bridget flashed through Dirk's mind. She would care that he wasn't coming home. Every year when he returned from camp, she had a stack of pictures she'd drawn for him. Usually pictures of him at camp. She thought he stood around playing a lot of volleyball in flowery fields. Bunnies often hung around watching him.

Leaving like this was so painful, and yet he didn't see another way. A clean break, that's what he needed. A new life.

By nine o'clock he'd made it to Staunton. Even though it was dark and he was tired, he had no plans to stop. He needed to put as much space between him and Virginia as he could.

Dirk's first hint that something was wrong came in a flash of dragon vision. He was so good at minimizing his dragon sight, at pushing it away so it didn't distract him, he didn't sense the dragon until she was nearly on top of him. Kihawahine was gliding high above the road, coming toward his car. Through her vision, he could see her purple-tipped wings stretching through the air. She was searching for him.

In an awful moment of clarity, Dirk realized he had never checked the interior of his car for a tracking device. That's where his father put it. He might have even placed it in the car before Dirk went to camp. Maybe Dirk should have expected that, but sending a dragon after him—well even now, Dirk was surprised. It wasn't often his father let the dragons out to fly around, and this was undoubtedly the longest flight one had taken since they'd come to America.

Dirk swore and sped up. It was no use. He couldn't outrun the dragon and there was no place on this stretch of road to hide. Not enough trees. He needed more time to think, to come up with a plan.

The headlights in either direction were far and few between. Would any cars notice what was happening? Would the tabloids report tomorrow that a dragon had dived out of the sky and attacked a Beemer?

Dirk tried to connect to Kihawahine. He slipped into her mind easily enough. It was familiar terrain. But he couldn't wrest his father's control away from the dragon. Dirk's thoughts knocked against her consciousness, unheeded. It was like trying to climb up a waterfall. He had nothing to hold on to. His father's will was too firmly affixed there.

Kihawahine gave a short yip of a screech, just enough EMP to wipe out the electronics of anything in the area. Dirk's car lights blinked out. The power steering was gone. The car slowed, worthless now.

The dragon was close enough that Dirk's powers kicked in. With his night vision he could make out shapes in the night. The slope of the shoulder. The scattered trees. A few cars in the distance. If their occupants chanced to look up at the sky, they wouldn't be able to see what was happening in the darkness. And even if they could see, the cameras on their cell phones were ruined now.

Through the rearview window, Dirk saw the dragon soaring toward him, almost to him. Her batlike wings spanned the sky, lazily flapping up and down. Each move of her neck and tail was graceful and precise. She enjoyed her elegance, enjoyed the chase.

He only had time to unbuckle his seat belt before she plunged down at him. The windows shattered; talons burst through the car, piercing its frame. Dirk covered his face with his arm to keep shards from flying into his eyes.

The car jerked upward. Kihawahine had lifted it off the ground. She swung the car around, turning it so quickly that Dirk's head slammed into his door. He grunted in annoyance. Where were the airbags when you needed them?

With powerful sweeps of her wings, Kihawahine flew upward. As soon as she got high enough, she would head to Winchester, bringing him to his father.

Dirk wouldn't go. He wouldn't let this happen. He had already made the decision to leave, made his clean break. Plan B: lose the dragon, hide out for the night, and hitchhike someplace safe.

Dirk crawled into the back of the car. The wind tore through the broken windows, making bits of ripped upholstery flutter around him. He was high in the sky now. The road below him was quickly becoming just a black ribbon. He flung open the back door and dived out. The night air rushed around him, welcoming him. No one at camp knew it, but all dragon lords could fly. He headed downward. The closer he got to the ground the better off he'd be. It was harder for dragons to maneuver near the land.

Kihawahine caught sight of him and hurled the car in his direction. He looked up and saw well over three thousand pounds of metal slamming his way. Was she trying to kill him? Dirk zoomed sideways to avoid being hit. Which was when Kihawahine swooped down on him, her talons closing around his middle.

Dirk struggled, pulled at Kihawahine's talons. It only made them tighten around his middle painfully. Even if he had some kind of weapon, he wouldn't have managed to get away. And he had nothing. He was caught.

The Beemer hit the ground with a thud of metal crumpling, followed by the scream of more glass shattering. It was the sound of his freedom being torn from him.

Tori was right, he thought. There was no such thing as a clean break.

Dirk wasn't sure how long it took for the dragon to fly back to his house in Winchester. The pain of having his middle squeezed by swordlike talons made it hard to judge time. It felt like forever. It didn't feel like long enough.

Finally Kihawahine flew onto his property. She passed over the house, then winged into the open enclosure. The structure was mostly underground and as large as a stadium. The smell of the enclosure was familiar, dank with the scent of death—the remaining bits and pieces of animals that the dragon ate lingered in the air. It didn't matter how many times the maintenance crew washed down those spots, the smell never really went away.

Above Dirk, the roof rumbled as it slid shut, erasing the stars. Kihawahine glided to where Dirk's father sat, stone still and expressionless, waiting. The calm before the storm. This was not going to go well.

With one quick motion, Kihawahine released her grip on Dirk, then sailed over to a perch of rocks. She landed there as gracefully as a duck on water, folding her wings to her side with a flourish. If dragons could purr, she would have done it.

Dirk used his power of flight to pull himself up to face his father. He couldn't walk. His ribs hurt too much. His jacket was ripped to shreds. So was his shirt. Even with the extra strength dragon-lord skin had, his middle was bruised, scraped, and cuts crisscrossed his stomach. If Kihawahine meant to hurt him, her talons would have gutted him.

Dirk's father stared at him, letting his gaze simmer. He was as large as Dirk and as strong, too. Beyond that, they didn't look much like father and son. His father had brown hair, gray at the temples now, and sharp features, as though they'd been carved with a knife.

He sat on a folding chair, the kind he used when he watched Bridget's soccer games. It looked odd sitting among the gray boulders, cement outcroppings, and bushes in the dragon enclosure. His father didn't normally allow any chairs in here. He thought chairs would lead to complacency. He was always emphasizing to Dirk that no one, dragon lord or not, could be complacent around dragons. Dragons weren't pets. They were predators, as wild as the fire they breathed out. If you slipped up with a dragon, if you lost control of its mind for even a few moments, you would be considering that mistake from the inside of the dragon's belly.

Dirk's father didn't leave his chair. Apparently this was a night for exceptions.

Dirk faced him, waited, kept his chin raised. He wasn't going to cower. He wasn't going to apologize. He would just take whatever punishment his father gave him and deal with it.

"So," his father said evenly. "Where were you planning on going after camp?"

"California."

"Why?"

"Because it's as far away from here as I can get without swimming."

His father's eyes darkened. His temper spiked. He stood up so fast, the chair tumbled over behind him. "You ingrate!" The words seemed to fill the entire enclosure and echo back in accusation. "I gave you everything you ever wanted. Money, a car, electronics, vacations all over the world." He snapped each word out as if it were proof he was laying on the table. "Any father could have given his son those things, but I gave you more. I gave you a chance to rule the future." He raised a finger, pointing. "And what did you do in return? You betrayed me to the Slayers—to people who were trying to kill me."

With a slash as sharp as a blade, Dirk felt guilt cut into him. When he had gone with his friends to raid the first dragon enclosure, he'd thought he couldn't possibly feel worse. It ate him up inside to pretend he was a Slayer, to pretend he was one of them, while he led them into a trap. He heard the panic in their voices when they realized they were caught in the enclosure. He heard their fear. And then when he heard his father's men shooting at Tori, it yanked something apart inside of Dirk. He switched sides and freed his friends. He not only knew the lock code for the roof door, he was one of the few people who could open its voice recognition software.

Dirk had been sure he'd done the right thing then—trading his future, his father's approval, for his friends' freedom.

Now, looking at his father's pained and angry face, none of it felt right. He'd only traded one betrayal for another. "No one tried to kill you," Dirk said. "They just wanted to destroy the dragon eggs." It was true. Before the raid the Slayers agreed they would do everything they could to avoid taking anyone's life.

"Destroying the eggs is trying to kill me," his father yelled back, "because the only way anyone will break those eggs is if they push my lifeless corpse out of the way first."

That wasn't the point. Dirk stood straighter, raised a finger of accusation of his own. "You promised not to hurt any of the Slayers and then you tried to kill Tori."

His father shrugged off the complaint with a wave of his hand. "My men shot at intruders. That's not even mildly wrong. It's allowed by the law."

"You promised," Dirk emphasized. "You knew I cared about Tori and you captured her, held her at gunpoint, and threatened to kill her."

Dirk's father narrowed his eyes. His voice was no longer raised in anger, just thick with contempt. "That's what this all boils down to, isn't it? Your feelings for Tori. You sacrificed the mission—our future—for a girl you just met." He paused, then gestured toward Dirk as though this were a casual conversation. "How did that turn out, by the way?"

Dirk didn't answer. He looked at the enclosure wall to his side with grim focus. Dark stains dotted the wall. Probably blood splatters the maintenance crew hadn't gotten around to cleaning yet. They could only come inside when either Dirk or his father were around to control the dragon's mind. Otherwise they'd be killed.

"I'm assuming you're a couple now," his father went on, "so close in fact that I ought to be considering her my future daughter-in-law. That will be awkward, I admit, bringing her over to meet your family after we've already shot at each other."

Dirk still didn't answer. He noticed that ripped pieces of his shirt had fallen to the ground and lay motionless around his feet.

His father didn't let the subject go. "Well?" he insisted.

Dirk knew his father hated Tori now. Hated her because she'd veered Dirk's feelings away from his duty. Maybe the truth would be enough to appease his anger.

"Tori and Jesse became a couple at camp. I didn't see much of her because in her free time Jesse was always teaching her the ins and outs of flying."

Dirk's father laughed, a deep sound that rolled through the enclosure. "What—you didn't volunteer to do that? You're still keeping your flying abilities from the other Slayers?"

"Yeah, I also didn't tell them I was the dragon lord's son sent to spy on them. Go figure. The time just never seemed right."

His father cocked an eyebrow. "I'm surprised they didn't figure it out themselves. They know Tori is your counterpart and she can fly, but they don't find it odd that you can't fly?"

Dirk shrugged. "They think she's Jesse's counterpart, too."

His father laughed again, so incredulous that some of the anger drained away from him. "And Tori and Jesse—they haven't noticed that they don't have the ability to sense things about each other?"

"They're in love. They think they do sense things about each other."

"Love," his father said the word as though it amused him. "A counterpart substitute. That's absolutely laden with irony."

"Yeah, ironic." That's all Dirk's life had become, an impenetrable maze of irony.

On her perch, Kihawahine laid her head on her front legs and curled her tail around herself, resting in a catlike pose. The lights of the enclosure made her blue and purple scales gleam. She always looked majestic in the light, like a living jewel.

Dirk's father eyed him silently. Dirk knew he looked pitiful, hardly able to stand, his clothes shredded, his torso bruised and bloody. He was beginning to feel that way, too, pitiful. He'd traded his future away, and what did he have to show for it? His father was furious with him; the Slayers had killed one of his dragons, Tori had fallen in love with his friend, and Dr. B wanted to replace him as A-team's captain.

"I assume," his father drawled, "that during the last two months you've had time to get Tori out of your system. Time to reflect on the value of her affections."

You would think so.

"Time to consider where your loyalties lie," his father went on. "I assume you withdrew a large sum from the bank and were heading across the country because you were overcome with shame for betraying me, your own father." He walked around Dirk, looking him up and down as though Dirk were a piece of merchandise that was defective, but perhaps salvageable. "I assume your guilt was driving that car. You couldn't face me because you didn't think you deserved my forgiveness. You don't, by the way. Your decision cost me a dragon. But it could have been much worse. I could have been killed. Everything we've worked for could have been destroyed—all because you had feelings for some girl."

Dirk felt another stab of guilt then. Could his father have been killed during the dragon fight? If Jesse had the chance, would he have done it? Dirk probably knew the answer to that question. If the Slayers could have, perhaps any of them would have killed his father. They were, after all, Slayers. It was bred into them to destroy dragons. Dragon lords just got in the way of their job.

Dirk's father's voice turned gentle, understanding almost. "You can't switch sides now. Your friends—would they ever trust you again if they knew you'd already led them into a trap once? Dr. B—who you admire so much—what would he do if he knew you nearly cost him his daughter's life?"

Dirk felt his throat tighten. His father was right. Dirk had known this all along, even if he didn't want to admit it to himself. He could have told Dr. B the truth anytime over the summer. Dirk hadn't, though. He hadn't wanted to see Dr. B's estimation of him crumble to dust. Dirk hadn't wanted to see his friends turn away from him.

"You might not like it right now," Dirk's father said, "but you're my son. A dragon lord. I love you and I'm going to forgive you. I'm going to pretend your betrayal never happened. And so are you." He put his hand on Dirk's shoulder, resting it there with a sense of reassurance. "Are we agreed about that?"

Dirk lifted his gaze to his father's eyes. His father did love him, was the only person who did, really. Everyone else loved the person Dirk was pretending to be.

Dirk felt tired then, resigned. His father wanted a better nation, and when his father grew too old to rule, it would be Dirk's nation. That wasn't such a bad thing.

Revolutions happened all of the time. The founding fathers' children hadn't refused to take part in their new country just because blood was shed in the process. The men who faced each other across the battlefield during that war—they might have been friends once, too.

"Yes," Dirk said. "We're agreed."

"Good." His father looked into his eyes for another moment,

seemed reassured by what he saw, and finally relaxed. "Were you able to copy the encryption algorithms and key for Dr. B's tracking program?"

Dirk nodded, felt numb. He had done that right before the raid.

His father smiled. "You have remarkable talent. You'll be an excellent ruler someday."

CHAPTER 7

Jesse hadn't planned on going to the Natural History Museum. He'd already shot down Tori's idea of meeting together, so there was no point in going. But he went anyway. If Tori made an appearance, he wanted to talk to her, to explain things better than he had at camp.

He showed up at eleven forty-five instead of twelve. The elephant display was in the middle of the atrium right in front of the museum entrance. The curators had posed the elephant in action, so it had a startled look to it—like it had just woken up, found itself surrounded by tourists, and was about to charge out of the room in a rampaging panic. Jesse didn't want to stand by it for the next fifteen minutes. He went up to the second story, he wasn't quite sure why, but he was used to following his instincts.

The second- and third-floor balconies wrapped around the atrium. Jesse wandered around near the railing, keeping an eye on the main floor without looking like he really was. As usual, the museum was packed with tourists, families, and kids on field trips. Constant noise, constant commotion. If there was something wrong on the first floor that his Slayer senses had picked up, Jesse didn't know how to figure out what it was. Too many people were coming and going.

Besides, Jesse didn't expect Tori to show up. She hadn't even wanted to talk to him at camp after he told her not to put her life on hold for him. She flew away, ditched dinner, and went off with Dirk somewhere. They didn't come back until late. Jesse knew how late because when Dirk came into the cabin, he shook his head at Jesse and said, "You are an awesome boyfriend. Wherever you learned your boyfriend skills—great job." Then Dirk had slow clapped.

That was the problem with counterparts. They were all fiercely loyal to each other. Even Alyssa and Rosa, who ignored each other most of the time at camp, would come to the other's defense the moment they thought another Slayer was too critical. And you didn't want to get them mad or they would both be slower than needed to heal your burn wounds.

Jesse and Tori were supposed to be counterparts, too, and there were times that he'd felt so sure of her, he was positive they were. But they didn't have the same abilities the other counterparts did. Maybe you couldn't be that with two people, and Tori was Dirk's counterpart before she learned to fly.

Twelve o'clock came. Tori didn't. Jesse wandered around looking at the signs for the butterfly exhibit and the gem and mineral section. The words he wanted to say to Tori ran in a loop through his mind.

I never said I didn't care about you anymore. I only said we needed to make sure our feelings didn't get in the way of our training. I said I didn't want you to sit home for nine months waiting to see me again. Most girls would appreciate a guy being unselfish about it. I never even said I was going to date other girls. And you didn't bother to ask.

Tori had assumed the worst; they were over and he'd never really cared about her to begin with. Jesse had meant it, though, when he told her he only wanted the separation to last until next summer. He had meant every kiss. It hadn't been just a pastime or an ego kick.

Jesse wandered back over to the railing and glanced down at the elephant again. Tori stood in front of the sign. She was here. She had come.

Tori stood out from the rest of the crowd. She couldn't help it. She was tall, graceful, and looked like a model. For a moment, he could only stare at her. He'd gotten used to seeing her in shorts and T-shirts, her hair always pulled back in a ponytail or braid. Now she wore a white skirt and a red-and-white top. Her long golden-brown hair fell around her shoulders in loose curls. She had not only come, she'd dressed up to see him. He smiled and turned toward the elevator, ready to push through the crowds.

Then he stopped. He knew why he had come up to the second floor instead of waiting on the main one. It didn't have anything to do with his Slayer senses or problems on the first floor. If Jesse went and saw Tori right now, they would go somewhere private. He would apologize, explain, and basically bend over backward to show how much he cared about her. They would end up kissing and he would promise to meet her wherever and whenever she wanted.

Jesse was Team Magnus' captain, and Tori was supposed to become A-team's captain. She was new to all of this, but he was supposed to have some self-control. He'd been taught, trained for years to keep his feelings for the other Slayers in check. During a dragon fight, he couldn't favor one Slayer over the other. He was only supposed to think about one thing—killing the dragon.

How could he be objective about Tori in a battle if he couldn't even keep his feelings in check long enough to stay away from her a few days after camp ended?

Down on the main floor, Tori glanced around at the people streaming around her. She walked slowly around the elephant exhibit.

It wouldn't hurt to see her this once. Maybe twice. Really, what did it matter if they saw each other over the school year? He was allowed to have a life, wasn't he? And that stuff he'd said about her dating other guys—that clearly had bad idea written all over it. The girl was gorgeous. Other guys should stay as far away from her as possible.

Jesse walked toward the elevator and then thought of the night the Slayers raided Overdrake's compound. Jesse had led that mission. After Overdrake trapped them in the compound, Jesse felt . . . it had been worse than fear, worse than despair, because he knew the failed mission was his fault. He'd been sure he would see his friends die. Knowing that he would die with them didn't bring him any relief. His death meant no one would be there to stop the dragons when they attacked. His death carried more deaths with it.

Jesse had to be careful. He had to be unselfish and think about what was good for everyone else.

Tori had come full circle around the elephant now. A group of kids in matching blue T-shirts streamed around her on their way to one of the halls. How long would she wait for him?

Jesse took another step to the elevator and another and then was mad at himself because he knew going downstairs was the wrong decision yet was doing it anyway. He couldn't be objective about Tori. Dr. B was right. Having a relationship was only going to make things more dangerous for both of them.

He should break up with her—not for the school year, but permanently. Or at least until the dragons were killed. Of course, that would become a permanent breakup, because when Jesse went down there and told Tori they needed to officially end their relationship, she was never going to speak to him again.

He stopped, leaned against the railing, and watched her. If he could prove to himself he had enough self-control to stay up here, then it meant he had enough self-control to be an objective fighter. He wouldn't need to break up with her. They could be together next summer. Maybe even after that, when he was at college. He just had to be sure he could master his feelings, keep them in their place.

Tori walked over to one of the benches at the side of the room. She pulled a book out of her purse and read while she waited. Or maybe she wasn't really reading. He never saw her flip a page. He stood there, watching her watch the entrance. She waited until twelve thirty, longer than Jesse had expected. Then she got up and walked out the door without looking back.

Jesse stayed on the second floor for a while longer. He leaned against one of the pillars and let the crowd wash by him. He felt strong, capable of being a captain, and horrible at the same time.

CHAPTER 8

Tori's parents spent the entire ride to the White House lecturing her on etiquette. What she was allowed to say. What she wasn't. "Thank the president and first lady for inviting you," her mother said, "and make sure you talk to all of the teenagers there, not just your friends. You don't want people to think you're cliquish."

Tori sat in the backseat of her family's Lexus, tapping her newly manicured nails against her armrest. She'd broken all of her nails off at Dragon Camp and still wasn't used to the acrylic ones. It was one more reminder that life wasn't the same anymore.

Tori's mother turned toward the backseat to make sure Tori was paying attention. Her blonde hair was swept up into a French knot, her makeup immaculate. If Tori had worn the same shade of bright red lipstick, she would have looked trashy. On her mother it looked glamorous. Her mother had a way of making everything work. That was her talent, making all the many things she did look effortless. Reporters could say completely horrible things to her mother, and she would laugh it off and then redirect the conversation to her husband's positive message for America.

"Are you listening?" her mother asked.

"Yes," Tori said.

Aprilynne, Tori's older sister, had her phone out, texting one of the guys who regularly orbited around her. She was obviously not paying attention to the conversation, but then she didn't have to. Aprilynne hadn't told a reporter last week that he should get a job that didn't involve stalking her family. Which Tori probably shouldn't have done. That was another effect of spending two months training to fight. She didn't feel like suffering fools anymore.

The fact that Tori's father had officially announced his candidacy for the next election only made all of the reporters worse. They lay in wait for her family like piranhas.

"Whatever you do," Tori's father said, sending her a look through the rearview mirror, "be polite to the president."

Tori's father was tall, with the same honey-brown hair and green eyes she'd inherited. Blogs had been written about his green eyes. One magazine had dubbed him the most kissable candidate—which Tori thought was creepy because, hello, strangers were talking about making out with her dad. She didn't think of her father as handsome, just as dependable, strong, and calm.

"You don't have to give me this lecture," Tori said, tapping her fingernails again. "I'm always polite to the president."

Aprilynne let out a snort of laughter.

Tori rolled her eyes. "Honestly. You're never going to let me live that down, are you?"

Her mother's voice took on a patient tone. "You posted online that the president wasn't two-faced, he was dodecahedron-faced."

"I was ten," Tori pointed out. "Most parents would be proud that their ten-year-old knew what dodecahedron meant."

"The post went viral," her mother reminded her. "Reporters were talking about it in China."

"I wouldn't have posted it on Dad's account if you guys had let me have my own." Tori smoothed out a wrinkle in her skirt with an air of nonchalance. "Besides, I was only telling the truth. The president acted like Dad's friend in private, and then told the media Dad wanted to starve old ladies and kick kittens."

Aprilynne put her phone away. "And so now the president doesn't act like Dad's friend in private. That's better."

Tori fluttered her hand, waving away her sister's words. "Big loss. Who wants to be friends with President Dodecahedron-face?"

"Victoria"—her dad said her name with equal parts pleading and warning—"be on your best behavior."

"I will," Tori said. Really, her parents didn't need to look so worried. She had seen the president a dozen times since that event. Christmas parties, senate family parties, and the occasional times like this one where the president was trying to schmooze big business leaders.

Unless you counted the time when Tori was eleven and threw an Easter egg at the White House—and okay, she'd also thrown one at an especially surly secret service agent—she had always behaved beyond reproach. And in Tori's defense, the agent had been standing so far away, she didn't expect to actually hit him. She hadn't realized back then how accurate her aim was becoming.

"Good," her mother said. "The last thing we need is some sort of incident while the president is around."

The car stopped at the guard station in front of the White House. A marine strolled up to the car, checked her father's papers, and took an account of everyone inside the car. Another marine with a German shepherd sniffed around the outside of the car. When the guards were assured that they weren't smuggling terrorists inside, they waved the car through.

A few minutes later, Tori's family walked into the White House.

Tori had been here before, and she'd certainly been in enough mansions and historic homes that she shouldn't have felt awed. She always did, though. The colonnades, sweeping grounds, the portraits of presidents in the hallways—the whole place was saturated with history. John Adams, Thomas Jefferson, and Abraham Lincoln had walked these halls. Dolly Madison hung out her laundry here. How could Tori not be impressed with the White House?

When her family got to the East Ballroom, they took their spot at the end of the reception line. From the looks of it, it would be twenty minutes before they could greet the president, pose for the obligatory photo, and go mingle with the other guests. A couple hundred people milled around underneath the ornate crystal chandeliers. Women confident in their silk dresses and pearls. Men exuding power in crisp designer suits. The whole room smelled of expensive perfume.

Tori wished she could skip the line altogether and find some friends. She didn't suggest it. Her mother would only point out that they couldn't appear to be snubbing the president—not since the dodecahedron incident.

You would think the leader of the free world would get over an insult from a ten-year-old, even if it had made the news when it happened. But no. He always found some subtle way to remind her about it. Last year he asked her if she was taking geometry in school. When she told him she was, he said, "I'm sure you'll do well. You've got your shapes down pat."

The president's son, Clint, made the whole thing more awkward. He was Tori's age and always went to the same private schools. When she and Clint were thrown together, he usually found some way to give her grief. He had been the catalyst of the whole Easter egg–throwing spree. Of course, he didn't admit it when a herd of angry secret servicemen descended on them, weapons at the ready. No. He was just an innocent bystander and not the boy who bet her twenty dollars she couldn't hit the presidential seal on the balcony. And he never paid up, either. The deadbeat.

Tori was probably the only child in the history of White House Easter egg hunts to be publicly chastised by the Easter Bunny.

She glanced around the room. Clint stood by Penny, a senator's daughter, who went to their high school. Tori usually hung out with her at these functions, but if Penny was going to stand around flirting with Clint, Tori would find someone else.

Maybe Clint was kind of good looking if you were into skinny guys with hawkish features, but really, the way he acted you would think he was the president and not his father.

The chatter in the room seemed especially noisy and intense. Tori wished she could put in some earbuds and listen to music instead. Her parents probably wouldn't consider that respectful behavior while waiting to greet the president.

Tori had always had good hearing. It was, she realized now, part of her Slayer abilities. She not only heard what the dragon heard, she heard everything better. The skill came in handy if she wanted to eavesdrop, but being in noisy crowds like this could be overwhelming. She had to concentrate in order to follow one conversation and keep the rest from twisting into her attention. The fact that she also had to deal with Overdrake's playlist going in her mind didn't help matters.

As she looked around for someone to hang out with, she heard a song she liked. That was a nice change. Someone in Overdrake's compound had brought in music from this decade.

Tori liked the song, so she let the music grow louder in her mind. She still didn't see anyone in the room she wanted to hang out with. These events crawled by when she had no one to talk to but her parents. Her mom and dad were always too busy working the floor to pay attention to her.

"Why are you humming?" Aprilynne asked.

"Oh, sorry. I didn't realize I was."

Aprilynne regarded her suspiciously. "You don't have some sort of wireless earbuds, do you?"

"No. I just . . . feel like humming sometimes."

Aprilynne leaned in toward Tori and lowered her voice. "If you have earbuds, I want some, too. I swear, if I have to listen to the president give one more speech about bipartisanship . . ."

"I don't," Tori said.

"Right. You're tapping your foot."

Before Tori knew what she was doing, Aprilynne reached out and snatched Tori's purse from her hand. "Are there more in here?"

Aprilynne turned away so Tori couldn't grab her purse back without making a scene. Tori was tempted to grab it anyway. She eyed her parents ahead of them in the line. They weren't paying attention. Neither was the president. The secret servicemen scattered around the room, however, all seemed to be watching her.

Tori patiently held out her hand to her sister. "Give me my purse back."

Aprilynne pulled out the black plastic watch from Tori's purse and held it up. She shook her head sadly. "I can't believe you brought this thing with you tonight. It's clearly time for a fashion intervention."

Aprilynne was right about the watch. It was too big, too clunky, and the tiny pink crystals Theo had glued around the face didn't do much to make it look like a woman's watch. Pretty much it looked like a man's watch in drag. Which was why techno geeks shouldn't design watches.

Tori kept her hand stretched out. "I'm not wearing it. I just put it in my purse and forgot it was in there. Give it back."

Dr. B insisted on phones that doubled as watches because he thought Overdrake wouldn't know they were phones and therefore wouldn't try to bug them. Which might be the case unless Overdrake had seen enough pictures of Tori in the media to wonder why she'd stopped wearing her Rolex in favor of something that was made of gaudy black plastic. Then he might suspect something.

Aprilynne turned the watch over in her hand. "A guy must have given this to you. Was it that hot guy at your dragon geek camp?" She meant Jesse. Aprilynne had met him at the beginning of camp.

"Actually, no."

Aprilynne smiled knowingly. "Right. I bet there was a tender exchange when he gave it to you."

Theo had given Tori the watch and the exchange had been:

> Tori: This is a prank, right? You and Bess came up with this together, didn't you?
>
> Theo: Don't wave it around like that. It's expensive.
>
> Tori: People at my school will openly mock me if I wear this.
>
> Theo: Stop whining. I put crystals on yours so it would look all bling.
>
> Tori (*trying to flick off one of the crystals*): What if this watch accidently fell underneath the wheels of a moving car? Would you make me a different one?

Instead of an actual answer, Theo had let out a stream of threats about what would happen to her should any harm come to her watch-phone.

As if. Even without her extra powers, Tori could have taken Theo out with one well-delivered kick.

Aprilynne held the watch between her thumb and finger as though it were a small animal that had suddenly died. Pathetic and probably germ ridden. "I'm all for romantic tokens," she said, handing it back to Tori, "but couldn't he have given you something with more . . . I don't know . . . class . . . elegance . . . basic fashion sense? It makes you wonder about his taste."

Tori snatched her watch back, then took her purse as well. She shoved the watch inside and snapped the clasp shut. "Jesse didn't give it to me." It shouldn't have bothered her to say this. She felt a sting, though. Her mind said the words she hadn't. Jesse hadn't given her anything.

The line moved forward, taking Aprilynne's attention away from Tori. They were almost to the president. A new song came on in her mind. Taylor Swift's "Picture to Burn." An angry breakup song. For once Overdrake had matched his music to her mood. As Tori concentrated on the words, the music automatically grew louder.

Tori's father shook hands with the president. Both men were all smiles. Tori's mother was next in line.

Aprilynne nudged Tori and gave her a warning look. "What are you muttering? 'Burn, baby, burn'? What's that supposed to mean?"

Oops. It meant she'd been singing out loud. "Nothing," Tori said.

Aprilynne didn't comment. It was her turn to greet the president. Aprilynne shook his hand, then turned and posed for the photo. After that, she glided down the line to the vice president.

Tori stepped over to shake the president's hand. He smiled at her, all teeth and polish, then called to her father, "Your girls just get prettier every time I see them." The president put his other hand on top of Tori's so her hand was sandwiched in his grip. Leaning toward her confidentially, he said, "You have a beautiful face, which is a good thing because, unlike some of us, you only have one, eh?" He laughed at his joke, but there was an edge to it.

"Yeah. Again, sorry about that." Again, not really.

"Don't get me wrong," the president said, prolonging her turn with him, "I admire a person who speaks their mind." At least until it went viral. Then he was considerably less admiring. "Once you're educated about the issues, you'll be able to do some good in the world." Implying, of course, if she didn't agree with him she was ignorant and worthless.

She smiled at him anyway. And that's when Tori heard it. A sound that wasn't part of Taylor Swift's song, but had come from the same location. A screech. High pitched like wheels squealing. But longer, animal like. Dragon like.

Tori let out a gasp. Her eyes flew wide open and her heart slammed into her chest. Had an egg hatched?

The president jerked his hand away from her. He looked behind him to see what she was staring at. The motion caused a ripple of movement among the secret servicemen. They were on alert, scanning the room, hands on their weapons.

"What's wrong?" the president asked her.

"Nothing." Tori strained to hear other noises among the chorus of the song. Had it been a dragon, or something else? "I just remembered I hadn't done my calculus homework."

The president relaxed. "That's what you think about while you're talking to the leader of the free world—your homework?" He let out a sound that was nearly a chuckle, although less amused.

She nodded, barely hearing his words. The noise couldn't have been a dragon. Not yet. It was something else. A cart moving near the eggs maybe. She took a deep breath. Everything would be okay.

And then Tori heard a second screech. An angry, rumbling sound that was immediately joined by another screech—two dragons. They'd both hatched. Tori stiffened, horrified. This couldn't happen yet. If the dragons had hatched, they would be mature within a year. She wasn't ready to fight them. She only had one summer of training.

The president looked nervously around again. The chatter in the room lessened. People noticed his reaction, noticed Tori. In another moment, her parents would come over to see what was wrong.

"What?" the president asked, all the humor gone.

She knew her eyes were still wide, staring at him in shock. She couldn't help herself. "Um . . ." She gulped hard. "I've got a French essay, too."

"Well," the president said, clearly offended, "I won't take any more of your time then." He turned his attention to the next person in line, dismissing her.

The security agents nearest the president glared at her, as if she were trying to create a scene. She walked woodenly over to where her parents stood waiting for her. Aprilynne had already gone off to find friends, or cute guys, or both.

The music was so loud in Tori's mind that she barely heard her father's voice. "What was that all about?"

"Nothing," she said.

Tori's mother brushed a piece of lint off Tori's shoulder, giving her an excuse to stand closer. She had a rigid smile, the kind ventriloquists wore. "It didn't look like nothing. It looked like you did something to upset the president."

"No," Tori said. "Not really." She didn't hear any other sounds in her mind. Just the music. But then, she shouldn't expect dragons to cry for food like baby birds. When dragons hatched they were the size of lions and could hunt just as well.

"Not really?" Her mom's eyebrows arched. "I had to keep your father from marching over there to see what was wrong." Her voice took on a staccato rhythm. "That's not the sort of scene we want to make here, is it?"

"Sorry," Tori said. Really, all she'd done was gasp and stare. You wouldn't think a guy with dozens of security guards would startle so easily.

"You look pale," her father said. "Are you feeling all right?"

"No," Tori said. "I mean, no, I'm fine." If her parents thought she was sick enough to leave the president's dinner party, her mother would take her home and hover around her for who knew how long. She needed to go someplace where she could call Dr. B.

Tori's mother kept talking, but Tori only half listened. She opened her purse and dug through it. If the eggs had hatched, Dirk would have seen it. Maybe he already called Dr. B. Maybe Dr. B sent out a message to the Slayers and Tori hadn't gotten it because she wasn't wearing her watch.

"What are you doing?" her mother asked in exasperation.

Tori found the watch and pulled it out. The face wasn't lit up. That meant she didn't have any messages. At least not yet. Tori slipped the watch onto her wrist. "I don't want to lose track of the time."

Tori's mother let out a frustrated sigh. "Fine," she said, clearly abandoning whatever point she'd been trying to make. "Go find your friends." She turned and looked around the room locating the people she wanted to talk to.

Tori's father studied her for another moment. "Our table is near the podium."

Tori wasn't sure whether he was telling her this so she could find them at dinner or whether he was warning her she would be in the president's line of sight.

Her parents turned and walked toward the middle of the room. Her mother's dress swished elegantly behind her, every movement calm and regal. Her father was already smiling at someone, heading toward him with an outstretched hand. Tori strode out of the East Ballroom, looking for a private place. There weren't as many of those as you would expect in the White House. Not with secret servicemen and marines stationed everywhere.

She headed to the ladies' restroom. As soon as she stepped inside, she knew she couldn't make a private call from here. Even the restrooms in the White House were tourist locations. The room was decorated with portraits of the first ladies, and several women were perched on the chaise lounge in the sitting area, snapping pictures of themselves with the paintings in the background. A line of women waited for their turn in the stalls. Someone was bound to notice if Tori went into one and started a conversation with herself about dragon hatchlings.

Tori went back out to the Cross Hall. The large hallway connected the East Ballroom and the State Dining Room, and also gave people access to the Blue, Green, and Red Rooms. It had chairs along the walls and large columns that a person could stand behind. A few scattered secret servicemen were around, making sure guests didn't wander off where they weren't supposed to.

As Tori strolled over to the closest column, she took off her watch and pretended to reset the time. Three buttons curved around each side of the watch. She pushed the first one once, the second twice. Dr. B's call code.

After only a moment, Dr. B answered with a "Hello?" His voice came out louder than she'd expected. A button on the other side of the watch controlled the volume. She pushed it a few times, lowering the sound so it was barely audible, then held the watch to her lips. "It's me, T-Bird. Do you copy?" As a security measure, Dr. B had given them all code names, something Tori thought was pointless since Overdrake already knew their first names.

"I copy. What's wrong?" Dr. B's voice was calm. If she hadn't known that he always sounded that way, she would have thought he was unconcerned.

"I heard noises that sound like hatchlings screeching. Has Hawk called? Has he seen anything? Over."

One of the security men was staring at her. Tori brushed her hand through her hair, pretending she was just out here primping—while still holding her cheap black, unmatching watch. Yeah, he probably didn't think she was acting odd at all.

"I haven't heard from Hawk," Dr. B said. "I'll call him and call you back. Over and out."

Over and out. Even after training at camp Tori still wasn't used to the military way of signing off. What was it with guys that they couldn't come up with a decent way of saying good-bye? But then, maybe the phrase was more accurate. Maybe guys just wanted things to be over and for themselves to be out. Clean breaks.

While Tori waited for Dr. B to call back, she fiddled with her watch. Her thoughts made panicked circles through her mind. Within a year of hatching, dragons were full grown. Overdrake probably wouldn't wait long after that to attack. And the Slayers didn't know how many eggs there were. They had assumed it was two because dragons laid their eggs in clutches of two—one male, one female. But there could be more.

Tori twisted the watch strap between her fingers, her dread picking up speed. It was the end of September now. Even if Tori got another summer of training in, it wouldn't be enough. Dr. B would have to call some interim training sessions. How would she explain it to her parents? How could she ever be ready to fight flying, carnivorous monsters?

Tori looked up and noticed Clint and Penny walking down the hall toward her. Penny's dark hair had been swept up onto the top of her head so that her dark curls fountained down around a garnet-studded clip. She was looking at Tori, but walking possessively close to Clint. He held a plate piled with shrimp from the appetizer table. He dipped one into cocktail sauce as he strolled up.

"There you are," Penny said. "What are you doing out here by yourself?"

Clint took a bite of his shrimp. "Besides making all the secret servicemen nervous, that is."

"What?" Tori asked. She tucked her arms behind her back, hiding the watch. "I'm not doing anything." She knew it sounded lame. She had never been a good liar.

"Right," Clint said. "You were just talking into your watch for kicks."

"No," Tori said, her hands still behind her back. "I . . . I wasn't."

Clint picked through the shrimp on his plate. "I don't blame you. Hey, what fun is life if you can't jerk around the president's bodyguards once in a while? Everybody needs a power trip now and then."

Penny tilted her head at Tori. "Are you acting all suspicious to get back at the president for his dodecahedron comments?" She shook her head with disapproval. "You really shouldn't make him nervous. You'll get in trouble."

"I'm not," Tori insisted. "I just came out here to get some fresh air. I wasn't feeling well."

Her watch let out a chime. Dr. B had called her back. Tori ignored it. Maybe Penny and Clint would think it was coming from somewhere else. "Well, it was great to see you guys," Tori said, prodding them to leave. They didn't. Her watch chimed again.

Clint raised his eyebrow at Tori. "You're ringing."

Penny shook her head again with even more disapproval this time. "You snuck in a cell phone? If it goes off during the president's speech, you'll never hear the end of it."

"She's right," Clint said. "Amy Carter is still getting grief for roller skating in the East Ballroom and scratching the floor. It's the reason my dad won't let me skateboard in there."

Tori's watch chimed again. Clint and Penny weren't going to go away, and apparently Dr. B would keep calling until Tori answered. She sighed, pressed the speak button, then held up the watch to her ear. "Yes?"

"I spoke to Hawk," Dr. B said. "He hasn't seen anything to indicate the dragons have hatched."

"Good," Tori said. Clint and Penny were both watching her, clearly questioning her sanity.

"It's possible that Hawk is connected to different eggs than you are. It's also possible Overdrake is keeping the dragons in a completely dark room. Although it's much more probable that Overdrake is playing screeching noises near the eggs as a sort of psychological attack on you. Perhaps he wants to make you anxious. Or perhaps he wants you so used to dragon noises you won't notice when the eggs really do hatch."

That didn't seem likely. It would be hard to fool both her and Dirk. Tori didn't comment on Dr. B's theory, though. She couldn't in front of Clint and Penny. "Okay," she said cheerily. "Thanks for letting me know."

She ended the call without over and outing, something she would probably hear about later from Dr. B. She shoved the watch back into her purse.

Penny and Clint were still staring at her.

"You know," Clint said popping the last of the shrimp into his mouth, "the secret service guys aren't big on practical jokes. Unless you want to spend a portion of the evening spread-eagle against a wall being frisked, I wouldn't do that sort of thing again." He turned to Penny. "I'm done with my shrimp. Let's get some caviar."

"Eww." Penny wrinkled her nose. "That stuff is so gross." She turned and went with him, leaving Tori alone.

Tori leaned against the column, limp with relief. The dragons hadn't hatched. They might not hatch for years. She had time to train. And what's more, she had time to find Ryker Davis so he could train.

That had been her goal from the day she left camp, and this evening's scare made her more determined than ever to find him. Granted, Dr. B had been searching for seventeen years and hadn't turned up the whereabouts of Ryker's family, but Tori had an advantage. Her father had access to government databases.

Strictly speaking, senators weren't supposed to use their government connections to find people. When Tori had asked her father to track down her camp friend's address and phone number, he'd given her a lecture about privacy, ethics, and security. Tori was forced to go on and on about how Ryker had asked for her number, and then she'd left before she could give it to him, and he'd given her his phone number but somehow she'd lost it. Ryker's parents didn't let him do any online social sites, so she had no way to contact him. He would think she didn't care and she would die heartbroken because of all of this.

Tori's father was decidedly unconcerned about her dying of heartbreak. He did finally consent to look up Ryker's address, though.

Once Tori had it, she would send it to Dr. B so he could recruit Ryker. An extra Slayer could mean the difference between success and failure, between life and death for any of them.

Now Tori pulled herself together, tried to match her mother's self-assured composure, and went back into the East Ballroom. Everything was normal. Everything would be fine. She minimized the sound near the eggs as much as she could to block out Overdrake's sounds. It didn't matter. Half a dozen times during the president's dinner speech, the screeching shrieks pierced through Tori's mind. Sometimes they were accompanied by bangs or thuds, as though there were two dragons and they were fighting—or something was crashing around trying to get away from them.

Every time Tori heard these sorts of noises, she startled. She automatically focused on the sound, making the volume in her mind shoot up, which in turn made her flinch. People around the room kept glancing at her as though she looked pained and twitchy because of the things the president was saying. Her mother nudged her under the table. Aprilynne leaned over and whispered, "Would you stop doing that. What's wrong with you?"

"My dress," Tori whispered. "Something keeps poking me."

Her father sighed and pointedly ignored her. Every time the president's gaze wandered in Tori's direction, he sent her a cold glare.

What a great night this had turned out to be.

Was it a coincidence that Overdrake started playing the screeching noises when Tori was in line to talk to the president? If it wasn't coincidence, how did Overdrake know when to play the new noises? The only people who could have known the exact moment she was meeting the president were other people in the room.

It wasn't a comforting thought at all.

CHAPTER 9

The screeching in Tori's mind eventually stopped. Then it started again at two in the morning, accompanied by more banging. By then Tori was so used to the sounds, she only woke up long enough to groan and minimize the sound in her mind again. She grabbed the white-noise maker from her nightstand and put it on the pillow next to her. Eventually she fell back to sleep.

All through school the next day, Tori had a hard time focusing on her classes. She kept waiting for the next hungry, high-pitched shriek to cut through her mind. She looked for a pattern, some sign the noises were repeating themselves. If Overdrake was playing a recording, the screeches would repeat themselves at some point. They didn't, not that she could tell.

So was it some sort of random, horrible noise generator or something else?

Tori wanted to talk to Dirk about it, wanted his reassurance that the eggs really hadn't hatched. Would it constitute an emergency if she needed to call him for her own sanity?

Tori was pacing back and forth in front of the living room windows when her father came home from work. Out in the front yard, the wind rustled through the maple trees. She barely noticed them. She kept searching the sky. It was stupid, really. Even if the dragons had hatched, they wouldn't be flying around her neighborhood. She knew this. Still, she kept watching the clouds as though any moment they would scatter out of the way to reveal a growling dragon. It was probably some inborn instinct she inherited from her Slayer knight predecessors. *If you sense danger, look up. That's where it's coming from.*

Her father patted his coat pocket. "I have something for you. About that boy from camp."

"Dirk?" she asked. His name came to her first because once or twice a week he sent a letter to Tori by way of her father's office.

Jesse had never written to her, probably wouldn't ever consider bending the rules that way, but Dirk's first letter had come the day after she got home. She realized from the postmark that he'd mailed it from D.C. the day they'd all left camp.

Her father's staff always opened his letters before they passed on any to him, something that Dirk must have known would happen, because he didn't mention any of the Slayer stuff.

"I know you weren't expecting to hear from me so soon," he'd written—which was an understatement. She hadn't expected to hear from him until next year at camp—"I still remember how hard it was to adjust to normal life after spending the first summer away, so I thought I'd write you. Don't worry, pretty soon you won't think of camp that much. You'll be able to go out in a crowd and not search for one of us. Spend time with your friends. Do everything you did before camp. Even though none of it seems important right now, it is. Normal is important. If you want to write me back, you can send a letter to 12 S Braddock Street, Winchester, VA.

"P.S. Stop moping about Jesse."

The letter had made Tori smile. She wrote Dirk back, feeling a little wicked for knowing his address, but special, too. It meant he trusted her. It also meant she wasn't completely adrift in the normal world. She had a link to camp, to her Slayer friends.

Since then, Tori's and Dirk's letters to each other were frequent, but always short and vague. They never had any information in them that would let anyone know they were part of a covert group. To be on the safe side, though, Tori kept Dirk's letters hidden in the wall safe in her bedroom.

Now she expected her father to produce another letter from his coat pocket. He didn't.

Upon finding his coat pocket empty, he reached into his pants pockets. "Not Dirk," he said. "That other boy."

Tori's heart missed a beat. "Jesse?" Was it possible that he'd written her?

"Jesse?" her father repeated, searching his suit pockets now. "Who's that?" He pulled out a folded piece of paper. "And how many boys were you seeing at that camp?"

Tori felt her hopes sink silently back to the floor. She should have known Jesse hadn't written.

Her father unfolded the paper. "Ryker Davis," he said. "I've got his address narrowed down to one of three. Did he come from California, Colorado, or New York?"

Tori went and peered over her father's arm at the addresses, doing her best to memorize each of them. "I'm not sure. Are there that many Allen and Harriet Davises?"

"Yes," her father said, clearly frustrated. "These were the ones left over after we narrowed down the age bracket. Your friend never mentioned, say, the Rocky Mountains, or surfing, or the Empire State Building?"

Tori shrugged apologetically. "Can't you find out which of them has a son named Ryker? Wouldn't that be on their tax returns or something?"

Her father made an unhappy grumbling sound in the back of his throat. "Isn't there anyone from your school that you like? What about Roland?" Her father seemed to have just noticed it was Friday night and Tori was at home. "Aren't you seeing him anymore?"

Tori had dated Roland before she went to camp, had liked him a lot actually. They were almost boyfriend and girlfriend. Now, though, the relationship seemed pale and anemic. Jesse had talked to Tori about life and duty. She had soared through the forest with him, glided through the starlit sky to mountain perches. Roland talked to Tori about French homework and whether the school should have a polo team.

Jesse knew who Tori was, what she was, and what she was capable of. Roland knew who her friends and family were and that she was pretty. Roland still talked to her at school and texted once in a while, but every time he asked her out, she told him she was busy.

Tori kept staring at the addresses in her father's hand. "Roland and I are just friends. I really need to know where Ryker is." She gave her father her most winning smile. "Please, can't you check the tax records for me? I know he thinks I've blown him off. I have to talk to him."

Her father sighed and tucked the paper into his pants pocket. "I'll see what I can do. But if you really are that keen about Ryker, you ought to tell that Dirk fellow to stop writing you."

"Dirk and I are just friends," she said.

Her father took off his coat and headed toward the coat closet. "Some friend. Why haven't you given him your cell phone number? It's not that my staff doesn't like going through your personal correspondence—actually, as a parent, I like it better that way—but wouldn't it be easier and faster for him to text you?"

"It's complicated," Tori said, and then she left the room before he could make more comments about her love life.

All through dinner, Tori kept thinking about Dirk. Every time a shriek interrupted her thoughts—less often now, and they were shorter, barely squawks—she wanted to talk to him. Was his dragon sight exactly the same as it had been before? Had he experienced any changes?

She kept fingering her watch-phone. If she called Dirk, Dr. B would see a record of the call on his phone. He monitored them. He'd wonder why his assurance hadn't been enough for her.

Besides, Dr. B thought their last phones had been compromised somehow. The same thing could have happened with the new phones.

It would be better, safer, if she went to see him in person. She knew his address after all. She'd memorized it even though she hadn't tried to. If Overdrake ever captured her, there wouldn't really be a difference between her knowing the address and visiting the place. The location was shot either way.

Tori went back and forth with the idea. Dirk would have told Dr. B if he'd seen anything unusual. And Slayers weren't supposed to see each other. It was one thing to write letters. It was different to completely disregard the rules.

On the other hand, Tori should talk to Dirk about what she was hearing. Ultimately the country's safety was at stake. And what was wrong, really, in going there? She would make sure no one followed her.

She wanted to see Dirk, wanted it more the longer she thought about it.

And so it became the right thing to do.

Half an hour later, Tori told her parents she was spending the night at Penny's, she told Penny to cover for her because she wouldn't be in until really late, and then Tori was driving to Dirk's house. She wished she'd left earlier. It was an hour and a half trip, which meant she wouldn't get there until eight thirty. She had been held up because she had to run an electronics sweep on her car before she left, and okay, she spent a little time touching up her hair and makeup. She hadn't seen Dirk since August, and she'd been a total mess over Jesse back then. Tonight she would show him that she was her usual confident, collected, over-Jesse self.

It felt odd to drive into Winchester. The place was full of dark memories. Overdrake's first compound had been on the outskirts of this city and the last time Tori came here the Slayers fought him and failed. Of course, Overdrake was long gone now. He moved everything off his property on the night of the raid. Still, Tori nearly expected to see him—black suit, helmet covering his face—lurking in the shadows of the streetlamps.

It must be hard for Dirk to live here, knowing that the dragons had been so close. Dr. B said that's why Dirk had always had such a strong connection to them. He grew up with dragons nearby.

When Tori pulled onto Braddock Street, she realized Dirk's address wasn't residential. It was in downtown. Which meant Dirk hadn't given her his home address after all. She slowed her speed, looking at the old-fashioned brick buildings on both sides of the road. Where had her letters been going? She finally pulled up to the address. La Niçoise Café. A restaurant.

Did Dirk work here?

Tori felt her expectations deflating. Dirk might not even be here tonight. She might have driven all this way for nothing. Still, she supposed she might as well go inside and see if she could find him. She parked her car, gave one last look around to make sure no one had followed her, and walked inside.

The café had a quaint French feel to it. Lace curtains, flower boxes, and small elegant tables. Strains of French music lapped gently through the room. It smelled of something savory, of things cooking.

Two people stood at the hostess station talking. A girl about Tori's age in a uniform and an older woman in a business suit. As Tori walked over, the woman looked up and smiled. "Welcome to La Niçoise Café. Table for one, or are you waiting for someone?"

Tori glanced around the room. No sign of Dirk. "Can I request a waiter?"

The woman's gaze ran over Tori, making a mental note of her designer clothes and her Gucci purse. "Certainly," she said. "We're happy to accommodate our guests anyway we can."

"Thanks. Is Dirk working tonight?"

"Dirk?" The woman's smile faltered. It wasn't confusion, just reluctance. "I'm sorry. We don't have any waiters by that name."

"Oh," Tori said. "Does he work in the kitchen then?"

The woman shook her head, eyeing Tori suspiciously now. "No. There are no Dirks in the kitchen."

Tori flushed. She'd sent letters here and Dirk had gotten them. He made comments about her letters in his. Which meant this lady had to know who he was, or something very odd was happening.

Tori shifted uncomfortably. "Dirk is a friend of mine. We met this summer and he gave me this address to write to him. I was in town and wanted to surprise him."

The manager raised an eyebrow at Tori. "What did you say Dirk's last name was?"

How could Tori explain that he'd never given her his last name, that he couldn't. "I . . . It's embarrassing. I've forgotten it. You must have seen my letters come in, though."

The manager's expression turned cold, guarded. "I've never seen any of your letters. You must have your addresses mixed up."

"No," Tori started, "I'm sure I—"

The woman held up her hand to stop Tori's protest. "I'm sorry. I can't give out personal information about the staff here." She picked up a menu, indicating the discussion was over. "Will you be staying for dinner?"

Tori didn't know what to say. She didn't want to, and yet at the same time she had the vague hope that Dirk might walk in and see her. "Can I look over the menu?" she asked.

"Certainly." The woman handed Tori the menu and walked away, heading toward the kitchen.

Tori scanned the dinner items without really paying attention to them. Filet mignon . . . grilled duck breast . . . what now? Should she call Dirk on her watch-phone? If she did, should she admit she came looking for him? Maybe she should just write Dirk and ask him in a coded way what he saw with his dragon sight. Hey, she could write him a note right now and leave it at the hostess station. It might not get to him, though. Maybe he was finding some way to intercept the mail before it got here. Could he be working at the post office?

The hostess leaned toward Tori. "I don't blame you for looking for Dirk," she said in a confidential tone. "The guy is hot."

Tori's gaze snapped up. "You know Dirk?"

"I'd like to," the girl said. Her name tag read, "M. J." "Me and every waitress in the place." M. J. looked over her shoulder to make sure no one overheard them. "Dirk's father owns the restaurant. That must be why he gave you this address."

"Oh." Tori perked up. "Do you know how I can get a hold of him?"

M. J. shook her head. "He only comes in about once a week. His dad doesn't *work* here. He just owns the place. So every time the Everetts come in, we're supposed to be on our best behavior and comp every-thing. Seriously, though," M. J. said with a sly smile, "I would comp Dirk's meals anyway."

The Everetts. That was Dirk's last name. Tori wasn't supposed to know it. She felt a pang of guilt and supposed this was why Dr. B didn't want them contacting one another outside of camp. It was too easy to find out personal information. She appeased herself by promising she wouldn't ever reveal it. Especially not to Overdrake. But now that she knew it, should she check the White Pages to see if she could find his home phone number? The hostess would probably tell her Mr. Everett's first name if she asked.

Tori folded the menu. She shouldn't ask. She should turn around and go home before she learned anything else.

"So you're Dirk's summer fling?" M. J. asked, clearly curious. When Tori didn't answer, M. J. added, "The postman drops off the restaurant's letters at the hostess station, so we see them before Mr. Everett's assistant picks them up. Personally, I think it's sweet that you keep writing Dirk."

"Um . . . ," Tori stammered. "Did Dirk . . . is that who he says the letters are from—his summer fling?"

M. J. shrugged apologetically. "He calls you his fan girl."

"His fan girl," Tori repeated.

"Listen, you seem nice, and you'd have to be blind and immune to charm not to fall for Dirk, but I should warn you—every time he comes in here for dinner, he's with a different girl." M. J. gestured around at the restaurant. "And the guy didn't even give you his real address. That says something."

"Yeah," Tori said. *Every time Dirk came in, he was with a different girl?* Tori shouldn't be bothered to hear this. The uncomfortable feeling in her stomach came from being lumped in with Dirk's groupies, from looking like some sort of pathetic, lovelorn girl who didn't know when her summer romance was over.

Tori was clearly not that sort of girl because she knew her romance with Jesse was over. Even if she had gone to the Natural History Museum in hopes that he would change his mind and meet her.

Sheesh. Now that she thought about it, maybe she really was as pathetic as one of Dirk's groupies.

The hostess was staring sadly at Tori, perhaps because she hadn't moved. What was even worse about all of this was that when the hostess got the next letter to Dirk, she was going to think Tori was doubly pathetic. If Dirk wanted her to keep writing to him, he would have to get a P.O. box just so Tori wouldn't imagine M. J. shaking her head and telling the waitresses about what a pitiable idiot fan girl was.

Tori forced a smile and handed the menu back to M. J. "Thanks for the information. I guess I won't stay for dinner. I only wish I'd gotten to talk to Dirk in person about all of this."

M. J. let out another sympathetic sigh. "I shouldn't say anything else, but if you want to see him, go to a John Handley High football game. Dirk has a letter jacket."

More personal information. Now Tori knew what high school he went to.

"Thanks," Tori said. She turned and left the restaurant before she could learn anything else.

Without letting herself think about it, she checked John Handley High's website on her phone. They had a home game tonight. Tori could be there in a few minutes.

She'd come this far. And she probably wouldn't learn anything else that M. J. hadn't already told her in her advice for the lovelorn.

Besides, why shouldn't Tori see Dirk play football? She was his fan girl.

CHAPTER 10

Tori nearly laughed when she caught sight of John Handley High. It was a sprawling brick building with so many white columns, it looked like it had been dropped down from Mount Olympus. BMWs and Mercedes littered the school's parking lot.

And the other Slayers had given *her* a hard time for being rich. Dirk had apparently been keeping a few secrets from everybody.

Tori walked down to the bleachers and found an empty spot near a group of girls. They glanced at her, slicing her up as a potential rival, and then ignored her. She got that a lot from girls. It was still better than sitting by guys, though. Guys always asked questions, flirted, and tried to attach themselves to her side with barnacle-like insistence. Tori didn't want that right now.

The air was cold, crisp with the sense of autumn. Her jacket didn't offer a lot of warmth, so she tucked her hands into her pockets. Her gaze slid across the players. John Handley was in maroon shirts with white pants. A glance at the bench told her that Dirk wasn't sitting there.

At camp she probably would have been able to tell which player he was through her counterpart sense. She wasn't sure how strong that ability was now that she'd been away from him for so long. It would be odd to see Dirk and not sense things about him.

Martinsburg's quarterback snapped the ball a dozen yards down the field to a receiver. With a few quick steps, a JHH linebacker plowed into the receiver, sending him sprawling. Tori's gaze zeroed in on the linebacker. He held out a hand to help up the downed player. Perhaps it was his self-assured walk, or maybe her counterpart sense worked as well here as it did at camp. She knew the linebacker was Dirk a second before the announcer called, "Tackle by forty-four, Everett."

Tori relaxed, smiled, and watched the last fifteen minutes of the game. Dirk made two more tackles. One of the cheerleaders, a lanky blonde who was fond of leg-kicks, seemed especially excited when this happened. John Handley still lost by three points. The crowd clapped at the end of the game anyway, the band played, and the team marched off to their locker room.

Most of the crowd headed toward the parking lot. Parents and friends wandered to the edge of the field waiting for the players. Tori joined them, suddenly nervous. What would Dirk do when he saw her? He'd said in one of his letters that he wished he could see her, but he might feel differently about her showing up at his football game.

Dirk hadn't given her his real address; he'd taken steps to protect his identity. And she had not only learned his last name, she also knew where he went to school. This wasn't just bending the rules. It was pretty much taking a sledgehammer to them.

Tori stood behind a clump of parents who were talking about the game. "So close," one of the fathers said. "It's a heartbreaker."

Tori's breath came out in cold puffs. She wrapped her arms around herself and shivered. Maybe this had been a bad idea all along and she was only making it worse. Maybe she should go before he saw her.

The players emerged from the locker room, done with whatever pep talk or lecture their coach had given them. They strolled over to talk to the people at the edge of the field. She caught sight of Dirk in the back of the group, talking with another player. His helmet was off and his shaggy blond hair was dark with sweat. Grass smudges and dirt covered his arms and uniform. She stared at him, drinking him in. Even dirty he was utterly handsome.

Tori looked toward the parking lot. The manager of La Niçoise Café would probably tell Dirk that a girl came by and asked for him, but Tori could leave before he found out that she had gone to his high school. He was nearly to where she stood. She moved a little farther behind the cluster of parents so she wouldn't be visible.

The lanky blonde cheerleader swept up to Dirk and gave him a hug. "You played a great game," she cooed. "You should have won."

"Thanks." He gave her a quirk of a smile and kept walking down the field.

He hadn't seen Tori yet. His gaze was trained on some people a few yards to her left. She glanced at them and then quickly glanced away. It didn't matter. The image stayed in her mind.

A middle-aged man with smooth dark hair stood next to a beautiful brunette woman. The man had to be Dirk's father. He had the same height and build as Dirk, the same face shape. The woman didn't look old enough to be his mother. She must have been, though, since she had her arm looped through his father's arm. She wore a form-fitting black coat with white fur trim and a matching hat—probably bought at some chic skiing villa somewhere. An elementary-aged girl waited beside them. She had long brown hair like her mother and waved excitedly at Dirk.

Tori had seen Dirk's family. This visit just kept getting worse. Why hadn't she realized his family would be here? That was the sort of thing families did.

Tori would draw attention to herself if she turned and bolted off the field now. She would let Dirk walk over to his family and then she would drift downfield to an exit. No one had to know about this unfortunate incident.

Dirk kept his gaze on his family. His father called out, "If your coach had let you play offense *and* defense, you would have won." He had an accent, a familiar one, although Tori couldn't place it. British maybe or South African.

"Yeah," Dirk called back. "What's up with the coach letting other people have playtime?" He was walking by Tori. She lowered her head as far as she could while still keeping an eye on him.

The smile dropped from his face and he abruptly stopped walking. "Tori," he said. His gaze swung to the bleachers behind her, searching the groups of stragglers making their way down them.

Tori froze. He had sensed her. She couldn't hide.

She stepped out from behind the group of parents. "Hi, Dirk."

He turned to her, surprised.

It felt like a long time—waiting for his surprise to fade and his real reaction to show itself.

He smiled broadly, a smile that lit up his face. "What are you doing here?"

She kept her voice low. "Um . . . breaking a lot of rules."

Dirk walked over, still smiling. "I knew you had a rebellious streak."

"I wanted to talk to you." She shrugged apologetically. "I didn't mean to end up here. It just sort of happened." She knew Dirk's parents were watching. She felt their gazes. They were probably inwardly groaning that their son had been detained by yet another groupie. "I know you're busy right now. This was a bad idea to begin with—"

"No," he said. "It's okay. What did you need to talk to me about?"

Nothing that she could say in front of a crowd of people. "Your family is waiting for you. I'll just . . ." She didn't finish the sentence. She wasn't even sure what she meant to say. *I'll just . . . talk to you some other time?* She couldn't. *I'll just . . . ask Dr. B to call you again like I should have done in the first place?*

"It's fine," Dirk said. "Wait here. I'll explain to my parents."

He turned to go speak to them. His sister was already bounding over. She had a wide smile and blue eyes like Dirk's: mischievous blue. She flung her arms around her brother. "You won!" she chimed.

He patted her shoulder. "Actually we lost. Thanks for paying attention."

Mrs. Everett strolled over. "Bridget, don't. He's filthy." She grimaced at the way Bridget clung to Dirk's sweaty jersey and mud streaked pants.

Bridget let go. "I thought you won. You were ahead most of the time. What happened?"

Mr. Everett sauntered over as well. "It doesn't matter who's ahead most of the time. It only matters who's ahead at the end. Unfortunately, tonight that wasn't your brother." Mr. Everett had been speaking to Bridget, but he smiled at Tori, waiting for an introduction.

"Dad," Dirk said, and there was a twinge of nervousness in his voice. "This is Tori. A friend of mine."

"Ah yes." Mr. Everett held out his hand to shake hers. "From camp."

Tori shook his hand and blushed. He knew she was from camp. Which meant he knew her as that pathetic fan girl who kept sending letters to Dirk at his restaurant. And now she'd shown up at Dirk's football game. This probably earned her stalker status. No wonder Mrs. Everett wore an expression of cold distaste.

Bridget giggled at Tori. "You're pretty."

"Thanks," Tori said. This was so awkward.

Mr. Everett was still staring at Tori with an amused smile. "So what brings you here?"

Well, no one has issued a restraining order yet, so I thought I would show up at random places where your son would be. "I was in the area," Tori said.

Please don't ask me what my father does, she thought. She didn't want to say anything that would make Dirk's parents remember her. She would rather fade in with the ranks of the lanky blonde cheerleader and all of the rest of Dirk's forgettable groupies.

"Tori and I are going to hang out," Dirk told his parents. "So you don't need to wait around for me."

Mrs. Everett turned to her husband, her eyebrow cocked. "I think we've just been dismissed."

Mr. Everett laughed and put his hand on her shoulder. It was deep and familiar. Or maybe it seemed familiar because there was something of Dirk in it, a sort of private amusement of the situation.

"Don't take it personally," he told his wife. "Teenagers are always embarrassed by their parents." He gave Tori a parting smile. "Pretend you never saw us. We don't exist."

Ditto, she thought.

Dirk's parents walked toward the parking lot. Bridget turned and waved over her shoulder. "Bye, Tori!" she yelled so loudly that several people looked at her.

Dirk ran a hand through his already mussed hair. "So that was my family."

"Yeah," Tori said. "They seem nice."

"They have their moments."

Mr. and Mrs. Everett were a few yards away by that time. Tori shouldn't have been able to still hear their conversation, but her extra sensitive hearing was always at work.

Mrs. Everett said, "That was dangerous. You shouldn't have talked to her."

"Quiet," Mr. Everett said in a low voice. "She'll hear you."

A chill went up Tori's spine. Had Dirk told them about her hearing? What did Mrs. Everett mean by dangerous?

Bridget said, "I'll hear what? What's dangerous?"

And then Tori relaxed. Mr. Everett meant Bridget, not Tori. Of course, Dirk hadn't told them her secrets.

Mr. Everett spoke to Bridget in a teasing way, "You'll learn when you're older. It's always dangerous to talk to girls your son likes." And then he was too far away for Tori to hear anything else. Which was a good thing, because she needed to pay attention to Dirk. He was looking at her expectantly, waiting for an explanation for her surprise visit.

"I shouldn't have barged in on you like this," she said. "Dr. B isn't going to be happy that I met your family. Or that I know which high school you go to . . ." She glanced around nervously, as though their camp director might suddenly appear to chastise her. "And I know your last name . . ."

"We won't tell him," Dirk said. "Look, I've got to shower and then I'll be right out." He took a few steps toward the locker room. "Don't go anywhere."

"Flee the scene of the crime, you mean?"

"Right," he said.

"I'll be here," she said.

Fifteen minutes later Dirk was opening the door of his car for Tori. A black Porsche. She slid in. It still had that new car smell to it.

Dirk got into the driver's side, turned on the car, and pulled out of the parking lot. "What?" he asked her. "You keep shaking your head."

"I was just thinking about all the times you gave me grief for being rich."

"I never gave you grief for being rich."

"Yes, you did. One time when we were all running, you shouted,

'Hey, Hampton, see if you can use your platinum cards to buy some speed.'"

"Leaders are supposed to motivate their followers."

"If I was the last one out of my cabin in the morning, you yelled, "Get your Diored butt out here."

"Again, that's leadership."

Tori ran her hand over the soft leather seat. "If you give me a hard time at camp next summer, I'm going to out you, rich boy."

"I never give you a hard time."

That wasn't even mildly close to the truth. After Tori and Jesse had started seeing each other, Dirk had ignored her for a solid week and then spent the next week looking for reasons to give her extra work. Jesse finally talked to him about it, and then after that she and Dirk had a truce, which eventually transformed back into a friendship. The last month of camp, Tori only sometimes caught the glimpses of anger Dirk felt about her choosing Jesse over him.

She supposed he had a right to be angry. On the second day of camp when Tori and Dirk discovered they were counterparts, Dirk kissed her. And Tori kissed him back. It was wrong of her, but in her defense, Dirk was gorgeous and an amazing kisser, and she was overwhelmed by the whole counterpart-suddenly-having-a-bond-with-him thing.

She told Dirk afterward that they shouldn't have done it. And really, she was sure even now that it was just his pride that had been hurt. He wasn't used to girls choosing his friends over him. Once Dirk kissed a girl, she probably followed him around mesmerized.

And even if Dirk's feelings for Tori had been more than just a passing whim—well, judging by his eating habits at La Niçoise Café—Dirk had gotten over her quickly.

Outside the car window, the manicured lawns of Winchester went by. Everything looked charmingly colonial. Orderly and safe. "Your mom and dad seem nice," Tori said.

"Stepmom and dad," Dirk corrected. "Bridget's my half sister."

"Oh." Tori wanted to ask if he always lived with his dad and where his mom was, but stopped herself. She wasn't supposed to ask identifying things about another Slayer's family.

Dirk glanced at her and must have sensed her curiosity. "My mom left my dad when I was six. From what I gather, it wasn't a real happy marriage before that. My dad told her she could leave and have a generous alimony, but I had to stay with him. I haven't heard from her since."

Tori let out an "oh" of condolence. "I'm sorry." She automatically reached out and put her hand on Dirk's knee, then dropped it away self-consciously. "Have you ever tried to talk to her?"

"I don't know where she is, and my dad doesn't like talking about her. He thinks we're better off without her." Dirk said the words evenly, casually. He was closing the subject.

"Do you want to find her? I could help if—"

"It's really not a big deal," Dirk cut her off. "I don't remember much about her."

"Part of you does," Tori said, keeping her gaze on him. "That's probably why you have such a hard time committing to relationships."

"What?" Dirk's gaze swung back to her. "Who said I have a hard time committing to relationships?"

"Well, I hear you bring a lot of different girls to La Niçoise."

Dirk turned his attention back to the road. "That doesn't mean I have commitment issues. Who have you been talking to, anyway?"

Tori glanced at the passing houses and the streetlamps standing sentinel along the road. She couldn't tell how close they were to downtown. "That reminds me, you're not taking me to La Niçoise, are you?" She gave Dirk a pointed look. "I can't go back to your restaurant. The waitresses already think I'm some pathetic summer fling who can't get over you."

A smile played at the corners of Dirk's lips. "Only the hostesses know about you. I had to come up with a reason I hadn't given you my phone number."

Only the hostesses knew about her? Dirk apparently had never realized how gossipy girls were. "Your family knows about me," Tori reminded him. "Do they call me fan girl, too?"

Dirk reached into his pocket and took out his phone. "This is why my family knows who you are." He turned it on and handed it to her. The background was a picture of her, snapped unaware. What's more, she could tell by the topaz studs in her ears it was a picture taken on her first day at camp. She hadn't worn jewelry after she started training.

Dirk had taken a picture of her before they even found out they were counterparts. That was a surprise. He had only seen her as the pampered new girl back then. "You have my picture?" she said, still staring at it. "We weren't allowed to take pictures of each other."

"Yeah, I don't think you're really in a position to lecture me about keeping rules."

"Probably not since I'm about to break another one." She dialed her phone number from his phone. Then, when her phone rang, she took it out of her purse and saved his number as a contact. She did the same for him on his phone. "Now we can text each other so your restaurant staff will stop thinking I'm a loser." Before putting her phone back in her purse, Tori took a picture of Dirk. It only seemed fair since he had one of her.

Dirk drove to the edge of Winchester, away from the homes and streetlamps. The only light now came from Dirk's headlights. "About the restaurant staff," he said slowly. "What else did they tell you about me?"

Against her better judgment, Tori flipped through the other pictures on Dirk's phone. The first was a picture Bridget had taken of herself making a goofy face. "They didn't tell me much. Just your last name and where you went to school." The next picture was a red-headed cheerleader, licking her lips. "And you know, the stuff about you being a womanizer."

Dirk made an unhappy grumbling sound. "It sounds like someone needs to be fired."

"Don't bother," Tori said. "I already knew that about you." The third photo showed the blonde cheerleader, puckering up for the camera.

"And how would you know that?"

"Please. I'm your counterpart. I can tell."

Dirk shook his head. "You don't know as much about me as you think you do."

"Oh. Well, maybe I figured it out from all of these pictures on your phone. You've got a whole cheerleading squad on here." The next photo showed a girl who'd held the camera at an angle to get as much cleavage as possible. "Wow. That one is really . . . um, interesting."

"What?" Dirk took the phone from Tori's hand and glanced at the picture. Sighing, he pushed the delete button. "I wish they'd stop stealing my phone."

Dirk turned off the road and drove up to a gated entrance. Although what it was an entrance to, Tori couldn't guess. From what she could make out, it looked like empty fields dotted with trees.

He rolled down his window and typed a pass code on a keypad. The metal gates slowly swung open and Dirk proceeded through.

"Where are we going?" Tori asked, craning to see through the darkness.

"My dad bought this land to develop into subdivisions. He's waiting until the market is better before he builds anything. Sometimes I like to come out here and look at the stars."

He pulled over to the side of the road, parked, and pushed a button that slid the cover off the car's sunroof. Then he leaned his seat back.

"The stars are brighter out here away from the city lights—just like they were at camp."

Tori looked out the sunroof. He was right. The stars were thick and brilliant out here, a bouquet of lights. She didn't lean her seat back. Instead she turned so she could see Dirk better. "You bring girls out here and use this as your own private make-out spot, don't you?"

Dirk put his hands behind his head and tilted his face to the night sky. "Nope. Your counterpart sense is failing you again. Or"—he grinned over at her—"were you suggesting activities?" He sat up and stretched lazily. "Fine, I'm game. Do you want music? Oh wait—you come complete with your own playlist, don't you?"

"Overdrake's playlist, not mine. That's what I came to talk to you about, actually." Funny, since she'd seen Dirk she hadn't paid attention to the sound in her mind. She'd completely blocked it out. Now she listened for it, let it grow louder. The music was there, an instrumental, with a soft, swaying beat. No animal shrieks. "I keep hearing things that sound like baby dragons—squawks, screeches, thumps. Are you sure you haven't seen anything odd—anything that might mean they've hatched?"

"That's why you tracked me down? To ask me about dragon sounds?" Instead of looking worried, Dirk grinned. "You already know what I said about that." He tilted his head down in mock offense. "You just came to see me because you wanted to make out, didn't you?"

He leaned toward her, only half teasing now. His lips would be on hers in a moment. She pushed him away. "This is serious. The noises don't sound like recordings. If the dragons have hatched, we need to get ready—to train more, to go get Ryker."

Dirk didn't return to his seat. He slid his hand on top of hers, caressing the skin there. "We don't know where Ryker is."

"I do. Well, I almost do. He's either in San Diego, Denver, or Crown Heights, New York. I'll know exactly where soon."

This stopped Dirk's advances. "How?"

"You can hide from a lot of people, but you still have to pay taxes."

Dirk nodded, impressed. "Let me know when you find him. I'll personally go talk to him."

"Dr. B should be the one to contact Ryker."

"Uh—that didn't work out so well last time. Ryker should hear about us from someone his own age, a team captain." Dirk intertwined his fingers with hers. "If only you knew how to get a hold of a captain . . . oh wait, you do." He leaned toward her again.

She put her hand on his chest to stop him. "The dragons," she said.

"Haven't hatched," he finished. "You know Overdrake likes to mess with your mind. That's what he's doing now. Besides, if the dragons were really screeching, they would send out electromagnetic pulses that would fry Overdrake's music system. Have the songs ever stopped for long periods?"

"No," she said, feeling foolish for not realizing this before. "I didn't think of that."

Dirk leaned over and let his lips brush across Tori's cheek. "You don't need to make up excuses to see me."

"I didn't," she said. She didn't push him away again, though. His lips made a trail across her cheek to her ear. Her breathing was suddenly unsteady. Sparks of emotion went off inside her. It felt warm and comfortable to have him so close. "We shouldn't do this," she said. She still didn't push him away.

Jesse hadn't wanted to see her, but Dirk did. And Dirk was handsome, and funny, and was sending electric waves of pleasure down her neck. Her hand tightened on his chest. How had she gone from pushing him away to clutching his shirt so quickly?

"You don't see anything out of the ordinary?" Tori asked, just to make sure.

"I see you." He ran his hand across the nape of her neck, tangling his fingers through her hair. "And when I shut my eyes, I still see you. I can't see anything else."

He didn't say more. His lips had found other things to do and she was too busy kissing him back to ask more questions. It was easy with Dirk, easy to abandon herself to this. He knew her so well, sensed what she wanted, didn't rush her. He made it seem like they had all the time in the world.

When Tori's sanity returned enough that she realized she needed to push herself away from him, she could barely speak. "Um . . . ," she said. "You should, um, take me back to my car."

Dirk kept his arms around her waist. "Not yet," he murmured. "I need to spend some time working on my commitment issues." He leaned in toward her again. "I think I can commit to this."

She laughed and pushed him away. "That's easy for you to say. You know you won't see me again until next summer."

"It doesn't have to be next summer." Dirk took her hand, intertwining his fingers with hers. "I'm not Jesse. I want to see you. We can work out something."

Dirk also knew what to say to make her want to stay. He was dangerous that way. He could use the whole counterpart thing to his advantage. He already had, kissing her like that.

"This is happening too fast," she said. "Us as a couple—that's something we need to think about."

He raised an eyebrow at her. "I assumed you were thinking about it while you were kissing me."

She blushed. "Well, okay, I was. But now I'm thinking about it logically and I think we need to take this slowly. Things will already be awkward between Jesse and me when we go back to camp. I don't want that to be you and me. I don't think I could stand it." She also couldn't stand to be hurt again. Every time she thought about Jesse, it still slashed her insides. The way Dirk went through girls—if she handed her heart to him now, she should expect to have it handed back to her in bleeding shards by Christmas.

Dirk groaned, but didn't argue the point. He scooted into the driver's seat and started the car. His jaw was clenched tight, his motions stiff and deliberate.

She held up her hands apologetically. "I've never been good at that let's-just-be-friends thing. I turn into the bitter ex-girlfriend. You don't want that. You'll end up sabotaging some mission in order to get rid of me."

Dirk put the car into drive and turned back toward the gate. "You know, Tori, I don't think I'm the one with commitment issues."

 CHAPTER 11

Instead of driving into his family's six-car garage, Dirk parked his Porsche behind the dragon enclosure. The car was an upgrade from the BMW that Kihawahine had trashed—his father's way of making a peace offering. Dirk walked past the security checkpoints and went inside to talk to his father. Dirk found him—right where he knew he would be—behind the soundproof glass looking into the nursery. That's what his father called the rooms the fledglings were kept in: the nursery. The rooms were small compared with the stadium-size enclosure their mother lived in—only four stories high and a hundred and fifty feet across. Enough room for the baby dragons to roam and fly a bit, but not soar. They couldn't go too far away.

"Like all children," his father had said when the two of them put the fledglings in these rooms, "dragons need to be taught obedience before they're given freedom." His father had looked pointedly at Dirk while he said this.

Dirk's father may have forgiven him for changing loyalties last summer, but he hadn't forgotten about it, and he wouldn't let Dirk forget about it, either.

Now his father stood in front of the partition that separated the dragons' rooms, checking messages on his phone. Jupiter, the male dragon, and Vesta, the female, were both resting, wings tucked around their bodies so they seemed to be nothing more than boulders. Fledglings were always grayish brown, sometimes with fuzzy patches of green that looked like moss. The camouflage kept them safe until they became bigger than anything that might attack them. In a few months their adult colors would come in: red, green, blue, or black.

Dirk's father heard him walk up and he looked over his shoulder. "Good. You're home. Now I can do something besides keep the dragons quiet." He gave Dirk an amused smile. "I trust you had fun on your date with Tori."

"You shouldn't have talked to her," Dirk said. "She could have recognized your voice."

"And if I had refused to talk to her—she wouldn't have thought *that* was suspicious?"

"You could have at least tried to hide your accent."

His father finished with his phone and slid it shut. "And then Bridget would have asked why I was talking oddly and drawn even more attention to my voice. The best way to hide something is to act as though you're not hiding anything. Ordinary people don't recognize a face if it's in an unexpected place, let alone a voice." He put his phone into his pocket with smug satisfaction. "Tori is as ordinary as everyone else."

Dirk didn't contradict his father. There was no point.

Inside the nursery, Jupiter opened his golden eyes, shook his head, and snapped his jaws. He was no longer connected to a dragon lord's thoughts telling him to rest, and apparently he didn't feel like resting anymore.

Babies of most species were cute. Nature had overlooked this trend when creating dragons. Hatchlings had loose, baggy skin that accommodated their quick growth spurts. Their mouths were proportionally too large, had to be in order to rip off the amount of flesh they ate. Later they would be beautiful. Sleek as birds, graceful as snakes, with scales that glistened like sunlight on water. Now they looked like a cross between a shar-pei and an overgrown crocodile.

Jupiter's eyes focused on Dirk. He opened his mouth, shrieking. Angry, not hungry. The remains of a cow still lay in the corner of the room.

The polycarbonate see-through wall was three inches thick, unbreakable for a dragon of this size. Dragons, however, were slow learners when it came to recognizing their limitations. Jupiter spread his wings, opened his mouth wide, and leapt. He slammed headfirst into the wall, righted himself with stumbling steps, then glared at Dirk and screeched again.

Jupiter probably would have kept at that for a while but he caught a scent from Vesta on the other side of the nursery. He turned in that direction and in an angry frenzy of flapping wings, threw himself at the wall that separated them. Which was why Dirk and his father had separated the dragons as soon as they'd hatched. A dragon lord had to work with dragons for months to overcome their immediate attack instinct, and even then, the beasts were unpredictable unless a dragon lord was connected to their minds and could guide their actions.

Dirk had reached into dragons' minds enough times to understand how they thought. Dragons had one goal—to rule their territory, undisputed. Any perceived threat to that goal resulted in claws and fire.

It was no wonder, really, that his father loved them. His mind worked in roughly the same way.

Dirk's father took hold of Jupiter's mind and the dragon immediately calmed. He swished his tail, sat down, and folded his wings. His eyelids closed in a sleepy daze.

When Dirk connected with the dragons, he thought of the power as a hand, one that held the dragon's head and firmly turned its thoughts in the direction it should go. His father's connection was like a spear. It shot into the dragon's brain and blocked all other input. His father was faster, more effective, more ruthless than Dirk was.

"So," his father said, "what brought your girlfriend out of hiding? Did she miss you?" He used the term "girlfriend" sarcastically, and yet Dirk liked hearing it. Whether she admitted it to herself or not, Tori had missed him.

"I put on some romantic mood music for you," his father went on. "I thought you would appreciate it."

Dirk did actually, but didn't say so. "Tori wanted to know if I'd seen anything that indicated the dragons had hatched. She's worried about the screeches she keeps hearing."

His father grunted. "I hope you didn't come here to tell me we need to keep them quiet. The only way that will happen is if one of us is here nonstop. And I'm too busy for that."

Dirk took a step closer to the enclosure. Vesta slept so soundly it didn't look like she was even breathing. "I told Tori the dragon lord was messing with her mind. If real dragons were screeching, they would send out electromagnetic pulses that would fry the stereo system. The music hasn't stopped, so the dragons aren't real."

Dirk's father let out an appreciative "ahh," the way he did when he admired his art collection or listened to a symphony blending together until it became a thing of perfection. "I've only been using the music to block out identifying sounds and here it's worked to ensure your lie is believable." He chuckled under his breath. "Dr. B doesn't know the EMP doesn't work until the dragons' vocal cords are bigger?"

"Apparently the medieval records left that out."

"And his traitor father must not have known about it."

Dr. B's father had worked as the cattle boss on the Overdrakes' plantation in St. Helena. That's how Dr. B had gotten most of his information. After his family fled the island, Dr. B's father told him every-thing he knew about dragons.

"To ignorance." Dirk's father held up his hand as though offering a toast. "And the never-ending supply of it this nation has. It works in our favor again."

Dirk didn't say anything. He couldn't celebrate the fact that he had just lied to Tori. It was for the best, he knew. He had saved her from being freaked out every time she heard a screech. Eventually, though, she would know the truth. All the Slayers would. Dr. B—who trusted Dirk as much as he trusted his own daughter—he would know that Dirk had been a traitor all along, a bomb waiting to go off. The thought made Dirk feel like he'd swallowed acid.

"Oh, come on," his father said, turning away from the nursery wall. "Tori is pretty, but not nearly as pretty as power." His father walked past the desk where the vets recorded their data and went to the cupboards filled with medical equipment. Well, mostly medical equipment. One held liquor and glasses. "The White House has one hundred thirty-two rooms, thirty-five bathrooms, a swimming pool, a movie theater, and its own bowling alley. I don't even bowl, but I'm going to use it, anyway."

His father took out a bottle of red wine and poured himself a drink. "Take extra care that the dragons don't damage anything in the building when we attack. You can destroy the president, but not the rose garden."

Cassie, Dirk's stepmom, had banished most of the alcohol from the house. She couldn't drink it now that she was pregnant. She was almost three months along—had gotten pregnant after the Slayers' attempted break-in last summer. She said she hoped it was a boy this time. Dirk didn't have to ask why. The threat was implicit. When his father at-tacked a city, he needed another dragon lord to help him control the dragons. If Dirk didn't cooperate, before long he'd be expendable.

His father poured a small amount of wine into a glass. Alcohol didn't affect a dragon lord's abilities like it did a Slayer's, but his father hardly ever drank much. He didn't want to dull his mind or cloud his reasoning. He liked to have a tight control of everything, including himself. He swished the dark liquid around to release its scent. "There's no shortage of pretty girls," his father said, refusing to let the subject of Tori go.

"You promised you wouldn't hurt her," Dirk reminded him. Dirk had already had more than one talk with his father on that subject.

His father kept swishing his glass. "Your mother was stunning. Absolutely gorgeous. But when she couldn't appreciate my vision for the future, I had to let her go. It hurt. I don't mind admitting it. It was a year before I could even entertain the idea of trusting someone enough to start another relationship." He took a slow drink. "And now I have Cassie. A beautiful woman who's my partner in every way. Eventually, when you're old enough, that's what you'll need. A partner, not a rival."

Dirk didn't like hearing about his mother. Not this way—with his father using her as an object lesson of failure. It made him wonder what she had to say on the subject of her ex-husband and son. Was she telling some other child about Dirk as if he were an experiment that didn't turn out right?

Dirk's father took another sip of wine. "I'm going to take this country from the ashes of its own impotent uselessness, and I'll make it great again." He gestured with his glass, emphasizing his point. "What the people need is a decisive leader, one that demands respect. I'll be that leader, and"—he favored Dirk with a meaningful nod—"I'll train you to take the reins the same way I taught you to ride dragons."

This was probably not the best analogy his father could have used. The first time Dirk rode Kihawahine solo, he slipped from the saddle during a backward dive. In his confusion, he broke his mind link with the dragon. She nearly ate him before he could get control of her again. Still Dirk nodded back at his father. His father wanted to fix the country's problems: the corruption, the gridlock, the staggering debts Congress had amassed that would bankrupt the people. The country's real problems came from 535 self-invested people in Congress, trying to lead the nation. What it needed was someone who could get things done.

Dirk's response must not have been enthusiastic enough. His father walked over to him, an unsaid tsking hanging on his words. "You worry too much. This revolution will be mild compared to others." He made a motion with his hand like a broom sweeping away little puffs of concern. "I won't have to destroy many cities before the people agree to my terms. The burning buildings, the dragons wiping out a few military combatants, my men marching through the streets—that's all for show. Once the fighting is over, the people will realize they're better off."

Dirk's father leaned in to him, sniffed, then pulled back. "You smell like perfume. Must have been an interesting talk you had with Tori."

Dirk rolled his eyes like it didn't matter. "Interesting enough."

His father finished his drink and put his cup on the desk. His gaze on Dirk was crisp now, penetrating. "I know you couldn't help becoming friends with the Slayers at camp. It's only natural that you don't want to hurt them. That's why I'm doing things the way I am. You have to cooperate this time, though. You can't switch sides when your friends are in danger. If they don't lose their memories now, they'll lose their lives later."

"I know." It would be better if his friends couldn't fight, better if their Slayer thoughts and experiences faded away like smoke from a fire that had been put out. They would be safer that way. "But leave Tori out of it. Don't drug her." Any dose of drugs that was strong enough to cause unconsciousness always carried the risk of permanent brain damage or death for Slayers. That's how Dr. B's younger brother was killed. When Dirk's grandfather found out the kid was a Slayer, he drugged him and ended up killing him.

"We have to drug Tori." Dirk's father looked upward and his voice took on a weary tone as though he was already tired of arguing this fact. "She's the most dangerous Slayer to us."

"She's not a Slayer," Dirk said. "You know as well as I do that she's a dragon lord. You practically told her she could fly before she knew it herself. Drugging her won't do any good."

Dirk and his father had disagreed about the subject before. Tori flew, heard what the nearest dragon to her heard, and didn't burn. Last summer she'd been hit with a fireball that seared though her jacket and shirt but only left a red mark on her shoulder. Dragon lord qualities.

The evidence that she wasn't a dragon lord, however, was equally strong. Girls were almost never dragon lords. The only female dragon lords ever recorded were so far back in history that they might have only been fiction—might have been the creation of disgruntled dragon lord sisters who wanted a heroine who could do what they couldn't.

Tori seemed to have Slayer instincts. She wasn't drawn to dragons, she feared them. And equally as telling, her powers faded when the rest of the Slayers did. Dragon lord powers lasted longer. Dirk could be away from the dragons for hours and still fly.

Dirk's father held up a hand as though conceding a point. "All right—Tori might be some sort of Slayer and dragon lord hybrid. I talked it over with a few of the scientist ilk and they think girls might actually inherit dragon lord powers but are—for whatever reason—unable to access them. Those powers are like an underground river. There, but unreachable.

"Because Tori is also a Slayer, her brain made new pathways, developed new abilities and those pathways cut right into the underground river of dragon lord powers. That's why her powers fade at the same time the Slayers powers do. So"—Overdrake clapped his hands together as though he were at the start of a new project—"if we destroy the Slayer pathways in her brain, her dragon lord powers will probably disappear at the same time. Problem solved."

The theory made sense. It explained everything. Even the long-ago female dragon lords. They could have been dragon lord–Slayer hybrids, too. And yet Dirk still didn't like the idea of drugging Tori. Dragon lords didn't react to drugs like Slayers did, which meant his father might have to give her larger and larger doses as he tried to blot out her memories.

"She's not a threat to us," Dirk said. "She's only had one summer of training and doesn't know anything about controlling dragons' minds. She doesn't even know she can do it. And even if she could do it, she couldn't take control of our dragons during a fight."

Once a dragon lord was inside a dragon's mind, it was somewhere between difficult and nearly impossible for another dragon lord to enter the same dragon's mind and give it instructions. By the time Jupiter and Vesta were full grown, they would be so used to taking instructions from Dirk and his father that they would do it without resistance. Entering their minds would be like walking down a familiar road, something that didn't take much concentration. Tori wouldn't have that advantage.

"That doesn't mean," Dirk's father said stiffly, "that Tori can't break in here some other time and steal a dragon, or worse—turn it on us. Do you really think she won't figure out that you're my son after the rest of the Slayers are neutralized?"

"She won't if you do the job right."

"And then what?" His father raised a hand in frustration. "I hate to put a damper on your romance but I think she'll realize something is wrong when she shows up to fight the dragons and sees you riding one of them."

"She's my counterpart," Dirk said. "I can change her mind about the rest. I can make her understand about the revolution."

His father rubbed his forehead and groaned. "Why do you insist on making this harder than it is?"

"Don't drug her. I don't want her to lose her abilities." He didn't want her to lose her memories. He wanted Tori to remember that she sought him out tonight, that she kissed him, and that while her arms were wrapped around him, they were perfectly in sync.

"Your counterpart," his father muttered. "She's your enemy, and by this point, one of you should realize that."

Vesta lifted her head, saw Dirk, and opened her mouth. Probably shrieking. She stood—her back arched—and readied herself to pounce. It made Dirk miss Tamerlane. Dirk had grown up with that dragon, had spent so many years training him, that Tamerlane knew him by sight. Tamerlane had stopped challenging Dirk when he came into his enclosure. He'd been downright domesticated for a dragon.

These dragons would keep trying to attack him for months—at least until they were full grown. Dirk's father cast a look at Vesta, and then turned and headed toward the door. "If you want the dragons to stay quiet for Tori, you'll have to keep them quiet yourself."

Dirk quickly slipped into Vesta's mind and murmured assurances to her. Everything was fine. She was sleepy. She needed to rest. "When are you attacking the Slayers?" Dirk called after his father. He was nearly to the door.

His father paused, considered. He hadn't given those details to Dirk before. In fact, he'd pointedly told Dirk he wouldn't tell him. *Just in case you're tempted to double-cross me again and warn your friends*, he'd said.

Dirk finished calming Vesta. "Tori told me she's close to finding

Ryker's location. He's either in San Diego, Denver, or Crown Heights, New York."

Dirk's father smiled. "That's good to know. I'll have some men check those locations."

"You'll want to wait until after we find Ryker to attack the Slayers," Dirk said. "Otherwise you'll have to find a way to take him out, too. It will be harder once he knows you're coming after Slayers."

Dirk's father rested his hand on the doorknob while he weighed these words. "The dragons will be ready to attack by this spring." That was another way ignorance was helping them. Dr. B thought it took a year until the dragons were full grown; it was closer to six months. "Some of the Slayers might evade my men during the first attack so I need time for a second, maybe a third or a fourth."

Dirk wasn't sure why he wanted his father to postpone the attack on the Slayers. No, that wasn't right, he did know. Years of going to camp had turned him into a Slayer. During the summer, days would go by when he would completely forget that he was a spy, a traitor. He didn't just pretend to be a team captain, he was one. He trained, fought, and strategized with the other Slayers. Sometimes that part of him still surfaced. That part always hoped that if he delayed the inevitable, it wouldn't happen.

"You shouldn't drug the Slayers until we're ready to attack," Dirk said. "Otherwise Dr. B might find a way to restore their powers."

The loss was reversible, or at least the stories the dragon lords passed down said it was. Given enough time away from the effects of drugs, the pathways in a Slayer's brain could regrow—the abilities and memories could flow through new passageways again.

It didn't usually happen. If a person didn't remember they had to abstain from alcohol and other drugs, they didn't. And those pathways were eventually completely destroyed.

According to the old stories, Slayers could regain their powers in another way, something fast. In the Middle Ages, there were accounts of fights where a dragon lord thought he had neutralized Slayer knights—only to have them flare back into battle, their powers restored.

Dirk's father opened the door, then turned back to him. "Isn't Dr. B already looking for a remedy? He must want to help Leo and Danielle."

Leo and Danielle were two Slayers who lost their powers and most of their camp memories sometime before last summer. The ironic thing was that they did it to themselves. Both started drinking. They must have turned into quite the partiers since at some point they'd drunk themselves unconscious.

Dirk shrugged as though it weren't important. "If Dr. B was looking for a cure, he never told us about it. He thinks he has enough Slayers to do the job." This was only partially true. Dr. B was searching for a cure. All summer, his office was littered with books and printouts, old documents he scoured for clues. But he also thought the Slayers left were capable of killing dragons. That was one of Dr. B's problems: He always thought people were better than they really were.

Dirk's father mused on that for a moment. He seemed to know why Dirk wanted him to hold off the attack. He smiled coldly. "Within a month, my men will drug the Slayers. I'll tell them to take out Jesse first—my gift to you. Less competition for Tori."

Dirk stared at his father, unsure how he meant the statement. Did his father really think Dirk wanted his best friend in the Slayers attacked first—that Dirk would appreciate having Jesse out of the way? Or was his father being sarcastic? Did he know how much losing Jesse's friendship meant to Dirk and that's why Jesse was first on the list?

Dirk supposed the fact that he didn't know the answer to these questions said something about his father. "When?" Dirk asked. "When will it happen?"

His father just nodded vaguely. "You don't need to worry about that." He turned and walked out of the room, leaving Dirk alone.

So, his father was setting plans in motion, but he didn't trust Dirk enough to give him details. Even if Dirk wanted to warn the Slayers, he couldn't have told them anything except to be careful. And they already knew they were supposed to be doing that.

CHAPTER 12

Over the next few weeks Tori and Dirk texted each other every day. He addressed her as C, for "counterpart." Tori called Dirk G for "glasses." It was her own code name for him because he had four eyes in his head. His and a dragon's.

It probably shouldn't have made her day—seeing the letter G pop up on her screen, but it always did. It wasn't just because he was good-looking, knew her inside out, and could make her laugh anytime he wanted. Talking to him was a reminder that the secret part of her was real, that it had all happened, that she wasn't alone in carrying the burden of being a Slayer. And it was sweet the way he always checked up on her, the way he worried about her safety.

When he found and friended her on an online social site, she felt only a twinge of guilt accepting him. She didn't post identifying information so there wasn't really any harm in it.

Tori's dad came home one night and handed her a slip of paper. "If anyone asks, you didn't get this from me." It had Ryker's address on it. He lived in Rutland, Vermont.

"Vermont?" she asked.

"Turns out none of those other Allen and Harriet Davises were the right one. Ryker's father's name is actually Charles Allen Davis. Don't ask how many staff hours it took to figure that out."

After Tori finished hugging her dad, she locked herself in her bedroom and used her watch-phone to call Dr. B. She was too excited to sit down. She paced back and forth, a bounce of happiness in each step.

"I know where Chameleon is," she said, as soon as Dr. B answered. Chameleon was Ryker's code name because he'd hidden for so many years. She knew Dr. B wouldn't want her to give his address over the phone so she said, "I'll overnight the address to you."

Dr. B made all the Slayers memorize his P.O. box number in case they ever had something Slayer-related to send him. Tori folded the paper carefully so she could put it in an envelope. She had already memorized Ryker's address and now it was scrolling on her heart with looping, triumphant script. "I recommend the team captains go with you to meet Chameleon," she said. "It will be easier for him to believe everything if he sees us in action. And since I'm going to be a team captain one day, I think I should—"

"T-Bird," Dr. B interrupted her. "We have to proceed carefully." He let out a reluctant sigh. "Perhaps I should have told everyone this before now." There was a pause, one that clearly didn't understand her impatience. "Chameleon contacted me over the summer."

"He what?" She didn't think she'd heard right and turned up the volume on her watch.

"He confronted his parents about the website." The Slayers knew about the Ryker Davis website. Theo had even mentioned that it had consistent hits, but there was no way to know who was reading it. They had all figured it wasn't Ryker, or he would have commented, contacted Dr. B, done something.

"Unfortunately," Dr. B continued, "His parents forbade him to communicate with me. Chameleon won't be able to train with the rest of you until he's eighteen. Then he'll come."

"Eighteen," Tori repeated. She was one of the younger Slayers. She didn't turn seventeen until January. But even the older Slayers like Jesse, Dirk, and Bess didn't turn eighteen until nearly the summer. "By then it might be too late."

"Let's hope not," Dr. B said.

"One of us should go meet with him. If we could convince him—"

"He called me from a disposable cell phone and told me not to contact him again. He doesn't want to talk to us, and I can't force anyone to join us."

Pinprick words. Ones that deflated her. Tori didn't know what to say. It hadn't occurred to her that Ryker might refuse to even talk to them.

"I didn't tell everyone about Chameleon's phone call," Dr. B went on, "because I didn't want anyone to hold it against him—that he knew what he was and didn't come." Dr. B waited for Tori to say something. When she didn't he added, "You won't hold it against him, will you? We can't expect him to run away from home."

Yes, they could. If it meant saving lives, why shouldn't he leave home a few months early?

She stayed silent, let the words seethe inside her head.

"Tori, sometimes it takes time for people to realize who they are."

More pinpricking words, this time stabbing her with guilt. Dr. B was reminding her, in his ever gentle way, that she hadn't wanted to be a Slayer when she first found out what she was. "I won't hold it against him," Tori said slowly. She would give him the benefit of the doubt, at least until camp started next year. If he didn't show up by then, she would personally take a trip to Vermont and have a long talk with him about patriotism while dragging him from his house.

"It's best not to tell the others about this," Dr. B said, "so keep it a secret."

"Okay," she said with a sigh. Dr. B was right. The other Slayers had barely forgiven her for leaving camp one day to repair fireball damage to her hair. They weren't going to forgive Ryker for skipping out an entire year—for waiting until it might be too late—to show up to camp.

The next day she sent the address to Dr. B anyway. She hoped Ryker didn't change his mind and disappear again.

A few days later, Dirk asked her if she'd learned anything about Ryker's location. She hesitated, then texted back. "My dad ran into dead ends." She didn't like lying to him, but really, Dirk would be Ryker's biggest tormenter if he knew the truth. Last summer, Dirk routinely had Kody freeze Bess' belongings into giant ice cubes—and he and Bess were friends.

So Tori would let Ryker stay hidden for a while longer. As long as the eggs hadn't hatched, the Slayers still had time left.

CHAPTER 13

Jesse sat in front of a computer in the White Oak Library and wished his mother wasn't his Honors English teacher. Seriously, the woman assigned essay topics just to pry into his life. This one was on leadership and what sort of qualities the next president should have. "The election is only a year away," she had told the class cheerily, "and most of you will be of voting age by then. You need to start paying attention to the candidates' messages."

The class was supposed to write about issues that were important to them, and then list the candidates' views on those issues, citing at least three references such as newspapers, transcripts, or magazines in the bibliography. A freaking bibliography. It was enough to make Jesse miss the essays from last year where he only had to do things like talk about the symbolism in *The Scarlet Letter*.

But no. His mom had noticed him following news stories about Senator Hampton's campaign and she was afraid he was defecting. She was such a Democrat that she'd had a donkey tattooed on her rear during some protest in college. Not after the protest, not before—during. Must have been a really boring protest if tattoo artists had been milling around selling their services.

Jesse could have told his mom that politics had nothing to do with his interest in Senator Hampton. Jesse was only looking for Tori. Sometimes she was there in the pictures. Sometimes the camera panned to her during one of his speeches.

Jesse had put off writing the essay because reading political speeches was the most boring thing on earth. Unfortunately, the paper was due on Monday and his mom had already told him no paper—no Halloween party. So he was spending his Saturday afternoon flipping through stuff in the library.

He picked up one of the newsmagazines and skimmed through an article on presidential hopefuls, looking for some concise, bullet-point lists about where they stood on the issues. No such luck. Ditto for the next magazine. And the next.

Jesse grunted, dropped the pile of magazines next to the computer, and wrote the title of his essay.

What I Did This Summer and How It Relates to Politics

This summer I went to camp with Senator Hampton's
daughter. Even though camp has a strict rule against
pairing off, we did. A lot. No guy who has ever seen Tori
Hampton would blame me. I have no idea where her
father stands on this issue.

Jesse deleted the paragraph almost as soon as he wrote it. He considered calling Tori on his watch-phone, asking her about her father's views on a few issues, and then writing his paper about why he agreed with those things. It would make his bibliography much easier. Primary source all the way.

Dr. B wouldn't approve of Jesse using the emergency channels for homework questions, and besides, Tori was probably still mad at him.

Jesse minimized his paper and went back to his Internet search of the candidates.

"Dude, are you still stalking that Hampton chick?"

Jesse only knew someone was walking up behind him a few seconds before he heard his friend Diego's voice. Not a good thing and more proof he should stop obsessing about Tori. Part of being a Slayer was having heightened senses. It never really wore off, even after being away from the simulator for months. People usually weren't able to sneak up on him.

"I'm not stalking anybody," Jesse said. "I'm researching Senator Hampton's political positions."

Diego sat down in the chair next to him and leaned closer to the computer. A picture of Tori and her sister, Aprilynne, was framed on the screen. Some posh fund-raiser. Tori wore a dress that showed off her long, well-defined legs. "Right," Diego said with a laugh. "I doubt those are the positions you're thinking about."

"Shut up," Jesse said. He exited out of the screen. Another one of Tori was underneath it. In this one, she stood with the rest of her family at a convention.

Diego shook his head. "Bro, she's way out of your league. Besides, you shouldn't even think about messing with girls whose fathers can set the secret service on you."

"Yeah, yeah." Jesse noticed a man in a suit cross the room. The man looked at Jesse, watching him for a couple seconds longer than was normal. When Jesse glanced at him, he awkwardly looked away. The man walked over to an empty chair on the other side of the room and self-consciously fingered the book he was holding. Jesse kept staring at the guy, maybe because Diego's comment made him wonder if Senator Hampton really would send somebody to check out Jesse. Did Tori's father know they had gotten together at camp?

Jesse dismissed the thought. Tori wouldn't have told her parents about him, and even if she had, she couldn't have given them his last name. She didn't know it.

The man in the suit held his book open, staring at it as if he was reading it. One hand was hidden behind the book, and Jesse could tell from the shivers of movement in the man's wrist that he had his cell phone out and was texting someone.

Weird.

"So what brings you to the library?" Jesse asked Diego.

"Same thing as you. Finding some BS for your mom's essay. I hate to say it, bro—especially since the woman has given me more cookies than my own mother—but this year, I seriously hate your mom."

"Join the club. Oh wait, you already did. It's called Honors English."

Diego pulled his car keys from his pocket, proof that his ancient Camry had made it through yet another day. "You got a costume for Bailey's party yet?"

"Right now, I'll be the invisible man. I can't go until my paper is done."

"Just write some crap about Senator Ethington. That's what I did. Your mom wants him to be the next president. Easy A."

None of Jesse's As from his mom were easy. Still, Diego was right. His mom was always more forgiving of sentence structure when she agreed with your topic. "I've got my iPad in my backpack," Diego said. "You can work on your paper while I drive home. You gotta come with me tonight. You're my babe magnet." Diego motioned to Jesse and then to himself. "They come over to talk to you, yes, but I'm by your side to pick off the leftovers. I'm fine with that."

"That's sort of . . . what's the right Honors English vocab term?"

"Cunningly resourceful?"

"No . . . lame."

Jesse exited out of the last screen and stood up. He might as well go. He wasn't going to get anything done here. Not with pictures of

Tori one click on a search engine away. Jesse noticed as he picked up his backpack that the man in the suit stood up, too. He carried his book in one hand, holding on to it oddly—like he was concealing something in the pages. Another guy who had just come into the computer area turned and sauntered slowly in the direction of the door. He wore a hoodie pulled up so it concealed half of his face.

It set Jesse's nerves on edge, the two of those guys walking the same direction. It was probably nothing. Coincidence. Still he kept track of both guys out of the corner of his eye.

Jesse had heard that dogs could smell fear. Slayers could, too. Their senses picked up on someone's tension, adrenaline, rise in sweat, breathing, and heart rate before they attacked. A Slayer might not consciously realize what was happening, but his instincts would kick in, warning him that something was wrong and he needed to be on guard.

It was happening to Jesse now. He immediately calculated the area around him, looking for weapons and exit routes. He zipped up his leather jacket. It was thick enough that it would offer some protection against knives. He slipped his backpack on his shoulders. It would be hard to fight with it on, but it shielded his back.

Jesse noticed an oversize, thick book lying on top of a shelf. He picked it up as he went by, holding on to it tightly. Diego had been talking about his costume. He glanced over to see what Jesse had grabbed. "'*Mothers of Faith*,'" he read from the title. "What do you need that for? Are you going to dress up as your mother for the party?" Diego snorted. "That would be funny. You could pass out failing grades to everyone."

The guy in the hoodie slowed his walk so that Jesse would catch up with him. The man in the suit quickened his pace. In a few seconds, Jesse and Diego would be flanked by the strangers.

Who were these guys?

"Are you actually going to check it out?" Diego asked, gesturing at the book.

"I forgot something." Jesse turned sharply and walked toward the nearest shelf. That way, if the men attacked him, they wouldn't be able to do it from both sides at once.

As Jesse walked, he flipped a button on his watch that erased the time and turned the face into a mirror. He kept his back to the men, letting them think he wasn't paying attention. Jesse reached for a hardback on the highest shelf, a George Washington biography. He checked the watch reflection as he did. From the sound of the men's footsteps, Jesse knew where each man was, where Diego was, too. The mirror let him see what the men were doing with their hands.

The guy in the hoodie realized Jesse wasn't heading toward the door anymore, and turned back around to see where he was. The man in the suit paused, then swiveled toward Jesse and lifted his hand. Whatever he'd concealed in his book was now pointed at Jesse's neck.

Jesse spun around. He simultaneously flung the Washington biography at the man's head and lifted the thick *Mothers of Faith* book in front of his neck to block the fire.

The man in the suit got off a shot. Not a bullet, thankfully. A small dart struck the center of the book cover. Then the biography slapped into the man's face. His head snapped back, and he let out a yell of surprise. He took a stumbling step backward, and the book that had covered his gun fell to the floor.

Jesse didn't have time to follow through on his attack. The hoodie guy pulled a gun from his sweatshirt, aiming it at Jesse. Again, at his neck. Must be another dart gun, or the guy would have gone for his chest. These had to be Overdrake's men. They'd come to drug him, not kill him.

Jesse rushed toward the guy, swinging the book up to shield his neck as he did. The shot went off and another dart embedded itself in the cover. Two steps later, Jesse kicked the gun from the assailant's hand. He followed that move with a roundhouse kick into the guy's chest. The man let out a muffled yell, which was nowhere near as loud as Diego's startled exclamation.

Diego stood about ten feet away, staring wide-eyed at the scene. Jesse didn't have time to do more than glance at his friend. The man in the suit was facing Jesse again. A trickle of blood ran down the man's nose, and a red spot over his eye was already turning into a welt. He pointed his gun at Jesse's legs. The determined scowl on the man's face told Jesse that if he missed this time, he'd use his fists.

Instead of trying to swing the book low to protect his legs, Jesse sprinted up the bookshelf in front of him, using it like a ladder. Books spit from the shelves, spilling everywhere. When Jesse neared the top, he pushed off, swung his arms, and backflipped through the air—still holding the book out like a shield. On the way down, his legs slammed into the man in the suit. The stranger's arms flailed, then he crumpled onto the floor.

The guy in the hoodie retrieved his gun, but by this time, the people in the library noticed what was going on. A teenage girl yelled, "They've got guns!"

The panic was instantaneous. Almost in unison, the crowd by the checkout stand turned and rushed toward the library doors. Mothers grabbed their children. People pushed to get ahead of one another. A couple of kids screamed.

The hoodie guy paled and swore. He realized he wasn't going to have an easy time getting through the stampede he just created. Without firing another shot, he turned and ran toward the door.

This only increased the level of screaming from the crowd.

The man in the suit still lay on the floor by Jesse's feet. His gun had fallen and lay next to some scattered books. Jesse reached down to grab hold of the man's shirt. The guy wasn't going anywhere until Jesse found out how Overdrake had located him and what else he knew.

Jesse wasn't fast enough. With one swift move, the man kicked Jesse's feet out from underneath him. Jesse fell to the ground, knocking into the bookshelf as he did. A couple more books thunked onto the floor.

Irritating.

Jesse turned to grab the man again. The guy had gotten to his feet, was out of reach and about to sprint to the front door. Jesse went for the gun on the floor, yelling to Diego, "Stop him!"

Diego stared at Jesse, hands raised in disbelief like he'd just told him to cut off a limb. The man dashed by Diego unhindered.

Useless. You'd think after all those war video games Diego played, he would be better in a fight.

Suit man ran toward the door—along with everyone else on the floor. Jesse picked up the dart gun, only hesitating for a moment because he knew he was wiping the man's prints off and adding his own. The police wouldn't need the guy's prints. They would have the entire guy.

Jesse glanced over the gun, taking a few seconds to figure out how to fire it. He would get in trouble for shooting it. The police stopped considering shots self-defense when your attacker was fleeing. Didn't matter, though.

A bottleneck had formed at the doors, people shoving to get outside. The book scanners in front of the doors let off shrill beeps of protest.

Jesse didn't have to hurry to catch up with Overdrake's men. They were caught in the crowd. That's what happened when you got too eager to make a shot. The men should have waited until Jesse was outside so they could get away without any problems.

Jesse aimed at the man in the hoodie first. The guy had nearly shoved his way through the crowd to get to the door. It was a tricky shot and Jesse didn't have a feel for this gun's timing. The last thing he wanted was to hit a bystander—or worse, a child. He didn't know what was in these darts. It could even be poison.

Jesse heard Diego striding up to him, but didn't worry about it. Diego was a friend not a threat. Which was why Jesse didn't move out of the way before Diego hit the gun out of his hand.

"Are you crazy?" Diego demanded. "You can't shoot into a crowd."

Jesse went for the gun again, knowing as he did it would probably be too late. It wasn't just a matter of aiming anymore. He would have to get away from Diego in order to shoot.

"Now?" Jesse growled. "Now, when I'm trying to stop the bad guys, you spring into action? Where were you when I needed you to tackle that guy?" Jesse picked up the gun and scanned the crowd.

It was too late. The hoodie guy was gone and the man in the suit was disappearing out the door.

Diego held out both hands, left them there hanging in the air. "You don't tackle armed hoods!" He waved his hands for emphasis. "What's with you? Suddenly you're flipping from shelves and flinging—put down the gun!"

Jesse thought about sticking around until the police showed up. What could the police do, though, except ask Jesse a lot of questions he couldn't answer? He slid the gun into his jacket pocket. No point leaving it here when it had his prints on it. Besides, if the police wanted to investigate, they could look at the darts. Two of them still stuck out of the *Mothers of Faith* book.

"Let's go," Jesse said. He strode toward the door and Diego went with him, looking over his shoulder nervously as though there might be more crazed gunmen hiding out in the nonfiction section.

Jesse picked up his pace. He had to get somewhere private so he could call Dr. B and report the attack. He had to decide what to tell his parents. He had to figure out if his home and school were safe for him now.

Somehow, Overdrake had found him.

CHAPTER 14

Dirk held a sword in one hand and *shuriken* in the other. Should he play the part of pirate or ninja for Halloween? Maybe he should go to the party as a normal teenage boy. That was a costume in and of itself.

On second thought, drunk guys and weapons were a bad combination, and there were bound to be a lot of drunk guys at the party. Half the football team was coming. Dirk put both of the weapons back in his closet and went to the kitchen to get something to eat.

Even though it was only three in the afternoon, Cassie was at the stove cutting up vegetables for stir-fry. Chicken strips sizzled in a nearby pan. It was early for dinner. She must have decided to get the meal and trick-or-treating done quickly so she could put Bridget to bed as soon as possible. Cassie felt sickest at nighttime—pregnancy stuff. Dirk didn't ask much about it.

Bridget stood by the island, bouncing on the balls of her feet, a bundle of impatient energy. She was already wearing her cat ears and a leopard-spotted dress. When she saw him, her voice went pouty, accusing. "You're supposed to go trick-or-treating with me."

"I will." Dirk took an apple out of the fruit bowl. Cassie couldn't yell at him for eating before dinner if it was something healthy. "We've got to wait until later. It's not even close to dark yet." His party didn't start until nine and Bridget would be tired by seven, seven thirty tops.

Bridget's expression didn't change. "Mom says you won't take me. She says Nora has to, and I don't want to go with her." Nora was the fifty-year-old housekeeper who didn't have much patience for children, especially if they were the messy variety.

"I can take you," Dirk said, biting into his apple.

Cassie kept cutting up the bok choy. Her knife thwacked in rhythm with her words. "You won't have time, and I can't do it. I already want to go lay down."

Bridget leaned her elbows on the island. "Why can't Daddy take me?"

"Daddy is busy tonight."

"I'll have time," Dirk said.

"No, you won't," Cassie said blandly.

Bridget folded her arms with a humph. "I hope when he gets here, our baby brother will go trick-or-treating with me."

"Our baby brother?" Dirk repeated, turning to look at Cassie.

She pushed the bok choy to the edge of the cutting board and smiled. "Didn't your father tell you? We found out from the doctor yesterday. It's a boy."

Dirk didn't let any emotion show on his face. He wasn't even sure what emotion he felt. A brother. Another dragon lord. Maybe Dirk's replacement if he stepped out of line. "Cool," he said. "That's what you wanted."

Cassie kept smiling, self-satisfied.

"I wanted a sister," Bridget reported to no one in particular. "I wanted to put insy-winsy bows in her hair."

That's when the alarm on Dirk's watch beeped. It was the

stuttering sound of a warning. The face read, "Code 2." One of the Slayers had been attacked. No backup needed. It was an alert for the rest of them to be cautious.

The message had come from Jaybird. Jesse.

So whoever Dirk's father had sent hadn't managed to drug Jesse. Dirk felt a smug sense of triumph about that. The Slayers weren't as easy to take down as his father supposed. And now everyone else would be watching for danger.

The triumph didn't last long. This wouldn't be the end of it. His father would only move on to his second plan.

Cassie pulled a couple carrots onto the cutting board and sliced through them with a forceful chop. "I told you that you wouldn't have time."

Dirk stared at her and felt his stomach sink. It was here. The time he'd been dreading. The part he didn't want to play—traitor.

# CHAPTER 15

When Tori got the warning alert on her watch, she was dressed in a Supergirl costume and standing in a large, decorated conference room at the George Washington University Hospital. Her father and his staff were putting on a Halloween party for the children there. The Supergirl costume was her own private joke. She was a flying superhero now. She might as well get the cape and shiny red boots to match.

A look at her watch codes told her Jesse had been attacked. Jesse, who was always so careful; Jesse, who wouldn't even give *her* any of his contact information. How was it possible that Overdrake found him?

She stared at her watch, worry mixing with fear in her stomach. Not for herself—her father had secret service agents in the building. Over- drake's men wouldn't get in here unless they were less than five feet tall and wore medical ID bands around their wrists. She wanted to call Jesse, needed to hear his voice to reassure herself that he was all right.

That wasn't procedure. She was only supposed to use her phone if she had something to report, not to check up on people. Besides, Dr. B was probably talking to Jesse right now and she shouldn't interrupt.

The desire to call didn't go away. She stared at her watch so long that Aprilynne texted her, "We're not even halfway through the party yet. Suck it up."

Tori and Aprilynne were running the fishing booth. It was a five-foot-tall screen, decorated with happy-looking fish frolicking through turquoise waves. Tori was sitting behind the screen next to piles of toys. On the other side, Aprilynne—dressed in a stunning Snow White costume—handed out fishing poles to the line of waiting children. Tori clipped stuffed animals on the hook for the little kids, books or games for the older ones.

It was impossible not to notice that these children weren't well. They didn't move with the same frenzied intensity that regular kids had on Halloween. Some were attached to IV poles. A couple sat in wheelchairs. The room smelled bleakly sterile.

Tori didn't answer Aprilynne's text. She stopped staring at her watch, stopped waiting for more information to appear on its face.

A moment later her cell phone vibrated. She pulled it from her pocket and saw a text from Dirk. "Are you okay?"

"Yes," she texted back. "Do you know what happened?"

Since Dirk was a captain, Dr. B gave him more information than he gave the rest of the Slayers. After a moment, he wrote her back. "Some guys came after Jaybird with a dart gun. Be extra careful today. Stay home."

Too late for that. She had to attach toys to fishing lines. "Don't worry about me," she texted back. "I can take care of myself."

His next text contained only a number: 12.

"12?" she wrote. "What's that supposed to mean?"

"That's the number of times you were killed during surprise attacks at camp. Trust me on this one. Stay home and lock your doors."

He had counted the number of times she'd died? She hadn't even counted the number of times she'd died.

She would have liked to retort with the number of times she had survived camp's surprise attacks, but she hadn't kept track of that number, either. "I'll be fine," she wrote. When it counted, she knew how to be careful. Really, he worried about her too much.

# CHAPTER 16

Dirk tugged his shoes on with more force than the task required. "It's Halloween," he told Cassie. "Couldn't Dad do this a different night?"

Bridget sat at the kitchen table next to him, arms folded, a frown on her face. Dirk gestured to his sister. "Halloween only comes once a year."

Cassie stirred the vegetables, unconcerned. Spurts of steam hissed in the wok. "So which do you think is more important than the country's future—your party or your sister's trick-or-treating?"

Dirk tied his first shoe. "Bridget has looked forward to this for months." He could complain about his dad disappointing Bridget without getting in trouble. Dirk couldn't say what he really thought—which was that the whole thing was awful. At moments like this he didn't care about the country's future. He only cared about his friends' futures. It was selfish and shortsighted, but he couldn't stop himself from feeling that way.

Cassie poured more sauce onto the vegetables. "We'll make it up to Bridget."

Typical. They'd probably buy her a new pony and think everything was good.

"Your father will call soon," Cassie went on, "and tell you what you need to do." She turned to look him in the eyes. "You'll follow through this time, won't you?"

"Yes," he said stiffly. He yanked his last shoelace so hard the end snapped off. He swore, kicked off the shoe, and then undid the other. He'd have to wear a different pair. "So what exactly is the plan?"

Strips of meat were in a frying pan beside the wok. Cassie dumped them into the vegetables and stirred them around. While she spoke, she cast a glance at Bridget, measuring her words so as not to say too much. "Your father's men are picking up one of the Slayers. They'll hold her until the other Slayers come for her."

"Who?" Dirk asked. "Which Slayer are they going after?"

Cassie shrugged. "I don't know. I'm sure your father will tell you when he calls."

Tori. It was going to be Tori. His father would take her to ensure Dirk did exactly what he was supposed to.

Dirk swore again and stalked out of the kitchen.

"Dinner is ready!" Cassie called after him. "You need to eat something before you leave!"

How could she do that—talk about kidnapping his friends in one breath and act all motherly and concerned in the next?

Dirk went to his bedroom and grabbed a pair of shoes from his closet. While he was putting them on, Dr. B called his watch-phone. Dirk stared at it in dread. He didn't want to answer. He didn't want any of this to happen.

Seconds went by. Dr. B wouldn't think it was odd that he hadn't answered. The Slayers were supposed to go to private locations before they answered their phones.

He shut his eyes and repeated the mantra he had been saying since he got home from camp: It's better for my friends to lose their memories now than their lives later. I'm helping them, not hurting them.

Dirk hit the receiver button. "Hello?"

"I have bad news," Dr. B said. His normally calm voice had an edge to it, a fear that seeped through despite his best efforts. "Overdrake's men captured Alyssa."

Alyssa. His father had taken Alyssa, not Tori. Dirk shouldn't have felt relieved at the news, but did anyway. He needed to respond—a Slayer response. Surprised. Upset. "How do you know they have her?"

"She turned on her watch-phone while it was happening. I heard it."

"Why didn't you call the rest of us for backup?" It was a real question, one sprinkled with agony. If Dirk had left home before his father called him, Dirk might have been able to avoid his father's instructions. It was a small thing, and probably pointless, but he would have felt better not being a part of the trap.

"Alyssa was too far away and it happened too fast. I'm putting out a call for everyone to assemble." Dr. B paused. "Overdrake hasn't drugged Alyssa yet because he wants her to give him information about the rest of the Slayers. We can attempt a rescue, but . . ." His voice faltered as though he couldn't say more.

"But what?" Dirk asked.

Even over the receiver Dirk heard the low breath Dr. B let out, a breath punctured with worry. "How can I send the rest of you into danger?"

"Uh, isn't that pretty much the point of being a Slayer? We go into danger."

"I've told you all along that you need to know when to cut your losses. You need to think about things logically—and yet I can't. Alyssa is alone, afraid, and Overdrake will hurt her if she doesn't cooperate. How can we stand by and do nothing?"

Dirk slipped his shoes on. "We'll think of a way to help her."

Dr. B didn't seem to hear him. "If anything happens to the rest of you, though—you could be killed. What would I tell your parents—that I trained you to do these sorts of things, that I purposely put you in harm's way?"

Dirk tied one set of laces, careful not to break them this time. "None of us will be killed." His father had promised that. "And you're not putting us in harm's way. We vote on these things. It's always our choice. You've just trained us so we know how to use our powers."

A pause, and then Dr. B let out a resigned sigh. "I'd better put out the call to the other Slayers."

In another moment the call would end. Dirk suddenly realized this might be his last chance to talk to Dr. B privately before everything changed. "Dr. B . . . ," Dirk said, and then couldn't think of what to say next—how to put it best. "Anything that happens later on—none of it is your fault. You're a great leader. You've always been my role model. I just wanted you to know that."

It was probably a suspicious thing to blurt out. Dirk never got sentimental. Dr. B didn't question it, though. "Thank you," he said. "You're a good captain. You've always been like a son to me. You should know that, too."

Dirk did. That's what made this so hard.

CHAPTER 17

While Tori's mom assembled the kids in the front of the room for story time, Tori and Aprilynne set things on the tables. When the kids were done listening to stories, they would come back here and paint pumpkins to look like jack-o'-lanterns.

Aprilynne placed paintbrushes on a table. "So what time is your party?"

"What party?" Tori asked.

"You must be planning on going somewhere or you wouldn't keep checking your watch."

Tori set out bottles of glow-in-the-dark paint on the center of a table. "I'm not going anywhere. I'm just . . . I think my watch might be breaking. It's making odd noises." She added the last part in case any more alarms went off.

"Well, what did you expect?" Aprilynne asked. "It's a piece of junk." As she put a water cup by a seat, she sent Tori a sly smile. "I bet if you asked Roland, he would get you a nice watch for your birthday."

Tori kept her voice low. "Roland and I are just friends." Tori didn't add that Roland wasn't happy about that fact and kept trying to change their status.

"Hmm," Aprilynne said, moving around the table with the cups. "Does the fact that you're just friends have something to do with the hot blond guy who appeared on your phone?"

Tori sent Aprilynne a sharp look. "You shouldn't snoop around on my phone."

"It's not snooping. It's sisterly love. So, are the two of you some sort of item?"

Tori picked up the water pitcher and poured a small amount into one of the cups. "I'm not sure. Things are complicated between us."

"Oh," Aprilynne said, her interest peaked. She loved drama and didn't understand why Tori didn't date with the same gusto for the sport that she had.

"It's never as complicated as you think," Aprilynne said. "What sort of car does he drive?"

"A Porsche."

"Go for him."

Tori laughed. Aprilynne had a completely different standard for judging guys than she did. A low, insistent beep from Tori's watch cut her laughter short. She felt frozen for a moment, standing there with the water pitcher in her hand. That alarm meant there was an emergency situation. The number one showed up on her watch face. The code to go to the exhibit room at the Jefferson Memorial.

Had Jesse been attacked again? Was it something worse?

At the thought of danger, Tori's senses grew even sharper. The smell of paint punched through the air; her mother's voice intensified. Tori noticed the fan vents pushing warm air into the room and heard the rustle of Aprilynne's costume as she moved around the table.

Tori had to answer Dr. B's call with a code of her own, telling him that she could come now, come later and meet up with the Slayers wherever they were at the time, or not come at all. Her gaze swept over the crowd of kids. Her parents were both busy right now. She couldn't ask them if she could leave. What excuse could she come up with anyway? Her parents wanted her help with the party and it would go on for another hour or two.

Then again, if Dr. B needed to gather the Slayers together, something was wrong. Something important. Tori couldn't wait out the party, go home with her parents, and then turn around and drive back to downtown D.C. The George Washington University Hospital was within walking distance from the Jefferson Memorial.

Tori pushed in her reply. "I've got to go," she told Aprilynne. "Cover for me with Mom and Dad until I get back."

Aprilynne sent her a humorless glare and kept putting cups on the table. "You're kidding, right?"

"It's an emergency." Tori looked down at her costume. Was there a way to look less conspicuous? Her jacket was locked in the hospital director's office. She wouldn't be able to get it.

"An emergency?" Aprilynne put one hand on her hip. "Tori, I heard your watch alarm go off. You must have set it to let you know when you needed to leave. That's not an emergency, that's called ditching. Where are you going?"

Tori checked to make sure her cell phone was still tucked inside her pocket. "Tell Mom and Dad I'll be back in a little while. If I don't get back before the party ends, tell them I'll take a cab to the house. They don't need to worry about me."

Aprilynne continued to glare at her. "Oh, I don't think worry is the emotion they'll be feeling."

Tori took a step away, and then turned back to her sister. She was so on edge she wasn't thinking straight. "Can I borrow some money for cab fare home?"

Aprilynne rolled her eyes, then reached for the purse that was slung around her Snow White costume—a small bag shaped like an apple. "You're lucky this went so well with my outfit that I wore it." She pulled out three twenties and handed them to Tori. "Is the hot guy going to be at your emergency?"

"Yes, actually."

"Well, at least it's for a good cause then."

Tori didn't say more. She walked out of the room, past the security detail, and into the hallway. She didn't look back until she was outside.

It was quarter to four when Tori walked around the tidal basin to the Jefferson Memorial. The trees lining the walkway were beginning to lose their leaves. Small puddles of them were gathered under their shade, a reminder that autumn was here. Cold air pushed against her legs and exposed midriff. She wished she'd chosen a warmer costume. Something that covered all of her thighs. This was why girls should want to become astronauts, doctors, and scientists. None of them had to wear miniskirts.

Tori's cell phone rang. It was her parents' ring tone. She didn't answer. They would only chew her out for leaving and tell her to come back.

Not many people were milling around the monument. The ones that were, all stared at her as she went by. *Yes*, she wanted to say, *I'm here on superhero matters. Go about your business, citizens.*

This was one more thing to thank Overdrake for.

Tori made her way to the underground exhibit beneath the rotunda. A few people browsed through the bookstore at the other end. A couple people sat in the room where the Thomas Jefferson videos played. A few more stood in the hallway outside these two places reading the timeline of Jefferson's life displayed on the wall.

None of the other Slayers had arrived yet. Procedure dictated that

Tori keep a low profile until Dr. B and the others assembled. Hard to do in a Supergirl outfit. She glanced at the doors that led outside, one on each end of the hallway, then turned and read the plaques that hung high on the walls.

The last hope of human liberty in this world rests on us—Thomas Jefferson, 1811.

She smiled. That quote, she supposed, was the reason Dr. B had chosen the monument as the Slayers' first meeting place. He wanted them to read that phrase while they waited. She walked down the hallway a bit. Another plaque read: *Knowledge is power . . . knowledge is happiness.*

That quote didn't engender the same response. It reminded Tori of a conversation she'd had with Overdrake during their confrontation.

They had been in the forest, both high in tree branches. She had a rifle trained on him—which wasn't much of a threat since he was dressed completely in bulletproof clothing. He talked to her, not because he was afraid of her, but because he wanted to taunt her.

He didn't insult her. He was too smart for that. Tori would have ignored insults and forgotten them before she went to sleep that night. Overdrake spoke in riddles, and those repeated endlessly through her mind as she tried to figure them out.

"Who is your source?" she had asked, her rifle held firmly in her hand. "How do you know things about me?"

"You go to one of those private elitist schools, don't you?" he called back to her. "Let's see if the tuition is worth it. Do you know what the sign in the Greek temple of Delphi says?"

"No littering. In six languages. I went there last summer. Now answer my question."

"The sign says, Know thyself."

She thought he was stalling. She'd already shot one tree branch from underneath him. He'd only managed to keep himself from plunging twenty feet to the ground by flipping through the air and landing on another branch. "Okay," she said, "I know I don't have a lot of patience." She looked into the sight of her rifle, aiming at the tree branch he stood on. "You might not be so lucky the next time you fall."

Overdrake shook his head. She couldn't see his expression through his helmet, but somehow still knew it was condescending. "When you understand yourself, you'll be a lot closer to figuring out who my source is."

It made no sense. The one thing she knew was that *she* wasn't his source.

"Who are you, Victoria Hampton?" he'd asked. "Where do you come from?"

Where did she come from? She came from Virginia. She came from a home that, despite her father's political position, was remarkably normal. Two kids and a dog. How did any of that have to do with Overdrake's source?

Tori didn't speak to him for long after that. She went to fight the dragon. When that was done, Overdrake was gone.

Tori knew he never meant to give her any information. He was only trying to get her to doubt herself. She ought to have been able to dismiss his words as easily as insults. Heaven knew she brushed off enough of those in high school.

But maybe that's why Overdrake's comments bothered her. Average people spat out random insults. The smart ones, the ones that really wanted to hurt you, they mixed truth in with their insults. Those were the barbs that penetrated and stung.

So what was the truth in Overdrake's words?

Tori knew who she was. She was a Slayer. She was a person who cared about her country and would fight for it.

She moved around the room, reading a history of Jefferson that hung on the wall. She sensed Dirk before she saw him. He was walking up behind her. "Nice costume. I'm glad to see you kept my advice about being careful and staying home today."

She turned and smiled at him. He wore jeans and a black leather jacket. His hair was shorter than the last time she'd seen him, the summer highlights gone. He was as handsome as ever, though—more actually, because now when she looked at him she didn't just see his perfectly formed features and light blue eyes; she saw the weeks of texts he'd written her. Funny ones, caring ones, ones that asked her out to dinner at La Niçoise so she could show the staff she was making progress with him.

Without saying a word, Tori hugged him. She would have hugged any of her friends from camp. Dirk held on to her for longer than normal, and she let him. It felt good to see him again.

He ran his hand along her cape. "Where were you today that you needed this?"

Tori pulled away from him. "I was helping my parents throw a party for some kids at a hospital."

"Giving candy to babies," he said, still looking her over. "That's probably why your father scores so high with the four-to-eight-year-old constituents." Dirk smiled as he said this, but Tori could sense the tension in him. The worry.

"What's wrong?" she asked.

Dirk put his hands in his pockets. "Dr. B will give us the details when he gets here. We'll feel the simulator when he gets close."

Tori had asked what was wrong with Dirk, why he was so tense. She didn't clarify herself, though. He was probably just nervous about the mission. She was, too.

She took the edges of her cape and wrapped them around herself. "This is the real reason superheroes wear capes. You've got to have something to keep you warm when your outfit consists of twelve inches of material."

She had expected Dirk to laugh. Instead he took off his jacket and draped it around her shoulders. The gesture was so sweet she didn't even make a token refusal. "Thanks," she said, and slid her arms into the jacket, enjoying the warmth. It smelled like his cologne. It felt like putting on a hug.

"Oh," he said, "I'd better get my phone."

He slipped his hand into the pocket to retrieve his phone. He was so close. She wanted him to be close and at the same time didn't. The rest of the Slayers were on their way. Jesse was on his way. That thought alone brought up a whirlwind of emotion inside her. This wasn't the time for her and Dirk to figure out what their relationship was.

Dirk put his phone into his pants pocket and looked around for other Slayers. A few more people had wandered inside the exhibit hall. No one Tori recognized.

"I'm sure more of us are coming," she told Dirk. "They'll be here soon." Dr. B knew who had replied. The rest of the Slayers didn't.

Dirk was silent as some tourists walked past them to the door, then said, "This is one of those times when we could use Ryker. Did your dad have any luck finding him?"

Tori hesitated. She didn't like keeping things from Dirk. "That's still up in the air."

"I called every listing for an Allen Davis in San Diego, Denver, and Crown Heights. Each time somebody answered, I asked to speak to Ryker." Dirk shook his head. "No one had heard of him."

"You did that?" It was touching and sad to think of Dirk calling all those people, each time hoping to speak to Ryker.

"I even searched some older records, in case they had gotten rid of their landline. I thought maybe I could find an address."

Tori had to tell Dirk something. Next he'd drive to the cities and go on a door-to-door search. She stepped closer to Dirk and lowered her voice. If any of the other Slayers came in, she didn't want them to hear this. "His dad's name isn't actually Allen. He's one of those guys who goes by his middle name. You should have been looking for a

Charles Davis—although it wouldn't have done you any good. Their phone number is unlisted."

Dirk straightened, surprised. "You found Ryker's address?"

She paused, didn't answer.

"Tori—" Dirk prompted.

"You have to promise not to be mean to him."

Dirk lifted an eyebrow. "I'm never mean to anybody."

"How many times last summer did you throw Lilly into the lake?"

"That wasn't mean," Dirk insisted. "If you use all the hot water in the showers, you get thrown in the lake. It's a posted rule."

"Yeah, but waiting until after she did her hair and makeup to throw her in—that's mean."

Dirk rolled his eyes. "Fine. If I throw Ryker in the lake, I'll do it before he beautifies himself. Where does the guy live?"

Tori glanced around to make sure they were still alone. "Rutland, Vermont. The problem is, Ryker's parents won't let him train. He has to wait until he's eighteen and he can legally leave on his own. That won't be until next summer."

"Next summer." Dirk considered this. "That's not too far away. The important thing is that we found him." Dirk's words were calm but Tori felt a surge of emotion run through him. Satisfaction, and then something else. Something that was harder to identify.

Dirk glanced at his watch, looked around the room, then put his hand into his jeans pocket and fiddled with his cell phone. An almost electric current of energy, of restlessness, ran just underneath his surface. He reminded Tori of one of those caged panthers at a zoo that paces back and forth in their cages.

"You're too tense," she told him and reached up and massaged his shoulders. His muscles were hard, thick. Slayer muscles. "Relax a little. It's not like *I'm* leading A-team on the mission. You'd have a reason to be tense then."

He forced a smile. "I'm just remembering our last mission."

"We'll win this one." She stopped kneading his shoulders and motioned to her costume. "As an experienced superhero, I can tell you that good always conquers evil."

Dirk let out a grunt. "Who said this is a fight between good and evil?"

She hadn't expected that reaction from him. It seemed so cynical. "Of course it's between good and evil. We're good and Overdrake is planning on using dragons to take down the government. Last I checked, that qualifies as evil."

Dirk's gaze went to a portrait of Jefferson on the wall. "Wars aren't ever that clear cut. You don't think everyone who fought on England's side during the Revolutionary War was evil, do you?"

"That was different. The British soldiers fought because their king ordered them to. But even then, they were in the wrong. Americans deserved to have self-determination. We deserved our freedom."

"Freedom?" Dirk asked, turning back to her. "Runaway slaves fought for the British troops. England promised them their freedom— something that didn't happen in America until the Civil War. And that war is still America's bloodiest."

Tori never considered this before and it bothered her. The colonies were fighting for their freedom while denying freedom to some. Then again, none of that changed what was happening now. "So what are you saying? That you don't want to fight Overdrake or that you wish you were British?"

Dirk turned and studied the pictures of Monticello. "All I'm saying is that conflicts aren't usually about good and evil. They're about the decisions people make when they're ambitious, when they're angry"— his gaze cut back over to her—"when they're in love. The fate of nations can change from the roll of the dice. Who's to say the world is worse off because Egypt fell to Alexander the Great or because William the Conqueror took over England?"

"This is about good and evil," Tori said. "I'm not risking my life over something that's no more important than a roll of the dice."

Dirk looked like he was going to say something, then changed his mind. "Sorry. I didn't mean to upset you." He reached out and took her hand. His was warm, comforting. "I'm just stressed."

She wondered if this was how soldiers felt before they went to battle—did they question the cause they were fighting for? Did they weigh it against their life and wonder if it was worth it?

She squeezed Dirk's hand. "It will be all right."

He smiled and squeezed her hand back, but wasn't convinced. Another emotion joined his others: a sadness she didn't understand. Were these emotions stronger than the ones he usually felt, or was she getting better at reading him? Even his light blue eyes seemed darker now, muted.

"It will be all right," she told him again, so softly it was no more than a coo.

He pulled her a step closer and leaned down to say something. She waited for the feel of his breath brushing against her ear. He never got the words out.

A voice interrupted them. "Well, I'm not the first one here after all."

Tori blushed even before she turned. She had been so wrapped up in Dirk, she hadn't heard Jesse come in, hadn't sensed that anyone was there.

Jesse wore jeans, a tan jacket, and an expression that said he didn't like that she and Dirk were holding hands. He walked toward them, a wry look in his eyes. "I guess I shouldn't be surprised. After all, I've always known how fast Dirk is."

CHAPTER 18

It had been almost three months since Tori saw Jesse at camp. When she'd thought of him, she pictured him standing against the canopy of sunlit trees, as much a part of the forest as the summer air and the emerald leaves around him.

It was odd to see him suddenly superimposed here in the real world.

That was the only reason she was staring at Jesse, the only reason she couldn't speak. It had nothing to do with the memories that rushed back at her—she and Jesse sailing through a sea of leaves and light, Jesse smiling at her as they sat by a campfire under the star studded sky, Jesse's hand on her cheek as he leaned down to kiss her.

Dirk didn't drop Tori's hand. He held on to it possessively. "Tori got here first. We've only been together for a little while."

"Oh." Jesse's gaze slid to Tori's eyes. His voice was accusing. "Sorry to interrupt you two then."

Tori felt caught, awkward. She didn't want to offend Dirk by pulling her hand away from him, but she didn't like this either—this feeling that Dirk was laying claim to her in front of Jesse.

She said the only thing she could think of. "Do the two of you need to talk . . . you know, as captains . . . to discuss strategy?" She dropped Dirk's hand and stepped away from him as though expecting him to walk off.

Jesse's gaze stayed on her. "Actually, I was just thinking that the two of *us* needed to talk."

Dirk folded his arms. He didn't move away from Tori. "I thought you said everything you needed to say to Tori on the last night of camp."

Jesse took a couple more steps over to him. "And apparently you said a whole lot to her afterward. Thanks. Thanks for being a friend."

"As I remember it," Dirk said, "Tori was the one who needed a friend that night."

"I bet she did," Jesse said. "How nice that you were there for her."

Tori's gaze bounced back and forth between them. She needed to put an end to this but didn't know what to say. She couldn't explain how things were between Dirk and her—didn't exactly know how they were herself. She couldn't decide on the spot and didn't want Dirk deciding for her. At the same time, she couldn't be disloyal to him. He had been there for her during the last three months. Jesse hadn't.

Tori pulled Dirk's jacket tighter around herself and addressed Jesse. "You have no right to be mad at either of us. You told me you wanted me to date other guys."

Jesse raised a hand in disbelief. "Yeah, but I thought you would wait longer than fifteen minutes. And I didn't expect you to start with one of my best friends."

She could have told Jesse things hadn't started at camp, and technically she and Dirk weren't a couple. Instead she said, "Sorry. After you break up with someone, you don't get to decide those things."

"I never—" Jesse didn't finish the sentence.

Rosa's voice called over to them from the doorway, "Is this where the Justice League is meeting?" She grinned and headed toward the group. "I must have missed the memo about our new superhero outfits."

Rosa wore faded jeans and an oversize jacket that made her look even more petite. She eyed Tori's outfit, shaking her head so that her long brown hair swayed around her shoulders. "Only you could make bright red, calf-length boots work." She gave Tori a hug, then turned and hugged Jesse and Dirk.

When she was done, Rosa said, "So, what did I miss?"

"I don't know," Jesse said. "I just got here. Apparently I missed a whole lot."

Dirk ignored Jesse's comment. "Dr. B only told me a few things. He wants to give everyone the mission details himself." Dirk didn't have to explain why. Dr. B didn't want the captains giving their opinions and swaying the vote. "I can tell you this, though, it will be an offensive."

Rosa nodded, suddenly business-like. "We should review offensive protocol for Tori." Tori only had one summer to learn the stuff the other Slayers had worked on for years. It wasn't second nature to her yet. She tried to pay attention as Rosa listed rules and procedures. She needed to wrap her mind around the mission and stop glancing at Jesse and Dirk to see if they were still glaring at each other.

Which they were.

Tori felt surprisingly horrible about this. Jesse and Dirk had been good friends before she came to camp. Now she was standing between them, figuratively and literally.

After another fifteen minutes of listening to Rosa talk about what constituted a need to use force, when property damage was justifiable, and which laws could be broken, Lilly made her way to the group.

Lilly was only an inch or two taller than Rosa, but she didn't come off as petite, or doll-like, or anything remotely soft and cuddly. She looked like the compact version of a roller derby queen. Lilly's bleached-blonde hair with dark roots seemed to be a lifestyle rather than a fashion choice. She'd worn nothing but tank tops and cut-off jean shorts all summer, kept her nails painted hooker red, and had a way of standing with one hip jutted out that indicated if you messed with her, she'd happily yank off one of your limbs.

Now she wore a pair of old jeans and a beat-up black ski jacket. A couple of bright red streaks ran through her hair. She walked over to the group while checking texts on her phone. "Do you guys know what's going on?" Her red fingernails tapped against the keypad. "I can't get a hold of Alyssa. It's worrying me."

"You can't get a hold of Alyssa?" Jesse repeated incredulously. "How are you trying to get a hold of her?"

Lilly flashed her cell phone at him. "We exchanged phone numbers a long time ago. Yeah, yeah, I know." She held up her hand to stop Jesse's protest. "It's against the rules. Dirk can make me run extra laps later. The point is, she's not answering her phone. We texted after the first warning and she was fine. She was on her way shopping for a costume and said she'd call me when she got to the store. She never did." Lilly went back to texting. "When Dr. B called the meeting, and I still hadn't heard from her, I called her watch-phone. She didn't answer that either."

"Did you tell Dr. B?" Rosa asked, her worry ratcheting up. She was Alyssa's counterpart.

Lilly nodded. "He said we'd talk about it once he got here." She looked between Dirk and Jesse. "Is this a drill or is it for real?"

"It's not a drill," Jesse said.

Lilly let out a long breath and put her phone in her jacket pocket. "Great." She looked around again. "Where's Shang?" Shang was her counterpart and the only Slayer besides Alyssa that Lilly ever listened to.

"He hasn't come yet," Rosa said. "Neither has Kody. Maybe they can't make it."

None of them asked where Bess was. She would be with Dr. B.

Tori's cell phone rang again. Her parents' ring tone. She still didn't answer. She was going to be in so much trouble when this was over. Her watch read 4:18. It felt like it had been longer. It felt like time was purposely dragging its feet and would keep them here, strung with suspense, forever.

"Dr. B is close," Jesse said at the same time Tori felt a surge of energy course through her, fill her. During missions, Dr. B hauled the simulator in a trailer behind the van. It was on and in range. She felt stronger, lighter, not cold anymore. Her senses grew even crisper. The room was brighter, louder, and she could smell whiffs of stale cigarette smoke coming from a couple of passing tourists.

Jesse's and Dirk's watches simultaneously beeped with new instructions. They both looked down and read their messages.

"I'll answer him," Dirk said.

While he called Dr. B, Jesse told the others, "We need to head to location two." That was the Lincoln Memorial. "Dr. B wants to meet privately."

At the Lincoln Memorial? The monuments weren't as crowded as they usually were on a Saturday. People were getting ready for Halloween. Still, any monument was a long ways from private.

Without questioning the logic behind this decision, the other Slayers headed toward the closest door. Tori followed. Lilly glanced behind them. "What about everyone else?"

Jesse was at the head of the group. "Kody will meet up with us later. Shang is out of the area." Dr. B apparently hadn't said anything about Alyssa. Tori wondered if that hinted at bad news. Lilly seemed to think so. She muttered unhappily and pushed ahead of Tori and Rosa to talk to Dirk.

The group made their way along the tidal basin toward the Lincoln Memorial. A few clouds had wandered in front of the sun, dimming the light and making the water even darker than its usual muddy green. There were no hints of the bright pink and white cherry blossoms the trees were famous for. That season was past. Now the trees stood about, average and unremarkable, waiting for winter to strip them down to their bark.

Dr. B liked the downtown area for Slayer meetings because the monuments were open twenty-four hours. So many tourists were always coming and going, that one more group walking around wouldn't be noticed.

Walking felt too slow. Tori itched to fly or at least to run. With her powers turned on, it wouldn't even be tiring. But the group wasn't supposed to draw attention to themselves. They had to look like a bunch of normal teenagers seeing the sights. Well, a bunch of normal teenagers and one girl wearing a miniskirt and shiny red superhero boots.

Rosa walked beside Tori, still giving her a refresher in protocol whenever passing tourists weren't within earshot. The group strode past the FDR monument: statues of people waiting in a line that never moved. Tori's father said it was really a monument depicting government speed.

The group next passed the marble likeness of Martin Luther King. Tori couldn't quite decide whether his expression looked hopeful or suspicious. One of the quotes on the inscription wall read, "I believe that unarmed truth and unconditional love will have the final word in reality. This is why right, temporarily defeated, is stronger than evil triumphant."

Right and wrong. Not just the roll of the dice. She felt buoyed by the words until she thought about the part that said right didn't always triumph. It seemed like a bad omen.

The group crossed Independence Avenue and walked over to the Lincoln Memorial, a hundred-foot tall Greek temple where a huge statue of Abraham Lincoln sat pondering the tourists. To Tori it would always be the place made famous by the back of the penny. As a child she had expected the monument to be copper colored and not made of pale white stone.

Bess stood near the mountain of steps that led up to the statue's room. She wore a jean jacket, cowboy boots, a western shirt, and a bandana looped around her neck. Her curly hair had grown out a little since the summer. It was long enough that she had put it in two short braids. She spotted the group, walked over, and hugged everyone—even Lilly, and they had never gotten along that well at camp.

In Lilly's defense, Bess did things like throw shields up while Lilly was tossing her lunch plate in the garbage can. Bess thought nothing was funnier than seeing bits of macaroni salad bounce back in Lilly's direction.

Tori looked around for Dr. B. "Where is your dad?"

"Waiting for us," Bess said. "We need to go around to the lower lobby." She headed in that direction and the rest followed. The Lincoln Monument, like the Jefferson Memorial, had a room underneath it full of information about the president: timelines, quotes, pictures, bits and pieces of the remarkable laid out to display. Definitely not the most private place to meet.

As she walked alongside Bess, Tori said, "I'm glad I'm not the only one wearing a costume."

"Costume?" Bess asked. "What are you talking about? This is how I normally dress."

"Right," Tori said. "Me too. Including the big S on my chest."

Bess laughed. "Okay, I don't actually dress like this, but Kody does. Seriously, the first time we did a drill in D.C., we had to make him ditch his cowboy hat. It was too conspicuous."

"It's a good thing I didn't make that mistake then. I'll blend right in."

"Don't worry about it." Bess glanced around to make sure no one overheard. "My dad brought our Kevlar outfits."

They needed their bulletproof gear. That wasn't good news.

The group walked into the lower lobby, weaving around displays until they reached the elevator. Jesse pushed the call button and after a couple moments the elevator doors opened. Tori walked in with the others. "Why didn't we just go up the stairs?" she asked Bess. "We were right there."

Instead of pushing the button that read "to statuary," Bess pulled a key from her pocket and inserted it into one of the keyholes on the panel. She twisted the key and the elevator went up. "You'll see."

Bess had a special key to the Lincoln Memorial elevator? How did a person go about getting one of those? No one else seemed surprised by all of this, but then, they'd done drills in D.C. before.

When the elevator stopped and the doors opened, the statue of Lincoln was nowhere around. A space not much bigger than the elevator stood in front of them. The group piled out and moved toward a built-in ladder that went up to the roof. Jesse flew up and opened a trapdoor. Tori watched him. "Um, is going up on the roof legal?"

"Define legal," Bess said.

"Will I be arrested for doing this?" Tori clarified.

"No," Bess said as though it were a ridiculous question. "No one will catch us."

It wasn't the most comforting of answers. "Couldn't we meet in the van?" Tori suggested. "Isn't that private enough?"

"Someone could have followed us," Bess said. "If that's the case, they'll think we went to the statuary and they'll look for us there. Besides, according to Theo, with the right equipment you can decipher what's being said inside a vehicle by picking up the sound waves hitting the windows." She shrugged. "Personally, I think Theo just likes making our lives harder." She took her place in the line for the ladder. "When you get up on top, stay low and follow the rest of us. We'll be far away enough from the edge of the building that no one on the ground will be able to see us."

Jesse flew through the trapdoor, stood on the roof, and held his hand down to help Rosa up. He did the same for Lilly. Dirk ignored Jesse's hand and leapt up onto the roof. Bess looked up as though contemplating trying to copy Dirk's move, but in the end she held her hand out to Jesse and let him help her up.

Tori flew up. By then the rest of the Slayers were carefully making their way around the skylights to where Dr. B waited for them. He sat cross-legged a few yards over, studying something on his laptop. Even in this simple act there was something of his signature demeanor: an odd mixture of intensity and mildness, of intelligence and inattentiveness. He was an operative who had a key to the roof of the Lincoln Memorial and yet was sitting up here wearing tan professor pants, bright white tennis shoes, and a jacket from a decade ago. Night vision goggles hung from his neck. It had probably never occurred to him that he didn't blend in.

His smile was tired, worried. "I'm glad you could all come."

"Alyssa isn't here," Lilly said pointedly.

"That's what we need to talk about," Dr. B gestured for them to come closer. "I'm afraid Overdrake has captured Alyssa. He wants to come after the rest of you, too. Now we need to decide what to do about it."

CHAPTER 19

Tori stared at Dr. B mutely. Alyssa had been captured? Lilly let out a high-pitched gasp. Her hand flew to her mouth. Her bright red fingernails contrasted against her ashen face.

"He hasn't hurt her," Dr. B went on. "At least not yet. We need to free her before he does."

First Jesse had been attacked, and now this. The safety of the normal world was shrinking, closing in on all of them.

Rosa paled. She reached out and took hold of Lilly's arm for support. "How did Overdrake find her? How did he find Jesse?"

"I don't know." Dr. B motioned for everyone to sit down. "Did any of the rest of you see anything suspicious? Anything that might indicate Overdrake was trailing you?"

The group all shook their heads. As Tori sat down, she said, "If Overdrake planned to pick us off, he could have already found me. He could have sent people to my father's events."

"True." Dr. B typed something on his laptop. "But you're also the most well-guarded Slayer. If you were attacked at a campaign stop, there would be a public outcry. The police would be pressured to find the perpetrator. Overdrake must not want that."

At least, Tori thought, *not yet.*

Bess nudged her elbow into Tori. "And an attack on you would give your father the sympathy vote. I bet Overdrake is a Democrat."

Dr. B sent Bess a look that indicated he didn't think her comment was helpful.

"What?" she asked him. "You're always telling us to pay attention for clues about his identity."

Dr. B turned to the other Slayers. "At 3:16, Alyssa sent me an emergency alert, and then turned on the phone function on her watch so I could hear what was being said. Overdrake had her by that point. He told her he wanted information about the Slayers—how many there were, names, and where you lived."

A chill went down Tori's spine. She remembered how frightened she was when Overdrake captured her, how he calmly talked about killing her. His voice was smooth, so cultured and civilized sounding with his nearly British accent.

"Overdrake," Dr. B went on, "said if Alyssa cooperated, he wouldn't hurt her. If she didn't, he would employ other methods to extract the truth from her. He gave her three hours to decide. From the noises I heard next, I can only assume he's gagged her. I haven't heard anything from Alyssa over her watch since then."

Jesse broke into Dr. B's speech. "Lilly, turn off your cell phone. And take the battery out."

Phones could be traced and Alyssa knew Lilly's number. If Overdrake had the right equipment, he could pick up the signal from Lilly's phone and tell where she was.

Lilly pulled her phone out of her pocket. Her hands were clumsy, her face still white. "Alyssa didn't tell him my phone number. Dr. B would have heard."

"Alyssa didn't have to tell Overdrake," Jesse said. "Your number is on her call history. You called her this afternoon."

Lilly pulled the battery out of her phone. "A lot of people are on her call history. My name won't be listed next to my number. He won't know it's me."

Dr. B looked at Lilly with such disappointment that even Tori felt the weight of it. "Did you leave Alyssa a voice message?" he asked.

Lilly gulped, seemed to shrink a little. "Overdrake won't recognize my voice. He's never talked to me."

Jesse spoke through gritted teeth. He was all captain now, expecting to be obeyed not contradicted. "We don't know how Overdrake knew our names in the first place. If he bugged the camp or listened in on our phones, he might recognize any of our voices."

Lilly pursed her lips. "My own mother doesn't recognize me on the phone half the time. Do you really think Overdrake can pick out my voice from Alyssa's voice messages?"

"Ever heard of voice recognition software?" Jesse asked.

"It doesn't matter now." Dr. B held his hands up, putting an end to the argument. "Lilly's phone is off and even if Overdrake was tracking it, he'd look for us by the statue, not up here. However"—Dr. B let his gaze sweep over the Slayers—"this is a good example of why the rules are in place. They protect all of us. You need to keep them, especially since we know Overdrake already gathered information about you. We need to make sure we plug leaks, not create new ones. Understood?"

Everyone nodded. Tori felt sick. She glanced at Dirk. The two of them had exchanged each other's phone numbers, too. Actually, she hadn't given Dirk a choice. She'd dialed her phone number using his phone and then added the contact information on both of their phones. Dirk returned her gaze and shook his head. He didn't want to bring it up. She supposed this wasn't the time for confessions. They needed to concentrate on a rescue plan now.

As soon as she had the chance, she'd tell Dirk they had to get new phone numbers.

It would be impossible for Tori to forget Dirk's last name and where he went to high school, and that bothered her. If Overdrake had kidnapped her instead of Alyssa, he might have been able to get that information from her.

Dr. B turned his laptop so the rest of them could see the screen. It showed an aerial picture of a large building and the parking lot that surrounded it. "Our big advantage," he said, "is that we know Alyssa's location. She's being held at this car dealership." He pointed to the building on the screen. "More specifically, in a room here."

Rosa was the closest to Dr. B. "How do we know where she is?"

"I can track your watches," Dr. B said. "Her signal is there."

Everyone stared at him for a moment, then Lilly spoke. "You told us no one could track our phones. Their signals are supposed to be encrypted."

"They are," Dr. B said. "No one else can track them, but I have the decryption program. I set it up for just such an occasion as this. There are times when I need to know where you are."

"And you never mentioned that to us before?" Bess asked in disbelief.

Dr. B enlarged the picture on his screen. "That information in the wrong hands would be dangerous. I certainly don't want Overdrake to know that I can track you, or that if he had the decryption key, he could intercept that information." Dr. B sent Bess a stern look and lowered his voice. "Which reminds me, we'll talk about where you went last weekend later."

Bess gulped and didn't say more.

Rosa leaned forward. "If we know where Alyssa is, why can't we call the police and have them go in and get her?"

"We'll consider that option," Dr. B said. "It may be our best course. That said, the police need a warrant or probable cause to search a place. We have no physical evidence of foul play, I'm not Alyssa's guardian, and she hasn't even been reported missing yet. Involving the police would mean involving Alyssa's parents." Dr. B shifted uncomfortably. "I don't think I could come up with a plausible explanation for giving one of my teenage campers a watch I can track. Any lie I attempted would most likely result in deep suspicions, a restraining order, and the police investigating whether I was fit to be a camp director. I would have to tell Alyssa's parents the truth about camp. I would have to turn over my laptop to the police."

Dr. B's gaze traveled around the group. "However, if we're able to take care of this ourselves, we'll not only keep our cover, we might be able to garner information about Overdrake and his organization. So let's take a vote. Do we try to handle this on our own first?"

"Yes," Lilly and Bess said in unison.

Jesse nodded.

Rosa said, "Alyssa wouldn't want us to blow our cover."

Dirk hesitated, then nodded as well.

Tori hated to be the last one to agree, but she couldn't help thinking of all the ways this mission could go wrong. They could fail, be hurt, be killed. Tori could be captured again. Or—almost as bad—the police could catch her breaking into a car dealership. To say the least, news stories that showed her being led away in handcuffs wouldn't reflect well on her father. The media, the people at her school, and late-night comedians would explode with commentary. And the president—Tori didn't even want to think about what he would say about her. Probably publicly. While smirking.

Would it be such a bad thing to let Alyssa's parents and a few police officers know about camp? It didn't mean the information would leak out to the public. It didn't mean Alyssa's parents would forbid her from training like Ryker's parents had . . . Well, it probably meant that, but it didn't *absolutely* mean that.

Tori had gone too long without answering. "If you don't want to come," Dr. B prodded gently, "you don't have to join us."

She imagined herself leaving the roof, going home, and waiting there to see how it turned out. She couldn't do it. Waiting would be torture. When it came down to it, she couldn't let her friends face Overdrake's men without her help. "I'll come."

Dr. B nodded and rattled off a list of the supplies he'd already put in his van. Rifles, tranquilizers, flash bangs, smoke bombs, infrared sensors, wire cutters, lock picks, neck microphones, earpieces, Kevlar outfits, and helmets. Booker, Dr. B's right-hand man at camp, would meet them with another van.

Booker was a middle-aged man who took care of the Slayers' horses and anything else that needed to be done. He was the gruff, quiet type that always made Tori a little nervous. It was hard not to interpret his silence as disapproval of life in general, and perhaps specifically teenagers. Still, he never seemed to be rattled by anything that went on at camp and was competent in everything he did, including breaking and entering.

Dr. B brought up a street view of the fence that surrounded the car dealership: Razor wire looped over the chain-link fence. "This may be electrified," he said. "However, it's only ten feet tall. Dirk will be able to jump over. Jesse and Tori can fly the rest of you over. If you have to get out fast, I don't want to risk anyone being caught on the wrong side of the fence. When you go over the first time, move one of the cars within leaping distance of the fence."

He didn't ask if they could accomplish this fact, which probably meant he knew about all of those times at camp when they had moved Theo's truck to different locations.

"Is there something we can do about the lights?" Bess asked. "It's as bright as day in that place."

"Not without alerting Overdrake that he's been breached. Surprise will be our most effective tool. Fortunately the rows of cars will provide good cover."

The discussion was beginning to have a feeling of déjà vu. Dr. B had said surprise would be the Slayers biggest asset when they broke into the dragon enclosure last summer. There was plenty of surprise in that attack, but they were the ones who'd been surprised.

Perhaps Jesse was thinking about that mission, too. "How do we know this isn't another trap?" he asked. "How do we know Overdrake didn't take Alyssa because he knew we would come after her?"

Dr. B switched to another street view of the dealership. "Overdrake has no way of knowing we can locate Alyssa. Before tonight, the only two people who knew I could track the watches were you and me." Dr. B regarded Jesse. "You didn't tell anyone else, did you?"

"I told Dirk," Jesse said.

Another flash of disappointment crossed Dr. B's features. It made Tori feel even worse about the rules she'd broken.

Dr. B turned to Dirk. "Did you tell anyone that I could track the watches?"

Dirk shook his head. "No."

Tori felt a spike of anxiety run through Dirk, a burst of guilt. It worried her. If he had told the truth, it wasn't the complete truth.

"Are you sure?" she asked him. "It could be important. We need to be certain Overdrake doesn't know."

Now all gazes were back on Dirk. His went to her. A warning was in his eyes. He didn't like being questioned and didn't want her to do it again. "Why would you think I told anyone about the watches? Did you ever hear me say anything about them?"

"No," she said. "It's just . . ." She didn't like feeling his anger and suddenly wished she hadn't spoken in front of everyone. She could sense Dirk's emotions, but not the meaning behind them. "You seemed so anxious for a moment."

"Of course I'm anxious," Dirk said. "We're about to break into a place where people want to kill us."

"Sorry," Tori said. "I misread you."

"Wait a minute." Bess' gaze ricocheted between Tori and Dirk. "Counterparts are pretty good at reading each other. Leo could tell when I was lying before all the words were out of my mouth. If Tori has doubts about you telling the truth, then I do, too. Did you or didn't you tell anyone that my dad could track the watches?"

Dirk grunted and held up his hands in a gesture of surrender. "Do you want to get a polygraph test going? Fine. Let's do that instead of rescuing Alyssa. I'm sure Overdrake didn't mean it when he threatened to torture her."

Dr. B looked directly at Dirk. "Did you tell anyone about the watches?"

Dirk looked at Tori, not at Dr. B. "No."

Everyone else's gaze turned to Tori then, waiting for her assessment of his answer. She told the truth. "All I can sense from Dirk right now is that he's mad at me." And she didn't need her counterpart sense to tell that.

Dirk smiled coldly. "Yeah, sorry, that's what happens when you announce to everyone that I'm lying."

Dr. B sighed and seemed satisfied with Dirk's answer. "We need to get back to our plan. We don't know how many guards will be around, although I assume they'll be both outside and inside. Check your infrared sensors before you go in."

Tori glanced at Dirk. He was looking at Dr. B, firmly ignoring her. She supposed she deserved it. Dirk wouldn't do anything to endanger anyone. During the last mission, he had been the one who freed the other Slayers, and when Overdrake had captured Tori, Dirk had come back to rescue her.

A memory flickered through her mind: Dirk and Overdrake on the enclosure roof yelling at each other. It was always a jumbled memory, one disjointed and mingled with the panic of that night—the men, the guns, the feeling of helplessness.

Overdrake hadn't thrown a net on Dirk, hadn't pointed guns at him. He just yelled, *What did you think would happen when you came here? What?*

Tori pushed away the memory and made herself concentrate on what Dr. B was saying, "Overdrake himself might be in the building. I'm not one to encourage you to break the law, but if the opportunity presents itself . . . well, you'll need to assess the risks and benefits of capturing him. Keep in mind that, according to Tori, he has extra strength and perhaps even leaping abilities like a Slayer."

Tori didn't like the way Dr. B made that sound—as though she didn't really know for sure. When she had been Overdrake's prisoner, he'd effortlessly picked her up and held her over his head. Later she saw him leap up and down from tree branches in a way that only Slayers moved. He was able to see well enough in the dark, too.

It was odd how the dragon lord's powers were so similar to theirs. Perhaps he had other abilities like theirs, too. Perhaps . . . a thought struck her for the first time. Perhaps a dragon lord could pretend to be a Slayer and they wouldn't even notice.

The thought burrowed deep inside her, made it hard to breathe. Because she had just remembered something else. Dirk's father spoke with an accent—a British-sounding accent, like Overdrake's.

Could it have been him?

No, she told herself. She would have recognized his voice when he spoke to her. But the next moment she wasn't sure. She hadn't expected to see Overdrake with Dirk at his football game. Had her expectations blinded her?

Dirk was wealthy, he lived in Winchester where the first compound had been, and his father knew who she was on sight.

It all fit together except for one thing—during the last mission

Dirk rescued the other Slayers. If he was Overdrake's son, why would he turn around and help them escape?

The memory from the dragon enclosure roof came back to her mind. This time instead of seeing dragon lord and Slayer facing off, she saw father and son.

What did you think would happen when you came here? What? Had Overdrake really asked the same question Tori was asking now? Why double-cross your friends and then rescue them?

It didn't matter to Tori—she didn't care whose son Dirk was as long as he was loyal to the Slayers now, as long as she could be sure about that loyalty—but here they were again, about to break into one of Overdrake's strongholds and Dirk knew information that could turn this whole thing into a trap. If Overdrake knew Dr. B would track Alyssa's watch, he knew the Slayers would come for her. Overdrake could eliminate most of the Slayers tonight without having to individually hunt them down.

She didn't realize she gasped until all gazes turned to her.

"What is it?" Dr. B asked her.

She couldn't answer him. She could only stare wide-eyed at Dirk. "Tell me this isn't a trap."

"What?" Dirk asked her. He was emotionally drawing back, trying to hide his feelings.

She needed to push him hard, to find out the truth right now. "Your father's accent . . . ," she said. "Tell me that you aren't Overdrake's son."

"What?" Dirk asked again, this time with an incredulous laugh. "You're not serious. Come on, Tori, why are you saying these things? You don't really believe that."

"I don't want to believe it."

"Then stop this." Dirk sounded angry, but Tori could sense the guilt creeping into his thoughts. The truth was in the guilt. She kept her gaze on his eyes, couldn't break the contact. If she stared at those familiar blue eyes long enough, she'd see an explanation in them for all the things she couldn't begin to understand. He was their friend, their captain. And he spent the last three months making her love him.

"Jesse," she said, and her voice was barely louder than a heartbreak. "Dirk betrayed us."

CHAPTER 20

For one breathless moment, everyone stared at Tori, unbelieving. She felt like the world had reeled in some horrible direction. The next moment everyone sprang to their feet. Dirk was the quickest. He backed away from the rest of the group. Most of the Slayers stood there watching him, caught by their uncertainty. They were waiting for an explanation.

They could have fought a dozen men, and taken them down, too—but one of their own?

"Dirk," Dr. B called. No anger, just confusion. Utter speechlessness.

Jesse walked toward Dirk. "What have you done?"

Dirk kept backing away. His gaze went to Tori. "You don't understand."

"Then explain it to me."

He shook his head and took more steps backward. He was getting close to the edge of the building. Tori didn't move forward, didn't want to push him closer to the edge. They were so high up. He wouldn't survive a fall.

Rosa, Lilly, and Bess all gaped in shock at Dirk. He and Bess had been friends for years. Dirk was Lilly's captain, and Rosa was simply incapable of thinking badly about any of the Slayers. They had known each other too long, fought together too many times.

"What have you done?" Jesse asked again. He was still walking toward Dirk, although slower now that Dirk was nearly out of roof.

Dirk turned his attention to Jesse. "Am I your enemy now? Just like that? Jesse, how long have you known me?"

"Apparently not long enough."

Dr. B stood at Tori's side. "Stop, Dirk. You're nearly at the edge. Come back here so we can talk about this. I'm sure there's been a misunderstanding."

Dirk stopped for a moment, glanced at Dr. B, then quickly looked away. Apparently he couldn't stand to see Dr. B's disappointment. "I saved all of you last summer," Dirk said. "I want you to remember that. I helped you fight the dragon." His gaze went back to Tori. "I saved your life." These weren't protestations of innocence. They were reminders that the Slayers owed him, that whatever else Dirk had done, the Slayers owed him for those things.

Dirk took another step toward the edge, barely paying attention to where he was walking.

Jesse took several more steps forward. "Is Overdrake your father? Tell us the truth. All of it."

"Dirk," Dr. B called to him. "We're your friends. We care about you. Come back here, please."

Dirk had backed up until he stood on the very edge of the building. He took off his watch and dropped it onto the roof.

"You have nowhere to go," Jesse told him.

That wasn't true. Tori knew what Dirk would do a second before he did it. He was going to step backward. The fall would kill him and he was going to do it on purpose. Her heart lurched into her throat. "Don't!" she yelled.

Dirk gave her a quirk of a smile, the same one he used whenever he was teasing her. "Bye," he said and leaned backward.

Before Tori could say another word, he was gone.

Someone behind Tori screamed. Dr. B yelled out, "No!" The sound of anguish. The sound that matched Tori's own unuttered response.

Jesse took to the air, diving after Dirk. Tori was farther away than Jesse, but she flung herself after them, knowing as she did that she wouldn't be fast enough to catch up to Dirk. It would only take him seconds to hit the ground. Could Jesse reach him in time? She willed it to happen, willed Dirk not to die. At that moment, grief cut such a huge hole through her that losing him seemed much worse than being betrayed.

She dived downward, searching for Dirk's falling body. She didn't see it. Jesse wasn't below her, either. He'd given up. He was flying sideways instead of downward. Panic washed over her. She only had moments to reach Dirk and she couldn't even find him.

And then she spotted him. Not down below her. Up and across the sky. It took her several seconds to realize what she was seeing, what it meant.

Dirk was flying. *Flying.* Dirk had pulled up and was zipping through the sky. Jesse sped after him, trying to catch up. The two rounded the corner of the Lincoln Memorial and headed across the reflecting pool toward the Washington Monument. Tori rocketed after them, the air rushing against her. Her anger was back, full force. Dirk had played them all as fools. She wasn't going to let him get away. Overdrake had a hostage—the Slayers were about to take one, too.

Dirk veered left, flying into the trees that lined the path along the reflecting pool. Tori wasn't sure whether Dirk meant to lose Jesse or whether he was just showing off. He zoomed around the trunks and branches, spinning, changing direction as fast as Jesse could. Dirk had been a flyer all along. He must have been practicing for years.

Tori trailed the two, twisting in and around the trees. She kept knocking into branches. Twigs waved at her like scolding fingers. Dirk and Jesse were both better flyers than she was, faster. Several people down on the ground noticed them. She heard people calling things, saw them pointing.

She pulled up so that she skimmed over the treetops. She kept her gaze on Dirk, not trying to catch him, just trying to keep up with him. Her hair fluttered every which way, annoying her every time it whipped into her face.

Why hadn't she known who and what Dirk was earlier? She was his counterpart. She should have known he was keeping secrets; she should have sensed his lies.

At the end of the reflecting pool, Dirk cut across to the World War II Memorial. Fifty-six granite pillars towered around an oval reflecting pool. The fountains in the middle splashed noisy, coating the area with a cold mist. He weaved in between the pillars, then streaked over a street full of lumbering cars and headed to the Washington Monument.

More people noticed them. Some yelled things. A few clapped like they were watching a show. This was all definitely against procedure—flying in public during daylight. But what else could she and Jesse do? If they caught Dirk, they would have some leverage against Overdrake.

Tori remembered when Overdrake first captured her on the top of the enclosure's roof. *You can't fly, can you?* he'd asked her mockingly. She wondered about that comment later. He seemed to know she was supposed to fly—knew it before she did.

Now Tori realized why. Overdrake knew she was Dirk's counterpart and knew Dirk could fly. It must have seemed so funny to him that she'd been caught on the roof.

Ahead of them, the Washington Monument jutted into the sky, a nearly six-hundred-foot white stone obelisk. Dirk went around the base, just above the flag poles. Jesse chased after him and then the two of them circled the building once, twice, each rotation traveling upward toward the obelisk's tip. Tori had reached them by the third time around. She couldn't catch Dirk, but she could intercept him.

She slid Dirk's leather jacket from her shoulders and then glided through the air higher than she thought he'd be when he came around next. She gripped the jacket and waited for her counterpart sense to tell her when he would appear around the side. If he was paying attention, he would know where she was, but he would think she was too far up in the air to reach him.

A moment later she felt him coming. Using every bit of her extra strength, she hurled the jacket down at him. It smacked him in the head and draped over his face. The leather wasn't hard enough to hurt. It caught him off guard, though, blinded him for a moment.

He tumbled, ripping the jacket off his face. "Tori!" he yelled in exasperation, as though she was the one being unreasonable.

Jesse plowed headfirst into Dirk, tackling him midair. They plunged downward, both twisting and grabbing at each other—a wrestling match that was falling to the ground.

Jesse had one hand on Dirk's head, keeping him from head butting. "Where is Alyssa?" he growled out.

When Dirk didn't answer his question, Jesse let go of his head and hit Dirk across his cheek. Dirk barely flinched. He took advantage of the fact that Jesse only held him with one hand, broke his grasp, and used the momentum to fling Jesse toward a flagpole.

Jesse smashed into the pole with a clang that made the group of bystanders wince. He slid downward several feet before he stopped his fall.

Tori went after Dirk. He darted away from her, flying by the pole. "Alyssa's fine," he yelled.

Jesse kicked off from the flagpole and shot back toward Dirk. "You think torture is fine?" This time when he tackled Dirk they both somersaulted through the air toward the monument. Jesse righted himself at the last moment, knocking Dirk into the wall.

Dirk's head snapped back. He recovered quickly and grabbed Jesse's shoulders. For a few moments they were at stalemate, spinning sideways against the wall as they struggled to break each other's grasp. Tori flew up to them, not sure what she could do to help Jesse. Neither guy was staying in the same place for more than a second.

"Where's Alyssa?" Jesse asked again. "If your father hurts her—"

Dirk cut him off. "Do you think he needs information from Alyssa? I already know everything she does."

The crowd around the monument kept growing as more and more people noticed the flyers. Two dozen people had their cell phone cameras out, recording the event.

Well, at least Tori had the right outfit for this activity.

Dirk tried to kick Jesse. Jesse flipped upward, dragging Dirk with him. It started another wrestling match, this one rolling upward along the monument wall. Tori skimmed along beside them, trying to grab some part of Dirk without getting pummeled in the process. Before she could, Dirk broke away from Jesse and pushed off the wall, plummeting in a backward dive.

The crowd below gasped.

Really, people? Tori wanted to yell as she and Jesse both zoomed after him. *He's not falling. Did you not notice before that he can fly?*

Just over the heads of the crowd, Dirk turned and straightened, soaring low. Jesse tailed, a few yards behind. As Dirk flew toward a group of teenage boys, he called to them, "Bet you can't stop the guy behind me!"

If Jesse had heard this, he would have had time to pull up higher, out of reach. Apparently he didn't hear Dirk's challenge. He wasn't prepared when the boys jumped up, trying to grab a hold of him. One of them hefted his friend into the air, and a boy caught hold of Jesse's leg as he went by.

The boy was yanked from his friend's grasp, where he hung, screaming, until Jesse managed to shake him off. By then Dirk was flying over Constitution Avenue.

Tori was closer to Dirk and she strained to keep up with him, to keep him in sight. He flew over buildings and traffic, then soared up to the Old Post Office Pavilion and disappeared behind the bell tower. Tori went after him, chasing him around the tower twice. From this height the buildings of D.C. looked like walls of a labyrinth laid out before them.

Dirk zoomed away from the pavilion and retreated behind the Smithsonian Castle. The Castle had always been one of Tori's favorite D.C. buildings. She loved the antique feel of its red sandstone bricks and the spires that sat like candlesticks on its roof. Now the building just seemed like an impossible place to keep track of someone. Dirk had nine spires to hide behind.

As soon as she flushed him out of one, he retreated behind another. And capes, Tori realized, were absolutely pointless. Hers did nothing but flap around her, getting in the way every time she changed direction.

Jesse caught up to them at the castle, but he kept losing Dirk. Tori had to yell, "Over here!" again and again. Dirk was close enough that she could always tell which direction he went.

Dirk must have realized he would never shake Jesse as long as Tori was around, because he finally flew around one of the spires, and instead of circling back to the roof, he shot off across the street. "This way!" Tori yelled to Jesse and went after him.

They darted over and around buildings, zooming one way, then changing directions and going another. Even though Tori was still calling out to Jesse, before long she left him behind. She didn't dare turn back to find him. The only thing that was keeping her on Dirk's tail was her counterpart sense. She didn't have to slow down or stop every time she went around a building to figure out which way he'd flown. She just knew.

After a couple minutes, Jesse called her watch-phone. "Where are you?" he asked.

"I don't know. I went by a baseball diamond a few seconds ago."

Jesse paused. "What direction are you going?"

"Um, toward a big parking lot—I think it's a hospital. It's not George Washington University. I'd recognize that one."

"I meant north, south, east, or west?"

Dirk zoomed down low so he could use the building as a screen. Tori followed. "I don't know. I don't have a compass on me."

"Your watch has a built-in compass, Tori."

Oh. She vaguely remembered Theo demonstrating that feature. "That's not one of the functions I know how to use."

Dirk went around the side of the building. Tori skimmed through the air after him, ignoring the windows she passed. If anyone was looking out, she didn't want to know.

"Do you see any street signs?"

"I can't read them from up here."

Jesse sighed, frustrated. "Are you still in D.C.?"

They were flying fast and D.C. was only ten miles long. "I don't know. I see a football field in the distance. Does D.C. have those?"

"Tori, how could you live your whole life here and not know . . ." Jesse took a deep breath. "Never mind. I'll put Dr. B on a conference call with us. He can tell me where your signal is and what direction you're going. Don't try to fight Dirk, just keep him in sight until I reach you."

"Okay."

Dirk glanced back and saw her talking into her watch. He twisted midair and missiled toward her. She hadn't expected that and didn't dart out of his way fast enough. He grabbed her wrist, tugging at the watchband. "This has got to go."

She tried to twist away from his grasp, at the same time aiming a kick at his side. Still holding on to her wrist, he jerked away to dodge her blow. The momentum spun them both, somersaulting them through the air for several feet. She noticed the hospital windows then, the patients lying in their beds watching TV. Only one young boy was looking outside. He stared at Tori, openmouthed. Yeah, after he reported this incident, his nurses would probably change his medication.

Tori kicked Dirk again, her anger hot and focused. This time the blow connected squarely in his chest with a powerful thud. He broke away from her with a grunt, ripping the watchband off her wrist as he did. It fell from her arm and tumbled downward, a black spiraling splotch that was her only contact with Jesse and Dr. B. She dived after it, caught it like a falcon grabbing hold of its prey, and then searched the sky for Dirk.

For a moment she didn't see him and cursed herself for going after her watch. She shouldn't have let Dirk distract her that way. Then she reached for him with her counterpart sense and spotted him darting over the roof.

She zipped that direction. When she reached the top, she sensed Dirk had gone left and low. She flew that way and spotted him soaring along the street toward some trees.

She slid her watch into her boot so Dirk couldn't take it again and then tore after him. All she had to do was tail him. Jesse would come. Dr. B and the other Slayers would follow in the van. Although, perhaps Dirk had thought about that, too. He was switching directions so frequently that the van would have trouble turning around and switching roads to follow him.

Tori glided over trees, lampposts, and a continual stream of traffic. It didn't matter where Dirk flew. She wasn't going to let him shake her off.

CHAPTER 21

Jesse flew high above the National Cathedral, watching for any sign of Tori and Dirk. They had to be down there somewhere.

"They've crossed Rock Creek Park," Dr. B said through the watch-phone. "They're flying northwest toward Bethesda. Go north. They're only a minute or two ahead of you."

Jesse zoomed that way. He still didn't see any sign of them.

"They're almost to Connecticut Avenue," Dr. B said.

Jesse couldn't read any of the street signs so he had to rely on Dr. B's directions.

"Too far north," Dr. B said. "Straighten up."

Jesse changed his direction slightly. He saw buildings and cars, sidewalks and trees. No sign of other flyers.

"They've changed trajectories," Dr. B said. "Veer right and pick up your speed. They're moving fast."

It was frustrating flying this way. Especially since speed worked against him. Twice he'd overshot Tori and Dirk. He'd flown by so fast he hadn't spotted them darting around trees and buildings. When he went slowly, they pulled too far ahead of him.

"Do you see them?" Dr. B asked.

"No."

Dr. B let out a sigh. "You and Tori have been out of the simulator's range for too long. You need to come back and recharge your powers."

"We can't," Jesse said. "If Tori flies away from Dirk, she'll never find him again. We need to get him now. Tori?" he said to get her attention. He hadn't heard from her in a while but figured that was because she was concentrating on Dirk and didn't want to interrupt Dr. B's directions.

Tori didn't answer.

Dr. B said, "Tori and Dirk are going to be on foot pretty soon. Tori, in five more minutes you'll need to stay close to the ground—even if you have to lose sight of Dirk in the process. Don't fly higher than you can safely fall. Jesse, come back, get recharged, and then when you go to find Tori and Dirk again, you'll have the advantage. I'm still out in Suitland on the parkway. Fly southeast. Understood?"

"Understood." Jesse flipped over and headed back the way he came. He knew Dr. B was right. Still it was aggravatingly hard to turn around when Dirk was so close and Tori needed him.

"Tori, understood?" Dr. B asked again.

She didn't answer.

"Tori?" Jesse called. The silence filled him with a growing sickness. He thought of all sorts of reasons why she wouldn't answer her phone, and none of them were good. "Could Dirk have captured Tori and put her watch on something else? A car, maybe?"

"Cars can't cut diagonally over streets," Dr. B said. "Tori's watch is flying."

It didn't make Jesse feel much better. Wherever Tori was, something was wrong.

# CHAPTER 22

The wind pushed against Tori, flinging strands of hair into her face every time she switched direction. Which she did a lot. Dirk wasn't making it easy to follow him. She soared over treetops and streets, past rows of homes, single-mindedly keeping him in sight.

Dirk flew behind the top of a tall church steeple and then stopped, hovering behind the point. The church below them was empty, the parking lot vacant. No one was around to see the two of them high above the ground.

He looked casual standing there, unconcerned. He might have been pausing after one of their daily camp jogs. "Aren't you tired of flying yet?" he called to her. "Let's take a breather."

Tori cautiously flew closer, glaring at him. It was unfair that he still looked the same. Handsome, open, achingly familiar. She kept the steeple between them.

He watched her and shook his head. "You're not even going to try and be understanding about this, are you?"

Understanding? Oh, she understood. She understood that he had just tried to lead her—to lead them all—into his father's trap. She pointed a finger at him. "You lied to me about everything."

He shrugged off the accusation with a smile. "No, I didn't. I probably only lied to you about fifty percent of everything. Is it my fault you couldn't tell the difference?"

That stung. "Do you know what I *can* tell?" she said. "I can tell where you are. You won't get away from me."

His eyebrows hiked up. "Tori, I have a hundred pounds on you and twice the muscle mass. Do you actually think if you took me on, you'd win?" He moved to the side of the steeple and motioned to her to come closer. "All right, I'm game. Go ahead and try."

He was right, and it irked her. She moved in the opposite direction, keeping the steeple between them. "I don't have to win. I just have to stick to you until Jesse gets here."

"Ah, until Jesse gets here." Dirk's voice lost its amused tone. "That's always been my role with you, hasn't it?"

Tori wasn't about to let him sidetrack her with that line of conversation. It wasn't the point, anyway. The point was innocent people suffering; freedom or war, right or wrong. Frustration made the words tangle in her throat so she hardly knew which accusation to fling at him first. "How can you do this, Dirk? How can you help your father attack your own nation?"

He didn't wince, didn't show even a flicker of guilt. "We're not so different, Tori. We both have fathers who are trying to take over the country. You help yours, why shouldn't I help mine?

"My father isn't planning on killing people."

Dirk slowly circled toward Tori. "You want to talk about our nation? Which institutions are you giving your life to protect? The Congress who's amassed a debt so huge our children's children will still be drowning in it? The endless bureaucracies? What?"

Tori circled the other way, keeping her distance from Dirk. "Our nation has its problems, but it's still the best in the world. We have freedom—"

"Oh, it's the freedom you're big on." He stopped, put his hands behind his neck, and leaned back so he looked like he was reclining in an invisible chair. "Let's examine some moments of freedom in our country's history. Ever heard about the Trail of Tears? How about the Japanese internment camps? Do you know what went on in Vietnam? The country sent its own sons to fight in a war and then turned its back on them. Do you know how many soldiers they left behind?"

Tori glided closer to the steeple. "And that makes it okay for you to attack innocent people? That makes it okay for you to betray your friends? You just pretended to care about us—"

He leaned forward, losing his relaxed pose. "The reason I turned on my father and freed all of you last summer was because his men shot at you. My father promised me none of you would get hurt—especially you. When he captured you, I went back for you. There was nothing pretend in any of that."

"Your father's men are waiting for us in that car dealership right now. How many of us would have been killed tonight?"

"None." Dirk held out his hands as though showing her something. "I don't want to hurt my friends. Not you, not any of them. But the Slayers have to lose their powers. Otherwise they'll be killed during a dragon attack. You can't win that fight."

"We did once," she said.

Dirk shook his head. "Tamerlane nearly killed you in the forest. The only reason he didn't was because I managed to enter his mind and push him away from you."

Tori remembered the dragon diving after her into the foliage. It had been so close she could smell his oily breath. "Tamerlane?" she asked. She couldn't believe Dirk had actually named the monster.

The lines in Dirk's face hardened. He was remembering that night, too, remembering it very differently than Tori did. His voice went low and was tinged with pain. "That was my father's punishment for turning on him. In order to save the rest of you, I had to help you kill my own dragon. I didn't betray you then. I watched Tamerlane die. You don't know what that was like, Tori."

The fact that he had done this sparked a flame of hope inside her. He was not completely lost. He helped them before, cared about them before. "You don't have to betray us now," she said. "Come back with me. You can help us." She held her hand out to him, fingers reaching for any little part of loyalty that was still left. "You can be one of us again."

Dirk moved closer to the steeple, staying only inches out of reach. "No, Tori. You come with me. You're my counterpart. Haven't you realized what that means?"

She dropped her hand, didn't answer him. A Slayer and a dragon lord shouldn't be counterparts. How could it be possible?

"You're part dragon lord," he said. "You have to be. Seeing what the dragon sees and hearing what the dragon hears—those were never Slayer abilities. Dragon lords have them because they can slip into a dragon's mind and control it."

Tori felt dizzy suddenly, weak. She stepped backward, forgetting that she was hanging in the air and didn't have to move that way.

Dirk held out his hand to Tori, beckoning her to come to his side of the steeple. "You've been fighting on the wrong side all along and didn't know it. You're the one who should come with me."

She didn't take his hand. Her breaths were coming too fast and she couldn't slow them. "I'm not a dragon lord," she said. "I'm not." She moved farther away from him, then looked around the sky. The sun was hovering just above the horizon, making puddles of light in the surrounding clouds. Where was Jesse? Why hadn't he come?

"Jesse won't come," Dirk said. "He can't. He's better at paying attention to details than you are. I led you out of the simulator's range nearly a half an hour ago."

Tori glanced reflexively at her wrist. Her watch was gone, lodged in the side of her boot. She could have fished it out or looked at the cell phone in her pocket. It wouldn't have done any good, though. She had no idea when they'd flown out of range or even what time it had been when they'd jumped off the Lincoln Memorial.

She looked down at the parking lot. It didn't seem like she was up that high—which went to show she'd become used to flying at high distances. Logically she knew a fall at this height would kill her. Still, if she moved to the ground, she'd lose Dirk.

She stayed put. "It hasn't been a half an hour." It couldn't have been more than twenty or twenty-five minutes since they'd flown away from the monuments, and they were in range of the simulator then. They didn't move out of range until they went over five miles away.

Dirk glided closer to his side of the steeple, closer to her. "Tori, you know you've always been lousy at keeping track of time. That's why last summer I always had to yell at you to get your Diored butt out of your cabin."

For a moment Tori worried he was right. She was in front of the highest part of steeple, with nothing to hold on to or break her fall if her powers vanished. She should move so she was over the roof. That way if she suddenly plunged downward, she'd at least have a chance of stopping herself before she rolled off the pitched roof. But moving to the other side of the steeple would put her within Dirk's reach.

He waited and watched her, not moving from his spot. "There's lots of room for you in the parking lot."

He was only trying to get rid of her. She would hold her ground, or rather—her place in the air. "It hasn't been close to a half an hour, or you wouldn't be up here."

"The reason I said you were *part* dragon lord," Dirk said as though they'd been discussing that topic, "is that you have some Slayer tendencies too—like losing your powers after a half an hour. Dragon lords, we don't do that."

"You're lying so I'll leave." Her heart was beating faster now. She wasn't sure.

"Tori," he said slowly. "I think we've already established that you can tell when I'm lying. Well, at least most of the time."

As soon as he said the sentence, she realized what else he'd lied about. Another wave of dizziness hit her. "The dragons," she said, horrified. "They've hatched, haven't they?"

Dirk tilted his chin down in frustration. "Dragons aren't evil. They're just dangerous when they're not controlled."

They were alive all of this time. They were already growing, would be ready to fight in less than a year. That wasn't enough time. She didn't have enough training. She couldn't take on Dirk, let alone his dragons.

The wind ruffled his hair. He looked so calm as he glided closer to her. "You're one of the few people who could be around them and be safe." His eyes had an intensity to them now, a sort of pleading. "You weren't born to be their slayer; you were born to be their caretaker. Will you at least promise me that you'll think about what I'm telling you?"

"Where are the dragons?" she demanded.

He let out a discouraged sigh. "You need to get to the ground. Your time is running out."

"How many eggs were there? Two?"

"Tori . . ."

"Four?" It infuriated her that Dirk knew this information and was keeping it from her. She tried to sense the answers from his reactions. "Will your father—"

She didn't finish. Dirk hadn't lied about how long they'd been out of the simulator's range. Gravity took effect, sucking her downward. She screamed. The church roof flashed by her in a blur of color. She was going to die, all because she was lousy at keeping track of time.

# CHAPTER 23

Jesse flew along the 395 heading toward the Slayer van. Dr. B was monitoring his progress and would tell him when he was within five miles of the simulator. He had to be close now.

"Tori?" Jesse asked into his watch-phone. He didn't know why he bothered. She hadn't answered the last ten times he'd said her name. His phone said he was still connected to hers, but it was hard to hear much while the wind whistled around his ears, and traffic constantly swooshed down below him. Every once in a while he heard muffled voices. He wasn't sure if that was Tori or the people in Dr. B's van.

Dr. B had said that Tori's signal was staying in the same spot now. He thought she had landed and was waiting for Dr. B to find her. Which might be true. Tori probably had no idea where she was or which direction Dr. B was.

On the other hand, Jesse couldn't forget that counterpart senses worked both ways. Dirk had a hard time hiding from Tori, but the same was true in reverse. And Dirk was bigger, stronger, and faster. What was to keep him from capturing Tori, chucking her watch somewhere, and toting her off to wherever his father was keeping Alyssa?

The more Jesse thought about it, the more likely the second scenario seemed. Why else wouldn't Tori be answering her watch? He never should have left her. He should have told her to stop chasing Dirk. What had they been thinking to let Tori tail him?

Over his watch, Dr. B said, "You're within range now."

Good. His powers were recharged. He flipped in the air and headed back toward Gaithersburg, streaking through the sky. He was going so fast he could hardly see through the wind clawing at his eyes. He had stopped worrying about capturing Dirk and just wanted to make sure Tori was safe.

That's when Jesse heard the scream from his phone. Tori's scream. Long and panicked. Jesse flew faster, even though he knew it was no use. She was miles from here and he was too far away to help. Then the scream abruptly stopped.

# CHAPTER 24

In Tori's fright, she didn't sense Dirk until he put his arms around her. He grabbed her around the middle, slowing her speed and transferring their momentum sideways. They flew along the parking lot and then back upward. Once Tori stopped screaming, she gulped in deep breaths and held on to Dirk's arms.

She had almost died. Those last moments had nearly been the end of her life. And the worst part was knowing that the media would have spent weeks speculating on how she mysteriously fell to her death, and everyone would know she died while wearing a Supergirl costume. How completely tacky.

Okay, that wasn't the worst part of nearly dying, just the first thing that came to her mind.

Dirk soared past trees and houses, kept going higher to get out of sight of anyone on the streets who might look up. "That's the third time I've saved your life. Most people would say thank you at this point."

"Thanks," she said, and then after a moment added, "although you wouldn't have had to save my life last summer if you hadn't endangered it first by leading me into your father's trap."

"A technicality," Dirk said. "Danger comes with superhero work. You should know that."

Even with Dirk's arms around her, the air rushing against her skin felt freezing. She had expected him to put her down on the ground somewhere, but he didn't. Of course he didn't. He wanted to capture Slayers tonight and now he had. Her.

"Let me go," she told Dirk.

"You don't really want me to do that. It's a long way down." And getting longer every second. Civilization was shrinking underneath their feet.

"Put me down somewhere safe. Please." She knew he wouldn't. How could she have been so stupid to let herself be caught like this?

"Where is your watch?" he asked.

"I dropped it."

"Right. I can tell that's a lie even without being your counterpart. You were expecting Jesse to find you, so you must have it on you somewhere."

An eight-lane highway came into view, the beltway that ran around the D.C. area. Rows of cars were slowly making their way in each direction. Dirk followed along above it.

"Where are you taking me?" Tori asked. She trembled and this time it wasn't from the cold. She couldn't fight Dirk. Not when he had superpowers and she didn't. She was completely at his mercy. "You're going to drug me, aren't you?" The thought hit her with surprising dread. She would be useless, unable to help the Slayers or anyone else, and she wouldn't even remember that it had happened to her. Everything she experienced over the last summer, everything that she'd become—it would be blotted out from her mind.

Dirk held on to her tighter. "I don't want you to lose your powers or your memories." The words were spoken softly. They would have been lost in the rush of the wind if Tori's hearing hadn't been so good. "When you came to see me in Winchester, I told you I wanted to be with you. Do you know why you couldn't tell I was lying?"

"Because you've had a lot of practice lying?"

"Because I wasn't lying. I told my father not to hurt or drug you. When all of this happens, I want you on my side."

All of this? Was that how he thought of attacks on cities, attacks on *people*—as if it were some sort of chess game? How could he think she would ever help him do those things? She shivered again.

He didn't notice. "You asked me how many dragons we have. The answer is there's enough for all of us. My father, me, you. If you work with us, your family will be protected. You'll have a position of power afterward. Isn't that what your father wants? We can give it to him for more than four or eight years." Dirk shifted her in his arms so he could see her face better. "Just agree to work with us. Say yes."

"I would," Tori said, "but you can tell when I'm lying."

Dirk's expression hardened. Anger flashed through his blue eyes. "You're so sure this is about good and evil that you won't even try to see my point of view. I'm just evil now, aren't I?"

Dirk tilted downward, flying lower, heading someplace now. She'd been foolish to make him mad. Maybe he changed his mind about drugging her. She swallowed hard. "Dirk, I care about you. You know I'm not lying about that. You can't really want to hurt innocent people—children, kids like Bridget. Don't do this."

"Child Protective Services," Dirk said. "That's one of many agencies my father will overhaul. I don't think abusive parents should have rights to see their kids again. Too many of them end up in garbage bins."

A huge castlelike building came into sight. The Mormon temple. The lights around the base made its white stone exterior glow, and its three-hundred-foot-tall spires seemed to pierce the coming night. A statue of a golden man stood on the front spire. He wore loose robes and held some sort of celestial-looking trumpet to his lips.

Dirk flew toward the temple. "You still want me to drop you off somewhere?"

"Yes." She didn't let herself feel either hope or relief at his question. He was asking, but not necessarily offering, and she could feel the ice in his tone.

He glided over until he hovered in front of the statue. "All right. Since you're so sure that you're on the side of good, you won't mind hanging out with an angel for a while."

This wasn't what she had in mind when she asked to be dropped off.

With one quick motion, Dirk tossed her toward the statue.

"Dirk!" she yelled, and grabbed hold of the angel's neck. She clung there, grappling to find footing. Stupid Supergirl boots. They didn't have any traction.

"What did you say?" Dirk asked with mock curiosity. "There's so much evil floating around I can't hear you."

Tori's boots scraped against the statue's robes. "If I fall and you have to save me, it so doesn't count as the fourth time." She finally found a foothold. Keeping herself pressed to the statue, she balanced her weight so she didn't slip. She let out deep breathes and held on tightly.

She heard Dirk's voice drifting away from her. "Don't worry. I'm sure Jesse will show up soon. Which means I should go. You know what they say, three is a crowd."

"Dirk!" She looked over her shoulder, attempting to reason with him one last time. "Don't go back to your father. You don't have to do this."

He turned and headed away from her without answering. If it hadn't been for her extra hearing abilities, she wouldn't have heard his parting comment: "You won't cry for me the way you cried for Jesse."

And then he was gone, disappearing into the darkening sky.

# CHAPTER 25

Dirk phoned his father while he flew toward Winchester. Instead of saying hello, his father growled out, "What happened?"

His father had been watching the Slayers' signals, waiting for them to converge on the car lot. When he saw Jesse's and Tori's signal take off across D.C., he must have known something had gone wrong.

"The mission is a bust," Dirk said wearily. "The Slayers figured out who I was. You'll need to get your men out of the car lot. Get rid of any evidence."

After a long pause, his father said, "How did they figure out who you were?" His voice dripped with accusation. He thought Dirk had told them, thought he'd thrown the mission again.

Dirk didn't expect sympathy, but he didn't deserve anger, either. He had been willing to go through with his father's plan even though he hated it. He gripped his phone harder. "Jesse told Dr. B that I knew he could track the watches. Dr. B asked me if I'd told anyone. When I said I hadn't, Tori knew I was lying. She started asking questions."

"And you couldn't think of a way to fool her?" his father drawled.

"You managed to hide your identity all last summer and when she came out for a visit. But you couldn't do it now, when it mattered most?"

Dirk hadn't had to lie about leading everyone into a trap back then. It was harder to pull off that sort of lie convincingly; he didn't point this out. His father would only see it as an excuse. "Tori remembered your accent," Dirk said. "She put two and two together." Dirk paused to let that bit of information sink in. "I told you that you shouldn't have talked to her."

His father grunted, unrepentant and unconvinced. "How lucky she recognized my voice right before the mission. It reminds me of her luck at the enclosure when you opened the roof to let the Slayers escape."

"I didn't throw the mission," Dirk insisted. "Did you notice Jesse and Tori flying, high speed, across D.C.? That was them chasing me."

Down below Dirk, the landscape crept by at a maddeningly slow pace. He couldn't fly any faster, though. The wind would make a phone conversation too hard to hear.

"Your problem is that you have split loyalties." His father's voice was cold, crisp. "You can't be completely loyal to me as long as part of you is loyal to them. Do I need to get rid of the competition so I can depend on my son again? Is that what it's going to take?"

Dirk felt the weight of the threat. His father had kept track of the Slayers' signals for nearly three months. He knew where they lived, went to school, and worked. He could send men to their homes right now.

"I didn't throw the mission," Dirk said again, more firmly this time. "It's a setback, but nothing we can't overcome. And it wasn't a complete loss," he added, hoping to distract his father from his threat. "Tori told me she found Ryker's address. He lives in Rutland, Vermont. His father's first name is Charles, not Allen. It won't be hard to find him. It's not a big city. You can have people ask around."

"Rutland, Vermont?" his father repeated, then paused for a long moment. A judgment lingered in that moment: a scale, a balance, and his friends' futures. Was Dirk's offering enough to protect them?

"Well," his father said, "it looks like I have work to do tonight after all."

Ryker didn't stand a chance. Dirk knew it, but couldn't bring himself to feel too badly about this fact. If his father's men were busy in Rutland, it would give the Slayers time to protect their families.

Ryker was a small price to pay for that.

CHAPTER 26

Tori clung tightly to the golden angel statue. She was numb from the cold. Her fingers were stiff, and she was developing what she was sure would be a lifelong aversion to the color gold. The parking lot off to the side of the building was half full of cars. Every once in a while people came out of the temple. She thought about calling to them for help, but couldn't bring herself to do it. What would happen if the news media showed up here? Exactly how would she explain her apparent angel fetish to the police, her parents, and the angry church people whose statue she was desecrating?

Yeah, if her parents were upset about her dodecahedron post going viral, wait until this story broke.

Tori's cell phone was in her pocket. She might have even been able to retrieve it without plunging to her death, but who could she call? She had to just hope that Jesse and Dr. B followed her watch's signal here.

She realized, with a shot of hope, that she hadn't ended her three-way phone call with Jesse and Dr. B. They might still be connected.

Tori lifted her leg as much as she could and yelled her location at her boot. Then she waited, ignoring the fact that raising her leg probably didn't make this scene look better from the ground.

She was barely able to hear Dr. B's faint answer. "Tori—thank heavens—are you all right?"

Well, that depended on his definition of all right. She was hundreds of feet above the ground, dangling from an angel statue. "I'm stuck on the top of a temple!" she yelled.

"We can't understand you," Dr. B yelled back. "Hang on. I've got a fix on your coordinates. Jesse is nearly there."

Hang on. Good advice.

"Is Dirk nearby?" he asked.

"No!" she yelled.

He understood that. He let out a groan of disappointment, then a moment later tried to soften it. "That's unfortunate. However, your safety is more important. You did the right thing to let him go."

Actually, she didn't let him go. She'd been holding on to him tightly until he tossed her at the angel. Tori sighed. Dr. B was not going to be happy when he heard the details of what happened. She was undoubtedly in for a really long lecture about all of this.

"Jesse has had trouble spotting you all night," Dr. B went on. "Do something to help him find you. Wave your hands or jump up and down."

"Or," Jesse's voice came over the phone, "you could wave your cape from the top of a temple spire. Good work, Tori. Hard to miss you up there."

At that moment, Tori took back everything she'd said about the cape. Capes were great.

A minute later Jesse flew up to her side. He took hold of her waist, easing her away from the statue. "Found a new guy already? You don't wait around long, do you?"

He was trying to make her smile. She couldn't, though. "Dirk put me here." She peeled her hands off the statue's neck and sunk into Jesse's arms.

He held her in an embrace. Neither of them moved for a moment. Flying was fastest when you did it horizontally or at least at an angle. Tori knew she needed to turn and face forward, but she didn't move and Jesse didn't twist her around. He held her and flew upward, away from the temple lights. It was dark enough now, no one would see them blending into the sky.

Tori couldn't stop shaking from the cold, even with Jesse's arms wrapped around her. She shut her eyes and leaned her face against his neck for warmth. He smelled the same as he had last summer.

"Are you all right?" Jesse asked again.

"Yes," she said.

"Where is your watch?"

"In my boot."

"Your boot?" he repeated, like she'd put it there on a whim. She hadn't noticed how worried he sounded until then. His voice grew low, turned into a ragged whisper. "You didn't answer when we called your name, and then we heard you scream. I thought you died."

"I'm sorry." She knew he deserved a better explanation, even if she didn't want to admit what had happened. "Dirk ripped my watch off my wrist and I didn't want to lose it, so I put it in my boot. I screamed because I was up in the air when my powers left. I sort of . . . plunged downward really fast."

"You fell?"

"Yeah. Dirk saved me."

Jesse's voice turned sharp with bitterness. "That was generous of him."

"He's not all bad." Tori didn't say anything else, couldn't defend Dirk more than that.

"I never said he was." Jesse turned her around then, keeping his arms wrapped across her stomach so she didn't fall. "But he still betrayed us." Jesse leaned forward and went faster. They soared off toward Dr. B's van, keeping high enough off the road that no one would notice them. The cars were lined up below, a slow stream of headlights inching along the beltway. "Dr. B is driving toward us. We'll be there soon."

The night air rushed against Tori's face. Her eyes stung and watered from it. She was still shaking. Jesse adjusted his grip on her, held her tighter. "Do you want my jacket? I could probably get it off without dropping you."

"No, it's fine. I'll be okay." She wasn't fine and nothing was going to be okay. "The dragon eggs hatched," she told him. "I've heard them since September. Dirk said he didn't see anything. He said Overdrake was just playing more of his soundtracks."

"The eggs hatched?" Jesse repeated. His muscles went taut like he'd been punched.

She knew how he felt. Dirk had put a hole through her, too. She'd been so angry at him before, she hadn't walked to the edge of that hole and peered down inside it. Now she did. It was deep, gaping.

"Dirk is gone," she said.

"I know." The wind took Jesse's words, took hers, flung them out into the night somewhere.

Dirk was wrong about her not crying. She broke down into tears then, sobbed really. Her powers came back when she got close enough to the simulator. She flew the last bit on her own, still crying until she and Jesse reached the van.

Dr. B had pulled over on a side street so that Tori and Jesse could land and get inside. Tori did her best to force away her emotions. It was time to start acting like a Slayer. All the Slayers were dressed in their black Kevlar mission suits. Kody had arrived at some point. He gave Tori a hug as soon as she got into the van. He was still all muscle in a cowboy-Hulk sort of way. His dark blond hair had been short cropped at camp. It was a little longer now. "Rough night?" he asked her in his Southern drawl.

"It's not over yet," Jesse said, climbing into the van behind her. He shut the door with a thud. "The eggs hatched in September."

This comment brought forth several gasps, a few swearwords, and a barrage of questions from the other Slayers. While Dr. B guided the van back onto the road, he explained what had happened in September. He sounded so tired as he spoke, as though every word were exacting a price from him. He had trusted Dirk and it had cost them.

"What are we going to do?" Rosa asked when he was done.

"What can we do?" Jesse said. "We keep training."

Dr. B glanced in the rearview mirror at Tori. "You and Jesse both need to take the batteries out of your watches."

"Why?" Tori finally pulled hers out of her boot. "Do you think Overdrake can track them?"

"Probably not," Dr. B said. "In order to get the decryption key, Dirk would have had to break into my cabin and hack into my laptop. It's just a precaution."

This wasn't the most comforting thought. Dirk's expertise was picking locks. Last summer he'd gotten into the girls' locked cabin more than once to steal Bess' stuff. That's how they ended up frozen into ice blocks. Dr. B's cabin wouldn't be any harder for Dirk to break into.

As Tori took her battery out, she wondered how Dirk's computer-hacking skills were.

"What about Alyssa?" Lilly asked. She sat next to Rosa in the middle seat, her gloved hands clenched. "We can't just leave Alyssa with Overdrake."

Bess grunted. "Well, we can't walk into Overdrake's trap, either."

Jesse put his watch in one pocket, the battery in another. "Dirk said Overdrake won't torture Alyssa. I'm not sure how much Dirk's word means, though."

While the group discussed their options, Tori took out her cell phone. She ignored the calls and texts from her parents and pushed speed dial five. Dirk's number. "I'm calling him," she announced to the van.

All gazes turned to her. "You have Dirk's phone number?" Jesse asked incredulously.

She didn't answer. Dirk had picked up.

"Hey, Tori," he said in a casual manner. "What are you up to—the top of the spire?"

She ignored the question. "I know your name, your school, your license plate number, and where your father's restaurant is. I probably could also find that land he owns. If you don't give us Alyssa back right now, I'll tell the police I saw you kidnap her."

"Nice to hear from you, too."

"Do you want the authorities poking around your house, looking through your dad's records so they can search all his properties?"

"No need to threaten," Dirk said. "If you want Alyssa, go to Tysons Corner. The parking lot by the theater. You'll find her in her car. It's a gray Hyundai."

"Tysons Corner?" Tori repeated. It was a large mall in Virginia. Dr. B flipped on his turn signal, changing lanes to head that way.

Dirk's voice became serious. "As soon as I'm done talking to you, I'm getting rid of this cell phone, but if you change your mind about things, post it online. I'll check."

"Don't bother," she said and hung up. While she relayed what Dirk had said, she turned off her cell phone and took out the battery. It felt good to rip something out.

Dr. B called out, "We'll be at Tysons Corner in twenty minutes. Tori and Jesse, get on your bulletproof gear. We'll have to be careful. This could be another trap."

CHAPTER 27

Dr. B took "careful" very seriously. As he drove, he called Booker on the phone, discussing safety and strategy. Booker had a suspiciously in-depth knowledge of firearms and SWAT team tactics.

The two talked for a while about whether the Slayers should get Alyssa or whether it would be better to call the police or her parents. Finally, Dr. B decided that since Overdrake wouldn't expect them to take chances, they probably could. Still, he sent Booker to the mall parking lot first to scope it out and cover for them.

It was six thirty when they got to Tysons Corner. They spent ten minutes scoping out the area with both infrared and high-powered binoculars. They didn't see anything out of the ordinary, but really, since so many people were coming and going to the mall and movie theaters, Overdrake's people could have blended in with them.

Alyssa's car was easy enough to spot. She sat in the driver's seat, her eyes closed and her head lolling back as though asleep.

When Dr. B was satisfied that no one in the parking lot or the surrounding buildings seemed to be armed, wearing Kevlar, or surveying the area, he let the Slayers out of the van. Dr. B didn't drive up to Alyssa's car. He was afraid that Overdrake might have men hidden somewhere with missile launchers, waiting for a vehicle to pull up to hers. So Dr. B dropped off the Slayers several rows back. They were instructed to keep low and close to the parked cars until they reached Alyssa's car. If their Slayer senses picked up any signs of danger, they were to retreat and take cover.

Up until that point, Tori had been pretty sure that the most humiliating part of the evening would be the time she'd spent clinging to an angel statue like a love-struck groupie, but no. At least when she had done that, no one was around to critique her performance. The same couldn't be said for the parking lot.

This early in the evening, a constant stream of people were walking by. Tori was dressed in a black Kevlar suit, a black helmet, black boots, and black gloves—which might not have been so bad if she hadn't also been crouching behind parked cars, surveying the area, and then darting to the nearest car.

Everyone who strolled past them stopped and stared. Many of the mall-goers felt the need to comment.

"Hey," one teenage boy called to Tori, "I think you need to go back to ninja school. I can see you."

"What a bunch of freaks," his friend added, and they both laughed.

A little girl shuffled by holding her mother's hand. "Mommy, what are those scary people doing?"

The mother glared at Tori and pulled her daughter closer. "Some Halloween thing. Ignore them and they'll go away."

Perfect. This was an awesome superhero moment: Tori in a mall parking lot, scaring children.

Jesse got to Alyssa's car first. That was the cue for the others to stop, take a position, and cover him. An empty space sat next to Alyssa's car. Tori dashed into that opening. She backed up to the next car and scanned the area around them. The Slayers had guns hidden in a slot of their boots. Tori put her hand on the butt of her gun, ready to pull it out. Jesse did a quick survey of the car, then tried to open Alyssa's door. It was locked.

Jesse tapped on the window. Alyssa's blonde hair was disheveled and she had a few mascara smudges on her cheeks. Her head flopped from one side to the other but she didn't open her eyes. Drugged probably. Tori had expected as much, yet it still made her stomach drop. Unless Dr. B found a way to reverse the process, the Slayers were down one more member.

Jesse inserted a pick into the lock. It looked like a metal centipede. He pulled a pin from the end, then fidgeted with the centipede legs, turning them. "Alyssa," he called. "Can you hear me?"

She didn't answer.

When Jesse had the legs aligned where they were supposed to be, he twisted one end. Nothing happened. He went back to fiddling with the little metal legs. Dirk was the expert at lock picking. They had depended on him for it. And now . . . Tori didn't let herself think of Dirk. She couldn't.

After a few more attempts, Jesse gave up on the driver's side lock and went around to the passenger side to work on that door. It remained locked. Jesse grunted and tried again.

A couple of middle-aged women walked by him. One of them paused and frowned at him. "Are you breaking into that car?" she demanded.

"No," he stammered.

She let out a disbelieving humph and marched off toward the theaters. "I'm telling the mall security what you're doing."

"I'm not breaking in," Jesse called after her. "It's my friend's car. See, she's sitting right there." Unconscious. Everything was clearly normal.

Kody got up from his spot and strode over to the car. He took a metal wire from his jacket pocket and worked it into the window seal, trying to open the door that way. Lilly was the next to abandon her post. She darted over to the car and banged on the window. "Alyssa! Alyssa, can you hear me?"

Alyssa opened her eyes, then shut them again.

After that, Rosa went over. "I'm her counterpart. Maybe I can get her to wake up." Rosa put her hands on the window near Alyssa's head and leaned toward it. "Alyssa, open the door. Reach out and push that little button. I know you can do it if you'll just wake up."

Bess sighed and left her post as well. "If Overdrake hasn't shot us all by now, I doubt he's here. But as long as the rest of you are gathered around the car like a willing target, I might as well put up a shield to protect us."

Which meant Tori was the only one unshielded. Was it better to stay here crouching by this car or should she join the others? The cramp in her leg decided the matter for her. She got up and slunk over to Alyssa's car.

As she did, Kody managed to push the lock button with his wire. He flung open the driver's side door. Lilly reached in and grabbed Alyssa's arm. "Alyssa, wake up!"

Alyssa opened her eyes, saw them, and let out a startled scream. She batted Lilly's hand, jerked away from the door, and screamed again.

Lilly pulled off her helmet. "It's me, Lilly. Are you okay?"

Alyssa stopped screaming and put her hand to her chest. "I was until you scared me to death." Her gaze darted between the other Slayers. "Who are the rest of you?"

"It's all of us," Jesse said. "The Slayers. You need to come with us. This isn't a safe place."

Alyssa squinted at him. "Jesse? What are you doing here? Why are you guys dressed like that?"

"Can you walk?" Lilly asked.

Alyssa looked around, noticing her surroundings for the first time. "Wait, how did I get here?"

"Sorry about this," Kody told her, "but it's gotta be done." He reached into the car, picked her up, and flung her over his shoulder.

"What the—" Alyssa yelled. "Hey, put me down!"

Dr. B had pulled up with the van. The door slid open. "Get in," he called to them.

Kody climbed into the van with Alyssa, the rest followed. Kody set Alyssa down in the middle seat, and everyone moved toward their seats or lookout positions. The door hadn't shut all the way before Dr. B was roaring through the parking lot toward the street.

"How is she?" Dr. B asked.

"We're not sure," Bess answered, making her way to the back of the van.

Alyssa looked at the group warily. "Okay, this has been a great Halloween prank—sneaking up on me and freaking me out with your costumes. Not nearly as good as that time Bess sewed up my sleeping bag, but still really good."

Kody had taken a gun from his boot and stationed himself by the front window, checking the cars around them.

Dr. B barely paused at a stop sign before he pulled onto the street. "Is anyone following us?"

"Not that I can see," Kody answered. With their night vision, the Slayers could see farther than Dr. B's rearview mirror allowed.

Bess peered out the back window. "It's clear back here."

Alyssa watched them and laughed in a forced sort of way. "This is fun. Really. And it's good to see all of you again." She gestured in a fluttering motion to them. "Are the rest of you going to take your helmets off, because they're still sorta freaking me out."

Everyone but Kody and Bess did. They kept theirs on in case they had to lean out of the window and exchange fire.

Dr. B made a quick turn, lurching the van onto another street. "Alyssa, what's the last thing you remember?"

Alyssa's smile dropped and her eyebrows knit together as she tried to remember. "I was going to a costume store . . ." She pulled out her cell phone from her pocket and checked the time. "Is it really quarter to seven?" She looked outside at the passing street. "Wait, what was I doing in the mall parking lot?"

Lilly was sitting beside her, straight backed and stoic. Tori could tell she was preparing for the worst while still holding on to threads of hope. Such thin, thin threads. "Do you remember anything about Overdrake taking you?"

"Overdrake," Alyssa repeated. "That name sounds familiar. Was he going to the party?"

The air went out of Lilly. She slumped in her seat, threads snapped.

One more Slayer was gone. Now, when they needed all the help they could get, they'd lost Alyssa.

Rosa's large brown eyes filled with worry. "You don't remember Overdrake?" She was really asking, *You don't remember you're my counterpart?*

Alyssa shook her head. "It's weird. I don't remember anything since I pulled up to the costume store." She ran a shaky hand through her hair. "Look, I appreciate you guys picking me up and taking me to"—she stared at their outfits again—"whatever party you're going to. I think I should go home, though. I don't feel good."

Dr. B switched lanes. "We'll take you home." His words were calm, but his grip on the steering wheel was tight. "You should get some rest. We'll talk about this later when you're feeling better."

"I live off Old Courthouse Road," Alyssa said. "It's not far from here."

She would have never announced her address if her memory was intact.

Lilly gulped. Her disappointment hung about her. "Alyssa, think hard. What do you remember about being a Slayer? There must be something."

Alyssa shrugged like she wasn't sure why Lilly was asking. "Slayers? That's what we called each other at camp while we played those games." She smiled in a nostalgic sort of way. "It seems like that happened so long ago, but it's only been a few months."

"What would it mean to you," Lilly asked, "if I told you the dragon eggs have hatched and they'll be full grown in less than a year?"

Alyssa shrugged again. "It means you're still really into dragon games." As she turned in her seat, she noticed the guns in Kody's and Bess' hands. "Those aren't real, are they?" She scooted farther away from them and laughed nervously. "You know, you guys are a little too intense for me tonight."

Rosa stared at Alyssa and made a pitiful sort of whimper. She'd lost her counterpart. Lilly had lost her friend. A-team had lost their healer. And new dragons had hatched. This fact kept presenting itself in Tori's mind, circling her with its immense desperation. Last summer, when they all fought together—with Dirk's help—they barely managed to kill one dragon. How could they fight three without Dirk or Alyssa? And how many other Slayers would Overdrake be able to pick off before the dragons attacked?

Alyssa felt her pants pockets. "Does anybody know where my car keys are?" She put her hands in her jacket pockets, and as she did the front of her jacket moved, revealing a piece of paper pinned to her shirt. She looked at it with confusion, ripped it off, and then held it up to read it.

"What is that?" Jesse asked, leaning over his seat to get a better look.

"Oh, this is nice," Alyssa said sarcastically. "You guys pinned your addresses to my shirt while I was sleeping in my car. I'm going to pretend I don't find *that* creepy."

"What?" Jesse grabbed the sheet from her hand and scanned it. His eyes widened with shock. "It is. This is my address."

Dr. B muttered something low and angry under his breath. "Overdrake tracked you."

Great. Dirk's computer-hacking skills were apparently as good as his lock-picking skills.

Alyssa kept checking her pockets for her keys. "You know, if you guys want to get together sometime, I need your phone numbers, not your addresses."

Tori took the paper from Jesse's hand. All the remaining Slayers names and addresses were listed. Jesse Harris. He lived in Silver Spring, Maryland. Kody Wright lived in West Virginia. Shang Lao lived in New York. New York? No wonder he wasn't here. Rosa Lopez, Alyssa Gustafson, and Lilly Schiete lived in Virginia. Bess Bartholemew lived in Maryland. Tori's address was listed in McLean, Virginia. "Mine is right, too," she said.

Rosa plucked the paper from Tori's hand, glanced at her address, and let out a short scream.

Alyssa blinked at Rosa, then scooted closer to the van's door. "Dr. B, um, you can just let me out here. I can walk the rest of the way to my house. I know the way."

Dr. B pulled a phone from his jacket, a small silver one that Tori had never seen before. He pressed a speed dial button on the phone and put it to his ear. "I need to talk to Sam. It's an emergency."

Sam. Jesse had told her last summer that Sam funded the camp. Judging from all the special equipment the Slayers had, Sam was wealthy. Beyond that, the Slayers didn't know anything about him—or her. They didn't even know if Sam was a real name.

Into the phone, Dr. B said, "It's a code two."

Tori was about to ask what a code two was when she noticed something was different. It took her a moment to realize what: The music by the dragons had stopped. For the first time in months, that part of her mind was silent. It didn't last. Overdrake's voice twined into that space.

"Hello, Tori. It's time for us to have a private chat."

Overdrake was by the eggs. He had stopped the music to get her attention.

She shut her eyes and let the sound expand in her mind. "Overdrake is speaking to me," she announced.

Jesse said something; she didn't hear what. She was doing her best to block out the other sounds in the van—Dr. B talking on the phone and Alyssa's nervous commentary about people who heard disembodied voices.

"I suppose by now," Overdrake went on, "you've had time to find Alyssa, get reacquainted, and noticed the note I left for you. As you can see, I know where the Slayers live. I haven't hurt any of you before because I promised Dirk I wouldn't. All bets are off now, though. I'm offering you one chance to surrender yourselves or your families will pay the price. Do you remember the land Dirk took you to? Bring the other Slayers there. Someone will be waiting for you who can relieve you of your powers. Then you can go home and return to your normal lives—the lives you should have had all along. Isn't that what you want, Tori—a normal life?"

One of the dragons screeched. Overdrake shushed it angrily and it fell silent. "You can't win," Overdrake said. "I know your plans, your strategies, and your weaknesses. I know everything you know. And now you're down by two more Slayers. Be reasonable. Persuade the others to go to the property. If it makes it easier for you, you don't have to tell them that my men are waiting for them. Tell them something else. You'll be doing them a favor, saving their lives."

Tori's heart pounded. Overdrake wanted her to betray the other Slayers, wanted her to finish what Dirk had started.

The music resumed. Tori opened her eyes. "He said we have three hours to go to Winchester and turn ourselves over or our families will pay the price."

"Not a chance," Jesse said.

Dr. B didn't say anything. Tori wasn't sure he even heard the ultimatum. He was still talking on the phone.

Kody made a growling noise in his throat. "Nobody had better mess with my family. I'll go after Dirk myself. What high school did you say he went to?"

"John Handley High," Tori said. "Although I doubt he'll be there on Monday. He'll disappear."

Lilly hit the side of the van with her fist. "We had him with us all summer." She turned to Tori, eyes narrow, her lips an angry red slash. "How come you didn't know then that Dirk was double-crossing us?"

"None of us knew," Jesse said.

"We weren't his counterparts." Lilly waved her hand at Tori accusingly. "When Shang's family moved, I could tell just from the stress he felt every time somebody talked about going back home or starting a new school year. Last summer, I could tell Shang's girlfriend dumped him the first time I talked to him at camp. How could you not know that Dirk was massively lying to all of us?"

Tori's stomach twisted. Lilly was right. Tori should have known, should have picked up on clues earlier. She had never felt that deceit from him at camp, though. All she could do was shake her head. "I don't know."

"You don't know?" Lilly repeated. "He and his father are trying to take over the nation. How did that fact slip by you for an entire freaking summer?"

"Stop it," Jesse broke in. "Blaming Tori won't do any good."

Lilly spun on him. "If you and Tori hadn't always been off in the forest, maybe she would have noticed Dirk was leading a double life. But no. She was too busy making out with you."

"That's enough!" Jesse's expression didn't leave room for argument.

Alyssa's eyes bounced between Lilly, Tori, and Jesse. She edged closer to the door. "I really need to go home. I mean, I have homework. And things." She leaned forward in her seat and waved to get Dr. B's attention. "Hey, you went past my street."

Lilly put her hand on Alyssa's arm. The anger she had just leveled at Tori and Jesse was gone. Her voice was earnest, pleading. "Listen to me, I'm going to help you remember who you are. You can't smoke or drink—not even those energy drinks—nothing with drugs. You need to let the pathways in your brain regrow." Alyssa tried to pull her arm away from Lilly, but Lilly held on tightly. "I'm going to come over to your house every weekend and make sure you don't inadvertently put more drugs in your system. It will be fun. We can hang out someplace where there's lots of security and not do drugs."

Alyssa slid farther away from Lilly. "I'm really busy during the weekends." She looked out the window again. "Dr. B, you need to turn around."

Dr. B had finished talking on the phone. He pulled the van over to the side of the road, then turned and attempted a smile. It looked pained. "I'm sorry, Alyssa. Something has come up, so I can't drive you home after all. Booker is in the van behind us. He'll take you where you need to go."

"Oh," Alyssa said. "Okay. See you guys later." She opened the van door and nearly leapt outside.

Dr. B leaned out the window to speak to her. "I'm sorry you aren't feeling well. Maybe we'll get together another time."

She didn't answer. She had already shut the van door and was going to talk to Booker. Maybe to insist that she would be safe enough to walk the rest of the way home. She probably would be. Overdrake had already taken her powers and her memory. She wasn't a threat to him anymore and wouldn't be again unless Dr. B found a way to restore her powers.

And in less than a year the dragons would be full grown.

Dr. B pulled the van back onto the street. He gazed briefly at the Slayers through the rearview window. "I've initiated identity breach protocol. It's not something I ever wanted to do, but we've no choice. With the exception of Tori's home, men posing as FBI agents will go to your houses. They'll tell your parents you witnessed a drug-cartel-related shootout. In order for you to testify against the drug dealers involved, you and your family need to be immediately relocated in the witness protection plan. They'll take your families somewhere safe tonight. Your possessions will be boxed up and put into storage for the time being. Sam will work with his contacts to get your parents new identities and jobs."

"Permanently?" Kody asked.

Dr. B sighed. "Permanently until Overdrake is caught or stopped."

"Just like that we have to leave?" Lilly asked. It wasn't really a question. "Our homes, our schools, our friends—everything."

"It's better than the alternative," Bess pointed out.

"What about Tori?" Jesse asked. "Why isn't anyone being sent to her home?"

Tori hadn't asked because she already knew. "My father works for the government. It would be too easy for him to check on the men's story. Besides, my father isn't going to change his identity."

"Tori's family already has security measures in place," Dr. B said. "For the time being, we'll have to hope that those are enough to keep Overdrake away." Dr. B punched in some numbers into his regular cell phone. "I'm calling Shang's home number. I sent him a message earlier to disable his watch, but I never heard back from him." He handed his phone to Kody. "Ask him if he's done it, and tell him about the FBI agents."

Dr. B picked up his silver phone again, about to make another call to Sam.

Rosa leaned forward in her seat. "Men posing as FBI agents? Why couldn't they have helped us when Alyssa was kidnapped?"

Dr. B's lips twitched as though he didn't like telling them the answer. "They're actually members of George Mason's drama department who agreed to help me should I ever need it. I couldn't send them to a place where Overdrake's men might shoot at them."

"What?" Jesse asked. "Overdrake is threatening our families and you're sending in drama teachers?"

Dr. B held up his hand to stop Jesse's protest. "Booker and a few of the other camp staff will be armed and doing surveillance. The drama teachers are just our front men, friends of mine." He cleared his throat, still explaining. "Throughout history, very few people have ever been double-crossed by drama teachers. They're obviously not the sort of people who do things for the money."

Jesse rubbed his forehead tiredly.

"Perfect," Lilly mumbled. "That's who we want watching our backs. Thespians."

In the front seat, Kody was nearly yelling into the phone. "I need to speak to Shang . . . Is Shang . . . is there somebody around who speaks English?"

"Tori," Dr. B said, finding her in the rearview mirror. "I'll take you home before I take the others to the safe house. I'll have Bess call your home phone tomorrow and give you any updates."

"Okay," Tori said.

Kody kept trying to communicate with whoever was on the phone. "Do you know if Shang's watch still works . . . The thing on his wrist that tells time . . . Um, just have him call this number as soon as he comes back. It's an emergency."

It seemed surreal that the others had to go to a safe house, that so much had changed in the space of a few hours, that Dirk was a traitor. *I know everything that you know,* Overdrake had said.

And then Tori remembered what else she told Dirk. She let out a moan.

All eyes turned to her. They must have thought that Overdrake was speaking again.

"Ryker," she breathed out. "I told Dirk that Ryker lived in Rutland. He's in danger now."

# CHAPTER 28

Tori's comment brought an immediate response from everyone in the van. None of it happy. Most of it confused. Tori didn't answer their questions right away. She was too busy chastising herself, too busy wallowing through pointed self-recriminations. How could she have trusted Dirk with Ryker's location? How could she have been so taken in?

Dr. B consulted with Sam, changed his course, and headed toward the airport. They had no way to call and warn Ryker that Overdrake's men would come after him. They had to go in person. Fortunately Sam had a private plane they could use.

As Dr. B drove, he told the other Slayers about Ryker's phone call. Then Tori told them how she'd had her father track down Ryker's address and what she'd told Dirk.

"So pretty much," Lilly said when Tori finished, "everything that's gone wrong tonight—Alyssa's capture, all of us being forced out of our homes, and Ryker being in danger—that all happened because Jesse and Tori can't keep a secret. They told Dirk things that Dr. B specifically warned them not to tell anyone."

Tori didn't answer, couldn't defend herself. She felt sick.

Bess let out a grunt. "You're one to talk. You and Alyssa exchanged phone numbers. The only reason all of this isn't your fault is that Alyssa wasn't the traitor."

"I didn't endanger everybody—" Lilly started.

Dr. B cut her off. "That's enough. It's time we all rededicate ourselves to keeping the rules."

"I think we need new team captains," Lilly said, still sounding wounded. "I don't care if the two of them can fly. The way things are going, they'll get us killed before Overdrake even attacks."

Dr. B kept his gaze on the traffic around him. "I've already called team leaders and you sustained them."

One of Dr. B's rules was that if a time came when more team members opposed the captain's leadership position than supported it, the captain would be asked to step down. There had been some moments at camp—usually when Dirk or Jesse had woken up everyone in the middle of the night for a surprise drill—that the Slayers would have cheerfully unsustained either of their captains. But the vote was only taken once: at the beginning of the summer. After that, if any of the Slayers complained, Dr. B reminded them that they had voted already and now it was their job to follow their leader's orders.

"I sustained Dirk," Lilly said, "Not Tori. You can't put her in as a captain now. I know more about leading a team than she does."

Tori nearly argued the point. She had worked harder than anyone last summer. During free time, while everybody else had been goofing off in the lake or relaxing in the cabins, Tori had been holed up memorizing strategies, hand signals, and procedures.

Tori didn't argue, though. She hadn't wanted to be a captain before tonight, and now that the weight of Ryker's fate hung on her—she knew she couldn't do it. She didn't want to be responsible for a team's safety. She didn't want to make decisions that could cost people their lives. Besides, with Dirk and Alyssa both gone, A-team consisted of only Tori, Lilly, and Kody. Lilly wouldn't sustain her, which meant Tori would never have a majority vote. "We should combine the teams," Tori said. "Jesse should be the captain of both."

Dr. B sighed, clearly not pleased with this answer. "Let's define the mission parameters before we decide that issue. Bess, there's a pen and paper next to my seat. I'd like you to keep the mission notes."

It was procedure before a mission to make one list of needed supplies and another detailing everyone's responsibilities. Since last summer, whoever kept the lists had to write them in code.

"What is our goal?" Dr. B asked, slipping into his role of teacher. Although, strictly speaking he was never a *real* teacher. Real teachers told you how to solve the problems they assigned you. Dr. B always wanted the Slayers to find the solution themselves.

Back at camp Tori hadn't minded this so much, even when it was clear that Dr. B knew the answer and was just waiting it out, prodding them in the right direction until they figured it out. Now Tori found it irritating. "Our goal is to warn Ryker," she said curtly. "His family will have to move."

"Do you know any drama teachers in Vermont?" Bess asked her father.

Lilly folded her arms, still sullen. "We should talk to Ryker before we talk to his parents. That way we won't have to admit that we illegally found his address and then screwed up and leaked it to Overdrake."

Not *we*. Tori had done that. She didn't look forward to telling Ryker about it.

Jesse stared at the floor in thought. "Our goal isn't just to warn Ryker. It's to convince him to come with us. More dragons have hatched. We can't wait until next summer. We have to train with him now."

"Yes," Dr. B agreed, "*that* is our goal. Suggestions?"

Kody cocked his head. "You're not saying we should kidnap him, are you?"

"That's one suggestion," Dr. B said. He gestured to Bess. "Write it down."

As Bess moved her pen across the paper, she muttered, "Commit a felony . . . risk jail time . . ."

"Other suggestions?" Dr. B called.

Rosa shifted in her seat. "We could talk to Ryker's parents and explain that the nation needs him."

Bess scribbled down another sentence. "Already tried that . . . failed miserably . . . Ryker's parents are unpatriotic slugs . . ."

Dr. B took his gaze from the road long enough to send his daughter a stern look. "There are no wrong answers in the brainstorming phase."

"Fine," she said. She tapped her pen against her paper, then wrote out a sentence. "Seduce Ryker . . . Get married. Have the state of Vermont declare him legally an adult."

Dr. B glared at Bess again. She ignored him and kept tapping her pen, waiting for more suggestions.

No one said anything for a minute. Jesse was still staring at the same spot on the floor, his brows pulled together in thought. Everyone else looked alternately at their hands, at each other, and at the ceiling.

Dr. B sped by cars, weaving in between them as he passed. It was one more example of his optimism when it came to human nature. He just assumed that people would make room for a speeding van that was hauling a trailer.

"We could tell Ryker's parents they won a cruise," Rosa suggested. "We'll tell them they have to leave immediately. Then while they're gone . . . we burn down their house, and move them to a secret location."

Everyone in the van stared at Rosa. Bess didn't write the suggestion down. Instead, she picked up the paper, surveying what she'd already written. "If Ryker's not bad looking, I'll volunteer to marry him."

"We have to talk some sense into his parents," Kody said. "We don't have another choice." He held up a hand to emphasize the point. "That means we gotta admit we put them in danger. There's no getting around it."

We put them in danger. Again, Tori.

Lilly shook her head. "They'll never let Ryker join us if we tell them the truth. We'll have to come up with a really compelling lie . . ."

"A compelling lie . . . ," Rosa repeated. Her face was blank. "I'm not good with lies."

Bess twirled the pen between her fingers. "We totally studied the wrong stuff at camp. Not once did we have a class on lying in order to lure people away from their homes."

Dr. B didn't say anything about the new direction the conversion had taken. He kept driving, waiting for them to come to a conclusion. And then—Tori knew from experience—after they came up with the wrong thing, he would gently point out to them why their plan was doomed to failure and make them start the process all over again.

Maybe it had been too long of a day, too emotional. Maybe it was because a dragon hatchling was awake now, screeching in the corner of Tori's mind. It sounded like metal being ripped from a car. It made it impossible to think. She had no patience left.

"Dr. B, just tell us the right answer," she said. "What are we supposed to do?"

He didn't answer for a moment. When he did, his voice was sympathetic. "Sometimes there isn't a right answer, only a better answer. I can't tell you what to do. The consequences will be yours, the choice should be, too."

Jesse lifted his head, finally rejoining the conversation. "Dr. B is right. This is a Slayer decision and the Slayer most qualified to make it is Ryker. We'll talk to him first. He'll know how to handle his parents."

"News flash," Bess said. "Not all of us know how to handle our parents." She motioned to her father. "If I did, I would get away with a lot more stuff."

Jesse reached over and took the pen and paper from Bess' hand. He flipped to a clean page and wrote the word "supplies" on the top. "If Ryker wants to join us, we'll find a way. He can run away and Dr. B's drama teacher friends will tell my parents the FBI assigned Ryker to be my live-in bodyguard. Ryker's parents won't find him at my house." Underneath "supplies," Jesse wrote the word "simulator." "And if Ryker doesn't want to join us, there's nothing we can do to force him into it."

It was 7:20 when they reached the Dulles airport. Dr. B drove onto the tarmac where Sam's plane was waiting for them, already fueled up. It was a sleek white Gulfstream, just big enough to fit the group and their gear.

The Slayers piled out of the van and began loading their weapons, the simulator, and everything Dr. B had brought for Alyssa's rescue mission. They didn't know what they would need when they tracked down Ryker. Overdrake's men might have beaten them to his house—or they might not show up for days. It all depended on how well Charles Davis had managed to hide his personal information.

While the Slayers were loading things, Dr. B came up beside Tori. "If you need to go home instead of coming with us, I'll understand."

All the other Slayers had a built-in excuse for being out late. They were meeting with FBI agents. But as far as Tori's parents knew, she had ditched them at the hospital, hadn't told anyone where she was going, and had refused to answer her phone. She was going to be in massive trouble when she got home, and taking an hour-and-fifteen-minute plane trip to Vermont was only going to make things worse for her.

"I'll go with you," Tori said. How could she not? It was her fault Ryker and his family were in danger. "I'll need to turn my phone back on long enough to text my mom that I'll be out late with friends."

Which was, technically speaking, the truth. No need to worry her parents with details about her possibly running into gun-toting men. Tori also reminded them to turn on the house alarm. Her hands shook a little as she did that. If it sounded cryptic, well, at least they would be careful.

They needed to be extra careful now.

Tori had expected a pilot to join them in the plane. Instead, Dr. B sat down in the cockpit. The others weren't surprised at all. As they settled into their seats, Rosa told her, "For a couple of years, Dr. B was hoping Sam's contacts would come up with a design for planes that could take off out of the range of the EMP and then rely on manual technology to maneuver in the air. He thought we might be able to fight the dragons that way. One summer we had to practice fighting while parachuting to the ground."

"They couldn't get a design that worked?" Tori guessed.

"Not one that could maneuver well enough," Kody said. "And the parachutes—yeah, we were pretty much just hanging in the sky like dragon hors d'oeuvres."

While the group flew to Rutland, they went over the remaining details of their plan. They would land at Southern Vermont Regional Airport, rent a van, and drive the five miles to Rutland. When they got to Ryker's house, Tori and Bess, dressed in their Halloween costumes, would ring the bell. If someone from Ryker's family answered, they would pretend to be from Ryker's school and ask to see him. When Ryker came to the door, they would clarify that they were new students moving into the area and ask to talk to him about the school.

Kody was flipping through pictures of girls on the Internet who listed Rutland High School on their profile pages. "Tell him that Paige Child told you Ryker was the guy to ask about the school. She looks nice. You know, the friendly sort."

Tori nibbled on some trail mix. None of them had eaten dinner, so they all went through the stash of snacks on the plane. "And you think Ryker will believe that? Out of the blue, two girls show up on his doorstep and want to talk to him?"

"If he's cute, he will." Bess reached over and stole some M&M's from Tori's trail mix. "Hot guys are used to girls throwing themselves at them."

"We don't know if he's cute," Tori pointed out.

Bess gazed upward. "If God is merciful, he is." She shut her eyes as though praying. "Ryker will be cute, single, and like girls with curly hair and a sense of humor."

Kody was still reading the Internet page. "Do ya suppose Ryker really knows Paige Child? I wonder if she's the type who'd go for a long-distance romance . . ."

"Back to the plan," Tori said. "I'm worried about just showing up on Ryker's doorstep. I mean, what if he doesn't want to go off somewhere private to talk to us?"

Jesse's gaze traveled over Tori. "With you dressed like that?" His voice was tinged with accusation. "Don't worry. He'll go with you."

Bess eyed Tori and let out an exasperated huff. "Jesse's right. This is totally unfair. I'm dressed as a cowgirl and you're dressed like a hooker with a superhero complex. Ryker isn't even going to look at me."

Tori blinked, offended. "Hey, I didn't design the outfit—DC Comics did. And it doesn't even show that much of my midriff."

Bess stole more of Tori's M&M's. "Never mind. It doesn't matter. If Ryker is the type of guy who's only interested in girls in miniskirts and halter tops, then I don't want him."

"This isn't a halter top," Tori insisted, tugging it down. "And I don't care what Ryker looks like. I'm not interested."

"Good," Jesse said. "Can everybody stop acting like this is speed dating, so we can finish planning the mission?" He put his pen to the paper. "Do we need to buy any supplies in Rutland?"

"Lipstick," Tori said.

"Lipstick?" Jesse repeated. "Why do you need that?"

"It's part of my cover. If I was really going to Ryker's house to hit on him, I'd touch up my lipstick first." She ran a hand over her hair. The wind had made it a mess. "I'll need a brush, too."

Jesse tapped the pen against the paper. "That's not worth a trip to the store. You'll have to manage without it."

"No, you won't," Bess whispered. She patted her jacket pocket. "I was going to a party with hot guys. I'm prepared."

Eventually the planning was done, and then everyone got up and made a second trip through the food cabinets. Everyone except for Jesse. He sat by himself, looking out his window. Tori grabbed a few things and went and sat next to him.

She offered him a soda. He shook his head. She held out a package of cookies. He shook his head at those, too. He had to be hungry. She was starving and she hadn't flown as far or as long as he had.

"Well," she said, surveying the food she brought over. "We know one thing about Sam: He isn't into health food."

Jesse didn't comment. The lines of his face were hard, angry.

"Are you thinking about Dirk?" she asked.

"I'm thinking about Alyssa."

He was angry at himself then.

Tori put her hand on his arm. "It wasn't your fault—telling Dirk about the tracking program. We all trusted him."

"But I'm the one who told him. Now we only have one healer. How many lives do you think that will cost?"

"If Dirk hadn't been a traitor, telling him that information could have saved all of our lives."

"*Could have* doesn't matter." Jesse went back to staring out the window. His gaze was fierce and determined. And worried. He didn't look at her, didn't speak again.

"I'm trying to make you feel better," she said. "You're making it hard."

"Sorry." He kept staring out the window.

She opened the packages of cookies and bit into one. Her stress made everything taste bland and chalky.

"You probably think it's ironic," he said. "I refused to break the rules with you during the school year, and then broke a rule that nearly got us all eliminated."

Tori hadn't thought of it that way. Now it stung. "You're right." She took another bite of the cookie, crunching it extra hard between her teeth. Jesse had trusted Dirk enough to tell him important secrets, secrets he'd never told her. Jesse wouldn't even show up at the Natural History Museum to have lunch with her.

And Dirk wasn't any better. He'd used Tori to get information about Ryker. He'd played her. "When you come right down to it, guys are jerks."

Jesse finally gave her his full attention. "Tori, you stink at making people feel better."

"Sorry, I stink at a lot of things." She took a cookie from the package and handed it to him. "Eat it," she said. "You'll need your strength."

CHAPTER 29

It was almost nine o' clock by the time Dr. B pulled onto Ryker's street. His house was on the east side of Rutland in a neighborhood that backed up to a forest. The yards were so large and the pine trees so big that you couldn't see one house from the next. Tori had hoped Ryker lived in a tract-home neighborhood, one that would be hard for Overdrake's men to converge on without being noticed by neighbors and trick-or-treaters. This house—an entire SWAT team could have hidden in the trees.

Dr. B parked down the street. Tori and Bess walked to the house, both of them surveying the area. The night was even colder now. Tori was grateful the simulator energy helped keep her warm. She would be shivering otherwise. The only jacket she had was the Kevlar one, and she couldn't very well wear that while pretending to be a trick-or-treater.

"I'm Courtney, you're Britney," Bess told her. "You're the pathetic stalker girl. I'm your normal friend that you brought along for support."

"I'm always the pathetic stalker girl," Tori mumbled.

"Also," Bess went on, "when you're off your medication, you do impulsive things. It can't be helped."

"Thanks," Tori said. "Thanks a lot."

Bess rang the doorbell. A few moments later a woman holding a bowl of candy answered the door. She was tall and trim with shoulder-length blonde hair and perfectly applied makeup. She had a professional air about her and looked so young Tori worried they had the wrong house. Could this woman be the mother of a seventeen-year-old? The woman held out a couple of miniature Snickers to Tori and Bess, then noticed they didn't have bags.

"Hi," Tori said sheepishly. "We're not trick-or-treaters. We were actually wondering if Ryker was home."

The woman didn't look confused or surprised by the name. They had the right house.

Before Mrs. Davis put the Snickers back in her bowl, Bess reached out and took one from her hand. "We're friends of his."

"Oh," Mrs. Davis said, looking them over more closely. Her eyes lingered on Tori's miniskirt with a twinge of disapproval. "He's not home right now. He went to a party at Jason's house."

"Jason?" Tori repeated, fishing for more information.

"Jason Ferguson," Mrs. Davis said.

A teenage girl walked up to the door. She was also tall and blonde, with high cheekbones and a build like a ballerina. Ryker's sister, most likely. She looked them over, probably expecting to recognize them and seemed perplexed that she didn't. Rutland was such a small city all the teenagers probably knew one another. Time to switch stories.

"You're Ryker's friends?" the girl asked.

"We're actually from Burlington." Tori said. "Ryker and I met at a football game, and he told me if I was ever in Rutland to stop by." She said it too fast, wasn't sure if it even sounded believable. If Ryker had a steady girlfriend, the next few moments were going to be very awkward.

Tori smiled and silently hoped Ryker's sister didn't ask anything about Burlington's football team. It wouldn't help their story if Ryker's family realized that Tori didn't know certain key facts, like the name of Burlington's high school or the name of their team.

"Oh," Mrs. Davis said again, and made another survey of Tori's costume. This time her eyes stopped on Tori's bare midriff. "What were your names?"

"Britney and Courtney," Bess said. She ripped open her Snickers and took a bite. "Since we're not from here, could you tell us how to get to Jason's house?"

The teenage girl stepped around Mrs. Davis onto the porch. "I can give you directions."

"Don't leave with them, Willow," Mrs. Davis said. "You're staying in tonight." The sentence was said in the tone of a parent who had grounded their child and wanted to make sure they remembered that fact.

"I won't," Willow replied, exasperated.

Mrs. Davis shut the door. Willow waited a moment, then glanced behind her to check that they were alone. She walked down the steps with Tori and Bess and lowered her voice. "Actually, Ryker's not at that party. So don't waste your time going."

"Oh. Okay," Tori said. "Where is he?" A chill breeze blew against her legs. No wonder Ryker's mother had kept staring at her costume. Clearly only crazy people and trampy girls would wear this little clothing on such a cold night.

"Probably on his way home . . . or maybe he just had to come back to town for something . . ." Willow seemed like the friendly type, not overly suspicious. That was good. She pulled out her phone and texted the words, "Where are you?"

Tori tried to catch sight of Ryker's number but was only able to glimpse a few numbers. "Don't tell him I'm here," she said. "I want to surprise him."

Bess leaned back on the heels of her cowboy boots, casually glancing around the front yard. "He's not out on a date, is he? That would be embarrassing. I mean, if he is—tell us where he's going so we don't accidentally run into him."

"He's not on a date," Willow said quickly. "He's just . . . out." She was withholding information. "Sometimes it's hard to get a hold of him. If he's not answering it probably means he'll be out until late."

Tori looked down at the ground and pushed a strand of hair behind her ear, pretending to feel reluctant. "I don't get to Rutland very often and I was really, really looking forward to seeing him. Can you at least tell us where he was going?"

Bess leaned toward Willow with a confidential air and motioned to Tori. "They're soul mates. Britney talked about Ryker the entire car ride up. Please help her see him or I'm going to hear about it all the way back to Burlington."

Willow fiddled with her cell phone, looked uncertain, then typed out another text. The way she held her phone, Tori couldn't see what she was writing. "Okay," Willow said, "but I'll have to ruin your surprise. It might be the only way to get him to reply."

Tori's stomach lurched. When Ryker texted back and said he didn't know any Britneys from Burlington, she was going to look really stupid. What could Tori do then? Laugh and joke about what bad memories guys had? Burst into tears?

"Are you Ryker's sister?" Tori asked, because it seemed like she should say something.

"His cousin. I'm staying here while my parents are working in India." Willow cast a look back at the door. "It's sort of like a prison sentence. I keep thinking it's going to be over and then find out that, no, I didn't make parole."

Bess nodded sympathetically. "Your aunt and uncle are strict?"

"Yeah," Willow said, like it was an understatement. She tilted her head, giving Tori a meaningful look. "Before you sign on as Ryker's soul mate, you might want to ponder his parents as your in-laws. Just saying."

At that, the door opened again. Mrs. Davis stuck her head out. "Willow, what's taking you so long?"

"I'm just telling them who to avoid at Jason's party," Willow called back.

"One more minute, and then you need to come inside." Mrs. Davis shut the door.

Willow's phone chimed. She glanced at it. "He's up at the ridge on Bird Mountain—the one where he goes hang gliding." She seemed to think Tori should know where that was, and perhaps a soul mate would. Willow headed back up the stairs, unconcerned. Either Ryker only answered Willow's first text message, or Willow's second text message didn't tell Ryker who was looking for him.

"Wait," Bess called to Willow. "How will we find him?"

"Look for his truck"—Willow put her hand on the doorknob—"and he'll find you." She went inside without another word.

He'll find you? Did that mean he would be waiting for them? And what was he doing up on a ridge on Halloween night anyway? Was he by himself?

Bess and Tori turned and walked toward the van, hurrying. Bess pulled off her bandana and shoved it into her jeans pocket. "Willow didn't think it was strange that you came from Burlington to see Ryker. You know what this means, don't you?" She smiled happily. "Ryker is totally hot. This is awesome. I am so ready to meet a Slayer who doesn't feel like a brother."

They climbed into the van. Dr. B moved it a little farther down the street so the Davises wouldn't see them parked in front of their house and become suspicious. While Tori and Bess put on their body armor, neck mikes, and earpieces, they relayed what they had learned about Ryker.

"And depending on what Willow texted to him," Tori finished up, "he might be expecting stalkers. Bess told her that I think Ryker is my soul mate."

"Well," Jesse said so softly that he probably didn't mean for Tori to hear him, "that's about how fast you move on to the next guy, isn't it?"

Tori shot him a sharp look to let him know that she'd heard him.

"We'll need to divide into two teams," Dr. B said. "One will guard Ryker's house in case Overdrake's men show up, the other will look for Ryker. Captains?"

At first Tori thought Dr. B had forgotten Dirk was gone. When she raised her gaze to Dr. B, he was staring back at her. He was waiting for her opinion.

She shook her head. She wasn't going to lead.

"I'll stay here to guard," Jesse said. "I want Kody and Bess with me. They'll be the most useful against Overdrake's men."

Bess let out a groan. "Seriously? The other three girls get to meet Ryker, while I have to stay here?"

"Sorry," Jesse told her. "No one else can throw a shield up that protects against bullets."

"Yeah, yeah." Bess adjusted her neck mike, then put in her earpiece. "If my fairy godmother shows up with a gown and some cool shoes—I'm totally out of here."

Dr. B had downloaded directions to Bird Mountain on his phone. "Depending on where Ryker is on the ridge, he's probably seven or eight miles away. That means while we're gone, Jesse's team will be out of range for part of the time." Dr. B frowned, unhappy about this fact. "I can't leave the simulator here, though. Tori's team might need their night vision to find Ryker. And besides, they'll need to show him their powers in order to convince him they really are Slayers."

Jesse strapped his rifle sling onto his shoulder. "If it looks like you'll be out of range for longer than a half an hour, drive back down here close enough to give us a recharge."

Dr. B nodded in agreement. "Bess, keep me apprised of any developments." Taking in Kody and Jesse with his gaze, he added, "If Overdrake's men show up, be careful where and what you shoot. You don't want to inadvertently hit trick-or-treaters."

"We'll try to remember that." Bess opened the van door and stepped out. "No sniping small children, guys."

Jesse and Kody joined her without comment. Dr. B turned in his seat so he could see Tori. He motioned to the passenger seat beside him. "Come sit next to me."

She did so reluctantly. He was going to talk to her about being A-team's captain and she didn't want the responsibility. She had thought it would always be Dirk's. He was so much better suited to that sort of thing—no, she wouldn't think about him. She looked out the window at homes, trees, and the occasional trick-or-treater.

As they drove through Rutland, she waited for Dr. B to bring up the subject of A-team's captain. He didn't speak, though. In the backseat, Lilly and Rosa were discussing Alyssa. "She's not as far gone as Leo and Danielle," Lilly said. "We just need to make sure she doesn't start going to keggers. We should be with her every weekend. I can take Friday nights. You shadow her on Saturdays."

"We don't even know where we're going to live now," Rosa pointed out.

"It doesn't matter," Lilly said. "We're her friends."

Finally Dr. B glanced at Tori. "It's hard to lose a counterpart," he said softly. "Perhaps it's even harder for you. Dirk . . ."

He didn't have to finish. They couldn't hope for a way to restore Dirk's powers like they could for Alyssa. Dirk chose to leave and betrayed them in the process. Tori didn't answer. She couldn't.

"When you met Dirk's family, how did his mother look?"

"Young, pretty, and rich."

The answer made Dr. B smile in a sad sort of way. "Bianca always was beautiful. Did she seem happy?"

Tori hadn't realized until then that Dr. B knew Dirk's mother. It made sense, she supposed. He and Overdrake had grown up together on St. Helena. "I met Dirk's stepmother," Tori clarified. "Overdrake divorced his first wife when Dirk was six. He hasn't seen her since."

A flash of surprise crossed Dr. B's expression. "I can understand why Bianca would divorce Brant Overdrake, but it's not like her to abandon her son."

"I don't think Overdrake gave her a choice."

Dr. B let out a disapproving grunt and shook his head. The van turned from one tree-lined street onto another. "I can't believe that Dirk is Bianca Fenton's son. I feel like I should have known, like I should have seen some part of Bianca in him. If I could have only . . ." He let the sentence drift off into a ragged, painful silence.

They had all loved Dirk. How did a person get over that sort of gaping loss? To stop her sadness, Tori concentrated on what Dirk had done. She concentrated on Alyssa, who couldn't help them anymore. On Jesse, who'd been attacked by Overdrake's men. On Ryker, who was in danger now.

Thinking of all of this only made her feel angry at herself. "I should have figured out the truth about Dirk last summer," she said. "We were together every day for months and not once did I ever feel like he was an enemy. When he was practicing with us—none of it felt like a lie. How could I have missed that?"

Instead of making excuses for her, Dr. B brightened. "Really? You never sensed any malice from him?"

She shook her head. "I knew he was hiding things sometimes, and I knew talking about his family made him tense, but I figured that was normal stuff."

Dr. B smiled. "That's wonderful news."

"That I'm clueless?"

"No. You couldn't have missed that much betrayal. That means after Dirk helped us escape from his father's compound, his loyalties were with us. For the rest of the summer he intended to help us, not fight us. His heart isn't as dark as I feared."

Tori hadn't considered this. She wasn't sure whether it made her feel better or worse. It made it harder to erase Dirk from her own heart. "What do you think changed his mind?"

"His father," Dr. B said simply.

"Why didn't he just tell us the truth last summer? We could have kept his father away from him."

Dr. B's gaze remained on the road. "I'm sure Dirk loves his father. Which of us doesn't? And when you're looking for approval from someone you love, well, sometimes you do things you shouldn't."

Over the last few months, Tori had done things that she knew she shouldn't have. Asking Jesse to meet her, giving Dirk her phone number, telling him about Ryker—they had seemed like little things at the time. Now the weight of them pressed down on her. "I should have followed your rules. I'm sorry"

"Are you?" Dr. B asked with surprise. "I was just wondering if it was wise to have that no-contact rule. You realized Dirk was Overdrake's son because you met his family. Breaking that rule helped us."

Again, Tori wasn't sure whether that made her feel better or worse. It reminded her of Dirk's commentary on wars—that more often than not they were decided by luck. The roll of the dice.

If luck were the deciding factor, the Slayers were in trouble. You couldn't depend on luck.

"I didn't tell you everything about Ryker," Dr. B said. "So there may still be things Overdrake doesn't know. For a short while I posted instructions on how to build a simulator on the Ryker website. He built one. He's been practicing. If Overdrake's men come here expecting an easy mark, they won't find it."

It was the first piece of good news Tori had heard all night. "Let's hope he's practiced a lot."

They left Rutland and drove up the road to Bird Mountain. Dr. B kept checking his odometer to see how far they'd gone. They climbed higher. The trees around them flashed into and out of the van's headlights. A few clung stubbornly to their leaves. Most were bare, staking the night sky with gray branches. Shadows flickered through the leaves and the tangled underbrush.

Finally Dr. B spotted a pickup truck parked in a grassy area at the side of the road. It was one of those tricked-up models that rode high off the ground. Something in the truck bed was covered with a tarp. No one was in sight.

Dr. B pulled up next to the truck, turned off the van, and everyone got out. The night smelled of autumn, of things changing. The Slayers not only had their body armor on, they wore their helmets as well. Dr. B insisted they wear them until they were certain Overdrake's men hadn't gotten here first.

Rosa, Lilly, and Tori walked around the truck, peering into the muted shapes of the surrounding forest. Dr. B put on his night vision goggles and joined them. Willow had said Ryker would find them, but nobody appeared from behind any of the trees. Maybe he wouldn't come near them as long as they looked like hit men.

"It might not be the right truck," Rosa said.

"It's the right one," Tori said, looking into a dense stand of trees. "He's got a simulator in the back."

"What?" Rosa asked. Apparently she and Lilly hadn't heard Dr. B tell Tori about that.

"A simulator?" Lilly asked, stepping toward it. "How can you tell?"

"I can hear it," Tori said. She'd heard the familiar thumping as soon as she'd stepped out of the van.

Dr. B adjusted his goggles. "Ryker must come up here to practice." After making a sweep of the area, he called, "Ryker, I need to talk to you! It's urgent!"

No one answered. The wind blew through the trees, picking up dried leaves and making them scurry across the ground. Branches creaked. Somewhere down below them an owl hooted.

After another minute, Dr. B called out, "Ryker, it's me, Dr. B!"

Still no answer.

Dr. B checked the time on his cell phone. "Spread out in standard formation. Walk ten minutes into the forest, calling Ryker's name in intervals, then report back to me."

The Slayers' neck mikes and earpieces were turned off now. While they searched for Ryker, they needed to hear him, not one another. They would turn them back on to report.

Dr. B peered around at the forest. "If we haven't found Ryker in ten minutes, I'll take our simulator back to his house, leave it for Jesse's team, and come back to help you look. Ryker's simulator should keep your powers working."

Rosa started off into the trees, but Tori and Lilly hesitated. "We don't have our watches," Tori reminded him, "and we took the batteries out of our cell phones. We'll have to estimate ten minutes."

"Right," Lilly said. "And we all know how well estimating time worked for you the last time."

Dr. B motioned to Lilly. "You estimate the ten minutes." Then he motioned to Tori. "You check back in five."

Man, you nearly plunge to your death once and people never trust your internal clock again.

Tori walked into the forest, her gaze constantly scanning the area. The helmet made it harder to see clearly, harder to hear. All around her, tree branches rippled in the wind, making a shushing sound. The constant motion was distracting. It made it hard to sense other things in the forest. Tori drifted upward an inch. Not enough so that someone seeing her would be able to tell she was flying, but enough so that the sound of her own footsteps didn't get in the way of the noises she was listening for.

"Ryker!" she called.

She got no answer except for the rustling of branches.

She glided farther into the forest, kept listening. In the back of her mind she counted off the minutes. She called Ryker's name three more times. If he was around, he was ignoring her.

When five minutes were nearly up, Tori heard a noise. Not one of the usual forest noises. Heavier. A thunk of some sort. Then she saw a shadow in the trees. A figure, perhaps. It disappeared behind a trunk. A deer? Or was someone hiding? It could be Ryker. It could be someone else, though. She didn't call out his name again.

She drifted soundlessly over to the spot, all the while watching the tree. Its leaves fluttered in the breeze, made dark, changing shapes. When she got to the tree, she quickly peered around the trunk. Nothing was there. She was sure she hadn't imagined the shape. She stood still, listening. A creaking noise like a footstep came from a thick-trunked tree a little ways off. Carefully scanning the forest around her, she went in that direction. When she got to the place, it too was empty.

She stood, looking around in frustration, then turned on her mike.

It was past time to report, and Dr. B was probably trying to get a hold of her. She was about to turn on her earpiece when she stiffened.

She only had a couple seconds' warning—a bristling of her senses telling her something was coming up behind her fast. She spun around and lifted her arms in protection. It was too late, though. A hulking figure plowed into her.

CHAPTER 30

Jesse surveyed Ryker's lawn from the top of a tree near the roof. Kody was stationed in the trees that bordered the Davises' back lawn. Bess was in a tree in the front yard. They all had binoculars to scope out the area. In their other hand, they each carried a tranquilizer gun. Killing was a last but necessary defense, so they wore rifles in slings on their backs.

Every three minutes the group checked in with one another. Jesse would whisper, "All clear." Bess and then Kody would echo the report.

Jesse tried to concentrate on this part of the mission, on the yard and trees and the sounds of the night. His mind kept turning to Dirk, though. Memories slashed at him. The two of them talking and laughing every summer, figuring out what they were supposed to do as captains. They had worked on drills, plans, procedures together. Dirk had undoubtedly given his father their entire playbook. Perhaps even more damaging, Dirk knew how each Slayer would react in situations. He knew their weaknesses. He knew that Lilly didn't always listen to orders, that Kody got hotheaded under pressure, that Tori was inexperienced, and that Dr. B—for all of his attempts at fairness—worried about Bess' safety more than the rest of theirs.

What did Dirk know about Jesse that he could use against him?

Well, Dirk knew Jesse cared about Tori. The thought stung. Dirk had already betrayed Jesse in that regard. The image of Tori and Dirk at the Jefferson Memorial sprang into Jesse's mind: the two standing close together, holding hands, Dirk leaning into Tori while Tori looked at him expectantly. Jesse forced his thoughts away from that subject, made himself think like a captain again.

How long would it take Overdrake's men to get here and what tactics would they use? Would they follow Ryker and try to catch him unaware like they did to Jesse? Maybe they'd do a home invasion; make it look like a robbery. If they didn't find Ryker at home, they'd wait. He'd come back sooner or later.

Kody's voice came over Jesse's earpiece. "I see movement in the forest behind the house. Someone is heading this way. Make that two someones."

"Kids?" Jesse asked.

"Kids would have flashlights," Kody whispered. "These guys are checking around the trees before they advance. They must have night vision goggles."

Bess' voice came over the earpiece. "That's got to be Overdrake's guys. I'm on my way." She dropped from the tree, hitting the ground as silently as a cat. She sprinted across the front lawn into the side yard.

"Body armor?" Jesse asked.

"Hard to tell at this distance," Kody said. "Looks like jeans and jackets. Could be some sort of Kevlar. They've got gloves and hats on, but their faces and necks are unprotected. Nothing we can't hit if we let them get close enough."

"Weapons?" Jesse asked.

"Handguns. The small kind."

Not well armed by Overdrake's standard.

Bess dashed to a tree on the edge of the property, her tranquilizer gun already drawn. "We'll surprise them before they make it to the house." She had placed herself on the opposite corner of the lawn as Kody. "Jesse?"

She was waiting for him to confirm the play or call another one. He hesitated—bothered by the thought that Dirk would call the same play if he were with them. Finally Jesse said, "Do it."

It was their best strategy right now. And besides, even if Overdrake knew their playbook, he didn't know they were here in Ryker's yard. "I'll cover you while I keep an eye on the front street."

They didn't want to be surrounded, and it only made sense that Overdrake would send someone to the front of the house. On Halloween, people opened their doors without checking to see who was standing there first. And if the neighbors saw a couple of guys go by wearing masks, or a strange car parked on the street—they wouldn't think anything of it. Just trick-or-treaters out late.

Now that Jesse thought about it, it seemed strange that Overdrake's men were coming through the forest at all. It would make more sense for them to come from the front and send a couple of people to the backyard before the invasion.

The street in front of the house remained clear of cars, of people. "I spotted more men," Kody whispered. "They're coming up behind the first two. Definitely wearing body armor and they're carrying guns that look like antiaircraft launchers."

That's when Jesse realized the men in the forest were looking for Slayers, not Ryker. Overdrake had known they might be here and he'd made provisions to take them out. The first two men were decoys, meant to draw the Slayers into position. The men behind them weren't just wearing night vision goggles. They wore infrared ones—which identified people as heat sources. Kody and Bess weren't hidden at all. And although Jesse couldn't see them, he was certain that the launcherlike guns the men carried shot out nets. Overdrake had used one on Tori when he'd caught her last summer. "It's a trap!" Jesse hissed, swooping down from the tree. "Retreat!"

CHAPTER 31

Tori flew fifteen feet before she slammed into the ground. Her head snapped backward and the breath whooshed from her lungs. The guy who had tackled her took hold of her jacket with one hand and pulled off her helmet with the other. She hadn't heard his footsteps. He must have leapt into her.

He stared down at her. "Start talking. Who are you?"

He had short dark hair that looked black in the dim night light. Even though he wasn't standing, Tori could tell he was tall and muscular. He was also handsome enough that Bess would consider herself right about her predictions of hotness.

"Hello, Ryker," Tori said.

He still held her pinned to the ground. "Somehow I doubt your name is Britney. Who are you?"

"Dr. B sent me. We need to—"

"Try again," Ryker said. "Dr. B and I already talked. He wouldn't send people. Who did?"

"Look," Tori said. "I'm happy to answer your questions, but I'd rather do it without you pressing your elbow into my lungs."

He didn't move. "Then talk quickly. I'm still waiting to hear who you are and what you want."

"I'm a Slayer like you."

His expression didn't change. "Prove it."

"I can see in the dark like you," she said. "I could show you some of my extra strength by throwing you into a tree, but it doesn't seem polite."

He still didn't move. "Dragon lords do both those things. Can you prove you're not one of them?"

She hadn't expected Ryker to know those details about dragon lords, and chided herself for not realizing it sooner. Dr. B had put a warning about dragon lord powers on Ryker's website after the fight with Overdrake.

Tori didn't answer. According to Dirk, she was a dragon lord–Slayer hybrid. All of her powers were dragon lord powers, too—extra strength, night vision, flight, and hearing what the dragons heard. Tori had no powers that were distinctly Slayer. Suddenly she realized she couldn't prove to her teammates, let alone to Ryker, that she wasn't a dragon lord.

Maybe she was.

Tori pushed the thought away and levitated off the ground, bringing Ryker into the air with her. After all, Ryker didn't know that dragon lords flew, too. And she wasn't about to mention it.

Ryker handled the shift in location calmly enough. When Jesse had first swept Tori off her feet and into the sky, she had screamed. Ryker watched the ground grow farther away and only said, "Point taken. You're a flyer."

Tori casually draped her hands around Ryker's neck. He had asked her to prove she was a Slayer, she was going to oblige. Still lying on her back, she shot upward until they reached the top of the trees. The stars blazed bright and clear above them, a million scattered lights staring down.

Ryker held on to her tighter. Didn't speak. She finally had his attention. "I know you told Dr. B that you wouldn't train with us until you were eighteen, but we can't wait that long. The eggs hatched back in the beginning of September. We have less than a year until they're full grown. You need to come and train with the rest of us."

He kept an eye on the trees below them. "I've been training fine without you."

"Have you? What's your extra power?"

He smiled. "Want to see?" Without waiting for her reaction, he sat up. The sudden movement jostled Tori. Ryker slid, tumbling into the night air.

Tori's heart lurched into her throat. She dived after him, straining to grab hold of him. He was going to die. And it was her fault. She would have to tell the other Slayers that she'd found Ryker and then accidentally killed him. She reached out and caught hold of his sleeve. He laughed and took off sideways, breaking her grip and gliding effortlessly through the air.

He was a flyer. She let out a long breath of relief.

Ryker wound his way through a few trees and landed on a branch not far away.

She flew over, hands on her hips, and hovered in front of him. "You just scared me to death."

"As you can see, I'm practicing fine without your help." He leaned against the tree trunk and surveyed her with dark eyes. "When it's time, I'll carry my weight. Until then, I'll stay here. That way my parents won't have every policeman from here to D.C. looking for me." He smiled condescendingly. "But it's been nice meeting you, Britney. Maybe we can be soul mates another time."

"You can't stay here anymore," Tori said. "Overdrake knows where you live. He'll come for you. It isn't safe for you or your parents."

Ryker cocked his head. "How did Overdrake find out where I live?"

Ryker leaned forward, his eyes narrowed. "For that matter, how did you find me?"

"Um . . ." She hadn't expected to tell him this. She had supposed that Dr. B would break the news to him in a diplomatic sort of way. She felt for her neck mike, realizing that it had been on the whole time. She had turned it on to report right before Ryker tackled her. Dr. B, Rosa, and Lilly undoubtedly heard her entire conversation with Ryker. "You should talk to Dr. B about that," she said and flipped on her earpiece.

"Tori," Dr. B said as soon as the sound came on. "Bring Ryker to his truck immediately. There's trouble at his house."

CHAPTER 32

Jesse only had a split second to make the kind of decision he hated most. Did he rescue Bess or Kody?

He swooped from his tree and headed toward Bess. She was closest to Overdrake's men, which meant she had a greater chance of being surrounded and captured. Besides, she had the power to throw force fields up. It was a skill the Slayers couldn't lose.

As he flew, Jesse swung his rifle forward and shot off a round, not at Overdrake's men—they were too well protected—but at Ryker's roof. The bullets wouldn't strike anyone up there, and the noise should alert the family that something wrong was happening. Hopefully they would call the police.

Bess and Kody abandoned their hiding spots. As Bess ran, she looked over her shoulder at the men. The decoys had dropped to the ground to avoid fire. The men behind them had rifles, but weren't using them yet. One of Overdrake's men dropped to his knee, pointed his shoulder launcher at Kody, and fired. A gray mass flew through the air toward him. The net opened in the air like a grabbing hand, stopped midair, made a crashing sound, and slid to the ground. Bess had thrown a force field up to protect him.

Jesse reached Bess, grabbed her, and darted upward. He didn't notice the net flying toward them until it was nearly on them. Its graying mouth opened wide to swallow them. Jesse dodged to the right. He wasn't fast enough.

Bess hadn't had time to slide the force field away from Kody to protect them. The net slammed into them, knocking Jesse backward in the air. He kept hold of Bess.

Tori had told the Slayers about the net Overdrake used on her last summer. The metal links were so strong she was barely able to rip them apart—wasn't able to make a hole in the net big enough to get through before Overdrake reached her. Superstrength magnets on the net had pinned Tori to the metal roof.

Jesse understood why Overdrake invented the metal-net launcher. His men needed it in case one of the hatchlings escaped when Overdrake wasn't around to control it. But the magnets always puzzled Jesse. Were the dragons kept in metal surroundings? What was the point of having magnets on the net otherwise?

Now it made sense. When the net curled around Jesse and Bess, the magnets connected both sides together, closing the net and trapping them. Still carrying Bess, Jesse righted himself and saw that a chain connected the net to the launcher. Two of Overdrake's men hung on to the launcher, skidding across the grass as they kept hold of Bess and Jesse. He was like the kite on the end of a string.

Bess yelled, "No!" The frustration in her voice told Jesse what had happened even before his gaze swung over to Kody.

When Bess moved the force field away from Kody to try to keep the net off Jesse and herself, one of Overdrake's men shot another net at Kody. He was down on the ground, the net tangled around him.

That was another thing Dirk knew about their strategy. Despite

Dr. B's instructions otherwise, instead of sacrificing one member of the group, the Slayers tried to save everyone. This time, instead of Bess saving either Kody or Jesse, they'd all been caught.

The only advantage the Slayers had was that so far Overdrake's men were only trying to capture, not kill, them.

Either Dirk's wishes still had some sway with his father, or Overdrake didn't want to have to deal with murders that would send the law snooping around in his direction.

Back when Tori had been caught by a net, the holes were big enough for her to put her fingers through. Apparently Overdrake had made improvements to his design. The holes were smaller now. Jesse wouldn't be able to rip his way free.

The gunmen who had acted as decoys stood up and jogged toward Ryker's house. Jesse didn't see where they ended up. He was watching the men who held on to his chain.

Jesse flew backward, pushing against the back of the net in an attempt to rip the launcher out of their hands. His anger gave him extra strength. He wasn't going to let himself be caught by Overdrake's men. He'd worked too hard to be knocked out of the battle before the real war even started.

Overdrake's men slid inch by inch across the lawn, tearing up the grass with the heels of their boots. Then a third man threw himself on the chain and stopped Jesse's progress.

Only one man had hold of Kody's chain. Kody couldn't fly, so he had no way to pull himself away from the launcher. The remaining two men in the yard ran toward Kody's trapped form. One man held a tranquilizer gun. The other held a rifle. A dart wouldn't go through Kody's body armor, but with Kody on the ground and trapped, it wouldn't be long before the men managed to take off his helmet, boots, or gloves.

Kody's arm wound back like he was pitching a baseball. The air shimmered with frost, and a freezing blast slammed into the man with the rifle. His head snapped back, his feet flew out in front of him, and he crashed to the ground. The rifle tumbled from his hands onto the lawn. The second man stopped advancing. Kody wound back his other arm and sent a fireball at him. For a moment, the man's head was illuminated, and his goggles reflected the light like holes in a jack-o'-lantern. The man stumbled backward, dropping his tranquilizer gun as he swatted at the fire.

"Hold on to my back." Jesse helped Bess get into position so his hands were free. He pushed his panic and anger away, relying on the years of training he'd had. Strategies and priorities clicked through his mind. He automatically evaluated each one. "Keep your shield between us and the guys holding on to that launcher." First priority: Jesse had to get Kody off the ground before Overdrake's men surrounded him.

As Jesse dived downward, the chain on the net went slack. He held his arms out and scooped Kody off the ground like a spatula taking a hamburger off the grill. It was a tenuous hold at best, especially since Kody kept moving. Jesse couldn't get a good grip on him. Still, with the Slayers all in one spot, they had a better chance of defending themselves.

Kody was pumping out blasts and fireballs quick and recklessly. A freezing blast hit the guy who'd dropped the tranquilizer gun. He flew backward through the air, knocking into the man behind him. Both fell to the ground.

"Fireball the guy on your launcher," Jesse said. He didn't have to explain why. Once the man started pulling on that chain, Kody would slip out of his arms. Jesse didn't dare fly high in case Kody fell. They were all dangling like a piñata over the lawn.

The man who held Kody's chain kneeled on the ground and leaned back, about to yank the chain. Kody whipped both of his hands forward, sending two fireballs in the man's direction. The flash of flames lit up the backyard. The first fireball hit the man's hands. The second hit the chain right above his hands, heating the metal chain.

The man yelled, let go of the chain, and peeled off his smoking gloves.

The men holding Jesse's chain were harder to shake off. When they saw what had happened with Kody's launcher, they dropped to the ground, lying on the launcher and chain so it couldn't be ripped from their grasp. Even if Kody fireballed the chain, the men's bullet-proof jackets would insulate them from the heat.

Inside Ryker's house, someone screamed. It sounded like a child. The noise made Jesse's stomach turn. Ryker's family needed their help, and they were trapped out here. Useless.

Jesse pressed against the top of the net, grunting with effort as he tried to lift the chain, launcher, and the men off the ground. It didn't work. Jesse was already carrying Bess, Kody, and the weight of the nets. He couldn't lift all that and the three men holding on to the chain.

A couple of the men on the chain pulled out assault rifles—high-powered ones. Apparently Overdrake's men were done playing nicely. Dirk knew what the Slayers' body armor could withstand, and no doubt Overdrake's men were carrying guns that could shoot through it.

"Set!" Kody called, indicating he wanted Bess to move her force field so he could send blasts at the men. With their hands on their rifles, the men weren't holding the chain anymore. If Kody could knock them off, Jesse would be able to fly Bess and Kody to safety. Kody waited for Bess to call back, "Draw," the code that meant the way was clear.

"No," Jesse said. It was better to let the men shoot into Bess' force field while Kody took care of the other men.

The men didn't shoot. Jesse immediately realized why. Overdrake's men knew the Slayer's calls, and when Bess didn't respond "Draw," they knew her force field was still between them.

Fine. It was a disadvantage that Jesse could turn into an advantage. He added it to his list of strategies.

One of the men Kody had blasted lay unconscious on the ground. Everyone else was still armed, which meant danger was coming at them from three angles. The men who held on to Jesse's launcher and the two men who were army crawling toward Kody's launcher. If they reached it, they would pull Kody out of Jesse's arms. Just as dangerous, the men could keep crawling across the yard until they surrounded the Slayers on three sides. Bess' shield was a straight wall; she couldn't curve it to wrap around them. And even if Kody didn't tire while sending out his blasts, eventually he would miss, mistime a blast, or not be able to see both gunmen at the same time. Overdrake's men would succeed in shooting the Slayers.

They needed to distract, attack, and take the advantage away from Overdrake's men.

"Kody," Jesse said, "freeze and flame the men's goggles coming at us."

Most weapons could withstand freezing cold or the blazing heat, but freezing and heating glass within seconds cracked it. Once the lenses broke, the infrared goggles would be ruined.

Kody pushed one hand forward, then the other, sending a freezing shock and then a fireball. The movement made him jiggle in Jesse's arms and Jesse had to keep adjusting his grip.

"Keep your shield in place," Jesse whispered to Bess. "Ignore my next command. Understood?"

"Yes." She was holding on to his back with one arm, and using the other to try to slash the net with a knife.

"Understood," Kody murmured. He sent out the last of his blasts. Both men pulled off their ruined goggles. It would be harder for them to see now. They would have to rely on the dim light of the streetlamp that made its way into the backyard.

Jesse raised his voice so it was loud enough for the men holding his launcher to hear. "Now take out the rest of the goggles."

"Set!" Kody called to Bess.

"Draw!" she responded.

The men holding on to Jesse's launcher raised their rifles and opened fire. Light flashed from the muzzles and even with the silencers on, Jesse heard the tapping sound of the shots. The bullets ricocheted off Bess' force field. The men didn't fire again. Their armor-piercing bullets had just backfired and pierced themselves.

All the men were still alive and lying on the chain. One grasped his shoulder. One stared at his bleeding hand and swore. The third was curled and moaning.

That left the two men still crawling toward Kody's launcher to worry about. "Shield in blue position!" Jesse yelled.

It was a made-up command. He was gambling that if the men didn't know where Bess' shield was, they wouldn't risk shooting.

The wounded men didn't take up their rifles again, and the other men kept crawling toward Kody's launcher. Served them right for using armor-piercing ammo.

Jesse didn't have to look over his shoulder to see if Bess had made any progress in cutting through the net. The net was made to withstand dragon claws. Knives weren't going to have any effect.

"Shoot a hole through it," he said.

Bess brought her rifle forward, rammed the barrel into the net. "Don't drop Kody," she said and shot.

The Slayers' rifles didn't have much kickback, but even the small amount of movement jarred Jesse so much that Kody slid in his arms. The bullets broke through the fibers of the net, leaving holes big enough that Bess could force her fingers through them. "We're in business."

Kody shot his net several times, aiming at the ground so he didn't accidentally hit Bess' force field.

"Swing," Jesse called, without knowing why he said it. It was one of the times his instincts took over. The call was for Kody and Bess to switch their defensive areas. Jesse sensed what had happened before he saw it. Their imminent escape had rallied one of the uninjured gunmen into action.

The man angled his assault rifle up and shot at them. Right into Bess' shield. The bullets rained back down with sharp thuds. One man rolled on the ground, cursing. The other barely moved at all.

With a grunt, Kody ripped the hole in his net until it was big enough for him to escape through. "I'm going for cover," he said. "Bess, watch my back." He jumped away from Jesse, before Jesse could tell him not to go.

Hotheaded.

They needed to stay in a group. If Bess covered Kody it meant she left Jesse and herself vulnerable.

Jesse helped Bess rip the hole. It was nearly big enough they could slip out of it.

None of the men on the ground shot at Kody. Perhaps they were more injured than Jesse realized or perhaps they just didn't want to take any more chances with Bess' shield. In seconds, Kody had crossed the lawn and made it to tree cover. While he sprinted, he shot his tranquilizer gun twice. Each hit its target: the faces of the men who had taken off their goggles.

Impressive shooting, even if it was hotheaded.

After one last tug, the hole in the net ripped wide enough. Jesse held on to Bess and flew out. He whispered, "Keep your shield in front of the men on the launcher." It was harder to give orders this way—to whisper sentences instead of calling plays. "Don't move it until I give the word."

He flew down toward the men and hovered in front of them. One was motionless now. One's hand was bleeding so badly, Jesse doubted he would be able to keep all of his fingers, let alone use his gun. The third man only had a shoulder wound. He raised himself up on his elbow and pointed his rifle at Jesse.

"Throw down your gun," Jesse told him. "And we'll call a doctor for you."

"Only one of you can shield," the man said in a raspy voice. "Surrender or I'll take out your friend and the tree he's behind."

The man shouldn't have bothered bargaining. In the time it took him to make his demand, Kody sent a cold shock that ripped the rifle away from his hand.

Jesse swooped down, dropping Bess as he did. "Cut," he told her, and rushed into the gunman, ramming him back into the ground. Jesse took out his tranquilizer gun, pulled off the man's night vision goggles, and shot his exposed skin. It would take a minute for the drug to work so Jesse grabbed the man, pinning his arms to his sides in case he had other weapons on him. The guy cursed and thrashed, but couldn't break Jesse's grip.

While Jesse waited, he turned around to see how Bess was doing. She'd already taken the other men's rifles and shot them with tranquilizers. The man with the injured hand didn't put up any resistance. Maybe he wanted to lose consciousness so the pain would go away.

She watched the man's head loll back onto the ground. The gunman that Jesse held raised his voice even louder, getting more creative with his curses.

Bess tilted her head at him. "Dude, you need an anatomy lesson. It would be impossible to pull somebody's heart out through their—"

"Call nine-one-one," Jesse interrupted her. "Police and ambulances."

She shook her head. "The phones won't work. I already tried mine."

Kody jogged over, joining them. "Overdrake's men must have a signal jammer somewhere."

That meant none of them could call Dr. B and report what was happening. Had he already tried calling them?

The man in Jesse's arms went limp. Jesse dropped him to the ground and walked toward Ryker's house. A light was on in the second floor. Judging from what he could make out in the large picture window, it was probably the living room. Overdrake's men were in there somewhere.

Jesse could run to a neighbor's house and use their landline to call the police. He didn't want to take the time, though. Not while people were in danger inside.

He took out his infrared scanner. "I saw two men go inside. More probably went in the front. They most likely have guards inside the front and back doors." Sure enough, a heat spot came up on the scanner right by the back door. But only one. That was good news.

Kody kept his voice low. "We can plow down the door easy enough."

Bess took out her infrared scanner as well. "We should find out where Ryker's family is being held first."

No one said anything else, because at that moment a crash sounded above them. Breaking glass. Jesse looked up and saw a coffee table and two of Overdrake's men flying out of the living room window. The men shouted, and for a moment Jesse thought they were performing an air assault. He yelled, "Shield!" and looked to see what sort of weapons the men were using. Their rifles tumbled with them, spun downward along with the shards of glass. When the men lay crumpled on the lawn, unconscious, Jesse realized they had been thrown from the window.

Who had done it, and how? It wasn't an easy thing to throw two armed men out of a window.

The lights in the living room suddenly went off. The heat signature of the guard who'd been at the downstairs door moved away. He was probably going upstairs.

"Kody," Jesse said, "break down the back door. Bess, cover him." Jesse refrained from adding, "Don't go anywhere you haven't cleared first." No point in being their mother. They'd been trained.

"I'll check out the window." Jesse was already off the ground and heading toward the living room as he said the last sentence. He flew upward, keeping off to the side of the window to be out of anyone's line of sight. His infrared scanner showed four people in the room, three lying on the floor, one standing in the middle of the room. Somewhere in the house a dog barked. It made it hard to hear anything else.

Jesse took a quick glance inside the window, ready to dive through the opening to tackle the figure standing. He expected it to be one of Overdrake's men. It wasn't. A teenage girl stood in the dark, at an angle to the doorway that led into the living room. Willow. She gripped an end table in one hand as though it were a club and was watching the door, waiting for someone to come through it.

The end table looked too heavy for a normal teenage girl to hold that way. And why had she turned off the lights?

Jesse's gaze went to the figures on the floor. Mr. Davis lay on his back, unconscious. Blood trickled from a wound on the side of his head. His wife lay next to him, propped up on one elbow. She had some sort of cloth pressed against his wound, but she couldn't see well enough to attend to him. A younger girl lay near them, crying.

"Stay down," Mrs. Davis whispered. "Be quiet."

Mr. and Mrs. Davis obviously hadn't helped Willow fight off Overdrake's men. Somehow, she'd managed to throw them out a window by herself.

No, not *somehow*. Jesse knew how—he should have known as soon as he'd seen her holding the end table that way. Willow had extra strength and she had turned off the lights to try and give herself an advantage. She could see in the dark. She was a Slayer.

Despite the grim situation laid out in front of Jesse, he smiled. He'd found another Slayer.

Footsteps sounded. Someone was coming into the living room. Before the man had even stepped inside, Willow hurled the end table through the doorway. Jesse caught sight of Overdrake's man, rifle drawn, just before the table smashed into his chest. Once he was on the ground, Willow picked up his gun. She didn't seem to know what to do with it or how to use it.

"There's another man coming from downstairs," Jesse told her, keeping his distance outside the window. The last thing he wanted was for her to attack him when Overdrake's man was about to come in the room.

Willow turned, saw Jesse, and was startled. "How are you doing that?"

"I'm a Slayer, like you. My friends might have already gotten the thug." Into his neck mike, Jesse said, "Kody?"

"The guy saw us," Kody said. "He's running in your direction."

"He's coming your way," Jesse told Willow. Then added, "Do you know how to use that gun? I don't want you accidentally shooting my friends." He glided through the window toward her. "Maybe you'd better let me take care of this."

"Gun?" Mrs. Davis called from the floor.

Willow turned and pointed the rifle at the door. "Stay down, Aunt Harriet. I'll handle this."

The next moment the man came through the door. Not of his own volition. He'd been hit by something in the back—probably one of Kody's freezing shocks. As he stumbled forward, Willow clubbed him on the back of the neck. Probably not the safest way to use a rifle, still, it did the job. The man hit the floor, moaned, then went unconscious. This caused the girl on the floor to let out a yelp. Mrs. Davis had moved so that most of her body covered the girl, shielding her from possible gunfire.

Into his mike, Jesse said, "Don't come in yet."

He walked over to Willow and held out his hand for the gun. "I'd feel a lot better if you gave that to me."

She didn't. "I'd feel a lot better if I knew who you were, and why you're in my house."

He kept holding out his hand for the gun. "My name is Jesse. I'm here to help you. Right now, I'd like to help you by making sure you don't accidentally shoot any of your family. I doubt the gun's safety is on."

She pointed the gun down at the floor. "There. I won't shoot anyone. At least not yet."

Instead of arguing the point, Jesse checked his infrared scanner for heat signatures. Two stood outside the doorway. Bess and Kody. He didn't see any others. "Are you picking up any heat signatures outside this room?" Jesse asked into his mike.

"Just a small barking one," Bess said.

"Two more Slayers are in the hallway," Jesse told Willow. "I'm going to tell them it's all right to come in. Don't attack."

Willow strode over to the wall and flipped on the lights. She looked more frustrated than grateful. "You came to help us?" She eyed Jesse, lingering on his helmet. He knew the helmet made him look ominous. It was hard to see his features through the tinted glass. But the Slayers couldn't take off their helmets until everyone was safe.

Willow took a step toward Jesse. "Where were you when four armed gunmen forced their way into our house, pistol-whipped my uncle, and threatened to shoot us?"

Bess and Kody walked into the living room. "We were outside in your yard," Kody said, "taking care of the six armed gunmen there."

"I gave you a warning," Jesse added, making his way over to where Mr. Davis lay. "I shot a round into your roof. Didn't you hear it?"

Willow planted her hand on her hip. "That was your idea of a warning? It's Halloween. We thought some kids were playing with firecrackers."

Mrs. Davis sat up, took the cloth away from Mr. Davis' head, and checked his wound. A small stream of blood dripped down the side of his face. "I need the first-aid kit," she called out. Her voice was high-pitched. Her hand shook. "It's underneath my bathroom sink. Somebody go get it. Willow, call the police. Call Ryker."

Bess turned and headed down the hallway. "I'll get the first-aid kit."

The young girl was rocking back and forth and crying. Her dark hair was pulled back in a bun, and she wore a long white dress with wings. An angel costume. It made her look all the more young and fragile. She already held a cell phone in her hand. "I called nine-one-one. It didn't work. Is Dad going to be okay? Should I get your phone?"

"You'll need a landline," Kody said. "Unless Overdrake's men took care of that, too." He pulled a pair of handcuffs from his pockets, then knelt by one of the unconscious gunmen. He flipped him over and cuffed his hands behind his back.

Willow was walking out of the room. "I'll check the phone in the kitchen."

Mrs. Davis pressed the cloth back against her husband's wound. "Willow, how long have you known you're a Slayer? Who else knows?"

Willow's voice came from the next room. "I found out when Ryker did. His simulator worked on me, too. I've been meaning to ask you, did my mom visit you in D.C. when you were both pregnant?"

Mrs. Davis let out a small gasp, which probably meant yes.

Jesse checked his scanner. Even though it wasn't picking up any new readings, he wanted to get everyone out of the house as quickly as possible. Overdrake could have backup coming. "Kody," he said, "stand watch outside the front door until we can evacuate."

Jesse turned to Mrs. Davis. "We need to leave. Overdrake might send more men." Without waiting for her response, Jesse bent down beside Mr. Davis. "I'll carry him to your car. We'll go to the hospital."

As soon as Jesse slid his hand underneath Mr. Davis, the man groaned and opened his eyes. He squinted at Jesse and then, with a jolt of clarity, pushed at his arms.

"It's okay," Jesse told him, raising his hands to show they were empty. "I'm here to help you. I'm going to carry you to your car so we can take you to the hospital."

Mr. Davis squinted at Jesse eyeing his helmet suspiciously. He sat up, wobbling. "Where's Ryker?"

Jesse took hold of Mr. Davis' shoulder to steady him. "We have four people on the ridge looking for Ryker right now."

Mrs. Davis held the cloth against her husband's wound again. Her hands were still shaking. "The ridge? Ryker's at a party."

"No, he's not." Bess came back into the room carrying a large plastic box with a first-aid sticker on the top. "He went up to the ridge." She opened the box and handed it to Mrs. Davis.

Jesse itched to leave, wanted to hurry everyone along. "We need to go," he told Mrs. Davis again.

Mrs. Davis rummaged through the first-aid kit and ripped open an antiseptic wipe. "Not until we get hold of Ryker. We've got to warn him."

She wasn't being rational, but he didn't want to pick her up and haul her out of here. At least not yet. He went to the window and checked the men lying on the lawn. How long would it be until Overdrake tried to communicate with them?

Willow came into the room holding a cordless phone. "This doesn't work either. Do you want me to go next door?"

Mrs. Davis taped a piece of gauze against her husband's wound. "Who are these men?" she demanded. "Why are they looking for Ryker?"

"They're Overdrake's men," Bess said, helping Mr. Davis to his feet. "The dragon lord isn't fond of Slayers. By the looks of it, you have two of those in your family."

Willow squinted at Bess helmet visor, trying to see beyond the tint. "You're one of the girls who came here asking for Ryker, aren't you? I felt my energy kick in and thought Ryker had come back to town. But it was yours, wasn't it?"

Jesse took Mr. Davis' elbow to help him as he walked. It would have been easier to pick him up, faster, but he could tell that Mr. Davis was the type that wouldn't appreciate being treated like a child. "Overdrake found out where you lived, so we came to warn Ryker. We need to talk to him, and . . ." Jesse sized up Willow again. "We need to talk to you, too."

"No." Mrs. Davis put her arm around her husband's waist, helping him across the room. Their daughter shadowed them, still clutching her cell phone.

"You want to take Ryker and Willow away," Mrs. Davis said. "You want to turn them into Slayers." She gestured back at the broken table and unconscious men lying on the floor. "Into this."

"Do you think this is over?" Jesse's voice rose despite telling himself to stay calm. The last five years of wondering about Ryker, of looking for him, were boiling up inside of Jesse. "Overdrake doesn't care that you don't want to fight him. He isn't going to leave you alone. You can't be neutral about this. Ryker and Willow both need to train with us. An attack is coming and the country needs them."

Mrs. Davis shook her head and kept shaking it. "If Ryker and Willow go with you, they'll be killed. Do you think it makes a difference to me whether they're killed defending the country?"

Jesse sensed someone was coming up behind him. He whirled around. A dark-haired teenage boy stood not far away. He was tall, muscular, and floating outside the window.

Another flyer. All the better.

"It makes a difference to me," Ryker said. Everyone in the room turned to look at him.

"Ryker!" his sister yelled and ran to him.

Ryker flew inside and caught his sister up in a hug, bending her wire wings. He carried her, one-handed on his side, as though she were a toddler and weighed nothing at all.

Mrs. Davis turned, let out a sob, and held out her arms to her son. Ryker came to her and embraced her with his other arm. Then he noticed his father's bandage and the blood that had leaked onto his neck and shirt. "Are you okay?" he asked.

His father nodded. Jesse wasn't so sure Mr. Davis was okay. He was pale and silent. He was either suffering from a concussion, or shock, or both.

The sister slid down from Ryker's side. "Dad wouldn't say where you were so one of the gunmen hit him with his rifle."

Ryker's expression tightened, went hard with anger. Whatever Ryker's reasoning for not joining the Slayers, Jesse could tell he wasn't a coward.

The sister gestured behind her at the spray of broken glass on the floor. "Willow picked up the coffee table and threw it at them. She knocked them out the window."

"Good," Ryker said and then turned to Jesse. "Those unconscious men in my backyard—they're Overdrake's men?"

Jesse nodded. "Kody is keeping watch in the front. We need to leave. More could come."

Jesse hadn't noticed that Ryker wore a neck mike—one of the Slayer's neck mikes—until he spoke into it. "The Slayers are inside with my family and a couple more unconscious gunmen. My father is hurt. Is the front clear?"

Jesse didn't hear the other group of Slayers on his earpiece. He knew what had happened. Dr. B tried to call Jesse, couldn't get through, and was afraid his team had been attacked. He drove back with the other team, using a different channel to coordinate with them in case Jesse's earpiece was in the wrong hands.

Ryker took his father's elbow and headed toward the front door. "The other Slayers are still making a surveillance sweep of the area around our house. As far as we can tell, everything is clear."

Dr. B tuned into Jesse's frequency. "Bess, do you copy? Are you okay?"

Technically, Dr. B should have been checking in with Jesse since he was the team captain.

"We were attacked," Bess said. "We're all okay, though."

It was probably a good thing that she didn't mention how close they'd come to being captured.

"Get Ryker's family to come out front," Dr. B said. "I'm pulling up to their house."

CHAPTER 33

The entire time Tori had scouted the forest around Ryker's house, her stomach was twisted into a ball of dread. One look at the Davises' backyard told her that Overdrake's men had attacked, and that Jesse, Bess, and Kody put up a fight. Dark scorch marks dotted the grass, remnants from Kody's fireballs. Nets sprawled here and there. Men lay unconscious. Shards of glass stuck out of the grass. A splintered coffee table lay on its back like an animal in rigor mortis.

It was only a couple minutes until Ryker found the Slayers inside and called in the all clear, but those had been frighteningly long minutes.

Tori considered Bess one of her best friends and loved Kody like a big, muscley brother. It was the thought of losing Jesse, though, that filled her with panic. All she could think was, *he was mad at me and we didn't have time to talk about it.* She never told him that she and Dirk hadn't gotten together the last night of camp. Tori hadn't moved on that fast. She wanted Jesse to know that she still wasn't completely over him.

After Ryker reported that the Slayers were okay, she sunk several feet in the air, limp with relief.

The Slayers then congregated in front of Ryker's house. Ryker took his parents and little sister in his truck. He wasn't about to leave his simulator sitting in the driveway. The Slayers, Willow, and the neurotically barking dog got into Dr. B's van.

Too many people were around for Tori to talk to Jesse. They drove a little ways down the street to a neighbor's house, Mrs. Davis called 911 to report the home invasion, then both vehicles headed to the doctor's office where Ryker's parents worked. His dad was the office manager so he had the keys, and his mom was a nurse. She would not only be able to sew up his wound properly there, they would avoid the lines at the emergency room, questions they couldn't answer, and they would be able to talk without people overhearing them.

While the Slayers rode in the van, they took off their helmets and introduced themselves to Willow. They had to do this loudly, because the dog barked so fervently he kept jolting himself off Willow's lap. She repeatedly petted his shaggy brown fur and murmured, "It's all right, Griffin. The police will take care of those nasty men."

Finally the dog's barks subdued into suspicious growling.

When Tori introduced herself, Willow raised an eyebrow. "Tori, not Britney? I guess this means you're not Ryker's soul mate after all?"

"Who knows?" Jesse said, answering for her. "The night is still young."

"No, I'm not Ryker's soul mate," Tori said, ignoring Jesse. "Although Ryker could be my counterpart since we both fly." The words felt like a lie. She was Dirk's counterpart and he was a dragon lord. She explained counterparts to Willow, then added, "Ryker could also be Jesse's counterpart. He flies, too."

"What about me?" Willow asked, letting her gaze sweep around the van. "How do I know who my counterpart is?"

"You're a flyer, too, right?" Rosa asked.

"No," Willow said, with a shrug of embarrassment. "I don't know what my extra talent is."

"It's got to be flying," Lilly said. "Being a Slayer is inherited and you're related to a flyer."

"Yeah, that's what Ryker and I thought, too." Willow kept stroking Griffin's head. "I can't tell you how many times Ryker dragged me around the sky telling me that I just needed to concentrate. It never worked."

Flying, Tori knew, had very little to do with concentrating and much more to do with feeling, with wanting to lift yourself through the air. When Tori's power of flight had kicked in, she had found herself soaring upward without any idea how she was doing it.

"She doesn't have to be a flyer," Bess pointed out. "Ryker's and Willow's Slayer ancestors could be through their unrelated parents."

Rosa considered this. "Maybe your power just hasn't manifested itself yet. Extra talents usually show up when you're in danger."

Willow let out a grunt. "Then I ought to have extra talent oozing out of my pores by now. If not from the armed gunmen who broke into my house tonight, then from all of the times Ryker dropped me while we were a few hundred feet up in the air."

"He dropped you?" Rosa asked, wide-eyed. "On purpose?"

"Yeah, on purpose. He claims he was helping me fly but sometimes Ryker is just a jerk." She fluttered her hand in Tori's direction. "That's another thing you ought to know about him before you become his soul mate."

"Counterpart," Tori said.

"Tori can't be Ryker's counterpart, too," Rosa said, leaning forward in exasperation. "That wouldn't be fair."

Bess nodded in agreement. She was twisted in her seat so she could see Willow. "Tori has been hogging the counterparts lately."

Bess meant Dirk and Jesse—technically not even close to *all* the counterparts. "It's not something anyone has a choice about," Tori reminded everyone.

Bess looked upward and sighed. "Tori will probably spend all next summer sequestered with Ryker training him."

Jesse straightened. "We can do a counterpart test right now." There was a challenge in his voice, as if he thought Tori was campaigning for the position. "We close our eyes, and Dr. B passes Ryker's truck—or not. When he says, 'now' we both point to where we think Ryker is."

Tori leaned back in her seat. "I doubt I'm Ryker's counterpart. I don't mind waiting to find out."

"Right," Jesse said. "I remember how you and Dirk figured out you were counterparts. This way is better."

Tori flushed. She never should have told Jesse about Dirk and her kissing that time.

Bess' gaze bounced between Jesse and Tori. "Wait, how did Tori and Dirk figure out they were counterparts?"

Tori glared at Jesse and didn't answer.

"You're blushing," Bess said. "So it's got to be a good story." She waved a disapproving hand in Tori's direction. "I can't believe you never told me." With an injured air, she turned to Rosa. "Did Tori ever tell you?"

Rosa shook her head. "Nope."

"Who's Dirk?" Willow asked.

"Fine," Tori said, "I'll do the counterpart test now. Dr. B, you can pass Ryker's truck whenever you want." She shut her eyes and hoped this would end the discussion about Dirk. It didn't. Lilly immediately began telling Willow all about Dirk.

"I'll do better than pass Ryker," Dr. B called back to Tori. "We're pulling into the parking lot now. I'll drive around and once I stop the van, tell me which direction Ryker is parked."

Tori kept her eyes shut tight and concentrated, trying to feel Ryker's presence. Mostly she felt Jesse's, though. She knew he was sitting across the van, ticked at her because he thought she was hogging counterparts. Okay, it was actually Bess who had said that. Jesse was just ticked at the idea of her being sequestered all summer with Ryker.

Did that mean Jesse still cared about her, that he was jealous? Probably not. He had been the one who told her she should date other guys. Jesse was only mad about her getting together with Dirk because Dirk was Jesse's friend. Or at least he had been Jesse's friend.

Tori revised the thought again. Dirk had never been any of the Slayers' friend. Not Jesse's, not hers. From the day Dirk enrolled in camp years ago, he planned to learn their secrets and betray them. It was a bitter, bitter thought.

The van stopped. "All right," Dr. B called. "Where is Ryker?"

Tori reached out with her mind, searching for his presence. It was no good. What had been so effortless with Dirk was absent with Ryker. "I don't know." Tori shrugged and pointed to her left.

"Tori isn't Ryker's counterpart," Bess announced, relieved.

Tori opened her eyes. Jesse, his eyes still shut, was pointing at the back of the van, which was where Ryker's truck was parked—right behind them.

"Jesse might be," Rosa said. "Or he might just be a better guesser than Tori."

Jesse kept his eyes closed. He moved his finger from pointing to the back of the van, to pointing to the back-left corner, and then slowly traced his finger along the left side of the van. Which made sense, because Ryker had gotten out of his truck and was walking along that side to talk to Dr. B.

"Okay," Rosa said. "Jesse officially wins. He's Ryker's counterpart."

Jesse opened his eyes, glanced at Ryker, and smiled triumphantly, not at Rosa or Ryker, but at Tori.

Which irked her because she never claimed to be Ryker's counterpart in the first place.

Tori smiled back at Jesse, amazed at how quickly she could go from gut-wrenching worry about his safety to wanting to throw something at him. "I might be Ryker's soul mate, though. As you said, the night is still young."

"Don't mind them," Lilly whispered to Willow. "They used to be an item and they haven't finished breaking up."

Tori wished she could argue that point, but she couldn't.

# CHAPTER 34

Jesse leaned against the office wall and watched Ryker pace back and forth in front of his parents. It was odd having a counterpart, odd being able to look away and still know where Ryker was. Back at camp, a part of him constantly kept track of Tori. When they were in a group together, he always knew where she was. He thought that awareness was a counterpart sense he shared with her. Now he realized that sort of attention didn't have anything to do with counterparts. That was love. This knowing where Ryker was—it was like knowing where his arm was.

Kody, Lilly, and Rosa were outside the building, standing watch. Everyone else had gone to the conference room at the back of the office. Willow, Bess, and Tori sat by Ryker's sister, Jillian, taking turns comforting her. Mr. Davis sat on the edge of the table while Mrs. Davis washed out his wound before she stitched it up. Dr. B stood next to Mrs. Davis, ready to assist her if she needed it.

Dr. B spoke for a few minutes, explaining who Overdrake was, that the dragon eggs had hatched, and that an attack would most likely take place in less than a year. Then the police called Mrs. Davis.

Judging from the things she said to them, the police were puzzled by what they'd found at the house and now had lots of questions, such as: who had shot the people in the backyard, why they were all unconscious, what had the nets been used for, and why did scorch marks run across parts of the grass?

Mrs. Davis worked on stitching her husband's wound while she spoke. "You know more about what happened in the backyard than I do. I haven't seen it." A pause. "I don't know. Maybe they were going to rob us." Another pause. "He knows even less than I do. The gunmen knocked him out right away." A longer pause. "Are you insinuating that our family had dealings with these people? We're the victims here. Why don't you ask the gunmen all these questions?"

Ryker sat down next to Willow. He glanced at Jesse. He'd done this off and on since he'd seen Jesse without his helmet. "I know you from someplace, don't I?"

"No," Jesse said. The other counterpart abilities were kicking in, he supposed. The ability to read emotions, to understand each other as though they'd grown up together. When Jesse had seen the other counterparts at camp working together, he'd envied their closeness, their support for each other. Now he couldn't help feeling uncomfortable, transparent. Ryker would be able to read him soon.

"I'm positive I know you." Ryker tilted his head as he tried to figure it out. "Which high school do you go to? Maybe I've played you."

"No," Tori said. "Jesse has only played me."

Jesse raised an eyebrow at her.

"What?" she asked him. "You can throw jibes at me but I can't throw them back at you?"

Ryker's gaze went from Jesse to Tori with puzzlement.

"They used to be an item," Willow stage-whispered to him, "and they're not through breaking up."

Dr. B, who had apparently been paying attention to this exchange, let out an unhappy grumbling noise. It was one more broken rule he had just found out about.

Jesse kept his attention on Ryker. "You probably feel like you know me because we're counterparts."

Dr. B had explained the concept to Ryker earlier, had even told him that he was Jesse's counterpart. Ryker didn't seem to fully understand it was a condition, not an assignment.

"No," Ryker said, narrowing his eyes in thought. "I know I've seen you somewhere. I'm good at remembering faces."

Willow snorted in disbelief. "Okay, if that were the case, you'd be asking Supergirl who she is." Willow smiled at Tori. "I just figured out why you look familiar."

"We don't divulge each other's identities," Dr. B broke in. "Secrecy is needed for safety."

"Oh," Willow said, casting another glance in Tori's direction. "Good luck with that."

No one else commented. Mrs. Davis had raised her voice, speaking sharply into the phone. "Look, I don't have time to answer more of your questions. I need to take care of my husband's wound." She nearly threw her phone down on the counter. "This is great," she said, tight-lipped. "The police think we're involved in organized crime. They can't imagine why else so many well-armed men would have attacked us."

Bess shook her head. "It's not true. Our crime isn't organized at all."

Dr. B ignored his daughter. "It isn't safe for you to live in Rutland anymore. Let us help you find somewhere else."

Mrs. Davis went back to her husband, cutting the thread on his last stitches. "And in return, you'll take my children? No thanks. I want them to live. We can disappear on our own."

Jesse inwardly groaned and fought the urge to grind his teeth. Was running away her answer to everything?

Ryker leaned forward in his chair. "That didn't work out so well last time, did it?"

Mrs. Davis spun on him. "We were fine until you and Willow started sneaking around using your powers. I bet that's how Overdrake found us. Someone saw you flying around the ridge. We all could have been killed because the two of you couldn't resist playing superhero."

Dr. B raised his hand in a calming gesture. "Nothing your children did brought Overdrake's men here. On the contrary, Willow's powers most likely saved your lives. Overdrake's men weren't expecting them. You should be glad she's been practicing."

Mr. Davis gingerly felt his wound. "How did they find us then? How did you know where we were?" He still sat on the edge of the table and hadn't said much since they'd come to the office. Jesse wasn't sure whether Mr. Davis was still groggy from his injury or whether he was entertaining the idea of letting Dr. B train Willow and Ryker.

Across the room, Tori tensed. She looked down at the floor.

"A fair question," Dr. B said. "Unfortunately, I can't divulge our sources."

"Well," Mrs. Davis said, folding her arms. "I guess you're entitled to your privacy and we're entitled to ours. We'll be more careful when we disappear this time. Please don't try to find us again. Don't contact Willow or—"

"Stop it, Mom." Ryker stood from his chair, a bundle of tension. "Overdrake's men broke into our home, clubbed Dad, and held the rest of our family at gunpoint in order to get to me. I'm not going to let him get away with that."

Mrs. Davis strode toward him. "This isn't a game. Do you really think a handful of teenagers can stop armed men, let alone dragons? You'll all be killed. It's the military's job to fight him, not yours."

Ryker folded his arms and used his height to look down at his mother—to send a message that she couldn't stop him. "I'm not running from Overdrake. Willow can go with you if she wants, but I'm going to D.C. to train with the Slayers."

Willow raised her hand. "If Ryker goes, so do I."

"You're both underage," Mrs. Davis said firmly. "And until you're eighteen, you will go where I go and do what I say. No arguments."

Ryker didn't move. Jesse could sense his frustration churning to a boiling point, perhaps Willow could, too. She let out an overly dramatic sigh. "Aunt Harriet, you're embarrassing us in front of the other superheroes." She turned to Bess who sat by her side. "I bet Batgirl's aunt never did this to her."

Bess nodded sympathetically. "You should see what my father does to embarrass me."

Mrs. Davis flushed with anger. It was clear she wasn't used to having Willow talk to her that way.

Ryker kept his arms folded. "You can't stop me. I'll find a way to go."

"If you think—" Mrs. Davis started.

"Ryker is right." Mr. Davis stood up and made his way over to his wife. "He and Willow need to train." The words were heavy somehow, weighted with a finality of what they meant.

Mrs. Davis stared at him openmouthed. Her insistence seemed punctured now and deflating while they all watched.

"We just had a taste of how Overdrake works," Mr. Davis said. "I don't want him ruling this country. We've got to try and stop him, even if that means letting Willow and Ryker go." He turned to Dr. B. "I'll sign any paperwork you need. You have my permission to train them."

Dr. B smiled and nodded at him. "Thank you."

Mrs. Davis kept staring at her husband. Her head made little shakes like trembles. "Ryker will die. You know that. And what will we tell your sister about Willow?"

For an answer, Mr. Davis stepped closer to his wife and gathered her into his arms. He held her that way, trying to ease her trembling.

"Overdrake will come after Ryker and Willow either way. It's better to die fighting than to die running."

Willow let out another sigh, a real one this time. She whispered to Bess, "Their faith in me is touching. Hello, I just saved them from armed intruders."

Jesse smiled, relieved. He didn't care what the Davises thought about the Slayers' chances. Finally, Ryker would join their group. A flyer. His counterpart. They would be able to fight so much more effectively with three flyers. And the Slayers would have Willow, too. That was especially important since their numbers kept shrinking.

Jesse relaxed in his chair, hardly paying attention to the details Dr. B and the Davises were working out. The whole day had been a string of horrible events, but things were finally looking up. The worst was over.

It turned out, he was wrong about that.

CHAPTER 35

Tori sat on the plane, watching everyone else talk to Ryker and Willow. Well, mostly Tori watched Jesse talk to Ryker. She should have been happy that Ryker was Jesse's counterpart—and she was. Even if it did make her feel like she'd been replaced.

Had she ever really been Jesse's counterpart? How could she have if he was Ryker's? What she thought was a counterpart connection might have been something else—a different emotion all together.

Bess and Rosa were trying to explain to Ryker what being a counterpart was like.

Ryker raised his eyebrows in disbelief. "So Jesse knows things about me just because he can fly, too? That's impossible." He motioned at Jesse. "Go ahead, tell me what you know about me?"

"I know you're skeptical," Jesse said.

Everyone laughed at that.

"I know you're smart," Jesse went on.

Ryker brushed off his words. "I had to be in order to build my own simulator. Anyone could have figured out those two things."

Jesse's eyes narrowed as though he was looking inside of Ryker's mind. "I know you don't like taking orders. In fact, you've got a stubborn resistance to it."

Ryker smiled. "Nope. You're wrong on that one."

Willow nearly spit out the soda she was drinking. "No, he's not. When we trained together, did you ever once let me be in charge?"

"Okay, maybe not," Ryker conceded. "But that's because you're indecisive and you kept interrupting training to answer text messages. It worked out better for me to be in charge."

Willow rolled her eyes.

"What else?" Ryker asked Jesse.

"You're a risk taker."

Ryker shrugged. "That's easy. You know I hang glide."

"And you have a problem with authority figures."

Willow laughed again. "No, as long as he's the authority figure, there's no problem."

Ryker cocked his head. "Do you only see bad things about me? Is that how this works?"

Jesse shook his head. His eyes were still focused on Ryker, studying him. "No, it's just what worries me most. Tori and I are the team captains. You have to do what we say."

Lilly stretched her legs out into the aisle. She was fiddling with one of the red streaks in her hair, twisting it around her finger. "Tori isn't officially A-team's captain."

"I'm not," Tori agreed, not even bothering to take offense at Lilly's lack of support.

Jesse gave Tori a long look, then turned back to Ryker. "Don't listen to Tori. She is the captain."

Ryker smirked. "First you tell me to listen to her, then you tell me not to. See, that's the reason I have trouble with authority figures." He turned to Tori, looking her over more thoroughly. "So you're my counterpart, too, right?"

"Nope," Tori said.

Ryker asked the inevitable question. "If you're Jesse's counterpart, doesn't that automatically make you mine, too?"

"I guess not," Tori said, keeping her voice light. "I can't sense things about you or tell where you are without looking."

Rosa spoke hesitantly to Tori. "You can't tell where Jesse is without looking. Are you sure you're counterparts with him at all? We thought you were because you could fly, but Dirk can fly, too."

Lilly unwound the red streak from her finger. "Yeah, I've been wondering about that. How is it possible for a Slayer to be counterparts with the dragon lord's son? Wouldn't Tori have to be a dragon lord herself to do that?"

The skin at the base of Tori's neck prickled. She stiffened. Here it was. The conversation she'd dreaded. "What are you insinuating, Lilly?"

"You hear what the dragon hears," Lilly said. "That's a way of connecting with the dragon's mind. You fly. So do the dragon lords." Lilly's gaze swept around the seats at the other Slayers. "Oh, come on. We've all thought it ever since we found out what Dirk was. Tori isn't a Slayer."

Bess waved away Lilly's words. "I don't care what Tori is. She's helping us. That's what's important."

"Dirk was helping us, too," Lilly said, "right up until the time he betrayed us."

Anger flashed through Tori. "Are you saying I'm a traitor, too?"

Rosa didn't let Lilly answer. "Tori is the one who told us that Dirk was a dragon lord. She wouldn't have done that if she was in league with him."

Lilly shrugged. "What I'm saying is that we need to make sure of everyone's loyalties. I'm not sure how we do that with a dragon lord as a team captain."

"She's not a dragon lord," Jesse said firmly. "She's my counterpart, too, and I'm a Slayer."

Lilly eyed him. "Are you sure you and Tori have counterpart abilities?"

"Yes," Jesse said. "We've always been able to sense things from each other."

Maybe Jesse was right, because Tori didn't have any trouble sensing that he was lying.

CHAPTER 36

After Dirk got off the phone with his father, he flew to Reston. One of his father's men met him there and drove him back to Winchester. Dirk didn't go in the house. Instead he went up on the roof, looked at the stars, and did his best to block out the events of the night.

So what if the Slayers hated him now? Let them be pious about their position. It wasn't any more worthy than his. Besides, he'd known one way or another his old life was ending tonight. This was just another move in the game. Emotions didn't matter. Not his, not Jesse's, not Tori's.

Dirk wasn't as good a liar as everyone thought. There was no way to make that lie work. He sat underneath the ancient stars and let his emotions rip through him until he couldn't feel anything else. Then when he was completely miserable, he went inside, got his laptop, and searched the Internet to see if anyone had posted pictures from his air chase with Jesse and Tori.

Several people had. Some said it must be a promo for a Supergirl movie. Most people speculated it was some sort of publicity stunt

Senator Hampton's office was doing. The girl in the Supergirl outfit was clearly a Tori Hampton look-alike.

Dirk watched the clips over and over. Stopped them frame by frame. He'd seen that look of grim determination on Jesse's face a lot of times, but never directed at him. And Tori. Her lips were set in an angry line. The same lips that had smiled softly at him earlier today. The same lips he'd kissed not that long ago.

Now that Dirk was out of the picture, it had probably taken Jesse about thirty seconds to get Tori back. After all, she saw Dirk as a villain, and girls never went for those. Until the villains won, that was. Winning changed everything. That's why Alexander of Macedon was known as Alexander the Great, instead of Alexander the Guy Who Decimated Persia, India, and Asia Minor.

Dirk walked into the living room and found Bridget sitting on the living room floor. He had expected her to be asleep. It was nearly ten o'clock. She had a jumbo variety bag of candy in her lap and was opening the candy bars and stacking them in front of her. She still wore her cat costume. The tail on her leopard dress was bent and the cat-ear headband was on crooked, making her costume look wilted.

"Did you get to go out?" he asked her.

She shook her head and ripped open a Baby Ruth. She laid it on top of the rest of the pile. "Mom was too sick to go. Nora said she'd take me, but she's mean, so I said no and Mom gave me this candy."

Which was why Bridget was ruining it all by making it into a pyramid. Dirk sat down beside her and picked up an Almond Joy from the stack. He took a bite. "Sorry."

"What happened to you?" Bridget asked. "Your eyes are all red."

He shrugged like he didn't know the cause. "Where's Dad?"

"Out," Bridget said. "Mom went to bed."

Dirk nodded, wondering if his father had personally gone to Rutland to oversee the search for Ryker.

"Do dragons eat candy?" Bridget asked. "I could give them mine."

"You know they only eat meat—and naughty little girls."

"Don't the baby ones eat candy?" Bridget was used to Dirk's threat about feeding pesky sisters to dragons, she didn't even react to it.

"Do you have any meat-flavored candy?" he asked.

Bridget stopped ripping the wrappers off her candy stash. "Can you take me to see Vesta and Jupiter?"

Dirk didn't want to, but Bridget had already had enough disappointments for the night. She was only allowed near the dragon enclosure when either he or their father was with her. "Sure," Dirk said. "Climb on my back and we'll fly over." He might as well spend time with Bridget. It was better than sitting around thinking about how the Slayers hated him now.

Fifteen minutes later, Dirk and Bridget had gone through the security checkpoints and walked into the nursery's observation room. A firmly locked door stood next to the window. It opened for only a few sets of fingerprints. Dirk's, his father's, and the head vets. The door led to another locked door, which opened for the same people. A desk and computer sat near the door. The vets recorded data there, checked schedules, and probably played a lot of games.

Bridget took Dirk's hand, refusing to walk across the room to the observation walls. Jupiter and Vesta both raised their heads—transforming their appearance from two boulders into dark scaly beasts with glowing yellow eyes. Vesta hissed at Dirk, and Jupiter flung back his wings menacingly.

Bridget scowled at this behavior. "I should have named them Grumpy Face and Mr. Mean."

"Yeah, Dad would have gone for that."

Dirk's father had scoured myths and legends with Bridget for an entire year before these dragons hatched, looking for the right names. Kihawahine was named after the Hawaiian dragon goddess and

Tamerlane was named after the medieval ruler who conquered Asia. "Names shouldn't be given lightly," his father had said. "I named my daughter, Bridget, after the Celtic goddess of fire, poetry, and wisdom. The name Dirk means 'dagger,' and that's what he'll be: a knife to cut away the evils of society. A knife that will slice through any who oppose us."

A knife in the back, too.

"Make the dragons nice," Bridget told Dirk. Jupiter screeched and leapt toward the glass in a flurry of stone brown wings, teeth, and claws. Vesta opened her wings in warning.

"I'll take care of Vesta," Dirk said, already slipping into the dragon's mind and calming her. "You try to reach Jupiter."

"I can't do it," Bridget chided. "Girls never can." In front of them, Jupiter bared his teeth in anger.

"Tori probably could reach into the dragons' minds," Dirk said, "and she's a girl." He had never talked with Bridget about Tori before—in fact, after the football game he avoided Bridget's questions about Tori. He wasn't sure why he was bringing her up now. Maybe speaking about Tori made him feel like she wasn't completely gone.

Bridget blinked at him, confused by this information.

"Girls might be able to reach into the dragons' minds if they have an ancestor who was a dragon lord and an ancestor who was a Slayer," Dirk clarified. Vesta tucked her wings at her side and settled back down on the ground, eyeing Dirk and Bridget suspiciously.

"What's a Slayer?" Bridget asked. She still hadn't let go of Dirk's hand, wouldn't until both dragons were subdued.

"They're people who are born to hunt dragons just like we're born to protect them."

Bridget wrinkled her nose. "You mean like those bad people who killed your dragon?"

"Yeah," Dirk said. Their father told Bridget that bad people killed Tamerlane. By an unspoken agreement, Dirk's father didn't mention that Dirk was there helping the Slayers. In return, Dirk didn't tell Bridget that their father used the dragon to attack him and his friends.

Bridget tilted her head. "How can people be protectors and hunters at the same time?"

It was called internal conflict. Dirk didn't say this. He shrugged instead. "I guess eventually they have to choose which to be."

Vesta lowered her head, laying it limply on the floor. Dirk had made her so drowsy she was half asleep and completely tame. He disconnected from her mind.

Bridget tugged on his hand to get his attention. "Does Tori have her own dragons?"

"No."

"Then what's the point of being a dragon lord?"

"There isn't one," Dirk said.

Bridget sighed as though this were a great waste. "Tori could come live with us and help you with the dragons."

Yeah, she could. But she wouldn't. Dirk reached into Jupiter's mind. It felt like a storm of aggressive impulses churning around him: Hunt. Pounce. Catch. Eat. *Nothing is threatening you,* Dirk told the dragon. *You don't need to fight. Lie down and relax.* The dragon obediently did, lowering the lids on his golden eyes while he preened the scales on his tail. His oversize talons clicked on the ground absently.

Bridget went to the glass then, putting both hands on the wall as she peered at the dragons. "Eventually they'll know I'm their friend."

"Dragons don't have friends," Dirk told her. It was something he and dragons now had in common. He would have to move again, have to cut all ties with his friends from Winchester so the Slayers wouldn't be able to track him down.

It would be easier for Bridget. She was homeschooled. Their father wouldn't let her go to a public school until she was older, until she could keep secrets.

Bridget turned away from the glass. "Can you take me for a ride on

Kiha?" Kihawahine was more dangerous than her children, much faster and more powerful. She was easier to handle, though. It was simple to slip into her mind, and she didn't fight Dirk's control. Bridget liked Kiha because she was prettier and more elegant then the fledglings. Her deep blue scales changed to purple at their tips, making her look exotic and beautiful.

Bridget wasn't allowed anywhere near the baby dragons. They were still too unpredictable, but Dirk could take Bridget for rides on Kihawahine.

"It's not a good night for rides," Dirk said.

"Why not?"

Dirk didn't have a reason he could tell her. "Kiha doesn't feel well."

Bridget cocked her head in disbelief. Dragons were rarely sick. "What's wrong with her?"

"She's tired."

"You're just saying that 'cause you don't want to take me." Bridget turned from the wall and flounced over to the computer on the desk. "I bet she's not even sleeping."

Well, she would be by the time Bridget checked on the cameras to that enclosure. Dirk reached his mind out to the dragon, severing the link he had with Jupiter and searching for Kiha's mind.

He couldn't reach her. His father must be with her, controlling her mind.

"Kiha is gone," Bridget said in confusion.

"Gone?" Dirk repeated. He felt a rush of dread. His father had been sure that the Slayers would head to Vermont to find Ryker. Although Dirk didn't say so, he thought the Slayers would get their families to safety before they did anything about Ryker. But what if they had come to the dragon enclosures instead? Tori could have stolen the dragon.

No, he told himself. The Slayers had no way of knowing where the backup enclosures were, and he had disabled his cell phone so they couldn't trace that.

Dirk strode over to the computer, telling himself it wasn't possible. Even if Dr. B had brought along some sort of tracking chips for the rescue mission, he hadn't handed out any supplies. The Slayers had no way to track Dirk. If anyone took Kihawahine, it was his father.

Dirk checked the cameras, hoping Bridget was wrong. When dragons slept, their scales darkened. If you didn't know what you were looking for, they could appear to be rocks.

Bridget wasn't wrong. From every camera angle, the room was empty. The dragon was gone. Dirk pushed the intercom button that connected him to the keeper on duty.

"Keeper One," the man answered. It meant he was the keeper assigned to enclosure one, where Kihawahine lived.

"This is Dirk. Where's Kiha?"

"With your father," the keeper said.

Dirk's father took the dragon out for rides some nights, but only when it was very late and never for long. This didn't seem like the night to give Kiha exercise. "What's my dad doing with her?" Dirk asked.

The man hesitated. "Taking care of some business."

"What sort of business?"

"I don't know."

He wouldn't tell, more likely. Dirk felt the sting of the man's refusal. It was another reminder that Dirk's father didn't trust him. "When will he be back?"

"Don't know."

Dirk grit his teeth in aggravation. "How long has he been gone? You were there when he left, weren't you?"

The man hesitated, then must have decided that it wouldn't hurt to tell Dirk. "About a half an hour."

Dirk cut the connection without saying good-bye.

What was his dad doing? Some sort of an attack? Where? Dirk ran his hand through his hair, noticing as he did that one of the computer screens showed information from the Federal Aviation Administration registry. He looked at the screen more closely. His father had been looking at flight plans from Rutland to Dulles. Somehow Dirk didn't think his father was checking on his men's flight home.

Bridget wandered back over to the glass wall to look at the fledglings. She leaned her head against the wall and sang to them. She liked to think she was a maiden from a fairy tale taming unicorns.

Dirk scanned the flight plan. A Gulfstream from Southern Vermont Regional Airport was slated to land at Dulles tonight. It wasn't one of his father's planes. The Slayers must have gone to Rutland and this was their flight back. Dirk glanced at the time. The Slayers would be so easy to attack—all together on a plane. His father must have seen it as an irresistible opportunity.

To check and make sure, Dirk accessed the security codes for the cameras in his father's hangers. Over the years, his father had amassed a collection of planes—a jet for personal travel, some retired C-130s for moving his private troops, and six cargo planes capable of moving dragons and releasing them midair.

One of the cargo planes was missing.

Earlier tonight his father said, *You can't be completely loyal to me as long as part of you is loyal to them. Do I need to get rid of the competition so I can depend on my son again? Is that what it will take?*

Dirk had thought it was a threat to keep him in line, not the next item on his father's to-do list.

In a horrible rush of understanding, Dirk knew what his father planned. His father would get close to the Slayers' airplane, then have Kihawahine intercept them. One burst of directed EMP and the plane's electric systems would be useless. A hit from the dragon, and the plane would plummet. It wouldn't even look like murder, just an unfortunate malfunction.

Would any of the Slayers have time to bail out? If they did, the dragon would be there to take care of that, too.

Dirk picked up the phone on the desk and called his father. He didn't answer. Dirk gripped the phone hard, listening to it uselessly ring. His father had promised he wouldn't kill any of the Slayers. That had always been Dirk's condition for spying. Apparently that promise didn't mean anything now that Dirk couldn't spy anymore.

He slammed the phone back onto the desk. He couldn't call Tori. She disabled her cell phone. He looked around the room, pointlessly searching for some way to stop this from happening. His gaze landed on the sleeping dragons.

Dirk's father would give Tori as little warning about the attack as possible. Last summer she knew a dragon was coming because, when Tamerlane got close enough, Tori automatically connected to his mind and heard what he heard. If Tori knew too soon that Kiha was coming after the Slayers, she would warn Dr. B. He would turn the plane around and land back in Rutland. To prevent that from happening, Dirk's father would take firm control of Kihawahine's mind and put her into a comalike sleep while she traveled in the plane. With the dragon's mind nearly an inanimate object, Tori wouldn't connect to it. Not until his father woke Kiha for the attack.

The upside of that was Tori was still connected to one of the fledgling dragons. At least Dirk hoped she was. He had no idea how long her range went. "Stay right here," he told Bridget. "I've got to go inside the nursery."

She brightened. "Can I come?"

"No. Cassie would kill me if I let you inside."

Dirk went over to the computer, put in one of the keepers' passwords, and opened the screen that controlled the nursery settings. His father didn't usually check the fledglings' day-to-day logs. Still, Dirk didn't want to leave any more evidence than he had to. He turned off the piped-in music, and hit the command that raised the wall between Vesta and Jupiter. He watched the dragons for signs of aggression. He didn't know which fledgling Tori connected to, so he would have to give his message where both dragons could hear him.

Vesta stayed asleep. Jupiter raised his head, sniffing the air. Dirk plunged into the dragon's mind and took control of its thoughts. There was no prodding this time, no gently directing Jupiter's thoughts to ease his resistance. Dirk told the dragon to stay down, stay calm, and stay quiet.

Jupiter bristled, fought Dirk's control, and then went limp on the floor. His mouth hung open as though he'd been hit.

Good. Dirk would be able to speak to Tori without worrying about a fight erupting. He hurried to the nursery entrance, put his hand on the lock pad, and impatiently waited for the scanner to identify his fingerprints. Bridget frowned at him, pouting.

Dirk turned away from her. He didn't have time to argue with her about this. He didn't know how long he had until his father's attack. It might already be too late. The door clicked open. He hurried through it, barely noting when the door closed and relocked. He didn't realize Bridget had snuck into the hallway behind him until his hand was on the lock pad of the second door. Then he heard her feet half tiptoeing, half running toward him.

Dirk swore and glared at his sister. Her blue eyes filled with tears. "I never get to see them," she protested. "How will they be my friends if they don't know I'm a nice person and not a nasty Slayer?"

The second door was opening. Bridget folded her arms stubbornly. Dirk didn't want to take the time to haul her back into the observation room. Instead, he picked her up and held her securely to his side. "You have to stay in my arms, and you can't make any sudden moves. Promise?"

She nodded, happy again.

As he strode into the room, he added, "And you absolutely can't tell Dad or Cassie I took you in here."

"Promise," she chimed.

The room smelled of raw meat, droppings, and cleaning detergent. Vesta surveyed him languidly. She was still in a lazy stupor, mollified by his earlier thoughts. Jupiter's eyes followed him, but he didn't move. Couldn't. Dirk still had a tight control on his mind.

Dirk didn't let himself think about what he was doing or what his father would say if he found out. "Tori," he said. "It's me, Dirk." Nearly as quickly he added, "Stop minimizing the sound to block me out. You're in danger."

"Why is she in danger?" Bridget asked.

Dirk made a shushing motion. With Bridget here listening, he couldn't tell Tori that his father was trying to kill her, so he used his father's real name. Bridget didn't know it. "Overdrake has a jet and his favorite weapon. He's going to intercept you in the air. If you're all on a plane somewhere, land or bail out because your plane won't be working for long."

Bridget eyed him over. "You don't have a phone," she whispered. "How are you talking to Tori?"

Dirk ignored his sister. "When you stop connecting with the fledglings and hear wind and wings—that means you're out of time."

Bridget leaned closer to Dirk's face, as though he had an invisible phone she could access near his lips. "Tori, you can come to our house and help Dirk with the dragons. They're nice."

"Shh," he told Bridget so she wouldn't elaborate on that plan. He stared at the ground, wanting to say something else, wishing he had a way to hear Tori's voice in return. He didn't, though. And he didn't know if he would ever hear her voice again.

"Don't try to fight," he told Tori, "just get someplace safe."

"Look," Bridget said, pointing. "Vesta is waving her tail at us."

CHAPTER 37

"Dirk, no," Tori said. The words were pointless. He couldn't hear her. Still, she wanted to yell at him. How could he stand by and let this happen? How could he stay with his father when the man was trying to kill people—starting with Dirk's friends?

Then she chided herself for forgetting so quickly. The Slayers weren't really his friends. This warning was only thrown in her direction so Dirk could appease his conscience. He had taken his little sister with him to deliver the message as if it were all a game without consequences.

Tori opened her eyes and the sound in the plane immediately grew louder. The Slayers were all staring at her. "Bad news," she said. The words sounded absurd even in her own ears. Getting a flat tire was bad news. Failing a math test was bad news. Finding out a dragon was going to attack your plane was something much worse. "Overdrake has a jet and a dragon. He's coming after us. Dirk says we need to land or bail out."

For a moment, the other Slayers stared at her in shock and then everyone spoke at once.

"We've got to turn the plane in another direction," Rosa said.

"We can't trust what Dirk says," Lilly insisted. "It's some sort of trap."

"How long do we have?" Jesse asked.

Ryker's gaze bounced between them. "How did Dirk talk to Tori? I thought you said counterparts don't have psychic powers."

Bess grabbed her helmet from off the floor. "How does Overdrake know where we are?"

Willow looked around the cabin nervously. "I really hope someone is about to tell me that there are enough parachutes."

The next few moments were just as loud and jumbled as people grabbed their gear and spoke over one another to answer the first set of questions.

"I don't know how long we have," Tori said.

"Air traffic control tracks all planes." Jesse handed Ryker and Willow bulletproof jackets, pants, and boots. Along with the extra pair Dr. B always packed for missions, he'd brought a pair for Alyssa. "Overdrake must have someone in ATC giving him information."

Bess got out the extra helmets. "Tori hears what the dragons hear. When someone is near the dragons, she hears what they say. Dirk knows that."

Willow kicked off her shoes and pulled the bulletproof pants over her jeans. "You know, when you asked if I wanted to be a Slayer, I thought I'd have a little more training before I faced a dragon. I'm seriously having second thoughts about my career plans." She tried to put the Kevlar jacket over her own, then took off her jacket, tossed it on her chair, and slipped her arms into the Kevlar jacket. "And I never thought I'd say this, but Aunt Harriet was right. This was not a good idea."

The floor tilted downward. Dr. B was lowering the plane. "Strap on your rifles and parachutes," he called. "Bess, bring me mine. Rosa, turn on the simulator. Lilly, give me the first-aid kit."

Most of the Slayers headed to the cabinets. Kody didn't. "Parachutes won't do no good. They're too slow. If the dragon catches us with those things on, we'll be nothing but a buffet of dangling Slayer kabobs."

"What other choice do we have?" Lilly asked, handing Dr. B a small blue box. It seemed pointless to take a first-aid kit. Sort of like taking an umbrella into a hurricane.

"Can't we make it to another airport?" Kody asked.

"If we have enough time," Dr. B answered. "Right now we're over the Catskill Mountains. Captains, what is our plan B?"

Tori didn't speak. She wasn't a captain. She snapped on her parachute even though it seemed meaningless. She could fly. Still, if the group bailed out over a populated area, people might wonder how she made it to the ground without one.

"Kody is right," Jesse said. "Parachutes are too slow. If the dragon gets around the flyers—and it will—everyone will be ripped to shreds. We'll only use them as a last resort." They had learned last summer that shocks and force fields weren't enough to hold a dragon back. "The flyers will carry the nonflyers," Jesse went on. "One person rides piggyback. We carry the other. We find cover on the ground and fight from there."

Fight? Hiding was a better option. Fleeing was a much better option. They didn't have any powerful weapons with them—only their rifles and knives—just like all of those practices at camp where Tori died first off. She didn't bring this up. When it came to fighting dragons, the other Slayers had an illogical optimism, a need to fight instead of retreat.

Which, Tori suddenly realized, might be one more indication that she wasn't really one of them.

"How will we know if we need to bail out?" Rosa asked, adjusting her straps. "We might make it to an airport. We can't jump out of our plane and let it crash just because we're spooked."

"You have a point." Bess handed a parachute to her father. "It's a long walk home and Tori is already out past her curfew."

To reassure herself, Tori listened to the sounds in the dragon enclosure. A dragon was shrieking angrily, the high-pitched sound like ripping metal she'd grown accustomed to. "Dirk said when I connect to Overdrake's dragon, we're out of time. I still hear the fledglings."

Lilly rolled her eyes. "And we can trust what Dirk says."

Jesse went to a window and peered out. Even though their night vision was working now, it was hard to see anything outside. "By the time we're sure a dragon is attacking us, it might be too late. If it comes at us from above . . . if the plane starts tumbling, we might not be able to open the door, let alone get out in time." He straightened and moved away from the window. "Team Magnus, get in formation by the door. I want to be ready." Everyone moved toward the door, including Tori.

"Tori?" Dr. B called from the cockpit. "What do you recommend for your team?"

"I recommend Jesse leads them."

Dr. B let out a frustrated sigh. But really, what was the use of putting Tori in charge of calling the plays for Lilly and Kody? They both knew the plays, strategies, and tactics better than she did.

"I'm not a captain," Tori said. "Call a vote if you want. Willow and Ryker aren't officially Slayers, and even if Kody sustains me, Lilly doesn't. It's a hung verdict."

Jesse was too busy arranging people into groups to follow Tori and Dr. B's conversation. He sent Willow and Kody to Ryker. "People who can block fire will be carried in front. People who can't, hang on to your flyer's back."

"It's not a hung verdict," Dr. B, called over Jesse's instructions. "You cast the deciding vote, Tori. You're on A-team, too."

"And you know how I vote," Tori said.

She already felt sick and jittery at the thought of facing another dragon. How many times in practice had she asked her team for a distraction and one of them had been killed doing it? She couldn't ask that of any of them now. She couldn't risk their lives to protect her own.

Lilly was in front of Tori's line, Rosa in the back. Jesse had given her the lightest people to carry. He was taking Bess and Dr. B. He had given himself the most dangerous job—Dr. B was the farthest from the door and would therefore be the last person out of the plane.

"Remember to slow down before you get close to the ground," Jesse told Ryker. "We'll be falling around one-hundred miles an hour. You don't want to take turns going that fast."

"Don't worry," Ryker said. "I've been doing this for five months." Rosa had given him a switchblade. He tested the catch. A five-inch blade appeared.

"Tori and I will stay on opposite sides of the dragon," Jesse went on. "When it turns on one of us, the other will go for the straps. We need to cut those and then blast through the chain underneath. Don't put yourself in danger unless you have a clear path and Tori and I aren't around to take it."

Ryker shut the switchblade and put it in his jacket pocket. "Don't you have any heavy artillery? Something in the way of a sticky grenade?"

"We do back in D.C.," Jesse said. "Right now we only have the stuff we thought we'd need for a rescue mission."

Bess nervously tightened her parachute straps. "Overdrake always catches us unprepared. Which is why I'm going to start carrying explosives in my purse."

Kody adjusted his helmet. "We don't know if grenades would even work. People hurled Greek fire at dragons back in the Middle Ages.

Didn't do 'em any good." Greek fire was the medieval version of a firebomb.

The sound in Tori's mind changed. The screeching turned off as if someone had pulled the plug on it. She heard the *whoosh* of the wind rushing by and a sound she recognized from last summer. The rhythmic beat of dragon wings.

"I can hear the dragon," she called. Her words hung in the air. Everyone looked at her, somberly taking in the news. This was it then. Dirk hadn't lied to them about his father's attack.

"Give me ten seconds," Dr. B said. "I'll lower the plane as much as I can."

The plane sloped sharply downward. Tori took a step to adjust her balance. She vaguely remembered hearing that if an aircraft was up too high, you couldn't skydive from it. The oxygen would be too thin. That would be just what they needed—to jump from a plane and then lose consciousness from too little oxygen.

Tori bent down so Rosa could wrap her arms around her neck. Then Tori picked up Lilly. In a few more moments Tori would be responsible for their lives, for keeping them safe while they fell. Her heart was already pounding with fear and adrenaline.

Jesse stood in front of the door. He hadn't picked up Bess yet, and Dr. B was still at the plane's controls. *Hurry and get ready*, Tori thought silently. *You need to be safe, not noble.*

Even if he could have understood her through some counterpart sense, he wouldn't have listened to her. He was too invested in being noble. "Stay as close to us as you can," Jesse told Ryker. "If the dragon comes at you from the side, use a zigzag pattern so it can't predict where you're going." On his way to Bess, Jesse leaned toward Tori. In a voice so low only she could hear it, he said, "If any part of you is dragon lord, keep the dragon away from us until we reach the ground."

He walked over to Bess before Tori could answer. She didn't know how to answer him anyway. She had no idea how to control a dragon's mind, or even if she could.

Dr. B stood up. "Time to go."

As Jesse reached for the door handle, he turned to Tori. "Do you have anything to say?"

"Yeah." She didn't care that everyone was listening, staring. She had to tell Jesse this. "I didn't get together with Dirk at camp. I only saw him once in September when we met to talk about the dragons. Dirk wanted to be a couple, but I told him no."

Jesse barely registered a response. She should have expected that. He was already in captain mode. "I meant, did you have anything to say as a captain." He opened the door and the wind screamed by. Without waiting for further instruction, Ryker stepped toward the opening, then jumped from the plane. Tori's last sight of his group was Willow clinging to his back, eyes shut.

"I know," Tori said, walking toward the opening. "But something might happen to one of us."

Holding on to Lilly tightly, Tori leapt out of the plane. She was immediately swallowed in a noisy rush of cold air. They were so high up it seemed like she could see the curve of the earth. The hills and mountains below them were only shadows.

Tori knew she was falling fast. The wind ripped at her. The cold found every exposed opening in her jacket and whipped into it. At the same time, she didn't feel as if she were moving at all. She had nothing to check her speed against. The ground didn't seem to be getting any closer.

She looked up and was relieved to see that Jesse had jumped with his passengers. He was angling his fall, moving closer to her and Ryker. The plane wouldn't last long unmanned, but right now it was gliding peacefully across the sky. She hoped when it went down, it only crashed into trees and not somebody's cabin. Tori took

Jesse's lead and pushed herself closer to Ryker, all the while searching for a dragon shape against the canopy of stars. She didn't see one. Maybe they would reach the ground before—she didn't finish the thought.

The dragon swooped down on the plane, a large dark figure, wings outstretched so they blotted out the stars. It had a long clubbed tail that moved up and down, serpentlike, while it flew. Tori knew what the dragon looked like even without seeing it clearly. She still saw the last one, vividly, when she dreamed.

It had an angular head, pointed ears, and a diamond on its forehead that would look like a horn because Overdrake had covered it in order to block the dragon's signal from reaching any pregnant women. The dragon's face was reptilian except for its glowing golden eyes. Those were the eyes of a cat—a lion, a tiger, something that wanted to eat you and would then lick its paws disdainfully afterward.

The plane suddenly looked small and vulnerable, toylike. This dragon was bigger than the last they'd fought, Tori was sure of it. The dragon grabbed the front of the plane with its talons, smashing the pilot's window. Tori heard the sounds as the dragon heard them: glass shattering. Claws ripping through the hull. Metal crunching, screeching like a living thing in pain.

She minimized the sound in her mind as much as she could. She didn't want to hear anything the dragon heard right now. It wrestled with the plane for another moment, tipping the hull over, then smacking the back end with its tail. Sparks and bits of metal exploded into the air. A fin broke off and tumbled away, disappearing into the night.

Maybe the dragon would destroy the plane and then leave. Maybe they would escape notice altogether. Even as Tori let this hope stir around inside, she knew the empty plane wouldn't fool Overdrake. It was what the dragon didn't hear that would give them away—no screaming, no human sounds at all.

The dragon released the jet. It plummeted downward, broken and spinning toward the mountains below. The dragon circled in the air, wings beating as it searched the darkness. It was looking for them.

It saw Jesse first. The dragon dived toward him—wings pressed against its body—like a hurtling comet. It was hard to maneuver while falling this fast, but Jesse wheeled to the left, avoiding the dragon's snapping jaws. As the dragon turned to go after Jesse again, Tori got a better look at it.

It was navy blue with luminescent eyes, a narrower face than the other dragon they'd fought and taut muscles rippling with every movement. A man in a black suit and helmet rode on its back. Overdrake. He didn't use a saddle like a horseback rider. The dragon was too wide for that. This saddle looked like a metal chair with compartments on its side for ammunition. The other thing Tori noticed was that the dragon's neck was covered in some sort of flexible plastic.

Tori couldn't read Overdrake's expression through his helmet, but she knew it was smug. The Slayers wouldn't be able to kill this dragon the same way they had killed the last one. Overdrake didn't think they had a chance now. And he might be right.

The dragon pushed toward Jesse a second time. Tori tried to connect to the dragon's mind, to feel something, to reach in and take control. She couldn't do it—didn't feel anything except frustration.

Bess threw a shield up between Jesse and the dragon. The dragon's head hit it, and the dragon went sideways for a moment before the shield gave way. The shield couldn't stop the weight of a dragon, but it had given Jesse the time to move farther away out of the dragon's immediate reach.

The ground still looked impossibly far away. The Catskill Mountains seemed like rolling hills, dark waves that were frozen in place. Tori didn't dare slow down yet for fear that the dragon would catch up to her.

The dragon plunged toward Ryker next. He dodged to the right, closer to Tori. Through the rush of the wind she could make out Willow chanting, "I need a power! I need a power!"

The dragon turned effortlessly in the air and made another lunge at Ryker, teeth bared. The dragon was so large. It could have snapped anyone of them in half. It could have eaten them whole. Ryker shot sideways, avoiding the dragon's mouth. He wasn't fast enough to avoid the dragon's tail. As the dragon went by, it lashed into Ryker, sending him careening. Willow was knocked from Ryker's back. She screamed and flailed, arms clawing at the air. Whatever power she had, it wasn't flying.

Tori sped in her direction. She had no way to grab hold of anything, and had to hope that if she got close enough to Willow, Lilly would grab her.

Ryker dived faster and reached Willow first. He tossed Kody upward a bit, grabbed Willow with one arm, then took hold of Kody's falling form by the other.

Impressive flying. He could be A-team's captain. Tori would nominate him herself.

Tori was close enough to the ground now that she had to fight against gravity and slow her speed. As she did, the dragon shrieked toward her. Her little group had no way to protect themselves against teeth and claws. Rosa healed burns and Lilly quenched fire. The dragon wasn't using fire yet. Tori supposed flames didn't do much good while they were all falling so fast.

Tori jerked to the left, flying that way. The dragon lunged toward her again. It was closer this time. She wouldn't be fast enough to get away, not while holding so much weight. She could escape if she dropped Lilly. It seemed the logical thing to do—save herself and Rosa instead of letting all of them die. Wasn't that what Dr. B had told the Slayers to do—the logical thing?

Maybe Lilly was thinking about this, too. She tightened her grip on Tori's arms.

Tori didn't let her go. She swerved as much as she could, staring at the dragon's nearing golden eyes. "Stop!" she yelled. The word was swallowed up in the rushing wind. "Leave!"

The dragon hesitated for a moment, tossing its head as though her words were bothersome flies. The hesitation let Tori slip out of the way of the dragon's passing jaws. It overshot her and she zipped off in the opposite direction.

Had her words worked? Had they made the dragon hesitate, or had it been something else? Coincidence maybe? Tori hadn't felt any sort of connection to its mind.

The ground was close enough that the landscape took shape. The hills grew. The trees looked like leafy-fingered hands reaching up to them.

The Slayers would be able to hide in those trees, disappear behind the sea of leaves, and yet Tori knew none of the group would. They would fight.

Tori watched the dragon, diving after Ryker now, just missing him. She'd forgotten how fast dragons moved, how effortlessly they turned in the air. She would be crazy to go anywhere near it, let alone try to cut off its straps with her five-inch switchblade. Last time when they fought the dragon they'd been lucky. And they had Dirk's help. The roll of the dice had been in their favor. It wouldn't be the same this time.

The Slayers had nearly reached the trees. They were still flying high speed. They couldn't slow down while the dragon was so close. They also couldn't sink into the tree cover going this fast. They wouldn't be able to maneuver around trunks and branches.

Jesse leaned forward, transferring his energy and speed that way. Tori followed. They needed to stick together. She looked over her shoulder in time to see Ryker try the same move. He tumbled for a moment, then recovered and zoomed after the other flyers. It took the dragon longer to change direction—it had more mass—but their lead wouldn't last long.

Your weapons aren't your greatest asset, Dr. B had told them over and over again while they trained. *Your mind is. You have higher reasoning. Dragons don't.*

The dragon might not, but Overdrake did. And he had a high-powered rifle as well. Now that they were all flying sideways, he swung it around to use it. Could Bess keep her force field in front of it while they were all racing across the tree tops?

Bess twisted in Jesse's arms so she could peer over his shoulder. Jesse slowed, let Ryker and Tori catch up to him so the force field would be behind them, not in front of them. Tori scanned the forest beneath them. Where was the best place to land? She couldn't remember whether it was tactically better for the nonflyers to fight uphill or downhill.

The dragon twisted in the air, whirling toward Jesse and pushing through Bess' force field. He dodged sideways, away from the dragon's snapping jaws and unfortunately into the path of its wings. The dragon clipped Jesse, flinging him through the air. He managed to keep hold of Bess. Dr. B slipped, sliding down Jesse's back, then caught Jesse's parachute strap. Dr. B held on that way. He dangled in the air, legs flailing.

So it turned out, it had been a good thing that everyone wore parachutes.

Overdrake swiveled his chair to face Jesse's group. He lifted his rifle to take aim.

"Mine!" Kody yelled. He hurled a freezing shock at the gun, knocking it sideways.

Immediately, the dragon jerked toward Kody and Ryker, turned on them. Ryker flew lower, switched directions.

Tori watched Jesse for a signal, hopefully a signal telling her he was landing. She wasn't sure how long Dr. B could hold on to Jesse's parachute strap.

The dragon breathed out a brilliant stream of fire that tore through the air toward Ryker's group. The mountainside suddenly lit up in sharp contrast to the night. The leaves on the trees were a carpet of yellows and oranges. The dragon wasn't navy blue, as Tori had first thought. Its scales were almost turquoise colored, darkening at their tips into purple. The entire dragon gleamed, jewel-like, in the light of the flames. Lilly extinguished the fire before it could reach Ryker. The dragon's colors faded into shades of navy again.

How odd that something so dangerous was so beautiful.

The Slayers had flown to a plateau. Jesse gave the signal. They would make their stand here.

The dragon kept after Ryker, and he zigzagged, changing his altitude and direction. Tori zipped along the tops of the trees, unsure where to deposit Rosa and Lilly. What if Ryker flew too far away—out of Lilly's range to quench fire? Did he understand that he had to stay where the other Slayers could see him? Tori couldn't keep lugging Lilly around, though. Tori needed to be able to maneuver and use her hands.

Jesse, she saw, had deposited Bess and Dr. B by a group of pine trees and was flying upward again. Bess leapt up through the branches so she could keep track of the fight. Dr. B stood behind the tree, rifle out.

Tori zoomed in their direction.

Fifty yards or so away, Ryker flew into the trees for cover, trying to shake Overdrake. He didn't let go of either of his passengers. He was probably afraid to with a dragon following so close. The dragon flew after him, mowing through the tops of the trees. So many branches cracked off, it looked like a giant wood chipper was plowing through the area.

Tori dipped down through the trees until she was only eight feet aboveground. "I'm dropping you guys," she said and released Lilly. At the same time, Rosa let go of her back. Both girls landed effortlessly on the ground.

Tori flew up past the tree canopy, pulling her switchblade from her pocket.

Jesse soared up behind the dragon, his knife out. Before he could get close to the dragon's straps, Overdrake swiveled in his chair, rifle raised. Bess gave the hand signal that said she'd thrown a shield up in front of the gun.

Overdrake apparently knew this signal, because he didn't fire. Jesse was safe, but he couldn't get through to the straps. He followed behind Overdrake at a stalemate.

Tori flew in the dragon's direction, gripping her knife. She needed to cut the straps to the Kevlar that protected the dragon's underbelly. Preferably without getting shot. The dragon was chasing after Ryker's group, breathing out another stream of fire. Tori kept her gaze on Ryker. She didn't want to see the dragon's jewel-like scales again, didn't want to think they were beautiful. Kody sent out a freezing shock at the blaze, blowing part of the stream away. Not all of it, though. Flames licked against Willow's legs before Lilly managed to extinguish them.

This was no good. Tori had to help Ryker before she tried to cut the dragon's straps. If nothing else, she could take one of Ryker's passengers. She was almost to him, could intercept him if he just stopped flying so fast.

Several branches in Ryker's wake caught fire, and for a few moments they looked like birthday candles on a leafy yellow cake. Then Lilly snuffed out those flames, too.

Blocked from shooting Jesse, Overdrake swung his rifle in Ryker's direction. Bess moved her force field. She wasn't fast enough. Muzzle fire erupted from Overdrake's rifle, spitting bullets into the trees. Jesse lunged at Overdrake, grabbing hold of the gun barrel. The two struggled over it, and more bullets cut upward into the air.

Tori was afraid someone in Ryker's group—maybe all of them—had been shot. As she flew into the trees she scanned the ground first for them. They were in the air just ahead of her, and the only blood she saw was a trickle on Ryker's calf. She flew alongside him. Before she could speak, the dragon sent another blast of fire in their direction. Heat ran up Tori's legs. Flames flickered around her shins, reached her knees, her thighs. She braced herself for the moment her suit succumbed to the fire and her skin burned. It didn't come. Lilly extinguished the flames before they even got painful.

Or at least painful for Tori. Willow moaned. The back of her pants had melted near her boots and the exposed skin was raw and blistered. Tori flew closer, took Willow's arm, and pulled her off Ryker's back. She had meant to lighten his load so he could go faster and they could both split away from the dragon.

Ryker was clearly not her counterpart, because he had no idea what she was doing. As soon as Tori had Willow, he threw Kody to her as well. Although in fairness, the dragon had stopped chasing them by that time. Overdrake, in an attempt to shake off Jesse, made the dragon roll so it flew sideways. Jesse, still holding the rifle, slammed into tree branches.

Ryker flew to help Jesse. Kody positioned himself on Tori's back. She threaded through trees so fast they flashed in and out of her peripheral vision. "I'll get you to Rosa," she told Willow. "She'll heal your burns. Do you feel any powers yet? Any strong desires to do something?"

"Only to scream," Willow breathed out.

That wouldn't be much help. "Okay," Tori said. "Once you're healed, your job is to protect Dr. B. Keep him as far away from the fighting as you can. If the dragon comes toward him, pick him up and leap out of the way. Kody," she said, directing her comments to him now, "try to heat up Overdrake's rifle so much that he drops it."

"All right," Kody said.

No, Dirk knew that trick. His father had probably taken measures to prevent it. "Maybe you should just cold-blast the gun out of his hand."

"Is that my priority?" Kody asked. "The gun?"

Tori hesitated. She wasn't Kody's captain. Earlier when the dragon came after her, she'd nearly gotten her entire group killed because she'd refused to drop Lilly. That decision had been both the wrong choice and the right choice, and Tori didn't want accountability for any of it.

"Yes," she told Kody. "Every time Overdrake lifts his rifle, send a freezing shock at the barrel. In the very least, you'll mess up his aim. Let Lilly and Bess take care of the fire."

Kody dropped to the ground and darted through the trees to get in position. Tori flew over to Rosa and gently set Willow down in front of her. "First patient. When she's healed, she's watching Dr. B. Everybody else, spread out. No one pay any attention to my hand signals. I'll only give out fake ones. Primary defense pattern." That meant that instead of working as a team with a specific goal, they would surround the dragon and do whatever they could to protect the flyers.

It was a basic command. One that anyone would have given. Tori still didn't like giving it. While the Slayers on the ground protected the flyers, they would be leaving themselves open to attack.

Lilly put her hand on her hip. "We should try something Over-drake isn't expecting. He knows what our primary defense pattern is."

"He knows *all* our patterns," Tori said, moving up through the air and away from the group. "Primary is the best one right now." She added, almost against her will, "That's an order."

She hated saying the words, hated what they meant. By taking the role of captain, she'd taken the responsibility for their lives. As she flew off, that weight pressed against her shoulders.

# CHAPTER 38

Dirk's gaze shot over to Vesta. He knew what a tail-wave from her meant. She was rippling her tail in excitement, the same way cats twitch their tails while they stalk prey.

Vesta's golden eyes were trained on him, her body a coiled spring. Dirk reached into her mind, knowing as he did he wouldn't be fast enough to stop her.

She pounced, a thousand pounds of teeth, scales, and claws, barreling toward him. He was used to making split-second battle decisions. This time the battle was different. This time he was holding Bridget. He couldn't take blows and he couldn't take chances.

Dirk dived underneath Vesta, nearly scraping along the floor as he flew forward. When Vesta landed behind him, Dirk pulled upward and flew halfway to the ceiling. From there he could survey both dragons and still had room to maneuver.

Bridget clung silently to his neck. She had been taught not to scream around dragons. It only made them target you as weak prey. Bridget was trembling, though. She realized they were in trouble.

Vesta turned, ready to chase them through the air. Dirk took hold of Vesta's mind with a firm grip, squeezing her will in order to extinguish it. *Down*, he told her. *Stay down*. She struggled against his command. She knew something foreign was in her mind. Screeching, she shook her head, as though she could knock him from her brain.

Jupiter was another matter. He'd gotten to his feet, growling and slashing his tail back and forth. Jupiter couldn't decide whether to tear into Dirk or Vesta first.

Dirk cursed himself for letting this happen. These dragons weren't like Kiha and Tamerlane, who Dirk could have given commands and expected them to stick. These dragons were young and untamed, too inexperienced to know there was no point in resisting a dragon lord. One defiant dragon was dangerous enough; Dirk had brought Bridget in here with two. He'd been so focused on getting a message to Tori he hadn't thought straight.

Dirk glided a little to his left, kept moving so the dragons knew he was alert. This wasn't going to end well. Even if the dragons didn't rip through Bridget and him, they were bound to hurt each other. How was Dirk going to explain those sorts of wounds to his father?

Bridget shivered in his arms. "I want to leave."

"We will. You'll be fine." He meant it. The dragons would have to tear Dirk to pieces before he let them have his sister.

Vesta hissed at Jupiter, raised her wings at him threateningly. This seemed to decide the matter for Jupiter. He would attack Dirk first. The dragon sprang upward wings outstretched. His gray coloring and oversize head reminded Dirk of paintings he'd seen of demons escaping from the bowels of hell.

Dirk dived downward. Vesta stood between Dirk and the door out, blocking an escape that way. The doors didn't have locks on this side. All you needed was opposable thumbs. Hopefully he would still have both of his when he needed them. Vesta watched Dirk, teeth bared, and hissed.

Dirk pulled up again and circled the room. Jupiter tailed him so closely that the wind from his wings fluttered Bridget's hair. Into Vesta's mind, Dirk said, *Walk away from the door. Go over to the corner and lay down.*

She started that way, still hissing and sending him resentful looks. Dirk's circle grew tighter. Bridget shut her eyes and buried her head into Dirk's shoulder. Behind him, Jupiter let out a stream of fire. He was too young to have a strong fire stream, still Dirk's shoes heated up and the air smelled of melting rubber and burning cotton. Which meant this was another pair of shoes and jeans Dirk would have to throw away. Since the dragons hatched, Dirk had gone through half a dozen pairs of both. Dragon lords were immune to fire. Bridget wasn't as lucky. The only thing she'd inherited from their father's ancestry was fire-resistant skin. She pulled her knees up to avoid the flames.

Dirk shielded her with his body, feeling the tingle of the fire on his calves as more of his jeans went up in smoke. Time to get out of here before Bridget was scarred by the dragon fire or by witnessing her brother's clothes burned off alltogether.

Dirk turned on his side, cut a corner, and pushed out toward the middle of the room. He zoomed right toward the observation room window. Jupiter followed, snarling and determined. Good. The harder Jupiter concentrated on catching him, the better. Dirk's father always said dragons, like horses, had to be broken. You had to show them who was boss, who was smarter.

Dirk reached the observation room window. Holding tightly on to Bridget's waist, he turned like a swimmer at the end of a lane. He kicked off from the wall and shot up over the dragon.

Jupiter didn't have the room or the experience to turn as sharply. In fact, he didn't seem to remember the window was even there. Until he slammed into it. Then he slid downward, flapping his wings feebly. A good crash always took the fight out of dragon for a few minutes.

Dirk didn't even check to see if Jupiter was all right. He flew to the door, commanding Vesta to run to it, too. He landed, opened the door, then dashed out. Vesta followed him, thrashing her head from side to side as though pulling against an unseen leash.

When Bridget heard the door click closed, she opened her eyes again. Then she gasped. "Vesta got out."

"I know," Dirk said. "I've got control of her." *Lie down*, Dirk commanded the dragon. *Don't move, and whatever you do, don't relieve yourself out here.*

"She's not supposed to leave the nursery," Bridget said reprovingly. His sister had picked a fine time to start obeying the rules.

Dirk flew over to the second door, still carrying Bridget. He didn't want to let go of her. Ever. "We named the dragon Vesta," Dirk said as he opened that door, "because she's allowed in vestibules."

Bridget kept her eyes on the dragon. "Nu-uh. We named her after the Roman goddess of fire."

Dirk should have known Bridget wasn't old enough to get the joke. He shut the door firmly behind him and walked to the computer. "I have to keep Vesta away from Jupiter until I put their wall up again. If they fight, they'll hurt each other."

Bridget didn't seem any more eager to let go of Dirk than he was to let go of her. She kept hold of his neck while he clicked through the computer controls. The wall went up. Music filtered back into the nursery. Jupiter folded his wings, turned his back on the observation room, and sullenly ignored them. *We will not speak of this again*, the dragon seemed to be saying. *You never saw me crash into the window, because I'm too dignified for that sort of behavior.*

Dirk needed to put Vesta back into her part of the nursery. He didn't move, though. That could wait. Vesta would behave as long as Dirk was still linked to her. Right now it was more important to rest his head against Bridget's hair, to reassure himself that she was safe and in one piece. She smelled of smoke. He would have to make sure she took a shower before she went to bed. He would also need to wash her clothes and throw his away.

"I'm never going inside the nursery again," Bridget announced. "Vesta is mean. She kept hissing."

Dragons are always mean, Dirk nearly said. *They're vicious, bloodthirsty, killing machines.* Bridget didn't need to hear that right now. Instead he shrugged. "All girls hiss. It's a prima donna thing. Anyday now you'll start hissing, too."

Bridget lifted her head from his shoulder, her fear finally fading away. "I will not."

Dirk pushed a strand of brown hair away from her face. He held her gaze to let her know that what he said next was serious. "We can't ever let anyone know what we did tonight. If you think those dragons wanted to rip us apart—wait and see what happens if Dad and Cassie find out you snuck through the door and I let you go into the nursery with me."

Bridget's chin drooped in a guilty manner. "They'll turn into Mr. Mean and Mrs. Grumpy Face."

"They'll turn into You're-Grounded-for-the-Rest-of-Your-Life Face."

Her chin drooped lower. "I won't tell."

Dirk lifted her chin so he could see her eyes again. "You can't tell about the things I said to Tori either."

Bridget's eyebrows drew together as she remembered that detail— Dirk had gone into the nursery to tell Tori she was in danger. "Is Tori okay?" Bridget asked.

He forced a smile. "Yeah, she's fine." The words felt tinny in his mouth, wrong. He had no idea if Tori was even alive.

CHAPTER 39

Tori flew toward the dragon. It had righted itself, and Jesse still had a hold of Overdrake's rifle. The two were struggling over it. Ryker flew up on the dragon's other side, his blade out. He was going for the straps. Tori hadn't seen Overdrake unbuckle himself from his chair, but he must have. He stood up to give himself leverage, then swung the rifle so that he flung Jesse into Ryker. Ryker tumbled backward, away from the dragon. The motion had given Jesse a better grip on the rifle. He nearly yanked it out of Overdrake's grasp.

The dragon turned its head and looked over its shoulder. It blinked its golden eyes and the next moment fire spewed from its mouth at Jesse and Overdrake.

Lilly and Bess weren't fast enough to stop the flames from reaching Jesse. Neither of them could have expected it—that the dragon would fry its own master. By the time Lilly extinguished the flames, they had already engulfed Jesse.

He toppled from the dragon's back, his body armor smoldering. Parts had melted away. He ripped at his chest where the steel plate inside the armor must have heated to an unbearable degree. Tori sped through the air toward Jesse. He couldn't right himself. She wouldn't reach him in time and he was going to crash. *No, no, no, no,* she repeated helplessly, and sped faster.

Before Tori could reach him, Ryker swooped down. He caught Jesse and zipped into the trees toward Rosa.

Tori turned her attention to Overdrake, expecting him to be burned, too. He wasn't. His suit smoldered, charred away in several places. It must not have heated to an unbearable temperature, though. Overdrake sat down on his saddle again, self-satisfied, and aimed his rifle at her.

In that moment two thoughts hit Tori. The first was that Overdrake's body armor was way better than theirs. They needed to figure out who his supplier was and buy from them. The second was that she was in between Kody and Overdrake. Kody couldn't send a shock to his rifle without hitting her first.

She dropped downward. Overdrake swung his rifle in that direction, still aiming at her. Then the rifle jerked sideways. Kody was taking care of her. Good. Unfortunately, there was still a dragon to deal with.

It roared and dived toward her. She shot straight up, hoping the dragon would glide by underneath her. It didn't. It turned and went up, too. Tori kept flying higher, darting slightly left one moment, then right the next. She wasn't sure what else she could do. If she turned too far in either direction, the dragon would catch up with her. It was gaining on her, anyway, would be on her in a few more minutes.

She should have told Dr. B when she first came to camp that attacking dragons was the stupidest thing anyone could do. Oh wait, she had. She had told the Slayers that they were training for short, quick deaths. But then Jesse had convinced her that her country needed her.

Somehow Tori didn't take much comfort in those words right now.

She didn't really see how her country would benefit all that much from her being chomped in half on this lonely mountainside. See, this is what she got for being taken in by Jesse's brown eyes. Attractive guys always got you in trouble.

Tori felt a pang of guilt then, remembering that Jesse was injured. She hoped Rosa could heal all of his burns. At least while the dragon was chasing her, it was leaving them alone.

Ryker, she noticed, was flying up behind the dragon. It wouldn't make any difference. He wouldn't be able to cut the Kevlar straps. Not while Overdrake was sitting there. He was facing Ryker and taking aim at him.

Which meant he wasn't watching what Tori was doing. She needed to take advantage of that, even if it would momentarily put her within reach of the dragon's mouth. She did a flip in the air, letting gravity help speed her flight back downward. The dragon snapped at her. Missed. It hadn't expected the sudden switch in direction. Her legs missiled straight toward Overdrake. His rifle was lifted and he shot off to the side a bit—the result of one of Kody's pushes.

Tori plowed into Overdrake's shoulder, knocking the rifle into the air. It turned end over end as it fell. Overdrake cursed and plunged off his chair to retrieve it. Ryker dashed after it, too. If Overdrake had the rifle, it would only be a matter of time until he shot some of them. The dragon stopped chasing Tori and dived after Overdrake, no doubt obeying some unheard command.

Good. It gave Tori a few moments. She flew after the dragon, shadowing its back. It was hard to position herself near a strap while the dragon tore through the air. She kept pace, did her best to catch the edge of a strap with her knife. The Kevlar was hard to cut through. Seconds went by without much progress. She wanted to yell in frustration. Even if Ryker managed to get the rifle, in another moment the dragon would catch him. Then it would turn on her. She wouldn't have time to cut one strap, let alone both—and they would still need to take care of the chains underneath the straps.

An angry sort of hopelessness filled her. They needed a better strategy, better weapons, some way to slow the dragon down. And then Tori realized she did have a way to slow the dragon down. She was carrying it around on her back.

Instead of working on the strap, Tori unhooked her parachute, looped it around one leg of the saddle-chair, then pulled the rip cord. White nylon shot from the pack, opening up until it looked like a giant jellyfish. The dragon jerked backward, slowed by the drag.

It turned its head and shot flames at the parachute. The flames never reached the nylon though. Lilly had been expecting the fire this time. She extinguished it as soon as it left the dragon's mouth.

Tori went to work on the strap farthest from the parachute. She forced her knife into the middle of the strap and pulled toward her, ripping the fibers. The dragon turned its head and lunged at the parachute. When it couldn't reach the nylon circle, it turned like a dog chasing its tail. As Tori stabbed her knife into the remaining part of the strap, she glanced down to check on Overdrake.

He and Ryker both held onto the rifle and they somersaulted through the air as they fought over it. Overdrake kicked Ryker hard in the chest, ripping the rifle from his hands. While Ryker spun toward the ground, Overdrake zoomed upward, aiming at Ryker—or at least trying to. Kody pushed the barrel sideways with one of his blasts. The shots streamed out into the forest.

Tori kept slicing through the cord. She was almost through it. She wondered why Bess hadn't put her force field between Overdrake and Ryker—until Overdrake smacked into the force field while he sped toward the dragon. Overdrake bounced backward several feet, dropping the rifle again. At camp, Tori had run into Bess' shields enough times to know how it felt. The faster you were going, the more it hurt.

Unable to bite the parachute, the dragon swung its tail at the offending circle. The straps made a pathetic popping sound and the nylon circle fluttered downward, deflated and ruined.

It had given Tori the time she needed, though. The strap gave way to show a chain underneath. She swung her rifle forward, aiming so intently, she didn't see the dragon's tail coming at her until it was too late. It swung into her side with the force of a battering ram, sending her reeling through the air.

The impact left her breathless and disoriented. She plummeted head over heels until she smashed into a tree. A second wave of pain went through her. Branches jabbed into her. Bits of bark rained down and a couple leaves fell off and landed on the front of her visor. She slid and bumped downward, then stopped, stuck in a tangle of branches. She caught her breath and took stock of the situation while extracting herself from the branches.

Ryker now had Overdrake's rifle. Overdrake sped toward him in one direction, while the dragon wheeled toward him from the other. Ryker fired at Overdrake's legs, attempting to disable him without killing him. The bullets didn't pierce his body armor. Overdrake kept coming at Ryker.

The Slayers so needed to get some body armor like that.

Ryker dashed downward, away from the nearing dragon. Jesse was back in the air again, healed and wearing what was left of his body armor. He held a parachute pack in his arms. He must have seen her strategy and decided to adopt it.

Bess threw a force field between Ryker and the dragon. It gave Ryker a couple seconds' lead before the dragon pushed the force field away and went after him again. Ryker dived lower and headed toward Jesse. As though they had coordinated it, Jesse flew higher and moved to intercept the saddle. With quick strokes, he attached the pack and pulled the rip cord.

The parachute ballooned out, tugging the dragon backward. While the dragon turned to see what had a hold of it, Jesse went to work on the second Kevlar strap. Overdrake saw what happened. He hung in the air for a moment as though he would turn and go after Jesse, then must have decided retrieving his gun was more important. He rocketed after Ryker again.

The dragon snapped at the parachute, snarling, then swung its tail to break the cords. It had figured out how to get rid of them pretty fast. Still, anything that slowed down and occupied the dragon's attention was a good thing. Tori sped toward the nearest Slayer. "Kody," she yelled, "throw me your parachute!"

He took the pack from his back and flung it toward her. It sailed through the air, going higher and faster than she'd expected. She had to fly up several yards to catch it.

Once she had it, she zoomed toward the dragon, circling it so she could approach it from behind. Free from the second parachute, the dragon swung its tail at Jesse. He jumped over it, and went back to cutting the strap.

Instead of disappearing into the trees, Ryker turned his attention back to Jesse and the dragon, checking on them. As soon as he did, Overdrake lunged forward, tackling him. With a yell of anger, the dragon lord grabbed his rifle, twisting it in an attempt to rip it from Ryker's hands.

Tori hesitated in the air, the parachute pack clutched in her hands. Who should she help? Ryker needed her more. She tucked the parachute under her arm, headed in that direction, then stopped herself. The dragon was her first priority. She had to do everything she could to get those straps off, even if it meant that Overdrake got his gun back. Hopefully Bess and Kody could help Ryker.

Tori flew toward the dragon again. Jesse had cut through the second strap and was swinging his rifle forward to blast through the chain. The dragon slashed its tail at Jesse, using it like a whip. He leapt upward. He wasn't fast enough this time. The tail hit him—not batting him away. The dragon wrapped its tail around him like a snake strangling its prey.

Jesse strained against the coil, pushing. He was able to keep the dragon from squeezing him to death, but couldn't free himself.

What could Tori do? She slung her rifle forward and shot at the dragon, not at the chains that held on the bulletproof plating; she wasn't in the right position for that. She was only trying to distract the dragon, to keep it from finishing its task.

The dragon barely flinched. Kody sent a freezing shock to the dragon's snout. Still the dragon didn't let Jesse go. How long would it be until the dragon overcame Jesse's strength and crushed him?

Tori's training told her to ignore what happened to Jesse and do her best to blow the chain straps away. But if she did that, the dragon would squeeze Jesse to death. He only had moments left.

She tried the only thing left to her. "Drop him!" she yelled.

The dragon turned and peered at her.

She maximized the sound window in her mind, hoping it would give her more access to the dragon's brain. "Drop him!" she yelled again, with every ounce of feeling and determination she had.

In that moment, Tori entered the dragon's mind. It was like the beast sucked part of her inside it and she was stretching now, trying on scales and wings. Tori still saw things from her perspective. She knew she was hovering in the air staring at the dragon, but another part of her saw out of the dragon's eyes. Things suddenly had more color, depth, and most odd of all, she smelled everything around her—the whiffs of smoke from the branches that had burned earlier, the slumbering life within the trees, the frozen ground covered in decaying leaves. She even smelled the Slayers—streaking bodies tinged with sweat, fear, and adrenaline.

All within an instant, Tori knew the dragon was a female, old enough to have laid two clutches of eggs. Overdrake called her Kihawahine, but she had no name for herself. She was fierce and powerful with strength she hadn't even tapped yet. She was a hunter as sleek and beautiful as a panther—hungrier, though. Much hungrier than a cat. The dragon didn't usually get to chase prey that flew, and she enjoyed this challenge, knew she would win. Flying had given her an appetite and her mouth was already watering for a taste of blood and bone marrow. Tori felt the intake of dragon's breath and felt the fire hot on Kihawahine's tongue, waiting to be released.

"Drop him!" Tori told the dragon, going closer.

Tori heard Overdrake's voice—not from his mouth; it was inside the dragon's mind. "The human in front of you is called Tori."

Overdrake knew she was in the dragon's mind. Tori could hear the rage in his voice. Slowly he said, "Kill her now."

Tori shot sideways, speeding away from Kihawahine as fast as she could. The dragon lunged after her, roaring. As Tori flew, she held on to the connection in her mind, telling the dragon, "Stop!" over and over again. It was as fruitless as waving to get a horse's attention when someone else held the reins. The dragon was firmly in Overdrake's control, always had been. Tori had only managed to temporarily distract it.

Tori let go of the connection and concentrated on fleeing. The dragon couldn't reach full speed while her tail grasped Jesse. She dropped him and raced after Tori, closing the gap between them in seconds.

Tori flew lower. She needed to slow Kihawahine down. She skimmed over the treetops, just above the reaching branches. The dragon chased after her, wings smacking into branches with every down beat. Bits of wood and broken branches flew everywhere. Tori had meant to fly down below the canopy, to lose the dragon there.

She couldn't hide from Kihawahine, though, not when the dragon could smell her. Flying around trunks and branches would delay Tori, maybe leave her trapped. One blast of fire, and the dragon would roast her.

Tori barely kept ahead of the dragon. If she wasn't already out of reach of the other Slayers, she would be soon. Bess couldn't shield for her. Lilly couldn't extinguish fire. Nothing ahead offered protection. Tori had to turn around, but couldn't; the dragon would catch her.

Kihawahine didn't shoot out fire. Probably because Tori would taste better uncharred. In another minute, the dragon's teeth would be on her.

Two months' training hadn't prepared her for this. Fighting the small mechanical dragon wasn't the same. Tori could only think of one thing to do. She curved upward a little, held the parachute over her head, and pulled the rip cord. She was immediately jolted backward. The opened parachute smacked into the dragon's face, covering it.

Tori let the parachute go, then flipped upward so the dragon flew by underneath her. The dragon let out a blast of fire that incinerated the parachute. By that time, Tori was over the dragon's back. She swung her rifle forward and in quick succession shot at the chains on both sides. It was sloppy shooting, but it worked. The chains gave way. The Kevlar shield fell from the dragon's underside.

Down below and far behind Tori, the other Slayers let out a shout. They had been running after her, she realized, trying to keep her in range. Tori would have joined them in celebrating if the dragon hadn't twisted around to come at her again.

For a fleeting moment Tori had a shot at the dragon's underbelly. Her rifle was raised. Her finger was on the trigger. She hesitated, though. Tori had been inside the dragon's mind. She had seen the beauty of its jewel-like scales. If Overdrake wasn't holding the reins, Kihawahine could be controlled. Tori could stop the dragon from killing people.

And then the moment was gone and the dragon was speeding toward her. Its glowing golden eyes fixed on her.

Tori zoomed back in the other direction, fleeing toward the Slayers. The dragon was already too close and her friends were so far away. She chided herself for not taking a shot while she had the chance. Even if her aim hadn't been good enough to kill the dragon, she might have at least hurt it enough to slow it down. Now Kihawahine roared behind her, faster and more powerful than Tori. She had only escaped before because she had a parachute. She was about to be eaten, and it was all because she'd hesitated to shoot something she'd shared brain-space with.

Jesse flew in her direction, rifle raised. He was still too far away to maneuver into a good shooting position. But she could help him.

Tori streaked upward. Kihawahine followed, exposing her now-unprotected belly. Tori glanced downward. The dragon was right below her, mouth opening, ready to snap its jaws on her feet. She could smell its oily breath overtaking her.

Jesse fired. The sound of gunshot punctuated the night like drum bangs. Tori couldn't tell whether he'd hit his target. Then the dragon's wings shuddered. Kihawahine's head lolled unsteadily, and she plummeted downward, wings convulsing. She screeched as she fell, fire streaming from her mouth. Her turquoise scales glittered in the firelight, winking like a crystal chandelier. The dragon stared at Tori with golden eyes, still fighting to fly upward. Instead Kihawahine sunk downward, hitting the ground with such force leaves and broken branches shot upward in an explosion.

Jesse flew down, and keeping a safe distance, emptied another round into the dragon's underbelly.

Tori finally stopped him. "You don't have to do that. She's dead."

"How can you tell?" Jesse asked, gun still trained on Kihawahine's quivering figure.

Blood streamed down the dragon's stomach onto the ground. Red blood. It looked wrong to Tori, too human. It should have been turquoise, something as unique as dragons.

Tori knew Kihawahine was dead because she couldn't connect to her at all. The dragon's mind, its breathing, its raw energy, everything was gone. That emptiness left a hollow spot in the bottom of Tori's stomach that felt nothing like victory.

"I don't hear what the dragon hears anymore," she said.

The music Overdrake always played next to the fledgling dragons was back in Tori's mind now. Classical music. Something with scolding violins.

Tori caught a flash of movement in the sky and looked up. Overdrake flew by. He knew what had happened, knew Kihawahine was gone. "The next time I see you," he shouted, "you'll wish you had died here!" Then he disappeared over the treetops.

Ryker wasn't far behind him. "Come on!" he yelled to Tori and Jesse, "We can catch him!"

Jesse flew upward to follow Ryker.

"Don't!" Tori called to them. "Come back!"

Jesse hesitated, then relinquished the idea. "She's right!" he yelled at Ryker. "Come back!"

Ryker nearly didn't listen. He flew farther away, then turned around and reluctantly glided back. He held his hands out in disbelief. "We could have caught him." The wound on Ryker's leg looked worse now. It hadn't stopped bleeding and a red trail made its way down his boot.

"No," Tori said. "Overdrake would have stayed out of reach until our powers ran out. Then he would turn on us and we wouldn't be able to protect ourselves."

Ryker grunted. "We could have caught him before then."

Jesse headed toward the other Slayers and motioned for Ryker to follow. "In a half an hour, you won't even be able to see in the dark. We need to get everyone off the mountain before our powers fade."

Tori followed after the two. They didn't have far to fly to reach everyone else. The Slayers were running toward them, cheering. Kody held his hands above his head like he'd made a touchdown.

Ryker swooped down and gave him a high-five. "You were awesome!" Ryker said. "The way you kept Overdrake from shooting—you saved us all, man."

Kody high-fived Ryker back. "Awesome is my job."

Tori and Jesse landed next to Kody, and he wrapped an arm around each of them in a group bear hug. "You guys rock!"

Ryker turned to the other girls. In their body armor and helmets it was hard to tell who was who. Lilly and Rosa were both petite and Willow and Bess were both tall. If Tori hadn't memorized the symbols on the back shoulder of their uniforms, she wouldn't have known who was who either. "Which one of you extinguished the fire?" Ryker asked.

Lilly raised her hand. "That would be me. Lilly."

Ryker picked her up and swung her around in a hug. "You saved my life. Thanks." He set Lilly down, and his gaze returned to the other girls. "Which one of you shields?"

Bess took off her helmet and shook out her hair with a smile. "Me."

With the same enthusiasm, Ryker picked her up and swung her around in a hug. "You saved my life, too. I owe you."

Bess laughed happily. "I don't mind that sort of debt."

Ryker set her down, picked up Rosa, and twirled her. "You're the one who healed Willow and Jesse. You're amazing!"

Ryker turned to Tori next, sweeping her up in a hug. "The way you got the Kevlar off—you can be my soul mate anyday."

As Ryker set Tori down, Willow put one hand on her hip and tilted her head at her cousin. "Don't even say it."

He gestured weakly at her. "And you did a great job, too, Wills."

She stamped her foot. "I did not. I didn't do anything. I don't even have an extra power. I thought those abilities showed up when you're under attack." She waved her hand at the dragon. "You don't get more under attack than having a huge flying carnivore chasing you."

Dr. B had finally caught up with the others. "Well done, Slayers!" he called. Without taking a new breath, he added, "Bess, put your helmet back on until we're in a safe location." He hugged her, then looked around at the others proudly. "Very well done!"

Kody elbowed Jesse. "That was nearly your epitaph. The dragon practically cooked you."

Without answering, Jesse walked over to Rosa, picked her up, and twirled her in a hug. "Thanks for saving my life."

Dr. B surveyed the group through his night vision goggles. "Does anyone have wounds that need attending?" He gestured to Tori's legs. "Are you burned?"

"No," she said, and then looked down to see why he'd asked. The bottom of her pant legs had melted away in places. The fire stream that had hit her earlier was stronger than she'd realized. She had been so intent on fighting she hadn't felt anything, not the burn, not the cold air pressing against her legs. Now she bent down to check for burns. There was nothing. Not even red, tender spots.

Slayers had stronger skin than normal people. It took more to burn or cut them. But this—was this normal even for a Slayer? She thought of Overdrake after the fire blast. Jesse had fallen off the dragon, scorched, but Overdrake had calmly returned to his seat. And Dirk—he had never been burned at camp. The absurdity of that finally hit her. How could he have fought a flame-throwing mechanical dragon for years and never once have been burned by it?

Dr. B didn't look at Tori's legs or offer an assessment. Willow had drawn his attention to Ryker's wound. "A bullet hit him," she said.

Dr. B took the small first-aid kit from one of the pouches in his coat. "How deep is it?"

Ryker brushed his hand over his calf. Blood streaked his glove. "A bullet grazed me. It doesn't hurt much so it can't be too serious."

Dr. B knelt in front of Ryker and moved his pant material to see the wound better. "It will hurt more after your powers wear off."

Tori moved a few steps away from them. She didn't want anyone noticing her legs, didn't want anyone wondering how she'd escaped being burned. The enormity of the situation hit her—she had been inside a dragon's mind. She knew its name. Dirk had told her the truth. She was a dragon lord and her unburned legs were proof for all the Slayers to see. Would they figure out that dragon lords didn't get burns?

You weren't born to be the dragons' slayer. You were born to be their care-taker. That's what Dirk had told her. Was it why she hadn't been able to kill Kihawahine? Would she ever be able to pull the trigger on a dragon?

Jesse set Rosa down and picked up Lilly in one arm and Bess in the other. He spun both around—Bess laughing, Lilly halfheartedly complaining. "This is a good tradition," Jesse said. "Thanks for saving my life."

He set them down and walked to Willow next. "Don't," she said. "I didn't do anything."

Jesse picked her up anyway, lifting her off the ground like a bride as he twirled her. "You protected Dr. B and that meant the rest of us didn't have to worry about him. Trust me, we know how much trouble he is."

Dr. B wasn't trouble—unless Bess was in danger. Then he became a father instead of a mentor. Since Bess hadn't been wounded, Tori imagined the most troublesome thing Dr. B had done was give Willow a nonstop stream of condensed Slayer fighting strategies.

Jesse set Willow down and picked up Tori next. He spun her in a tight hug. "You are an incredible Slayer."

I'm not, she thought, and was glad he couldn't see her face. "You're pretty incredible yourself. Thanks for saving my life."

Jesse held on to her longer than he had the other girls, didn't let her go right away. She thought he was going to say something else. Instead he let her go.

Dr. B finished cleaning Ryker's wound and taped gauze over his leg. "It's not deep. A few stitches should take care of it. Hopefully you'll be able to walk on it without much trouble." Dr. B glanced up at the rest of them. "I don't suppose any of you have been to the Catskills and know where we are?"

Rosa, Lilly, Kody, and Jesse shook their heads.

Ryker shrugged. "I've been snowboarding at Windham Mountain and cliff jumping at Kaaterskill Clove. This isn't either of those places."

"I've been to the Mohonk Resort," Tori said. "If anyone spots a castle by a lake, I know where we are."

Lilly shook her head. "Rich people," she muttered.

Dr. B he felt around his pockets. "I might have a compass in the first-aid kit."

Lilly turned and headed toward the dragon. "I want to take a better look at the dragon. Who's with me?"

Kody, Ryker, Jesse, Bess, and Rosa all went with her. Kody insisted that they make sure the dragon was "all the way dead, and fixin' to stay that way."

Willow and Tori stayed with Dr. B while he searched his things for the compass. Willow stayed because Dr. B was asking her questions, and Tori stayed because she'd already seen as much of the dragon as she wanted. In fact, she knew she would see it over and over in her dreams for nights to come.

A minute later, Dr. B found his compass. "We need to go!" he called to the group of Slayers, who had congregated at the dragon's side.

When none of them called back, he headed in their direction. Tori and Willow walked beside him. "Are you sure you're not overlooking something?" he asked Willow. "You didn't have *any* strong desires?"

"Let's see," Willow said, thinking. "We already went over my desire to scream hysterically and my desire to commandeer any passing armored vehicles. Besides that, no, not really."

Classical music was still playing near the fledgling dragons. The violins were insistent now, like a wail cutting through the melody. She wondered if Dirk was still there listening to the music. Was this a song of mourning? If so, who did he think he would be mourning?

"You wanted to heal Jesse," Dr. B reminded Willow.

"But I couldn't," she said. "When I tried to help Rosa, nothing happened."

"Maybe you just need more practice."

"I want to heal Ryker," Willow said.

Dr. B brightened. "Perhaps you're a different type of healer. Perhaps you heal something besides burns. Ryker!" he called. "Come here!"

Ryker flew back to them, hovering a foot off the ground.

Dr. B motioned for him to come closer. "We want to see if Willow can heal lacerations. Willow, see what you can do."

She walked over to her cousin, placed her hand over the wound, and shut her eyes. She stayed that way for an entire minute, her brows drawn together in concentration. Then she peeled off the top part of the bandage.

Tori couldn't see the wound, but she could tell from the way Willow's shoulders slumped that it hadn't worked.

"It's all right," Ryker told her. "I'll be fine."

Willow hung her head and let out a sigh. "For a moment, I was so sure I was a healer."

Ryker put his hand on her shoulder. "I know what will make you feel better."

"Yeah," she said, "but unfortunately no one brought chocolate."

"This is better than chocolate." In one swift motion Ryker lifted Willow into his arms. "Let's go poke the dragon with a stick. It's got wicked long claws. You've got to see them."

As they flew toward the dragon, Willow said, "You seriously underestimate chocolate."

Tori was finally able to smile. She was glad to have Ryker with them, and equally glad to have Willow.

CHAPTER 40

Tori didn't like seeing the dragon's limp form on the ground, seeing it drained of beauty and power. The whole time the group stood around examining it, she averted her eyes. Luckily, the Slayers didn't have much time to stay around and poke at the dead dragon. It was cold, they had no shelter, no protection, and they knew Overdrake would be back.

He had to come back and get his dragon. It wasn't the sort of thing you could leave around the mountainside for hikers to run into. If the Slayers could persuade the authorities to come up here before Overdrake could haul the dragon away, the government would have physical proof that dragons were real.

With that goal in mind, Dr. B put his battery back in his watch and made a call to 911 about a large violent creature up on the mountainside. The problem was that he wasn't exactly sure where they were. "You'll know you're in the right place," Dr. B said, "when you get to the middle of the spot where the electricity stopped working. Oh, and there are scorch marks on some of the trees."

He paused. "I don't know. Maybe a campfire got out of control."

Dr. B didn't dare tell the police it had been the work of a dragon. They would think he was a prank caller. They probably thought it anyway. Still what else could Dr. B say? Whoever went up the mountain needed to be armed in case they ran into Overdrake's men while they were there.

Dr. B also made a call to Booker telling him what happened. Booker would drive in the direction of the Catskill Mountains and trust that they could give him a better idea of their location by the time he got close to New York. The good news was that all the Slayers' families were safe and accounted for. After those calls were done, Dr. B disabled his watch again. He didn't want to give Overdrake any clue about which direction they'd gone.

The Slayers traveled the same way they'd left the airplane. Each flyer had two passengers and glided over the treetops. Dr. B figured if they kept going straight, eventually they'd run into civilization.

Rosa was happily optimistic about the night. "If the authorities find the dragon, they'll have to act. They'll study it and look into ways to protect the population."

"Or," Tori pointed out, "the government could track us down and arrest us for killing the most endangered species on earth."

Kody let out a scoffing sound. "No way. It was self-defense."

"Tori's right," Lilly said, bringing the total times she'd ever admitted this to . . . uh, once. "The public won't care that the thing is the world's largest and most dangerous carnivore. People love dragons. They'll be calling for our blood."

"I blame Christopher Paolini," Bess agreed.

After every mission, real or practice, Dr. B held a review session where he went over what had worked well and what needed improvement. Even though he was hanging off Jesse's back, he didn't abandon the practice. This time, most of what he said was praise. His only criticism, delivered in his usual mild tone, was that next time the

Slayers needed to keep in mind that Overdrake might have the dragon shoot fire in his own direction. "His suit apparently protects him from more than just bullets."

Tori probably should have said something then, should have told them her theory about dragon lords being immune to fire. She couldn't bring herself to do it, though. One of them would point out that it wasn't just Dirk who had never been burned during practice. What would the Slayers do once they found out the truth about her? Would they question her loyalty—her sanity? Should they? At some critical juncture would she fail to kill a dragon again? If she couldn't be trusted to slay a dragon that was attacking her, could she be trusted to slay one that attacked anyone else?

With his only reprimand out of the way, Dr. B said, "Both times we were attacked, we were unprepared and underarmed. However, by working as a team and improvising with the tools we had, we were able to kill the dragons. Excellent use of the parachutes, Tori."

"Thanks," she said, and didn't say more.

"The parachutes helped us this time," Jesse said. "But you can bet Overdrake won't give us anything to attach them to next time."

"We'll look into self-adhesive designs," Dr. B said. "Theo should be able to come up with something."

Jesse veered left, heading toward a break in the tree line. It might be a river or, hopefully, a road. "If any one of us hadn't been there," Jesse said, "we would have had casualties—would have failed, probably. The problem is, we're still in the preliminary round. How can we manage against two dragons and Overdrake's men?"

"Leave Overdrake's men to the military," Dr. B said, "and fight one dragon at a time."

Lilly kept shifting in Tori's grip. It couldn't be comfortable to be carried this way. "When we start to fight one dragon, Overdrake will call the other over."

"We need two teams," Bess agreed. "We need our lost team members back."

Dr. B sighed. His voice grew softer, sad. "I wish I could tell you that I'll find a way to restore powers before the dragons attack. Unfortunately, we have to make strategies based on what we have, not on what we wish we had."

Tori felt she had to say something then. "There might be more than two fledgling dragons."

The other Slayers turned to look at her. "Did ya hear more than two?" Kody asked.

"No," Tori said, "but we don't know how many eggs Overdrake started with. The others might not have hatched yet."

This theory didn't seem to worry anyone. The group began discussing which city Overdrake was likely to attack first, and how the Slayers could get there. D.C. was out. Overdrake knew that's where they expected him to strike. He would hit somewhere else first. New York or Boston. Maybe even a place on the West Coast.

Tori didn't press the subject of dragon numbers. She couldn't very well say, "When I was using my dragon lord powers to connect to the dragon's mind, I got the impression that Kihawahine had laid more than one clutch. It might have been my imagination, though. I didn't really ask her about it."

But that was what had happened. And it did worry Tori.

The Slayers were gliding along a paved road, heading toward the lights of a nearby town when their powers faded. They walked the rest of the way, stowing their weapons behind a tree before they reached the city limits. They didn't want to frighten the residents or give the police a reason to detain anyone. Tori felt vulnerable without their rifles, but the general consensus was that Overdrake would have all his available men working on getting the dragon off the mountain and keeping everyone away from the site until then. His men probably weren't scouring the nearby towns looking for another fight.

When they reached Monticello, New York, it was midnight. Dr. B found an all-night convenience store and bought a few cell phones and food for the group. While Jesse called Booker to report their location, Dr. B made another anonymous call to the police about the large violent creature up on the mountainside. He had a slightly better idea where the group had been, but his directions were still sketchy at best. They had no idea how many miles they'd traveled or the exact direction they'd been.

After he finished his call, Dr. B turned to the clerk. "Are there any car rentals open this late in town?"

The clerk shook his head. He was an older man, with a few days' worth of stubble on his chin. He hadn't stopped eyeing the Slayers the entire time they'd been in the store.

Dr. B ran his fingers through his hair wearily. He was silent for a moment, then said, "Do you know anyone with a van for sale?"

"Nope," the clerk said. Since Jesse's clothes had been burned completely through in places, Kody had given him his Kevlar jacket and pants. The clerk noticed that Jesse's boots had melted parts and Willow's and Tori's pants were burned at the bottom. "Are you some sort of motorcycle gang?"

"Junior firefighters from Scranton," Dr. B replied without hesitation. "We were doing drills up in the mountains and our truck had problems. Listen," Dr. B, scratched his ear absentmindedly. "I've called someone from the fleet, but it will take a while for them to arrive. I need to get these kids home."

Tori was pretty sure firefighters didn't come in fleets like ships. It wasn't the sort of mistake Dr. B generally made. The clerk didn't seem to notice the slip.

Dr. B turned so he could look out the glass door onto the parking lot. "Is that white pickup yours?"

"I can't take you nowhere," the clerk said. "I've gotta watch the store."

"Could it drive a few hundred miles without a problem?" Dr. B asked.

The man leaned against the counter. "Are you looking to buy it?"

"If it works," Dr. B said.

"She works like a dream. That's why I couldn't let her go for under ten thousand. You got that kind of money on you?"

Dr. B pulled out his wallet. "I do if you'll take a credit card."

The transaction took a few minutes. The clerk, it turned out, was also the convenience store owner and he was more than happy to take Dr. B's card once he knew the charge would go through.

Then the Slayers all walked out to the parking lot. The truck didn't seem like it was worth five thousand, let alone ten, and Tori didn't look forward to a long drive home where they were all huddled, without seat belts, in the truck bed.

Dr. B handed the key to Jesse. "I want you to drive Tori back to McLean. She needs to get home. I'll walk with the others down to that motel." He pointed a little ways down the street where a vacancy sign glowed. "We'll get some sleep while we wait for Booker to pick us up."

"All right," Jesse said, and without another word, he opened the truck door and slid behind the wheel. He put the keys in the ignition and waited for Tori to get inside.

"Jesse can stay with the others and go to sleep," Tori said. "I can drive myself." Dr. B had bought the clerk's GPS, too. She might not be able to navigate through D.C., but she could follow directions.

Dr. B handed Jesse some protein bars and a couple of bottled waters for the trip. "It's a five-and-a-half-hour drive and it's already late. I'll feel better knowing the two of you are helping keep each other awake. Besides . . ." He motioned for her to go to the passenger side.

"You can discuss captain things on the way home. I'm sure Jesse has a lot of information he can pass on to you in that regard. We've got two new Slayers to train."

On the walk to town, Dr. B had already told Ryker and Willow that they would live with his family for a while, so Tori doubted they needed much personal training from her. She walked around the side of the truck, opened the door, then with a sigh turned back to Dr. B. It wouldn't do any good to keep putting this off. She needed to think of a way to make him understand.

Granted, she had acted like a captain during the first part of the battle. She'd tried. But by the end of the battle she'd acted like a dragon lord. That wasn't the sort of captain A-team needed.

The other Slayers were already heading down the street. Bess said something and they all laughed. Ryker and Willow seemed to have blended into the group effortlessly. Tori used to belong with them. Still wanted to. But she wouldn't now, not really. She supposed the only way to make Dr. B understand was to tell him the truth, flat out. "Lilly was right about me," Tori said. "I'm part dragon lord. I went into the dragon's mind tonight."

Dr. B's eyes widened. "Could you control it?"

"Well, no. I never said I was a *good* dragon lord. Overdrake had control of Kihawahine the whole time."

"Kihawahine?" Jesse repeated, staring at Tori in a sort of horrified disbelief.

"That was her name. Oh, I also got the impression that she's laid more than one clutch of eggs. I don't know if they've all hatched yet." Tori sunk down onto the passenger seat. "I can't be A-team's captain. If the others knew what I was, they wouldn't even trust me, let alone follow my orders. They'd be afraid I was going to turn on them and join Dirk." She didn't add *Like he's already asked me to do.* But maybe it was there in her voice anyway.

With one hand planted on the truck roof, Dr. B considered her. His voice was soft, coaxing. "Are you going to join Dirk?"

"No." She looked down at her hands. The black gloves made them seem foreign, like they were somebody else's hands, not hers.

Jesse watched her and his eyes narrowed. "There's something else, isn't there? What aren't you telling us?"

For someone who wasn't her counterpart, he could read her pretty well. She shut her eyes, didn't answer.

"Tori?" Dr. B prodded.

She looked at her hands again. It was probably better to let them know everything. "After the dragon's bulletproof shield came off, she turned and for a moment I had a shot at her, but I didn't take it. I hesitated. I couldn't kill her. That hesitation nearly cost me my life. Next time it might cost someone else's. The problem is, I can't say I'll act any different the next time. Even though Kihawahine nearly killed me, I keep thinking about what a shame it is that she had to die. If Overdrake hadn't been controlling her . . ." Tori didn't finish the sentence. If Overdrake hadn't been controlling Kihawahine, she still would have wanted to eat one of us. She just wouldn't have been greedy about it and killed all of us.

That wasn't the sort of sentence that would reassure anyone about Tori's loyalties, and it was probably a sign of craziness that the thought had even popped into her mind. "What if I'm genetically programmed to protect dragons instead of slay them? What if in the end, I can't even fight them?"

Dr. B leaned closer to her. His gaze bore down on her. "No matter what your genetics are, you have the power to choose your actions. That's true for being a Slayer as well as a dragon lord. I have faith in you."

He'd had faith in Dirk, too.

Jesse sighed. She thought it was in disappointment until he said,

"So you have some built-in compassion for dragons. I can live with that as long as you're still fighting on our side."

"I'll fight on your side," she said. "But I can't be a captain."

Dr. B straightened. He put his hand against the small of his back, rubbing at some discomfort there. "We'll talk more about this later. You need to be on your way." Before he turned away, he added, "Tori, both times we fought dragons, you were instrumental in killing them. I trust you to do the right thing." He waved good-bye and then headed off across the parking lot toward the other Slayers.

Jesse started up the truck and drove onto the street.

Dr. B might trust her, Tori thought warily, but she knew herself better, and she didn't trust herself at all.

CHAPTER 41

Tori stole glances at Jesse while he drove. He was looking straight ahead. Neither of them spoke. The silence felt heavy, awkward. This was the first time she and Jesse had been alone since he saw Dirk holding her hand at the Jefferson Memorial. No, that wasn't right—she and Jesse had been alone after he had peeled her off the angel statue. But that didn't really count since she'd cried the whole way to the van. It was hard to talk to your ex-boyfriend about your relationship when you were sobbing over another guy.

This was the first time she and Jesse would be talking about everything that had happened, and they had five and a half long hours to do it.

Tori stared at the protein bars in between them. She offered one to Jesse.

He shook his head. "Later. When I'm tired."

She already felt tired. Well, not sleepy, just exhausted. She fingered one of the bars. She didn't want to be the one that brought up the subject of their breakup. All she could think to say on the subject was, why didn't you care more about me? Why couldn't you have wanted to be with me as much as Dirk did? That wasn't a question she could ever ask. She didn't know if it was the truth. Had Dirk wanted to be with her or had that just been part of his deceit?

At a red light, Jesse ran his fingers over the radio buttons, figuring them out. "Do you want to listen to music?"

"I'm always listening to music."

He dropped his hand away. "Oh, right."

"You can listen to something if you want. I block out Overdrake's music pretty well."

Jesse turned on the radio and flipped through a few stations until he found one he liked. "Is Overdrake still playing Bee Gees greatest hits?"

"No. When camp ended, the music changed. Sometimes it's even songs I like now." She realized as she said this what had happened. Dirk had taken her iPod at camp once. He claimed you could tell a person's IQ from their playlists and he wanted to see how she scored. He gave her a rundown of her music, adding points for songs he liked and subtracting for ones he didn't.

Dirk had been the one who had changed Overdrake's music selection. The songs Tori liked usually came on in the evening when she was relaxing and getting ready for bed.

This piece of kindness unsettled her. Had Dirk's father known about that?

Tori kept fingering her protein bar absently. "If you could have killed Overdrake tonight, would you have done it?"

"Yes," Jesse said. He didn't have to give reasons why. She already knew them: averting war, saving lives, protecting their families. "Wouldn't you?"

She didn't answer. "Dirk warned us of the attack. If he hadn't, we wouldn't have made it out of the plane before the dragon reached us. He saved our lives, and in return we could have killed his father."

This was the real reason she'd told Ryker and Jesse not to go after Overdrake. How would Dirk have lived with himself if his warning had caused his father's death?

It was another action on her part that hadn't been logic based, hadn't been captain-ish—hadn't even been Slayer-ish.

Jesse raised an incredulous eyebrow at her. "Overdrake attacked us. With a dragon. And an assault rifle. He was trying to kill all of us."

"I know," Tori said. "But I also know he has a seven-year-old daughter and a pregnant wife. I've met them. Bridget is this bouncy little girl with dark brown hair and blue eyes like Dirk's."

"I don't *want* to kill anyone," Jesse said. "But plenty of little girls will lose their fathers when Overdrake attacks."

"I know," Tori said. "It's just . . ." She looked out the window at the white lines that pulsed through the highway like the rhythm of a heartbeat.

"Now you have feelings for Dirk," Jesse finished with a note of bitterness.

"He's my counterpart," she said. "And he's Dirk. You can't tell me that when he left it didn't affect you, too."

Jesse's gaze swung round to hers. "Oh, it's affected me. I don't blame you for crying earlier. If I wasn't so mad at him, I'd be crying, too." It all came out then, a torrent of emotion from Jesse. Everything that had built up over the night. The deep cut of betrayal. Accusations. Questions. Disbelief. Sadness. Waves of rage.

Discussing Dirk got them through most of New York and Pennsylvania. Tori listened, agreed with Jesse, and added questions and thoughts of her own.

"I didn't only trust him with my life," Jesse said, "although I would have done that without even thinking it over first—I trusted him with everybody else's lives. I don't know who I'm angrier at about that. Dirk or me."

"We all would have trusted him with our lives," Tori said. "Maybe it's a good thing you told him Dr. B could track the watches. At least this way we found out the truth about him now, instead of after Overdrake attacked. We'll have time to change plans, hand signals, and the insignias on our body armor."

Jesse's profile looked stern in the darkness. "It doesn't feel like a good thing. Dirk was like a brother."

"Be glad he wasn't really. Otherwise you would have been sent to Dragon Camp as a spy, too."

"I wouldn't have done it," Jesse said.

Tori envied his assurance. She wanted to say she wouldn't have done it either, but her talks with Dirk about war had made her question that answer. A soldier's participation in a fight was usually determined by location, by timing, by pay. How often was it really a matter of conviction? How much of conviction was conviction and how much was other influences?

Tori reached out and put her hand on Jesse's knee. "Dirk didn't completely turn his back on us. He helped us when Overdrake captured us at his enclosure and he helped us tonight, too."

Jesse put his hand over Tori's. He gave it a squeeze and suddenly things felt comfortable between them again, the way they had at camp before Jesse broke up with her.

"Yeah," he said, without meaning it, "I'll thank Dirk for that sometime." Jesse kept hold of her hand. It was ironic that Dirk had come between them, and now his betrayal was drawing them back to each other, stitching them together with consolation.

They talked about other things then, normal things, like what classes they were taking in school. Jesse told her quite a bit about Springbrook High, probably because there was no point in hiding it now. He wouldn't be going there anymore.

Finally, when the sun was just beginning to lighten everything,

Jesse drove through the winding tree-lined streets that led to Tori's neighborhood. He didn't say much as he looked at the mansions and their sprawling, manicured lawns. She directed him to her street, then had him park a little ways away from her gate so they could say good-bye before he dropped her off. Once she punched in the gate code, her parents would know she'd come home and would most likely storm out of the house to begin their lectures.

Jesse turned off the ignition and peered at her home. It was a dark-brick two-story with high-pitched roofs. Her mother had wanted something that looked like a Swiss chalet. The home was so big, it actually looked more like a Swiss skiing lodge.

"So that's your house?" Jesse stared at it. "House probably isn't the right term, is it?"

"I don't care where you live," Tori told him. "You shouldn't care where I live."

"I don't care." He turned and looked at the property on the other side of the street. "I just don't want any butlers to come out and yell at me for loitering in the neighborhood."

"No one has butlers. They're called personal assistants now. And besides, this truck blends right in with people's landscaping crews."

"Oh . . ." Jesse was still gazing around as though the neighborhood were some sort of house museum. In another moment he would leave and then she wouldn't see him until next summer. Or until the next crisis.

She took hold of his hand again, casually intertwining her fingers into his the way they'd been for a lot of the drive. "About us . . ."

That brought his attention back to her. He turned in his seat so that he faced her. "Yeah, we should talk about that." He ran his thumb across the back of her hand. It was funny how such a little motion could make her insides tingle. "You said you and Dirk weren't ever a couple? You were . . . ?"

"Friends," she said. "Who texted and called a lot."

Jesse relaxed. "You didn't ever kiss each other?"

"Well, we kissed when I saw him in September."

Jesse considered this. "But it was just a friendly kiss."

"Um . . ."

Jesse's thumb stopped caressing the back of her hand. "It was just one kiss, though?"

Tori shifted uncomfortably. "Define one."

Jesse's eyes didn't leave hers. "Was it on a well-lit doorstep, in a semipublic place, with a foot of space in between you?"

"Actually, it was in his Porsche out on some property his dad owns."

Jesse let go of her hand. "You were totally making out with him, weren't you?"

"You broke up with me," she reminded him.

"And apparently we had different ideas about what that meant." He gestured to himself. "I was being a thoughtful boyfriend. I wanted you to socialize, casually, with guys from your school—the wimpy ones in pleated pants that I could beat up if necessary. I wanted you to go to the homecoming dance and the prom—not make out with one of my best friends in his car."

She folded her arms. "Do you understand what broken up means?"

Outside, an orange leaf fluttered down onto the windshield. "All right," Jesse said, "let's renegotiate those terms. Broken up is out. Instead, let's say that we're on a hiatus for the school year, and I don't want you kissing other guys."

Tori's mouth dropped open. "This isn't some sort of contract. You can't just redefine our status. I'm not a book that you can put down, ignore, and then pick up nine months later and expect the story to be the same."

"I don't think—" he started.

She didn't let him finish. "Do you know the reason I got together with Dirk?"

"Did it have something to do with his Porsche?"

She ignored that. "Dirk took the time to write to me. He wanted to see me. He texted. He called. I knew he cared." As Tori said the words, they sliced through her. "Well, at least I *thought* he cared. Okay, maybe using Dirk isn't the best example, but my point is, I want someone who's going to be there for me. That wasn't you."

Jesse still didn't want to be there for her. He wanted a hiatus. Tori looked out the front window at the autumn leaves that littered the street. She hated that being a Slayer meant more to him than she did, and she hated that she felt that way. He was so much better at being self-sacrificing than she was. Maybe dragon lords were naturally more selfish.

Tori could feel Jesse watching her. Finally he said, "I came to the Natural History Museum on the second Saturday in August. I told myself I wouldn't, but I did anyway."

She tilted her head at him in disbelief. "No, you didn't."

"You wore a white skirt with a red-and-white-striped shirt."

She blinked at him, stunned.

"I was watching you from the second-floor balcony. I nearly went down to meet you a dozen times."

He had been so close and hadn't gone to see her? "Why didn't you?"

Jesse paused. Whatever the answer was, she wasn't going to like it. "I figured if I couldn't control myself enough to stay away from you in a museum, there was no way I could be objective enough to fight dragons with you and not let my emotions get in the way."

And then it made sense to Tori. It was Jesse logic. If he couldn't fight alongside her objectively, then he couldn't be her boyfriend. She forced a smile she didn't feel. "I guess you managed to do both just fine."

"I didn't," he said. "Every time you got close to the dragon last night, I couldn't concentrate. It made me sloppy. After I cut through the last Kevlar strap, I didn't get out of the way when I should have. I knew if I didn't blast through the chains, you were going to come back and do it. So I stayed and managed to get myself caught in the dragon's tail."

Tori took a sharp breath. Jesse getting caught—that happened because he was trying to protect her? He nearly died. He would have if Overdrake hadn't decided to make Tori's death the dragon's first priority. Back at camp when Jesse told her they shouldn't let their feelings get in the way of their job, she hadn't thought his feelings ever would. For the first time she understood it was a real danger.

"You don't have to worry about me while we're fighting," she insisted. "I can take care of myself."

He lifted an eyebrow. "Before I shot the dragon, it was about to catch you."

"But it didn't," she said.

"Earlier in the night, you lost your powers and nearly fell to your death."

"But I didn't," she said, frustrated that she wasn't making her case very well.

"Do you know what it was like hearing you scream and not being able to do anything to help you?"

She put her hand on top of his. "All right, I made a few mistakes, but you still don't need to worry about me."

Jesse wrapped his fingers around hers, and as quickly as that they were holding hands again. "If tonight proves anything, it proves I can't be objective even if I want to. So there's no point making myself stay away from you." He squeezed her hand. "I want to be there for you. I want to call and text and meet you at the Natural History Museum."

She stared at him, didn't answer.

He pulled her closer. "And what was the other thing Dirk did for you? Something about an activity in a car . . ."

She meant to come back with a retort to that, but he leaned over and kissed her. His lips were soft against hers, gentle. He let go of her hand and his fingers slid around her waist, pulled her closer. She had kissed him dozens of times at camp. It should have felt familiar. Instead, it felt like the first time. Her heart pounded in her chest. A breathless sort of happiness filled her. It was hard to think at all while he held her. They sat like that in the truck for a few minutes, despite Tori's fear that one of her parents might come out of the house and see her. Kissing him outweighed fear.

Finally Tori pulled away from him. "You want to see each other outside of training—date like a normal boyfriend and girlfriend?"

"Yes." There seemed to be an unsaid "if that's what it takes to make you happy," attached to his answer. She knew he still thought it was dangerous.

She ran one of her fingers along his hand, tracing the curves of his knuckles. "And when the next attack happens you'll be able to concentrate on fighting instead of worrying about me?"

"I'll worry about you either way." He turned his hand to capture her fingers with his, then brought her hand to his lips. He softly kissed her fingertips.

He would worry about her either way, but if they dated, if they let their relationship grow more intense, it would be harder for both of them. It would be especially hard for Jesse because he thought he had to protect her.

Last summer at camp, he tried to tell her all this. But she hadn't understood it.

Tori took her hand from his and ran her fingertips down the side of his cheek. "We've spent so much time training, and now your family will have to move, start new lives—because we're trying to do what's best for the country. How can we endanger it all just because we want to see each other?"

Jesse let out a breath of exasperation. "Tori . . ."

She slid a finger over his lips to keep him from saying more. "I know. I was the one who got mad at you for saying the same thing at camp. But if I can sacrifice what I want most—you—to fight the dragons, then I know I'll be able to overcome any feelings I have about sparing the dragons while we're fighting. I'll be able to be A-team's captain."

She dropped her hand away from him, then leaned in and kissed him. She had meant it to be a quick good-bye kiss. Somehow she didn't move away from him, though, and he wrapped his arms around her and pulled her to him. His hands twined through her hair. Good-byes apparently were hard for both of them to say.

She pulled away from him and let out a breath. "I guess we'll have to finish this discussion later, after the dragons have been killed."

He leaned back against his seat, gave her a long look, then turned the keys in the ignition so he could drive through the gate to her house. "After we've killed the dragons, we'll discuss this a lot."

# CHAPTER 42

Dirk sat in the living room watching a movie on his laptop. He'd been up all night waiting for his father to get home. Every few minutes he scanned Tori's social website looking for an update from her—anything that would give him a hint of what had happened. She never posted anything. She hadn't blocked or unfriended him either. Some of the Slayers could be dead. All of them, maybe. How would he know?

If anything had happened to his father, he would have heard about it by now. Someone would have called and woken up Cassie. She would be wailing around the house. So his father was safe. Probably.

As light was breaking, Dirk's father strode inside. He smelled of smoke. His clothes and hair were covered in soot and dried blood. Dirk put down his laptop and stood up. "Are you okay?"

His father glowered at him. "It's not my blood. Your friends killed Kihawahine."

Dirk's stomach fell. He stared at his father, not knowing what to say. Kiha—always so easy to handle, so beautiful—she was gone. At the same time, relief seeped through Dirk. The Slayers hadn't all been killed then. Had any of them died? Could he ask his father about it without it seeming like he was more concerned about their lives than Kiha's death? "What happened?" Dirk settled on.

His father grunted, then headed across the living room to his den. Dirk followed him. "What happened?" he asked again.

Dirk's father went to the liquor cabinet in the back of the room, opening it with quick, angry motions. "The Slayers reached Ryker before we did. He's a flyer and his cousin is a Slayer, too, although an untrained one. I never saw her do anything except stand by Dr. B."

While Dirk's father took out a bottle of scotch, he began a terse rundown of events. He drank wine or sherry when he was celebrating, scotch when he was mad. He downed a glass while he related the play-by-play—adding lots of dark commentary. "Then your lovely little girlfriend shot off the chain straps and your BFF blasted Kihawahine. He didn't stop firing for a long time. He got a kick out of it, seeing her bleeding and helpless on the ground."

So Tori and Jesse were both still alive. None of the Slayers died. The worry that had tightened Dirk's insides all night loosened. He could breathe again without feeling like something was stabbing into him.

Dirk's father took out the scotch bottle again. "After that I flew back to the Catskills and spent the rest of the night getting rid of the evidence. We had to cut into Kihawahine's underbelly, plant explosives inside her, and then hack through parts of her scales. We moved her piece by severed piece." He poured himself another drink. "I've decided not to gun down Tori and Jesse. I'll capture them, drug them so they lose their powers, then throw them in the nursery and let the fledglings tear them apart." He put the bottle back into the liquor cabinet. "I'll wait until Jupiter and Vesta have already eaten so they're not hungry. That way they'll do it slowly."

Dirk eyed his father to see if he was serious. His father swirled the liquid in his glass, then took a drink. He didn't seem to be joking.

"You won't," Dirk said. "In return for my cooperation, you promised you wouldn't kill any of the Slayers."

His father slammed his glass down on the desk so hard the glass cracked and little splinters skidded across the wood. "Don't tell me what I'll do to my enemies!" He stepped closer to Dirk. The smell of the scotch on his breath mingled with the scent of blood and smoke. "That's what they are—my enemies—not your friends."

"It doesn't matter what they are," Dirk said softly. He knew he was treading on dangerous ground. "You made a promise to me, not them, and I'm your son."

His father turned back to the cabinet and took out another glass. He set it down on the desk with a thud and got the scotch out again. "Look, in the unlikely event that you can't find a girl you like at your new school, I'll drive you to a modeling agency, you can pick out whoever you want for your next girlfriend, and I'll buy her for you. But you've got to forget about Tori. Do you understand?"

"You can't buy a girlfriend," Dirk said.

His father took a drink. "Yes, I can."

"Well, you can't buy one who'll be my counterpart."

Dirk's father whirled on him. "Tori was in the dragon's mind tonight. I felt her in there, trying to wrest control away from me."

"Really?" Dirk was so surprised he didn't mask his admiration. It was hard to get inside a dragon's mind when another dragon lord was there first. Tori had done it without practice, without ever being in a dragon's mind beforehand.

His father waved his glass at Dirk, irritated he was missing the point. "She. Is. Dangerous. Do you understand that? The other Slayers can kill the dragons. She can take control of one and make it kill us."

"She could also be a powerful ally," Dirk said.

His father let out a huff of exasperation and took a drink. "I think we can deduce from the two dragons she's already killed that she's not interested in being an ally."

"You said Tori got Kiha's shield off but Jesse was the one who killed her. Why didn't Tori kill her? She had to be close enough."

"The dragon turned on her too fast." Dirk's father said, but his voice had a tone of hesitation to it, as though he wasn't quite sure.

"Tori couldn't bring herself to do it. Not after she'd been inside Kiha's mind. I was with Tori after Tamerlane died. She felt horrible about it and she hadn't even connected with him."

"She's a Slayer." His father gripped his glass harder. "And that means she needs to be stopped."

"She's a dragon lord. And you promised not to hurt her."

His father scowled.

"She can be turned," Dirk insisted.

His father swallowed the last of his drink, slammed the glass down on the table and stalked out of the room. He hadn't agreed to leave Tori alone, but then again, he'd stopped threatening to make her dragon food. It was progress.

Dirk returned to the living room, picked up his laptop, and went to his room to get some sleep. Before he crawled into bed, he checked the computer one last time. Tori had written him a message.

> Dirk,
>
> I suppose you'll count this as the fourth time you saved my
> life. Thank you. There, I said it, even if I'm still mad at you.
> How can you do this? You can't. Don't. Come back to our side.
>
> C

Dirk deleted the message so his father wouldn't see it. Tori was naive if she thought the other Slayers would ever take him back. They wouldn't forgive him, let alone trust him again.

It didn't matter. He wasn't going back.

He didn't write Tori. That was the nice thing about having her connected to the fledglings. Later on when Tori and he weren't so tired, he would visit Vesta and then Jupiter and explain in detail why he'd done what he'd done. You couldn't argue with history. Conquerors always won by using force. You had to get rid of the dead growth in order to have new growth.

Tori could be part of the new growth, part of the new world, instead of being cut down while she tried to protect a decaying system. She had to realize that.

Because she was the last person in the world Dirk wanted to cut down.

CHAPTER 43

Tori was grounded for two weeks. It could have been worse, especially since her parents weren't amused by all the videos on the Internet that showed her flying around the Washington Monument with Jesse and Dirk.

Tori told them she had rushed out of the Halloween party at the hospital because she'd forgotten she promised some of her camp friends that she would help them with a stunt project they were working on for a film class. They'd rented expensive equipment and had to get the project done right away. Then Tori told her parents that she'd fought with Dirk because he dropped her phone in the reflecting pool and ruined it, which was why she couldn't answer any of their phone calls. She ended up breaking up with Dirk and was so upset she spent all night talking with her other camp friends.

It was a lame excuse and Tori was lucky that her parents believed it. They spent so much time lecturing her about leaving without permission, and about not letting them know where she was, and about doing things that ended up going viral on Internet, they didn't ask her a lot of questions about other things. Her parents made several new rules including ones about what sort of videos she was allowed to be in. As if she needed to be reminded not to put on the Supergirl outfit again. Nearly everyone at Tori's school had left comments on the Internet videos—critiquing her performance, her outfit, and the obvious Photoshopping that had occurred when Dirk and Jesse had wrestled on the side of the Washington Monument.

Really, when had the public become so jaded?

Dr. B mailed Tori her old watch back with a note saying it was now secure and safe to use. She had been hoping that Theo would come up with something new and less tacky, but was glad to have it back anyway. It made her feel more secure to know she had a way to contact the other Slayers. She called Dr. B right away for an update. She hadn't heard anything in the news about a dead dragon being discovered in the Catskill Mountains and hoped the authorities were just keeping it under wraps.

Unfortunately, Dr. B's sources hadn't turned up any news about the dragon being found, either. "Overdrake most likely removed the telling evidence," Dr. B said, and then after a pause added, "at least I hope that's it. I hope Overdrake doesn't have people in our government who are covering up for him."

It wasn't a happy thought.

"In better news," Dr. B went on, "since the other Slayers' parents think their children are working with the FBI on a secret drug case, I've been able to hold several practices. Chameleon and Aspen are coming up to speed quickly." Aspen? Tori supposed that was Willow. "The group meshes together nicely," Dr. B added.

"That's good." Tori hadn't meshed so well with everyone when she first joined. And now she couldn't help but feel left out. All of them were together. Jesse was getting to know his counterpart and Willow.

Perhaps her feelings came through in her tone. Dr. B said, "We wish you could be with us, but of course it's a little harder to get you out of school."

"Which team will Chameleon and Aspen be on?" Tori asked.

"We'll decide later. Right now we're practicing as one team."

Tori heard Bess in the background, talking and laughing with someone. Was it Ryker? Willow? Maybe Jesse?

"I need to go," Dr. B said. "I'll call you as soon as we plan any weekend practices. Let me know if you hear anything new from the dragons."

He told her good-bye, and then Tori was alone in her room. Disconnected from the Slayer world again.

Tori hadn't meant to drive to the Natural History Museum on the second Saturday of November—her first official day of being ungrounded. In fact, when she thought about the day at all, it was only to reflect how sad it was that she and Jesse couldn't meet. Still somehow she found herself driving to downtown D.C. that morning.

It was just to reassure herself that Jesse wouldn't be there, she told herself. It was closure.

She parked her car at L'Enfant Plaza and walked to the museum. It was only eleven thirty, and she didn't want to stand around looking at the elephant for a half an hour—she'd already done that in August—so she went up to the balcony on the second floor and walked around while she waited. For closure, nothing else.

Jesse came in a few minutes later. He was dressed in jeans and a jean jacket. He was an achingly familiar face in the crowds that flowed around the first floor. He went and stood in front of the elephant display, glancing around the room. Searching for her. Would he look up here?

Tori moved behind one of the columns that stood on the balcony. She stayed there for a couple of minutes, until Jesse had time to scan the ground floor and the balconies, too.

Then she peered around the column again. Jesse was still standing in front of the elephant display, his hands thrust into his jacket pockets. He looked like he was reading the information on the elephant placard, but she knew he wasn't. He was waiting for her.

It would be so easy for her to go down the elevator and walk over to him. He would smile, hug her, and then they'd hold hands while they decided where to go for lunch.

Tori wasn't supposed to do that. She had told herself she wouldn't. The nation needed her. A-team needed her. If she was strong enough to give up what she wanted most right now, it would mean she had enough self-control to fight the way she was supposed to. To be logical. To do what needed to be done.

A foreign couple stood on one side of Jesse, snapping pictures of themselves with the elephant in the background. Farther down the display a group of teenage boys were pretending to throw spears at it. Jesse stood there, unmoving.

Tori watched him for another few moments, drank in the sight of him, and told herself it would have to be enough. She couldn't have a relationship with him while they both had dragons to fight.

Tori couldn't leave the building, not while Jesse stood between her and the only exit. She walked a few steps down the balcony until another column blocked her view of Jesse. Even if he looked up now, he wouldn't know she was here. She would watch the doorway until she saw him leave.

Minutes went by. Instead of feeling strong or proud of her self-control, she just felt sad, like a plant that had wilted. Self-control was way overrated. She wondered how long Jesse would wait for her, how long she would have to stand here silently, withering.

"Tori." It was Jesse's voice, right behind her.

She spun around, surprised. He was inches away. Rugged, handsome, and smiling at her.

"How did you know I was here?" she asked. "You couldn't see me."

She half hoped he would tell her his counterpart sense knew where she was.

He stepped even closer to her. "I couldn't see you, but the three guys a few feet away from me could. They couldn't keep their eyes off someone up here. I figured it had to be a really beautiful girl." He gestured to her with a sweeping motion. "And here you are."

"You're making that up."

"I'm not." He fought a smile. "Although I will admit that it helped when one of them said, 'Hey, isn't that Tori Hampton? You know, the chick from the Supergirl video.'"

Tori let out a sigh. "I hate the Internet."

"Your dad is running for president. You can't really be anonymous anymore." His smile won out then. He put his hands on her shoulders and dropped a quick kiss on her lips. "Where do you want to go for lunch?"

She didn't move. "You know, I was trying to do what you did. I was testing my resolve and being self-sacrificing. At this moment things are looking bad for the nation."

He slid his hand into hers. "If we stayed away from each other right now, would it really make you care about me less?"

She remembered how she'd felt when the dragon wrapped her tail around Jesse. Tori had known she should shoot through the chains. Instead she connected with the dragon's mind in an attempt to make Kihawahine let him go. "I guess not," Tori said.

"Then let's get lunch." Jesse tugged at her hand, leading her toward the elevator. "We don't know how many more moments like this we're going to have. We might as well enjoy them."

Tori gave in and walked with him. "I thought being self-sacrificing was what we were supposed to do. Now you've muddling my thinking. Apparently one of us is a bad influence on the other. I'm just not sure which of us it is yet."

Jesse stopped in front of the elevator and pressed the button.

"Maybe you were right all along when you told me we shouldn't break up."

She smiled over at him. "So you're saying I'm the one who's the good influence?"

The doors slid open. "I'm pretty sure I'm the good influence." Jesse sidestepped a woman with a stroller coming out, then towed Tori inside. "For example, I'm about to remind you that you really shouldn't be wandering around downtown D.C. by yourself when you know Overdrake is trying to kill you."

Tori pushed the button for the ground floor. "Do you think Overdrake comes armed to museums and I might run into him?"

Jesse tilted his chin down and gave her a look that said she was missing the point. "You're the only one of the Slayers that didn't pack up and disappear two weeks ago. Overdrake knows where you live. What's to keep him from stationing people outside your neighborhood to tail you?"

"Besides the fact that I watch for that sort of thing now?"

"He's probably just waiting for a time when you let your guard down. I think you should take one of your father's security agents with you whenever you go out."

Tori could have pointed out that she had better senses than her father's security agents, or that having one along today would have made the moment when Jesse kissed her really awkward. Instead she raised an eyebrow at him. "Are you going to keep lecturing me? I thought you wanted to enjoy these moments."

He sighed, smiled, and took her hand. "I do."

She squeezed his hand. "Good, because so do I."

Thank you for reading
this FEIWEL AND FRIENDS book.
The Friends who made

SLAYERS

FRIENDS AND TRAITORS

possible are:

JEAN FEIWEL, *Publisher*

LIZ SZABLA, *Editor in Chief*

RICH DEAS, *Senior Creative Director*

HOLLY WEST, *Associate Editor*

DAVE BARRETT, *Executive Managing Editor*

NICOLE LIEBOWITZ MOULAISON, *Production Manager*

LAUREN A. BURNIAC, *Editor*

ANNA ROBERTO, *Assistant Editor*

Follow us on Facebook or visit us online at mackids.com.

Our books are friends for life.